MURDER IN GOLD RUSH COUNTRY

ALEXANDRA D'ANGELO MYSTERIES

BOOK ONE

A contemporary mystery set in

the Sierra Nevada foothills of California

SUSAN M. SOULE

This book is a work of fiction. Names, characters, businesses, institutions, foundations, governmental organizations, events or locales in this novel are either the product of the author's imagination, or, if real, are used in a fictitious context, and with permission. Any resemblance to actual events, or to any persons, living or dead, is unintentional and entirely coincidental.

There is no such entity as the Jackson-Martell Police Department. And, sad to say, Bucky the library mascot is fictional too. Sorry.

The quote "Music has charms to soothe a savage breast" is from *The Mourning Bride*, William Congreve, 1697.

The Serenity Poem by Dr. Reinhold Niebuhr was never copyrighted.

Use of an excerpt from *The Hollow Men* by T.S. Eliot is allowable under fair use guidelines, as established on the publisher's website. ©Faber & Faber Ltd, London, UK.

Cover photograph of Butte Mountain by the author.
Front cover design by Jesh Designs, https://www.fiverr.com/jesh_designs.

First edition, Sacramento, California: Blackdeer Press, 2018
Version 1.1 (minor revisions), December 2021
Version 1.2 (minor revisions), September 2024
Softcover ISBN: 978-0-9988795-1-2

Dedication & Thanks

Dedicated to the memory of my wonderful husband, Bill, who was quite sure that I could do just about anything, even when I was overflowing with self-doubt. The courage Bill displayed in the face of insurmountable challenges continues to inspire me.

To my family, all the love and thanks in the world. You are my biggest fans, and greatest supporters. I am so lucky to have all of you in my life!

A huge thank you to novelist Gini Grossenbacher and the Elk Grove Writers and Artists for their enthusiastic and loving support of my efforts to bring this story to life. I couldn't have done this without you, my friends.

Many thanks, in alphabetical order, to: Eric Alvarez, Mary Ann Bernard, Robert M. Pacholik, James C. Sida, David Spitzer, and Stacey Taylor, for technical advice. Your words of wisdom are most sincerely appreciated.

Thank you, Carmen Ferreira, for your generous help in getting this book into the form it is today.

TABLE OF CONTENTS

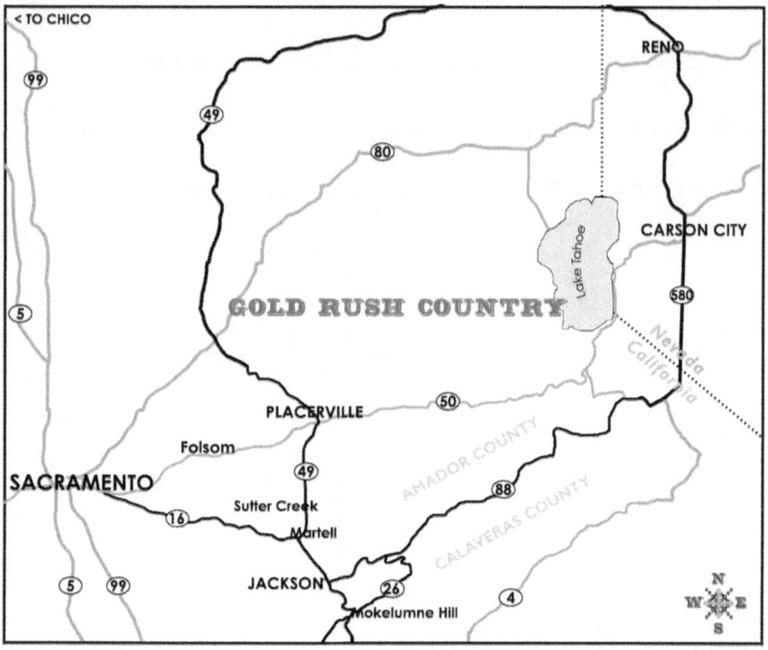

© Susan M. Soule

Highways mentioned in this story are numbered and indicated in black.

Chapter One

Summer, 2018 — New York City

Hands shaking, I stared in stunned disbelief at the letter I'd just opened.

Ms. Alexandra D'Angelo
D'Angelo Royston LLP and Affiliates
4 Times Square, Floor 24
New York, New York 10036-6522

Dear Ms. D'Angelo,
I regret to inform you that your aunt, Milagros A. Minero, unexpectedly passed away at her home in Jackson, California, on July 18th of this year.

A low animalistic moan roiled upward from the bottom of my soul. *Noooo.*

The strangest feeling washed over me, as if a wave of ice water had surged out of the carpet and engulfed me, chilling the entire length of my body.

I went back and started the letter again. *This is wrong. This is all wrong...*

The shaking in my hands trebled. The letter I was reading slid through my fingers and plopped onto my desk. I pressed both hands against the sides of my head.

My stunned brain struggled to process information before me. How could my aunt Millie be *dead*?

And, why—WHY—hadn't anyone called me to share this shocking news? None of this made any sense at all. What the *hell* was going on?

Millie was only in her early fifties, vibrant, living her life with gusto, and, as far as I knew, enjoying robust good health. If she'd had an illness, a serious health concern, surely she would've told me. Wouldn't she?

I snatched up the letter.

As I am serving as the executor of the estate, I must inform you that you are named in Ms. Minero's will as her sole heir. Accordingly, and pursuant to California Probate Code, I have enclosed copies of Ms. Minero's trust documents. Also enclosed, please find

I stopped reading, right in the middle of a sentence.

No. No. NO! This is impossible. It's got to be a mistake. But, despite my angry denials, tears overflowed and meandered in salty tracks down my face. Deep inside, I knew the truth was staring me in the face.

Oh, Millie! She had raised me and my twin brother Rudy. Millie was our rock, our safe harbor, our... everything.

And now she was gone. How could she be gone? It was unthinkable, impossible.

I am the only one left.

The realization left me lightheaded, disoriented. Welcome to a new existence, a new view of the world.

I slid my hands through my hair, sniffed hard to clear my nose, and grabbed a tissue to blot the tears tumbling down my face.

No. I clenched my fists, wrinkling the letter. This can't be real. I won't *let* it be real.

My attempt at magical thinking failed. I sighed, picked up the discarded envelope, and pulled out the copy of Millie's will. I quickly scanned the document. This was no sick joke, no outrageous scam. The document before me was real, and nothing could change that fact.

Millie had died, and she'd left her entire estate to me. The historic home where I grew up, and the fortune she'd amassed as an internationally acclaimed Western artist, all of it, now mine.

A cold, sweaty wave of nausea swept through me. I inhaled deeply, and searched hard for my emotional reset button. I was at work. I had things to do, meetings to attend. I had no time, as my long-departed grandmother often said, to shilly-shally.

I stepped out into the hallway, and headed towards the ladies' room so I could splash cold water on my face. Distracted, I flinched back when I realized that I was close to being run over by a looming figure that appeared out of nowhere. The figure resolved into the lumpy shape of senior partner and pompous gasbag James Royston who, as usual, was wearing a frown on his face and not watching where he was going.

Royston expected women and other minions to step out of his way as a matter of course, preferably in a deferential and expeditious manner. He always seemed startled and offended when I failed to do so.

He was pushing seventy, and his squarish face reminded me of an age-spotted sheet of corrugated cardboard. Add a tatty old mop to mimic his wiry white comb-over, and he and a beat-up old box would be twins.

He looked up to see who dared to encroach on his space, and ran an appraising eye the full length of my body.

"Good god above, Alex, you look like everlasting hell."

I couldn't tell whether Royston was grossed out because my face was red and puffy, or by the fact that I was wearing business casual. Just as surely as winter followed autumn, I could always count on him to be a paternalistic grump.

Old Cardboard-Face had founded the firm with my father, years back. I guessed the poor man probably missed the good old days, when the "girls" in the office knew their place, and realized intellectual fulfillment by fetching coffee for the big strong men. Early on, I'd adopted a policy of trying to imagine that this creature was actually a human being, and doing my best to ignore his grunts and grumbles.

But, this time, Royston's misogynistic snark proved to be too much for me. My emotions already frayed, I arrived at the proverbial bridge too far. I glared at him, focusing hard on his mottled beige face. Steel daggers were surely leaping from my eyes, racing forward, seeking to stab and maim.

His grumpy expression flickered through surprise into alert wariness. He might be a crank, but he certainly wasn't stupid.

"Jim." I decided to go with one of his favorite expressions, "Pack sand."

I was met with stunned silence.

What the hell. I'd already stuck my foot in it. Might as well do a good job. "Up yours. Get bent. You know. Stick it where the sun don't shine."

I made an abrupt U-turn back into my office, picked up my phone and buzzed my secretary. "Listen, Musu, I'm not feeling well. I'm going home. Rearrange as best you can and dump the rest on someone else. Thanks so much. You're the best."

I called Malcolm, my husband's driver, to come pick me up.

◆ ◆ ◆

By the time Malcolm got to my office, about an hour later, I'd had time to wash my face, and attain at least a superficial level of emotional control. He took me back to our trendy Tribeca loft and rode with me up the elevator, stoic and silent as ever. There was no point in asking him why he hadn't just let me out and gone back to his office on the garage level. He wouldn't have answered.

When we got to our floor, I stepped out of the elevator, only to find my husband, Mark, killing time in the foyer next to a stack of his stupidly expensive Louis Vuitton brown leather luggage.

I let my eyes linger on him for a moment, remembering the warm and handsome man of years past. Mark—tall, lean and athletic—had dark russet hair, and brown eyes that were a shade darker than my own. But now, his once-sensuous mouth seemed permanently curled in a dismissive sneer.

I often wondered what I had done to earn his contempt; I had no idea how to address it.

A flicker of surprise must have dashed across my face when I saw him pacing the foyer, obviously waiting for Malcolm's return.

"What's your problem," he said, and it wasn't a question. His voice sounded harsh, irritated. "I told you I was going to Sun Valley for those seminars."

So he had.

I approached him, and gave him a perfunctory peck on the lips. "Sorry, love, I forgot. I'm... I'm not feeling very good."

He flinched backwards, away from me. "You're not coming down with the flu, are you?" His voice shifted into his usual cold indifference. "The UN reception is next Tuesday. You know I'm expecting you to be there."

Yes, I knew. And suddenly, I just didn't care.

I turned away, and headed towards our front door. Mark stepped in behind me, and pulled me rearward into an embrace, the back of my head coming to rest against his pectorals. His muscular arms edged upwards, a little too close to my neck, and tightened, sending a clear message: Do not fight me.

Once upon a time, I would have relaxed onto his body, reveling in his closeness. Now, I only felt trapped, pinned like a withered butterfly displayed on a collector's mounting board. And I hated myself for being so passive. Instinctual self-preservation? Maybe.

"I won't forget," I whispered. "It's on my calendar. Don't worry. I'm just tired. And Royston was being unbearable. Things are crazy at work. I simply... got fed up and decided to let someone else deal with it for once. I'm sick of being their goddamned miracle worker."

He let his arms drop. "Get some rest. I'll be back Friday night. Or maybe Saturday."

Mark put a heavy hand on my shoulder to keep me from escaping and kissed me on the top of my head. Then he stepped back, pivoted on his heel and walked away. Malcolm picked up the bags and followed him into the elevator.

As I watched the shiny brass doors slide shut, I wondered why I hadn't told Mark about Millie.

◆ ◆ ◆

Within minutes of his departure, I'd padded into our bedroom, shucked off my work clothes and pulled back the covers on the bed. I plopped down on the mattress, grabbed my phone, and called Doc, a Jackson resident who'd been a friend of my family forever. Instead of the call connecting, I got a recording.

"All circuits are busy right now. Please try your call again later."

Well, shit.

I tried the phone number for the office of the lawyer who'd sent the letter. Same thing. Something big was going on in the Jackson area, if the phone system was down. Forest fire? Maybe. It happens from time to time.

Oh, hell; I'd deal with it later, or maybe tomorrow. It wasn't like I could actually *do* anything for Millie at this point. If there'd been an associated emergency, it was long over. And, like the phone circuits, my ability to cope had hit overload.

I wasn't hungry, it seemed too early to sleep, and seeking distraction, I wandered over to the movie player. When I pushed the power button, the soft buzz of a disc spinning up told me that Mark left a video in the machine. I reached toward the window to draw the drapes. A low, breathy moan floated out of the speakers.

I whirled around and looked at the display. *Good lord.* Had Mark been watching porn?

I gaped at the entwined naked figures, unable to comprehend the scene before me.

No. Please no. This couldn't be...

My knees buckled, and I collapsed onto the bed. I stared in horror at the image of my husband, displayed on the screen in all his sweaty, naked glory, vigorously bonking a writhing female.

She looked far too young to be viewed without revulsion at the unspoken implications, maybe high school age, perhaps even younger. Her arms were splayed outward, hands clenching the sheets. Her face, partially obscured by long, tangled blond hair, remained a mystery, but her other attributes were clearly on display. The girl's high young breasts jiggled like Jell-O with every jolting thrust of Mark's lean hips.

Moving in shell-shocked slow motion, I picked up the remote control from the night stand and, hands trembling, turned off the video. What had I just seen? What did it mean?

Oh, I'd always known that Mark loved the ladies. And I was thrilled and flattered when he left behind the inflated bimbos he previously favored and chose me—ME—to be his bride. And, I'd never had so much of an inkling, in all the years we'd been together, that he'd strayed. But... this... was more than straying. The girl in the video *was a kid.*

Shocking realizations rushed forward in my mind, shrieking for attention and demanding acknowledgement. Everything good that I'd ever believed about my husband disintegrated, and collapsed into a pile of bitter ashes.

It all made sense now.

I am, from time to time, mistaken for someone much younger than my actual thirty-four years. I'm barely five feet tall, small-boned, somewhat flat-chested, and perennially thin, like my mom, and her mother before her.

My stomach lurched. An adult who looked like a kid—I was the perfect solution for satisfying his secret proclivities. And now, here I was, creeping towards forty, and not looking so much like a kid any more. I'd refused to get my face botoxed when Mark had not-so-gently suggested doing so.

Well, then. Time for a replacement... ? Ditch the old hag, and the horror of her embryonic crows feet?

I stumbled into the bathroom, and vomited until I collapsed.

Long minutes later, when my strength allowed, I rolled over and stared at the blank white ceiling, waiting for my thoughts to settle and crystallize. The coolness of the ceramic tile floor didn't bother me; I felt suspended in space, separated from my body. The only things that seemed real were the furious thoughts raging through my mind.

For the second time that day, I faced a new reality. I knew I could not bear it if Mark touched me even one more time.

And then I also knew, with calm and clear-eyed surety, what I had to do.

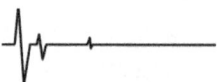

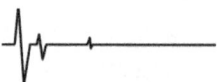

Chapter Two

I left a note on the bed, and the video paused at a particularly vulgar-looking frame. A copy of the video was tucked in my bag. Mark was to be away for four, possibly five days. With the help of a packing and shipping company, and despite the shocked entreaties of the whole of D'Angelo Royston LLP and Affiliates, I was ready to leave in three.

It took a while, but I finally got ahold of the lawyer. Doc's phone just rang and rang. It was impossible to dismiss my sense of unease at the uncharacteristic silence from his end.

Nevertheless, I felt a gritty sort of triumph, walking out the door at six a.m., the morning of the fourth day after The Discovery. The note I left for Mark did not state where I was going, only that my attorney would be in touch. Our shared assets would be divided up in a civilized manner. I was not on the warpath. I cared not for revenge. I only wanted to be gone.

Thanking providence that I'd maintained my own separate banking accounts, I kissed my life in New York City goodbye. Just like that. No regrets, no second thoughts, no moments of panicked indecision.

My sudden departure from the eastern seaboard would not cause a fatal rupture to occur in the city's space-time continuum. Life there would muddle along just fine without me. Some might say that running was a foolish act, tantamount to burning a bridge. So be it. I torched the sucker, and danced in the ashes.

I was free.

I was going home.

◆ ◆ ◆

My destination, on this fine August morning, was the city of Jackson, California.

Born during the hustle and tumble of the California Gold Rush,

Jackson sits nestled in a pleasant narrow valley in the Sierra Nevada foothills, southeast of Sacramento. I'd grown up there. Even after I'd left home, my heart refused to let go of the place. I may have appeared at ease in a tailored business suit, but inside, I remained a country girl. The closer I got to my old hometown, the louder my heart sang.

I'd left New York about a week before and camped my way across the United States. And now I was back in the embrace of the mighty Sierras. The previous night, I'd pulled into the familiar campsite near Hunter's Lake, and the verdant forest worked its magic, welcoming me home.

I'd camped here many times during my childhood, with my twin brother Rudy and my Grandpa John. This place, sheltered by lofty pines and mighty California blue oaks, felt as comforting as memories of my childhood bedroom. I didn't bother to set up my tent. I just let the warm evening air of August embrace my body. The wind whispering in the trees and the cascading rush of the little stream that ran through camp joined together in a soft lullaby. I fell asleep, and the night passed in peaceful serenity.

A sudden piercing pain in my eye shocked me awake. and my hands flew upward in an involuntary reflex. I jerked into a sitting position, confusion clouding my brain. I leaned back on my elbows and pulled in a deep breath of resin-scented air. Oh. That's right. Campground.

I rubbed my throbbing eyelid. Had someone thrown a rock at me? I swung my legs around and inadvertently placed my hand on the sharp top of a fat brown acorn. I hissed and snatched up my hand; the hard brown nut had punched a small divot in my skin. I flicked my hand with a reflexive jerk, and winced. A squirrel screeched in the huge tree above me, seemingly furious at losing its treasure.

I picked up the acorn and chucked it across the campground. It skittered along the soft surface of the ground and ended up in a clump of manzanita.

"Payback's a bitch, squirrel."

The squirrel paid no apparent attention to the lesson in life that I thoughtfully provided, and scuttled away, bounding up the tree trunk. I ran my fingers through my unruly hair, and listened to the fading sound of the squirrel's angry chattering.

Further musing on the life of a squirrel cut short as my bladder demanded my attention to other matters. I hopped up off the yoga mat that served as my mattress and hurried over to the campground pit toilet. I peed, holding my breath against the ambient stink of the place. I cleaned my hands with bottled sanitizer and meandered back across the powdery Sierra soil to my little nest.

No one would see me wandering around in just my tee shirt and panties, not that I really cared. Summer tourist season was almost over, and outsiders didn't know about this place anyway. I had the campground to myself.

The only sounds around me were the sighs of the wind through the dusty green pine branches above my head and the distant call of a scolding jay. I tilted my head back to gaze at the arc of the sky. In the patches of blue between the treetops, pink traces of sunrise faded into pale yellow and disappeared into the white clouds. Sierra sky is pearlescent, almost glowing, unique. It felt good to be home.

Why had it taken a tragedy to bring me here again? Everything around me brought bittersweet memories rushing back. I should have come home sooner.

◆ ◆ ◆

The campground sat on National Forest property, but the adjacent lake, owned by friends, did not. The lake wasn't visible from the campground, but I knew it was there. I'd spent a good portion of my childhood at that lake.

Once upon a time, long ago, I'd loved to sit on the boulders along the shore, perched high above the beach, while my twin brother Rudy hunted for bugs in the adjacent meadow. I didn't get down in the dirt with him on his entomological expeditions, at least not very often. It's not that I don't like bugs and such. Rudy could simply sit and stare at them far longer than I ever cared to.

But, Rudy was dead, had been for many years. Far too many people I loved had died too young.

Even now, Millie's death still didn't seem real. Tears welled up. Millie, of the flashing amethyst eyes, the long jet-black hair highlighted by time and nature with bold streaks of silver-gray. Yes, she was my great-aunt, but she was only a few years older than my mom, and the two were as close as sisters.

In my drive across the country, I'd had plenty of time to think about where I'd been, and where I was going. Millie's death might be blamed on the whimsies of fate and time, except for one thing—the strange letter from Doc McFarland that arrived in our mailbox the morning before I'd left.

He was a long-time friend of the family; I'd known Doc forever. Something about his letter bothered me at a very deep level. Why was the letter so cryptic, so unlike his usual self? The message between the lines seemed clear. He needed to tell me more. What in the world could be so horrible that he couldn't bear to write about it? Why hadn't he just called me?

I sent a letter back to Doc immediately; email was useless, he had no account. I knew now that he would never read it. Just days ago, while sitting in an internet café in a small town whose name I couldn't remember, an email arrived from his new medical partner, a Dr. Hunter. He regretted having to inform me that Doc had died of a massive heart attack shortly after Millie's death. I sent off a reply, telling him that I was on the road, and would be arriving in Jackson within the week. His response frightened me. He needed to talk to me as soon as I arrived in town. The message practically vibrated with urgency.

If that wasn't strange enough, then there was the weird reticence on the part of Millie's lawyer, the man who'd sent me the paperwork after Millie's death. I never did get a straight answer from him regarding cause of death, and had yet to see a copy of her death certificate.

The questions had gnawed at my guts for days now, and no reasonable explanations came to me. One thing was certain: I needed to find out what the hell was going on as soon as possible.

I shoved aside my morbid musings and jumped up to rummage around the campground, picking things up and tossing them back into my car, a used Mercedes SUV that I'd bought on my way out of town. The troubling thoughts persisted.

I had to fend off a descent into a dangerous mood. To distract myself, I belted out, at the top of my lungs, a favorite campfire song from my childhood. *Heeey Juuude...* The suspicions ducked around the musical roadblock and kept on eating away at me.

Stop! Just stop, right now. Of course, Doc had been cryptic! Poor man, Millie's death had broken his heart. He had known her for thirty or forty years, maybe more. And, then he had to sit down and write a letter to little Alexandra. To an eighty-seven-year-old man I probably remained a child, a babe, all alone in the world.

The song circled around in my head again. *Don't be afraid...*

Was Doc afraid?

Damn. All of a sudden, I sure was. Afraid that Millie's lawyer might be hiding something from me. Afraid that I'd made the wrong decision when I'd burned my bridges. And afraid that maybe this time I'd stuck my neck out too far.

Not that there was anything I could do about it now. I'd jumped off the cliff. Time to learn how to fly.

I straightened my spine, and marched about the campground, yodeling out the bouncy refrain, trying to set myself to rights. I stowed my gear, laid out my pink tracksuit, and grabbed a granola bar.

I sat on the back edge of the wooden picnic table, munching the peanut-buttery snack and swinging my feet back and forth like a little kid.

I had a whole stack of hours to kill before it was time to head down the hill to Jackson and see Millie's lawyer. I had to move, to do something before I exploded with impatience. I hopped off the table, got dressed, trotted over to the small path, and wound my way down the hill from the campground to the lake.

Small puffs of fine silt swooshed up beside my bare toes as I bounced down the little trail towards the lake. Around a little bend, and the view of the deep blue water opened up. The lake beckoned to me, shimmering, a small piece of heaven dropped into the midst of the forest.

The morning sunshine reflected off the glittery speckles in the huge granite boulders where, yesterday afternoon, I watched laughing teenage boys jump and dive into the lake. Now, no one but me disturbed the quiet peace. I heard no voices, smelled no smoke from other campfires. No one lived in the old stone mansion up on the bluff. I was alone with the blue jays and the whispering wind.

I ambled along the long narrow beach, listening to the pleasant crunch of the grainy sand rubbing my feet, and headed to the jumble of massive rocks that sat at the end of the stretch of sand. Picking my way with care, I climbed up to the top of the boulders from where the boys had leaped with such joyous abandon.

I plopped myself down on the top of the biggest boulder and dangled my legs over the side. The breeze sang sweet songs across the water, and tiny waves gurgled in counterpoint as they bumped against the rocks. Once again, I thought about my brother Rudy, and those long-ago sunlit days of childhood.

A famous author once said that you can't go home again. Was there a warning in his words? I didn't know, but here I was.

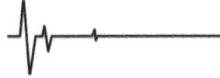

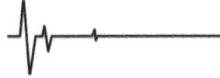

Chapter Three

A couple of hours later I pulled onto the highway and continued on down the road to Jackson, eager to meet with the lawyer, and finally get the keys to Millie's house.

Jackson is a town of venerable homes perched on steep hillsides, all looking down upon the row of businesses strung like multicolored beads along the ribbon of Highway 49.

I parked way up on Summit Street near the old courthouse, an ugly mustard-yellow Art Deco slab of a building that always gave me the giggles when I was a kid. I thought the brown-painted decorative trim pieces that stretched between the first and second-story windows were giant Legos. What were Legos doing stuck to the side of a building?

I exited the car, bent over, and stretched my flatlander leg muscles by touching my toes, preparing for the gallop down Court Street to the bottom of the hill.

Court Street runs sharply down the hill like a sluice, catching unwary walkers by surprise when it throws them into a run. At the bottom, the involuntary jogger can stop to catch their breath, then turn the corner and move at a more reasonable pace along the sidewalks of Main Street.

I turned right on Main and walked along until I came to the historic brick edifice that was my goal. A glass-paned door on the ground floor opened into a stairwell. Golden lettering on the etched glass told the visitor the name of the business occupying the top floor.

ANDREW GEORGE PICHL
ATTORNEY AT LAW

I stepped inside and started up the timeworn oak stairs. The building smelled of beeswax, lemon oil, and well-aged books. Like the bones of a very old man, the stairway creaked when forced to carry even the lightest of loads.

The squeaks and groans of the oak stair treads spoke of over a hundred years of footsteps, of thousands of treks up and down the wooden steps.

I had no interest in the antique ambience. I wanted to get those keys in my hands. I wanted to *go home.*

I made a hard-right turn at the top landing and continued on up to a small reception area. A few inexpensive-looking framed photos of historic Mother Lode locations—Sutter Creek, the Kennedy Mine, the little town of Volcano—graced the walls in a haphazard arrangement. A few wooden chairs sat along the wall across from a bare desk sitting forlorn, shoved into a corner.

The desk and chairs, massive pieces of scratched and worn golden oak, looked like were carted in from a second-hand store, dumped there and forgotten. The room had a sad air of neglect about it.

An inner door stood a bit ajar. I walked towards it. "Hello?"

"Yes." A cold and uninviting response rang out from the inner office.

"Mr. Pickle?" I'd asked a German-speaking friend how to pronounce the name, and she'd assured me that the silliest-sounding version was as close as I could get to the correct pronunciation.

"It's pronounced Pea-KEL," came the voice again.

I pushed the door open, and found a tall, gaunt-looking man standing behind a desk stacked high with papers and file folders. Mr. Pea-KEL looked exactly like a frowning version of the old farmer in Grant Wood's iconic painting, *American Gothic.* So much for the warm welcome.

Perhaps he mistook me for a lost tourist or something. I hadn't exactly dressed up for the occasion, and I knew my short dark hair bounced in wild, flyaway corkscrews, as it always did.

The lawyer's sour facial expression said, "Go away." His voice said, "What can I do for you?"

I turned on my patented meeting-a-client, megawatt smile. "Good morning, sir. I'm Alexandra D'Angelo."

The man's eyes widened. I held out my hand. He took it, and gave me a dead-fish shake. His hand felt sweaty and had a bit of a tremor. "Yes, yes. I've been, uh, expecting you. Andrew Pichl, at your service. And, yes, in case you are wondering, I *am* related to the great Czech composer, Václav Pichl."

"Oh," I said, startled by the odd non-sequitur, and trying to sound impressed. What response was he fishing for?

"Your aunt often spoke of your prodigious musical talents," he continued. "And, of course, anyone operating at that, uh, level in the august halls of the classical music community would have knowledge of all the major composers."

I decided to ignore his comments regarding my abilities as a musician. Yes, I could play a fair tune, but that was neither here nor there. "Of course," I said. "Your ancestor was one of the great ones. Pleased to meet you."

Mr. Pichl finally dropped my hand and stepped backwards with an off-balance lurch. It appeared that he intended to park himself in his wheeled desk chair. But he stumbled, knocked the chair a tad backwards and to the side, and failed to adjust his aim.

I held my breath and leaned a bit forward, wondering if I should try to grab him, save him from a catastrophic crash to the floor. To my relief, he managed to rescue himself with a clumsy sideways shuffle-scuttle. He seemed to not even notice this near-calamitous moment. Perhaps he liked living life on the edge.

I sat down in the hard, wooden chair across from him. Without making eye contact, Pichl turned and pulled out a huge folio of papers from the old credenza behind his chair.

"Well, then, let's begin. As you know, Ms. D'Angelo, you are the sole heir to the estate of Ms. Milagros Minero. The net worth is substantial."

He handed me a statement from a major investment company. I opened the envelope, and scanned the summary page. The balance was indeed noteworthy, but hardly surprising. Millie was respected internationally as a gifted artist. She'd done well for herself.

Once again, I wondered what response the man expected. Without comment, I slid the papers back in the envelope and set it on his desk. Pichl leaned forward and peered at me over the top of his wire-rimmed glasses. "The trust leaves, uh, nothing to her brother's children, you know."

Did he want me to comment on family dynamics? Sorry, but it wasn't going to happen. Millie set things up the way she set them up, end of topic. I didn't say anything, and hoped he'd get the hint. He didn't seem to notice my discomfort.

"Ms. Minero was, uh, extremely well-organized, you'll be pleased to know."

Yes, I did know, as a matter of fact. I nodded my head in curt agreement.

"You are, uh, also aware that the house is old, built well before 1900, and the plumbing last updated over fifty years ago, at the very least. I want to make sure that you, uh, know what you're taking on."

He stopped abruptly, and gazed hard in my direction. His studied pose brought to mind a worried old undertaker in a BBC television series, complete with hands clasped together in front of his chest.

"In fact," he continued, "I'm prepared to make a generous offer on the property. I've always had an interest in historic buildings." He shoved a real estate offer-to-purchase document towards me.

What the hell? Didn't he know that I grew up in that house?

Not wanting to convey even the smallest amount of interest in his offer, I didn't touch the document, didn't even glance at it. I said in a calm professional voice, "I'm not interested in selling the house."

A brief and uncomfortable silence hovered over us for a few seconds. Pichl shifted around a bit in his chair and resumed pulling out papers from the portfolio. I had to fight the urge to grab the stack out of his hands and start sorting through it myself.

He cleared his throat. "Thank you so much for signing and transmitting all the other needed documents back to me so promptly," he said. "Your name, as trustee, is now on the deed, on the bank accounts, the brokerage accounts, and on the car registration. This envelope has the keys to the house, to the car, and to the safe deposit box."

He set the envelope just out of my reach. *Jerk.*

"Yes. Thank you. Mr. Pichl, I'm wondering why you never provided any information regarding the specifics of my aunt's passing. I'm very interested in knowing the details—cause of death, and so forth."

"Umm. Well. The Jackson police department never, uh, transmitted that information to me."

My gut roiled. "Police department? Why is the police department involved?"

There it was again, that unsettling internal alarm bell that told me that something about Millie's death was off-kilter. First Doc, and now Pichl.

"Well, uh, the death being very sudden and unexpected, I guess they had to investigate."

"And you didn't follow up on that?"

"No need to. Since there was no impact on settling the estate, I just carried on."

He went back to pulling documents out of the portfolio, as if Millie's death was really no big deal. I wanted to slap him.

He launched into a tedious explanation of all the details in each of the documents. My temper rose even further.

Is this guy deranged? Why is he wasting my time? There was still a stack of papers he hadn't yet touched. I couldn't stand it any longer.

I grabbed the untouched papers, and began to flip through them, ticking them off against the checklist in my head. Vehicle transfer of ownership. Stock certificates. Bank account information. It wasn't difficult to verify that everything appeared to be correct and in order. And, as long as I did so promptly, I could always contact him later if I found an error.

"Mr. Pichl," I said, in a curt business-like tone, as I thumped the stack to straighten it. I handed the papers back to him. "Thank you so much for holding these documents and the keys for me. Since we both know there are no challenges to the terms of the will and the trust, and no problems are known to exist in conjunction with any of the other documentation, I won't take up any more of your time."

I smiled at him, pushed back the chair, and stood up. When he didn't respond, I turned my smile into a wide-eyed death-ray glare. He got the hint.

Pichl gathered all the papers together, placed them in the portfolio, and turned them over to me. Good thing, too. By this point, I wouldn't have been above breaking his arm to get them. I wanted out of there.

"I hope you have a pleasant rest of the day, Mr. Pichl, and thanks again for all your help." I extended my hand for another one of his dead-mackerel handshakes, turned and left his office. Halfway through the empty reception area, his voice rang out behind me.

"Miss D'Angelo?"

"Yes?" I didn't turn around.

"When you decide you want to sell that old house, let me know."

When I decide to sell? Where'd that come from? "I'll keep that in mind," I said. Like when hell froze over.

I walked out the door and across the landing. I lifted my right foot to start down the stairwell; an abrupt bump on my left shoulder sent me off-balance. I lurched, slapped at the railing to grab it, and turned, trembling.

Andrew Pichl stood there, his face bright red. "Oh dear, I'm so sorry. I, uh, just thought I'd see you out, and I tripped on the hall runner, there." He gestured towards the carpet. "Are you, uh, alright?"

Refusing to believe what seemed obvious—the jerk had tried to trip me—I muttered the standard words indicating no harm done. It seemed far easier to believe him only a bumbling fool. I turned and hurried down the stairs, and almost ran out of the building.

◆ ◆ ◆

I trudged back up Court Street's intimidating hill to my car, leg muscles protesting all the way. I drove down into the town via Water Street, turned right onto Main Street at the grand old National Hotel, and proceeded into the Downtown Historic District. Bit by bit, my mood improved.

I passed the old familiar downtown storefronts, many of constructed of brick following the Great Fire of 1862. Back in those days, Jackson was a roaring mining town, rich from the gold of the Kennedy and Argonaut Mines. These days, the place was much more sedate.

How many times had I walked along this street, holding my grandpa's hand? How many times had we stopped at the old hardware store and poked through the zinc-plated bins that held nails and screws and other magical things?

I pulled up to the signal in front of the historic former fire station and waited for the green light. I turned left on Hwy 49 to go to the grocery store. I bought only a few things—coffee, fruit, and a few other odds and ends. Unfortunately, the excruciating amount of time expended standing in line wasn't reflective of the size of the purchase.

Already riled by my encounter with Mr. Pichl, I found myself getting antsy, and then angry. The New Yorker inside of me fumed.

The clerk, relaxed as a fine summer day, chatted with each and every customer about their kids, the new movie at the cinema, where they'd gone on vacation, and even their choice of product brands.

My right foot started tapping. A nasty remark rested on the tip of my tongue. Get on with it, already. I bit off the comment just in time, before it came blurting out, laden with sarcasm. I'd forgotten. This was life in a small town.

Inhale. Count to ten. Smile. Ignore the clerk's odd look at my choice of coffee. Be glad the place even stocked it.

The clerk wore a name-tag that proclaimed to the world that her name was Chairish. I realized, with a shock, that I knew her from high school. I would have never recognized her without her label. She looked time-worn, older than her years.

We were never friends. She was in school because she had to be there, not because she wanted to be. I remembered wondering if she had a brother named Table-ish, or a sister named Sofa-ish. My adult-self cringed at my younger pettiness.

Chairish lifted her faded blue eyes to scan my face, and her expression glazed over with disinterest. Her eyes darted to see who stood in line behind me.

A chilling realization washed over me, and I bit back another impatient remark. How much of a New Yorker had I become? Did I want to be that person now? Rudeness wouldn't accomplish a darned thing except to put me on the community shit list.

I stowed the purchases in the back of the car, and spent a few moments taking deep breaths and re-centering myself. Only then did I pull out of the parking lot onto the highway.

◆ ◆ ◆

I drove south a short distance from town, past the old Butte Store, turned left, and proceeded up a steep unimproved road that ran along the base of Butte Mountain.

Clustered in majestic groves across the rolling landscape, ancient oak trees bearing the dusty grayish blue-green leaves of late summer greeted me. At the top of the hill, the trees on either side of the road gave way to patches of open grassland, rippling and golden in the strong light of late summer. This was the beloved landscape of my childhood.

I drove a few miles to a small, unremarkable junction where a narrow dirt lane branched off to the right. I turned. No signpost, no mailbox, no marker of any kind stood here, but I could drive to this place at midnight on a moonless night and not falter for an instant.

Almost there, almost home... Around the bend, past the big old oak tree, up the small rise, and there it stood alone, surrounded by an expanse of golden summer grass—Millie's big stone house.

My house. I'm home. At last.

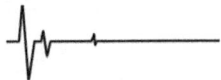

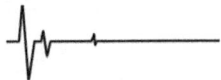

CHAPTER FOUR

The big old house faced southwest, overlooking the long ridges that reach from the Sierras like fingers stretching out to claw at the valley floor below. I loved the venerable structure. Constructed in the 1880s of heavy local rock and hand-sawn timbers, it was a remarkable structure, and a registered California Historic Landmark.

Rough-hewn natural granite blocks formed the solid back and sides of the building. Unevenly-finished swirling white stucco covered the front. Large double chimneys marked fireplaces on the east and west sides of the house. How many evenings had my family watched the sun go down, comfortably perched in the Adirondack chairs on the deep porch that crossed the front of the house?

From the time when I was just a toddler, I'd heard the story of how the Minero family came to be. The original familial patriarch and the builder of this house, was one Juan Minero, a young, well-educated Chilean who came to the Gold Rush country in 1849. It seemed he'd cut all ties to his homeland, for no records existed documenting anything of his original identity, not even his real name.

His name, 'Juan Minero'—John the Miner— was of his own invention. It originated as a pseudonym, an attempt to remain anonymous. The Minero name morphed over time into his true identity, recorded on legal documents, and passed along to his children. He'd survived the Chilean War of Calaveras County and, wounded, fled to Jackson. Here, he'd put down roots, and founded a dynasty.

Rudy and I reenacted this dramatic story countless times, with Rudy playing the heroic Juan Minero. I much preferred playing the role of the wicked miner who'd shot him, and who then went down in a hail of bullets delivered by our hero. Which probably wasn't what happened at all, but since when do kids worry about historical accuracy? I would die with great drama, lurching and staggering all over the place while Rudy shot about fifty thousand pretend bullets into my hide.

Rudy and I had also heard many times how the strong men of the Minero family had built the house, but never once did we pretend to be stonemasons or carpenters. Funny how that works.

I approached the house and anticipation—a mixture of hope and dread—heightened. The dirt road curved to the right in front of the rugged old building and wound around to the back. I followed it, circling into the parking area at the rear. Behind the house stood a large propane tank and an old barn long ago converted into a garage.

I hopped out of the car, pushed open the heavy sliding doors of the barn, then drove inside. The place was huge. I could've put ten cars in there if I'd wanted. A cool and earthy smell imbued the old building with an aura of home and history. Even now, years since animals were stabled there, it still smelled more of hay and horses than automobiles.

I parked next to Millie's little station wagon that sat shrouded in a heavy canvas cover. Her car remained protected to a certain extent, but spiders had already been busy at work, building complex webs connecting the dirt floor to the sides of the wheels. I stood with my hands on my hips and stared at it. I knew the car was almost new. But, to even consider selling it seemed disloyal, almost sacrilegious. I filed that thought away as a problem for another day.

I walked to the open doorway and lingered a moment, squinting into the bright sunlight, and savoring the sight of this old familiar place. Two stone outbuildings squatted to the right of the barn, each about twenty feet wide and forty feet long. The closest one, built as a bunkhouse for the crew of a working ranch, had remained unused for years. The intended purpose for the other small building was long forgotten, and had served as a general storage area for years.

Also to my right stood a tall windmill, with its large metal water tank high up on substantial legs. The windmill blades whirled with flashing speed, singing their distinctive humming song, pushed in endless circles by the slightest breeze. The piston driving the water pump thumped up and down in steady cadence. In the house, there would be running water, sweet, clean, wonderful-tasting well water—even if the power was shut off.

No garden of any sort graced the property. One hundred years ago, a vegetable garden would have been an absolute necessity for survival here. But Millie had no desire to engage in a never-ending difference of opinion with the black-tail deer, the jackrabbits, and all their hungry animal brethren. Even though home-grown vegetables are the best of the best, I didn't care to have that ongoing battle either. Store-bought veggies would have to suffice.

I left the barn and walked to the back of the house, up the steps, and across the small porch to the back door. Hand trembling, I inserted the key and heard the familiar snap as the bolt disengaged. I hesitated, took a deep breath, and walked in.

◆ ◆ ◆

The familiar scent of bacon and biscuits that was always present during my childhood failed to greet me. Instead, the pungent smell of Pine-Sol smacked me in the face. Someone had scrubbed the place to within a millimeter of its very existence.

I wandered around, opening cupboards. The beautiful vintage Franciscan Desert Rose dinnerware, the glassware, the pots and pans, the cooking utensils and flatware all sat lined up in their proper places. The refrigerator was cleaned out, everything perishable taken away. Every flat surface gleamed, every fingerprint removed from the ivory-toned painted cabinet faces.

Millie never gave two cents about being meticulous housekeeper. Who'd done all this for me?

The kitchen looked just the same as it always had—the jade-green antique wooden table and chairs, the ivory wallpaper printed with a soft pattern of green latticework and big pink cabbage roses. I walked across the bleached pine floor and ran my fingers along the rim of the enameled cast-iron sink and the top of the big, white 1940's gas range.

The house sat there empty, devoid of life. The tick... tick... tick... of the old pendulum clock in the front room rang out in the silence. That's when it hit me. Millie was... gone.

◆ ◆ ◆

How I had loved her! Our aunt swooped into our lives and became a surrogate mother to Rudy and me when we were only in kindergarten. Our mother's death was expected, dreaded, made inevitable by the cancer that ravaged her body. Millie was our savior, our rescuer, our provider of solace and comfort. Only as an adult did I appreciate the magnitude of her sacrifice.

I stumbled to one of the familiar green chairs, ran my hand over the top of it, and stared at the huge watercolor painting of burgundy, pink, and yellow roses that hung over the bricked-up stone fireplace.

Odd. The bricks sealing the old fireplace looked like someone had bashed at them with a sledgehammer. And the marks were fresh. A cold frisson of discomfort sent goosebumps popping up along my arms. The fireplace was bricked up years ago, the reason for doing so now lost in time. There was no reason for someone to damage the bricks.

The bashing of the fireplace suddenly seemed m to me to be an apt metaphor for what had happened to my family. One by one, my relatives were chipped away. Even now, was the invisible hammer of fate aimed at my head?

Oh well. I shook my head to free myself from my macabre thoughts. As with the car, the damage to the fireplace was a problem for another day.

I wandered into the hallway and walked towards the front of the house. There, in the living room, stood Millie's beloved satin ebony 1929 Steinway concert grand piano. I sat down on the familiar bench.

Music was my solace, my passion, and my most trustworthy companion. My fingers ran up and down the keys, playing scales and arpeggios, and drifted into Franz Liszt's haunting Liebestraum No.3.

O lieb' so lang Du lieben kannst...
Oh, love as long as you can!
The hour will come when you will stand at the grave and mourn.

Memories swept over me like a huge rolling breaker at the seashore, threatening to drown me. Millie should be here, dancing around the kitchen, humming a sweet, secret song. My brother Rudy should be here, crashing down the stairs to meet me, yelling, "Yo! Allie-Saurus!" just to piss me off.

But, Rudy was dead too, gone since our sixteenth year. Rudy died, under brutal, senseless, and mysterious circumstances. All these years later, it still hurt.

My mom, my dad, my brother, and now my aunt. All dead.
How long would it be before I'd be dead too?

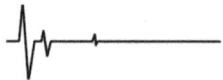

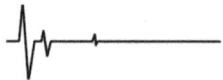

Chapter Five

It seemed that I'd been up for hours, and the day should be over by now, but lunchtime hadn't even arrived yet. The memories were knocking the stuffing out of me. But, there were places to go, and things to do. I pulled out my cell phone and called Doc's office.

The receptionist told me that she could get me in if I came within the hour, as they'd had a last-minute cancellation. Well. That was easy.

I found Millie's thick ivory towels stacked in the cabinet in the small bathroom off the kitchen, and shampoo and soap in the shower. The warm water coursed over me in a river of pure bliss, but since I had no idea how much propane remained in the tank, I couldn't indulge in a marathon shower session.

I practically bubbled over with smug self-assurance. A city slicker wouldn't have even considered the fact that the water heater ran on some sort of depletable fuel, and would have stood here shrieking when the hot water disappeared.

An immediate second thought erased the first one. It didn't actually occur to me to check the propane gauge until I was already soaking wet, standing there with shampoo running down my face. City slicker? Guilty as charged.

I dried off, dug through my stuff and found my last clean blouse and a pair of not-too-grubby jeans, got dressed and headed out. I gripped the steering wheel too tightly, wondering, once again, what horrible secrets would soon be revealed. Had Millie died of the plague, or Hantavirus, or... something even worse? Maybe that's why the house was scrubbed down. I shivered, imagining deadly microbes crawling all over me.

◆ ◆ ◆

Within seven minutes I strode down the echoing center corridor of the medical arts building. At the office door, I stopped, took a deep breath, and stepped inside.

Before I knew what was happening, I got crushed in a cushiony hug. “Oh, Holy Angels, look at you! My little chickie is all grown up. My goodness, but don’t you look fabulous!”

I found myself squeezed against the very ample bosom of Alberta ‘Bertie’ Strahan, Doc’s office manager for the last thirty years. Bertie was built somewhat like a walking feather pillow, and had plump pink cheeks, kind green eyes and flyaway graying hair. She'd known me since... well, since forever.

“He's waitin’ for you,” Bertie said, waving at one of the inner-office doors. “I know it's a bit too early to be thinkin’ about food, but when you're done talkin’ to him, let's go grab some lunch.”

“Sounds good.” My early morning granola bar seemed but a distant memory. I took a few steps in the proper direction, stopped, and turned back to Bertie. “What’s up with the ‘no problem with an appointment’ deal? Is he an asshole or something?”

A wicked little smirk danced across Bertie's plump face. “Well, his appointments were rearranged this morning because... well, things just got weird. You know. Things happen. Sayin’ we had a cancellation was easier than explainin’ the mess.”

Bertie glanced at her watch. “He’s only got about ten minutes or so to give you. But, as far as whether he’s a jerk or not, I'm just gonna make you find that out all by yourself.”

“Bertie! I thought you were my friend.”

Bertie grinned and shook her head. “You musta thought wrong, Chicken Little. Off you go.” She took me by the shoulders and pointed me in the general direction of his office door. “Good luck,” she added with a bit of drama in her voice. She gave me a soft swat on the butt.

I glared back at her over my shoulder. “Thanks a lot, Bertie. I’ll remember this.”

In a few steps, I was at Dr. Hunter’s office door. I knocked, and a deep male voice bid me to enter. I pushed open the door and saw a pair of hands holding a medical journal. The magazine came down, and two of the bluest eyes I’d ever seen stared out at me. Chris Pine blue eyes. I’d seen those eyes before. But, for the life of me, I couldn’t remember when or where.

A delighted grin lit up Dr. Hunter’s face. He stood, and held out his hand. Quite clearly, he expected me to recognize him.

I found myself mesmerized by his eyes. At last I came to my senses and returned his handshake. We settled into our chairs.

His face...There was something about it... A vision from the past flashed into my mind. Small children, running and splashing in the shallow

pick a table at the back, near a window. A bored-looking waitress with faded hennaed hair greeted us, set water glasses on the table, and rattled off the list of daily specials. The ceiling fan overhead squeaked at intermittent intervals during her recitation, punctuating the more salient points. When finished, she flashed us an insincere smile of strangely bright white teeth that looked like Chiclets. She plopped the plastic-coated menus on the table and walked away. I took a sip of water.

"Wow," said Bertie, "Does the library know that Bucky's teeth are missin'?" She was referring to the taxidermied beaver mascot at the children's library.

I snorted and got water up my nose. I wiped my face with the napkin. "How do you do that?"

"Do what?"

"Always make me laugh at just the wrong moment."

"It's called 'know your audience.' You know I used to work in an insane asylum. I'm super good with crazy people. That's why you and I get along so damned well."

"Bertie! You're awful!" I grabbed one of the little pink packets of fake sweetener out of the container on the table, and flung it at her.

She laughed with a wicked-witch cackle. "You have noooo idea," she said. "And while I'm bein' awful, I gotta ask. What happened in Greg's office? You were outta there like a gazelle with a bee up its butt. C'mon, sweetheart. Spit it out, like a good girl."

I laughed. Bertie was an absolute love. I rolled my eyes. "It's not worth talking about."

"Well, with the kind of reaction he got from you, it certainly must be. C'mon. I'm waiting."

I couldn't help it. I burst out laughing. Just like that, poof, my whole body relaxed.

"Oh," I said, "he was just pulling my chain. A return to childhood insults, and all that." And, for once, Bertie just grinned, and had the good sense not to push for every bloody detail.

As the meal progressed, Bertie's mood grew more somber. "Damn," she said. At my quizzical look, she said, "You know." She paused for a few seconds. "Doc."

"Yes." I nodded my head as memories swept over me. He visited us often, popping in with little gifts or treats, or a bundle of flowers for Millie. A Mark Twain lookalike, and born raconteur, Doc had entertained Rudy and me for hours with an endless stream of ridiculous stories.

"It doesn't seem quite right, does it," I said. "I mean, we all knew the man was getting up there. But I thought he'd still be playing golf at ninety-nine."

Tears came up in Bertie's eyes. "Lordy, I loved that man..." Her voice trailed off into a strained silence.

"Good grief, yes. We all adored him. He gave so much, to so many people."

"Yeah." Bertie did an odd little shake and seemed to force a smile onto her face.

As the diner filled up, the beaver-toothed waitress sent a couple of hard looks in our direction. We got the hint, I paid the bill, and we retreated to the outside patio, uncrowded due to the summer heat.

We settled in at a round wooden table. "Now," said Bertie, shifting to fit her well-padded body into the white plastic chair, "why are you *really* here?"

"What do you mean, *why* am I here? You know I inherited the house."

"Bull hockey. We both know that there's more to it than that."

From the determined look on her face, I knew it wasn't going to be as easy to wiggle out of this one. Still, I didn't say anything.

Bertie chose persistence over tact. "Listen, chickie, you didn't walk out on a gorgeous hunk of a husband and a big-time career just because you inherited some old dump."

"Dump! That house is not a dump. It's a wonderful historic structure, and..."

"Nope. Try again."

I couldn't lie to her. Tears welled up in my eyes. "It all fell apart. Everything. The marriage, the job, the career. My whole world was built on... fundamental dishonesty, deceit, and evasion, and..."

I had to stop for a moment. Breathe deeply. Stay in control.

"Mark is... *livid* that I left. I mean, out of control. He was the one who couldn't keep his pants zipped, and yet he's furious! He still doesn't know where I am, and I hope to hell he doesn't figure it out."

Bertie's face sagged in sad concern. She spoke in a soft, gentle voice. "What happened?"

I pinched my lips together and looked at the wooden ceiling for a few seconds before I could answer. How could I explain it? I didn't want to speak the words to describe what I'd seen on that video.

"I don't even know how to explain it," I said. "Let's... let's just call it a huge betrayal. He did some really reprehensible things, and yet somehow he sees himself as blameless."

Was that the definition of a borderline psychopath? Could be. As Mark's angry words came to mind, my temper rose. "You wouldn't believe the emails he sent! 'What will everyone think?' That's all he cares about! His stupid image, and his stupid career. You know." My voice slipped into a sarcastic sing-song, "What will the tabloids say when they find out you took off?"

I felt a tear overflow, and run down my face. I brushed it away with an angry flick of my hand.

"He made some pretty nasty threats. I was never scared of him in the past, but now, all of a sudden, it's... it's like I never really knew him."

I stopped, fumbled around in my purse for my handkerchief, and wiped the tears from my face.

"Millie saved me," I said. "Boom, right out of nowhere, here came the house, dropped in my lap, a gift from an angel. The perfect solution to the problem. And, so... here I am."

"Oh, chickie..." Bertie rubbed my arm, and gave me a few minutes to compose myself. She didn't push for any more details, and I felt grateful that she understood that I was still in the middle of adjusting to a new and difficult situation.

"Well," she finally said, as the comforting silence tailed off. "I've gotta get back to the office. Greg pays me to do stuff, you know."

I nodded. "And I have to get things set up at the house. Make it feel like home again, and all that."

Bertie drove me back to the office. I got in my car and drove away, but didn't head back home. There was one more place I needed to go.

• • •

The cemetery was at the top of the hill, not too far from where we'd had lunch. I parked the car, and walked towards the southern boundary of the graveyard, where I knew that I'd find Millie resting alongside my brother, Rudy.

The brisk wind, ever-present on the summit of the ridge, scudded around me. My hair blew wildly, dancing in and out of my eyes. I didn't bother to try to push it aside. I had other things on my mind.

I walked along the rows, not quite certain where to look. Years had passed since I'd last visited this place, and there were many more graves surrounding the family plot where he rested. And then, suddenly there he was. Rudy. Forever sixteen years old, deprived of the future that should have been his.

I didn't go looking for the graves of my parents. They were elsewhere. My mother was laid to rest in Sacramento. My father, cremated and buried at sea, off the coast of Cape Cod, where he loved to sail his little sloop.

Rudy rested alone in the family plot no longer. To the right of him were two newer graves, still marked with temporary plastic grave-markers. The first one was Millie's. The other one was... Doc? I was surprised. I would have thought that he'd be buried in his own family plot, wherever that might be. But here he was, alongside Millie forever. Somehow it felt right, and good.

Millie had not wanted a funeral, or even a brief memorial service. I'd honored her wishes. I had no idea if a service was held for Doc. I also had no idea if gravestones were ordered for either of them. I'd have to find out, and take care of it if needed.

I stood in loving and silent contemplation of the resting places of the people who'd meant so much to me. No regrets, no what-ifs rose up to batter at my soul. Such thoughts are pointless. As I walked back to my car, I felt an overwhelming gratitude that they'd enriched my life. I would miss them forever.

I'd done the right thing by coming home.

◆ ◆ ◆

I stopped at the nearby propane company after I left the cemetery. I arranged for the tank to be filled within a few days. No more wondering if the hot water would give out in the middle of a shower.

I drove down into town, gassed up my car, and considered choices for my first steps towards building my new life. No decision was ever easier. The sooner I got integrated back into the fabric of the community, the better. I drove up the hill to the parking lot next to the hospital, to the whimsical local wonder known as Demetra's Coffee House.

A dear friend of mine from high school owned the place. There, I knew, I could find a reliable wireless internet connection. Better yet, working electrical outlets were skulking around the place, too, always a big bonus when a dead phone battery crisis loomed.

The whimsy of the place never failed to bring a smile to my face. The building, designed to look like a funky little steep-roofed cottage, featured drunken lines of shingles, out-of-plumb walls, crooked windows, and a bent stovepipe protruding from the roof. A bouquet of enticing kitchen aromas vented to the outside, near the front entrance.

The seductive perfume of roasting coffee beans and fresh-baked pastries floating across the parking lot worked better than a tractor beam for drawing in customers.

Three large chainsaw-carved bears stood out in front of the place—a bemused Papa Bear wearing big round spectacles, a serene Mama Bear with a scarf on her head, and a mischievous Baby Bear, complete with sagging wooden diaper.

I needed to charge my phone and laptop, check my email, and charge myself with some of Demetra's wonderful coffee. The aroma of the coffee alone was reason enough to be there. Sitting and sipping the stuff was even better.

The only thing missing was Demetra herself. Damn. I'd been counting on seeing her, and finding out how many of our mutual friends were still in town. After being away for so long, I'd lost track of almost everyone.

It seemed odd to sit there in the coffee shop, and see not one familiar face. A small rush of melancholy swept into my brain. Maybe it's true, I mused. Maybe you really can't go home again.

I plugged in the laptop and opened my email. Scores of backlogged messages flew in. And a few of them were from Mark. I popped one open.

> You'd better think twice before doing anything foolish. If I find out that you've contacted anyone in the media, you will live to regret it.

In an instant, the crushing weight that had sat on my shoulders before I left New York returned with a vengeance. How had I ever believed that he loved me? I closed the letter and tried another one from him.

> Never forget that I know where you are. I will *always* know where you are. As the old saying goes, you can run, but you can't hide.

It seemed a sure bet that this was a bluff, that he had no idea where I'd gone. Still, the coffee turned into a churning puddle of acid in the bottom of my stomach. I'd always known that Mark had the potential to be a fierce opponent. He was a living legend among criminal defense lawyers. And now he attacked me with the same ferocity that he fought his cases.

And why? I hadn't threatened him in any way whatsoever. My two main goals were an amicable dissolution of the marriage, and to get the hell out of his life. And now all I could think of was the rumor I'd once heard that he had some close connections to organized crime figures.

I'd always thought that rumor to be ridiculous. Now I wondered if I was the most gullible idiot on the planet. And it hurt. This man had once been the light of my life. These messages were from a cold and heartless stranger.

Ignoring his emails wasn't an option. He would interpret silence as fear or weakness. I closed my eyes and considered my choices.

Yes. This would work.

> Did I happen to mention that I may have made a copy of the video that you left in the player?

That should shut him up. I sent the email off and hoped that I hadn't just made a huge mistake. The man was a far better poker player than I'd ever be.

Demetra maintained an informal leave-one-take-one lending library at the back of the shop. I stopped for a moment to look over the latest offerings. Unable to decide between *The Yummy Unicorn Pet Bakery*

Murders and *The Girl with the da Vinci Tattoo*, I left empty-handed, and headed home.

◆ ◆ ◆

Before I settled down for the night there was one thing I knew I had to do. I opened the front door and went outside. Arching over me was a sight I loved—the night sky displayed in all its cobalt glory. I'd spent too many years looking at a muddy-orange city sky, and had almost forgotten that the nighttime sky is actually the deepest of velvet blues.

I gazed up at the heavens, entranced with the myriad of stars, hidden from me for too many years. An increasingly cool breeze stirred my hair, but I didn't want to retreat inside. I'd not seen this view in far too long. I turned in a slow circle, drinking it in.

To the north, the great black hulk of Butte Mountain sat outlined against the sky, its size accentuated by the blinking red light at the top of the tower at its peak.

Lesser mountains and rolling hills dominated the view to the east and southeast. These black mounds made up the lower Sierra foothills, and were speckled here and there with a few stray points of light.

And, to the southwest and west, the pale yellow-orange glow of the cities in the distant valley lay flat to the horizon.

The sparkling vault of the nocturnal sky arched above it all. I drank it all in, savored it, and tried not to think about how very alone I was at the top of that hill.

In some ways, it seemed odd to be back here. In other ways, it seemed like I'd never been gone.

My mind skipped and jumped through the events of the past few weeks. I'd done what I could to rescue myself from a bad situation, and was very satisfied with the results. But there was someone else who needed to be rescued too. The memory of the young girl in Mark's video haunted me. How many other victims were out there?

If I called the cops on Mark, he'd know who did it. I didn't want to face the kind of trouble that would instantly come raining down upon me if I dared to—literally—expose Mark to the world. And I was ashamed of myself for being a damnable coward. But, on the other hand, Mark shouldn't be given *carte blanche* to be a predator, to ruin more innocent lives.

What could I do? I had no idea. But someday, somehow, I'd figure out something...

After a long while, I retreated back into the house, shivering from more than just the coolness of the night. I stripped off my clothes, pulled on my favorite oversized tee shirt, crawled into my bed, and pushed the pillow into the perfect spot under my head. Memories of Millie, tucking me in, singing a good-night song, washed over me, sending a comforting warmth to my heart.

A small popping noise in the ceiling broke in stillness of the house. A second, louder one caused my eyes to fly open. The heavy old wooden beam in the ceiling overhead groaned, as if some invisible pressure was suddenly released from it.

My eyes darted around the room; I could see nothing. And then I realized that I was holding my breath. I let the trapped air out in a soft swoosh; the slight sound seemed loud in the silence of the night.

I didn't hear anything more that seemed out of place. The odd creaks were surely just the sounds of the old house settling in for the night. Weren't they?

The emotional center of my brain reached for that comforting remembrance that had cradled me only moments before. I began to sing, in a soft, tentative voice.

Lavender's blue, dilly dilly
Lavender's green...
When I am king, dilly dilly
You shall be queen.

Such a wonderful memory... It made me feel a tiny bit better. Despite that, still a bit on edge, I didn't go to sleep for quite some time.

Chapter Six

BAM!

The thundering blast of a shotgun sliced through the silence of the morning air.

BAM-BAM!

I rolled over and scuttled my hand around, searching for my phone. I found it and squinted at the display. Saturday, September 1, 5:58 am.

BAM!

Oh... Opening day. That's what's going on. Dove season commenced a half hour before sunrise.

BAM!

It happens every year. September 1st arrives, dawn approaches, and any clueless newbie hanging out in rural California flies out of bed in a panic. March might come in like a lion, but September arrives with a *bang*.

I knew that by the end of the day, untold numbers of fat little birds ended up on barbeques, and untold numbers of grilled dove aficionados cracked a tooth on stray birdshot.

There was no point in trying to sleep through the dove Armageddon. I pulled on some jeans and a sweatshirt. I shoved my feet into my gray felt clogs, stumbled downstairs to the kitchen.

The coffee had just finished perking when I heard a vehicle pull into the yard. An old battered pickup came to a stop out back, and a familiar figure climbed out.

I opened the back door. "Greg Hunter!" I shouted. "What the hell are you doing up here? Only crazy people and hicks are awake at this hour of the morning."

The corners of Greg's eyes crinkled in good-natured harmony with his smile. "True," he said. He paused on the back steps, stomped the dust off his boots, walked into the kitchen, and hung his hat on a hook by the door. "So, which one are you?" he asked.

"Which one what?"

"Are you the crazy person, or are you the hick?"

I turned and looked up at him. "Both. Guilty as charged. You want a cup of coffee?"

"Sure." He set down the small cooler that he held in one hand, strode with confident assurance across the kitchen, and grabbed a mug out of the cabinet. I realized that he knew where everything belonged. He'd done this sort of thing before, right here in this kitchen.

"Greg!"

He stopped short and looked at me.

"You're the one who cleaned up the kitchen and emptied the refrigerator, aren't you."

He paused, and seemed to mull over the best answer. "Yes." He picked up the cooler. "You had breakfast?"

"No."

"Good." He went to work, cracking eggs into a blue ceramic bowl. Then he added, "The police made quite a mess when they were in here with their fingerprint powder."

Police? Fingerprint powder? First Pichl, and now Greg. My instincts hadn't lied to me. "I think we need to talk."

"Yup. We sure do. That's why I'm here. But first, we need to eat, while the grub is hot."

While he worked, I pulled the Franciscan ceramic plates out of the cabinet, and put them within his reach. I then set the old green table with Millie's thick, handwoven napkins and the flatware that had been in the family forever.

Greg carried the plates over to the table and set them down. "I need you to promise me something," he said. "There is going to be a secret between us. A big secret. It's very important." He stared at me, bug-eyed, until I nodded in agreement.

"You must never, ever, tell anyone—*anyone*—that Dr. Gregory Ian Hunter, sworn enemy of all things cholesterol-laden, fed you a bacon and Swiss cheese omelet."

I put my hand over my heart. "I so swear." I took a bite of the omelet and rolled my eyes back in ecstasy. "Whoa," I said. "You can come cook me breakfast *anytime*."

"Glad you like it." He stood behind me to refill my coffee mug, then walked around the table, and sat down facing me. "I have to thank you for something."

I tilted my head, puzzled.

"I really appreciate the fact that you took our Bertie out to lunch yesterday. She's had a rough go of it. I was so pleased when she came back from lunch with a grin on her face. She was everyone else's support system for a while, and, well, you know that's a tough roll to fill.

"After Millie died, Doc went into a sort of tailspin. He was a mess. Heck, we all were. Bertie stepped right up to the bat, and gave him a shoulder to lean on. Gave *me* a shoulder to lean on. I was proud of her. She kept us going."

He picked up the napkin, ran his fingers over the thick woven linen, set it down, and continued with his thought.

"And then Doc was gone too, and it was like the world had jerked the rug right out from under her. She took it hard. I kept asking her if she wanted some time off, but she said no, it was better if she kept coming to work. I could understand that, because I felt the same way. It seemed like an insult to Doc's memory to do anything less than our best.

"Anyway, what I'm trying to say is that you really did her a world of good yesterday, and I wanted you to know that. It was wonderful to see a real smile back on her face."

"Oh, good," I said. "I'm glad I helped, even if I didn't know what I was doing at the time." I stood up, and carried a couple of the plates to the sink. Greg followed, carrying the mugs.

"Hey country-girl," he said, "after we get this stuff cleaned up, let's go for a walk."

It was time to face the apparently grim truth of what had happened here the day my aunt died.

◆ ◆ ◆

Greg reached for the battered Stetson he'd hung on the peg, spun it around in an elaborate flourish, opened the back door, and with a broad sweeping gesture said, "After you, ma'am."

I glanced at the hat, and wondered how a city boy had conjured up an obviously genuine Western relic. He must have read my mind. "It was Doc's," he said. "Part of his Mark Twain *Roughing It* regalia."

I smiled, remembering long-ago days. When Doc's hair started turning gray, someone had told him that between his big hawk-beaked nose and his mustache, he was beginning to look a lot like Mark Twain. Doc seized that image with relish.

He allowed the mustache to flourish into an extravagant walrus bristle. He let his hair grow to just the right length. He took to wearing a white suit and black bow tie during the summer. In the winter, he favored the Old-West gold prospector theme. He was having fun. To him, life was a grand adventure. His loss left an aching hole in many hearts.

Greg and I walked across the back porch, down the steps, and started along the gentle slope of the dirt road. My mind shifted to all the questions that had plagued me for the last month. No time like the present. I blurted it out. "I need to know what happened to Millie."

His fine mood drained away, leaving his face still, his eyes sad. "Absolutely. And we'll get to that. But first, we need to talk about Doc."

"Doc? Is there a connection?"

"Yes. There is." Greg took a deep breath, and sighed. The melancholy sound seemed to come all the way from the center of his soul.

Cold prickles crawled down my arms, and I suddenly felt afraid of the unknown.

Greg's voice softened. "After Millie... died... Doc and I came up to the house here, so he could get his clothes."

I stopped in my tracks and looked at Greg. "His *clothes?*"

He stopped too. "Yes. He had a key to the house. So, we came in, and he went... up to her bedroom... so he could pack up his stuff."

"*Her* bedroom?"

"Yes."

I grabbed Greg's arm. "You are *not* telling me..."

"Yes. That's what I'm telling you. Millie and Doc were lovers. Had been for years."

I pulled back from him. "If this is supposed to be some kind of a joke, it isn't the least bit funny."

He looked at me, his face as still as a frozen pond. "It's not supposed to be funny. It's the truth."

"Greg! Doc was old enough to be her father!"

"That may be true, but they didn't seem to care. After I joined the practice, Doc pretty much lived up here full time."

"But... he was *old*."

"Think what you want, but they looked darned happy to me."

We began walking again, at a slow, deliberate pace. Small pictures from my childhood clicked together in my mind—the smile that lit up Millie's face whenever Doc came over to the house, the long walks the two of them liked to take together, the way they often held hands.

The sudden realization shocked me. Why had I never noticed that something special connected the two of them?

Of course, the underlying reason was pretty simple. Kids don't see the significance in situations that they don't comprehend. By the time I was old enough to put two and two together, I was so accustomed to Doc being around that the undercurrents were invisible to me. And, obviously, they'd been very discrete.

"Okay..." I said. "Go on."

"We came up here. I went into the kitchen and packed up the food in the pantry. Doc went upstairs, and then pretty soon I heard him coming back down. His footsteps sounded odd, sort of uneven, so I went out to the hallway to see what was going on. He was clutching at his chest. As soon as I saw him, I was sure he was having a heart attack. I grabbed him and hauled him out to the truck.

"Once I had him in the truck, I got on my cell phone and called the hospital. I headed straight for the ER. We both knew the prognosis looked bad. I debated if I should stop to give him CPR, but decided to keep on going. I sometimes wonder if I screwed up, and what would have happened if I'd stopped."

He took a deep breath and glanced over at me. "It all boiled down to the fact that the hospital is better equipped than the side of the road. They were waiting for us at the ER. They tried... everything..."

Greg's voice trailed off. A tight muscle flicked in his jaw. I took his arm, and pulled him over to a fallen oak tree, the bark long gone, its trunk burnished silver from years in the weather. We sat down side by side on the smooth wood. He slumped forward and buried his face in his hands.

I leaned against him, sharing the grief at the loss of a mutual lifelong friend. A hollow ache burned in my chest. Doc was one of those almost-magical people who lit up people's lives, just by being there. He'd been a truly good man.

A soft breeze wafted by, offering a caress to my sorrowful soul. An odd thought occurred to me, out of nowhere. "If they were lovers, why did they keep it a secret?"

Greg lifted his head. He didn't look at me. He stared off into the distance. "I don't know."

He finally turned to me, with troubled eyes. "Now, this is where we get to the bad part." He paused, pressed his lips together, and shook his head.

My stomach plunged. Whatever had happened, it wasn't good.

Greg took another deep breath. "Millie didn't die of natural causes."

I stared at him, speechless.

"There's no easy way to say this. Someone shot Millie in the back, not twenty yards from the north end of the house."

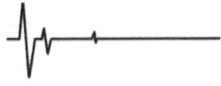

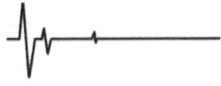

Chapter Seven

I fell apart. Collapsed.

Despite all the hints that something was strange about Millie's death, deep inside I'd wanted to believe that she'd suffered a heart attack, or a stroke. Simple. Straightforward. But this... How could it be true? First Rudy, now Millie. *Murdered.* No wonder Doc's letter to me had seemed so odd, so despairing.

Greg caught me before I hit the dirt. He held me right there in the road, let me cry, and stroked my hair to comfort me. After a while my sobs subsided, my breathing settled. We walked back to the house, his arm around me, and settled into the heavy Adirondack chairs on the front porch.

I'd run away from one nightmare, only to find myself trapped in the middle of a new one.

Greg watched over me with the eyes of an old friend, but also with the eyes of a physician. He wasn't a cold-steel sonofabitch like Mark. He stayed, held my hand, until he felt sure that I'd be okay, at least for the moment.

We sat there together as I struggled to comprehend the horror of my aunt's last moments of life.

The shotgun-toting dove hunters had long since packed up their guns and dead trophies and gone home. Shadows shortened as the sun climbed in the sky. The melodic lilting songs of the meadowlarks, and the rusty-hinge calls of the red-winged blackbirds echoed across the field.

The initial shock finally gave way to anger. I sat up straighter in the chair, and said, "Why didn't anyone tell me what happened!"

Greg's face flushed, the ruddiness emphasizing the blue of his eyes. He drew in a deep breath, and said, "I..."

"Oh, I don't mean *you,*" I said, with a wave of a hand. "You didn't have any way of knowing if I'd been contacted or not. And Doc tried. I don't understand why he sent me a letter though, instead of calling me."

I jumped up out of the chair. "I'm talking about *other* people, folks who should have known better, should have communicated with me in some sort of official capacity. I'm *pissed* because the neither the police, nor that damned little worm Pichl, had the brains to figure out that, you know, it might be nice to tell me that my aunt had been *murdered!*

I'd almost shouted that last word. It was nothing less than an obscenity. I suddenly realized that my whole body was shaking.

Greg stood up, and gave the top of my head another brief caress, a gentler version of the boisterous noogies of our childhood. "You're right," he said. I don't understand it either." He fumbled around in his shirt pocket and pulled out a business card with his personal cell phone number scribbled on the back.

"I hate to run out on you, but I've got some things I have to do at the hospital. That's why I came over here so early. Call me, any time. I have an answering service—you can have them wake me up in the middle of the night if it's urgent, or you can leave a message. Either way, it won't be a problem."

"Thank you," I said. "Everyone needs a friend they can lean on when things go south."

"Yup." He squeezed my hand, and walked away.

I watched his truck disappear down the road in a cloud of dry, wispy tendrils of dust, trying hard not to feel abandoned. I blinked back more tears of loss. I'd cried more in the last few weeks than I had in a long, long time, perhaps even since Rudy died.

What am I? A woman or a mouse? I found it hard not to be a mouse. A little, frightened, sniveling mouse.

No. Not true. I've never been a mouse, never will be a mouse. *I'm only hurting.*

Within the space of only a month or so, my whole world flipped upside down. As soon as things seemed to be settling down, I got sucker-punched again. I couldn't be upset with Greg for telling me the truth, though. I needed to know.

One by one, the people I'd loved most in the world had died, as if struck down by sudden lightning. Vibrant, and alive one moment, still and dead the next.

Rudy's death was made to look like an accident, though the family never accepted that interpretation. And now, for me to believe that there was anything accidental about what had happened to Millie? Impossible!

I jumped back up, stormed into the house, and called the police department non-emergency number.

"I'd like to make an appointment to talk to the detective handling the investigation of the death of Millie Minero. I'm the next of kin."

The stiff-voiced woman who'd answered the phone said, "Let's see now, that case is assigned to... Detective Newhall. N.C. Newhall. You can come in Monday, at 3:30, if that will be convenient for you."

Monday seemed like a century away. I wanted to scream. Instead, I said, "That will be fine. Thank you."

◆ ◆ ◆

I disconnected the call, sat down at the venerable Steinway, and let my emotions fly free. The dark chords of Richard Addinsell's *Warsaw Concerto* rang through the house. My fingers glided over the smooth ivory keys, and I savored the lush tones of the beautiful instrument.

Real Rachmaninoff followed the fake Rachmaninoff created by Mr. Addinsell for a movie. Haunting nocturnes, preludes, and etudes flowed from my fingertips. I played until exhaustion overtook me.

Millie. Oh, Millie...

I thought that Mark had ripped my heart to shreds, but I'd been wrong. He'd only lacerated the surface. Now my heart was flayed, ripped apart, bleeding.

I owed everything to Millie. *Everything*. The woman was an angel, a hero. She didn't deserve to be shot down like a rabid animal.

Fresh tears welled up, burning my eyes. I needed to get out of there.

◆ ◆ ◆

I gathered up my car keys and purse, and jogged out to the barn. I stopped and looked at Millie's shrouded little station wagon. Curiosity plucked at my impulse center until I gave way to it. I lifted a corner of the tarp, and what I saw took my breath away. I pulled the cover all the way off.

Millie had hand-painted the entire car with a Western panorama of rolling hills, golden meadows, blue skies and ancient oak trees. She had inscribed her initials and the date on the left rear fender. She'd finished it only about a month before she died. Not one single scratch marred the paint. The surface gleamed with a professionally-applied clear coat.

No way would I drive this car. *No way*. The vehicle was... what? Magnificent? Mind-boggling? No descriptors seemed adequate. My aunt was a true genius, a bright light in the universe, cruelly snuffed out by the hand of another.

I put the tarp back in place, started up my own car, and headed off to Demetra's place.

◆ ◆ ◆

I first met Demetra Herron in high school, and we'd remained close friends for years now. Tall, lean, and energetically engaged in wiping down countertops, she looked up when I walked in. "Lexie!"

No one else would ever be allowed to call me that. It sounded like something a person would name their car.

I paid her back with her own hated nickname. “Meter Maid!”

She ignored the taunt, popped around the end of the counter and wrapped me in a hug. “Damn, it’s good to see you! It’s been too long.”

Demetra’s lithe body made her look more like an athlete than a chef. She had smooth tan skin, green almond-shaped eyes, and golden-brown hair that bounced in springy coils all over her head, making my own wild hair look tame in comparison.

Her exotic beauty was completed by her warm personality and her uncanny ability to turn ordinary foods into extraordinary treats. When she’d opened her little coffee shop, with off-kilter décor in sync with the wacky outside appearance, it was an instant success.

“I’m dying for a chai latte,” I said, “and you’re my only hope.”

“Never fear, Lexie, dear. Help is on the way.”

In nothing flat, she had the luscious drink ready for me. The place wasn’t busy, so she sat down with me for a couple of minutes. I asked her about old friends, and if any of our little nerd-herd still lived in the area.

Demetra shook her head, making her curls bounce and sway. “Not many. Siren song of the Big City, and all that. I’ll see if I can scrape up some email addresses, so you can reconnect.”

“Super. Thanks!”

My friend trotted back to the counter to take care of another customer, and I opened up my laptop.

Mundane stuff first. I connected to the wireless network and checked the status of the crates I had shipped from New York. They were still “in transit.” Whatever that meant. Sitting in a storage lot in Newark? I’d have to call the company on Monday and use my lawyer voice on them.

I left the freight company site and pulled up the main webpage of the *Argonaut Ledger*. I typed the word 'obituaries' into the search field. I scrolled down the list that appeared on the page. July... Okay. There.

> MINERO, MILAGROS A. Noted local artist Milagros A. "Millie" Minero, age 54, passed away suddenly at her home on July 18th. A native of Jackson, California, she was a graduate of Kennedy Mine High School, Stanford University, and the Ruskin School of Drawing and Fine Art at Oxford University, UK. She was preceded in death by her parents, Rolando J. and Ella-Ruth Parker Minero, her sister Rosalinda Minero Womack, and her brother Joaquin R. Minero. Survivors include several nieces and nephews. Per her request, there will be no services. Interment at Valley View Cemetery will be private. Donations may be made in her memory to the Stanford University general scholarship fund.

Doc must have provided the information to the newspaper, because I sure hadn't.

Demetra appeared next to me and plopped a big chocolate brownie, fresh from the oven, on the saucer at my elbow. "Have some health food," she said. "You're too skinny." I laughed, and swatted at her in jest. She grinned and danced away, retreating to the kitchen.

My eyes drifted back to the obituary. Millie's legal name, Milagros, meant 'Miracles.' It suited my aunt in so many ways. And now she was gone, her life cut short by a contemptable coward. I took a deep breath, and did another search.

> McFARLAND, LINUS ALEXANDER. Local area physician Linus A. "Doc" McFarland, age 87, passed away on July 25th, while under treatment at a local hospital. A native of Bangor, Maine, McFarland was a graduate of the University of California at Berkeley, and the University of California, San Francisco, School of Medicine. He was preceded in death by his parents, Paul L. McFarland and Katherine Smithson McFarland, and two brothers, Emerson F. and Keating J. McFarland. He is survived by his wife, Suzanne Langford McFarland, of Ipswich, Massachusetts. Per his request, there will be no services. Interment at Valley View Cemetery will be private. Donations may be made in memory of Dr. McFarland to the general operations fund of Doctors Without Borders.

His wife? Doc had a *wife*? Is nothing in my life actually what I'd believed it to be?

I shut down the laptop, jammed it into its bag, and eyed the treat on the saucer. My appetite had fled, but I couldn't ignore it. I couldn't bear to hurt Demetra by leaving it untouched. I cut off a small slice, popped it in my mouth, and wrapped the rest in a paper napkin to save for later. A few crumbs remained behind on the plate as witness to my presumed enjoyment. I stood up, pasted a smile back on my face, and waved goodbye to my friend.

I got in my car and stared at the steering wheel for a few moments, feeling somewhat disoriented. For the very first time in all my years on this planet, there was nowhere I had to be, and nothing I had to do. What a strange and bewildering thought. I started up the car and drove up the hill to the beautiful old stone house.

◆ ◆ ◆

I let myself into the kitchen, and stood a moment, listening to the silence. I grabbed up the last of the stuff that I'd left downstairs the previous night and headed for the stairs.

The landing at the top of the stairs ran all the way around the second floor, forming a rectangular mezzanine. Rudy and I used to race our remote-control cars around the oak floor, treating it like a giant racetrack.

I stopped and looked out the north-facing window at the top of the stairs. The land on that side of the house rose gradually up a knoll topped by a large outcropping of granite. Millie loved to paint studies of the rocks at different times of the day, in different lights. Somewhere, right out there, Millie had died.

When the house was built, there'd been four large bedrooms upstairs. One of the bedrooms on the north end of the house was cut in half to make a bathroom when indoor plumbing became all the rage.

The remaining half of the former bedroom served as Millie's studio. She supervised the installation of large windows all around the studio, allowing it to be flooded with an artist's beloved northern light.

All the bedrooms upstairs were spacious and sunny. No point in looking for nostalgic traces of my childhood—Millie had fixed up the two extra bedrooms as guest quarters as soon as I left for college.

I stood in the doorway to my old room. Dark walnut furniture danced around the room in a rather haphazard arrangement that somehow ended up being quite pleasing to the eye. A comfy sofa, upholstered in sage velour, sat pushed against one wall. The walls were a pale yellow and showed off watercolor paintings of Lake Pardee.

The very faintest hint of Millie's beloved lemon oil furniture polish still hung in the air, or maybe I imagined that it did. I dropped my items onto the floor, and wandered through the upstairs area.

Rudy's old room, with the door immediately to the left of mine, was decorated in a similar fashion, but with a palette of pale blue and muted violet. The walls were hung with paintings of old barns, wagons, and houses.

I walked around the landing. The door to Millie's room stood ajar; I entered. I hesitated a moment just over the threshold, overwhelmed by the feeling that I'd intruded into her private space. I drew in a breath to fortify myself, and pushed forward.

The room still smelled of her favorite frangipani perfume. Dramatic oil paintings, rendered in vibrant jewel-like tones, covered the walls. Far different from those that brought commercial success to Millie, the paintings were oils of nudes, men and women, painted in thick impressionistic, almost three-dimensional, impasto strokes. Vibrant human figures leaped across the canvases, living, breathing, and enjoying life. The paintings bore Millie's bold signature in the bottom right corners.

Milagros

Millie's bright-colored clothes, her favorite novels, and even her bottle of hand lotion remained as she'd left them. Everything looked like she'd just run to town to go shopping, and would be back in a bit. The tears came again, and this time the mouse inside me won. I turned around, walked out of the room, and shut the door behind me with a soft click.

I spent all day Sunday unpacking the car, doing laundry, and moving in. The one item of no practical necessity that I'd brought along in the car was my portable electronic piano. I hadn't trusted the freight company to handle it with proper care. Now I wondered why I'd bothered to bring it with me at all.

I shoved it, still packed in its case, under my bed. With that wonderful old grand piano downstairs, why would I ever want to touch an electronic keyboard again?

◆ ◆ ◆

Monday afternoon, at 3:30, I found myself waiting on a wooden bench near the front desk at the police station. Wanting to make a solid, no-nonsense impression, I'd dressed in a pale lilac linen suit with an ivory silk blouse, heels and purse. Truth to be told, these were the only decent clothes I'd brought with me in the car, and I wore them almost by default. It just didn't feel right to go to such a meeting in my camping clothes.

The unmarked door on the other side of the room opened, and a sloppy blob of a man walked through. I was stunned. Didn't the police department set healthy weight standards for their officers? This man appeared to be a good sixty pounds overweight, if not more, and his clothes looked like he'd slept in them. His soft face flushed a deep pink as he stood there, panting. I was a bit confused, too, because I could have sworn I was to meet a female officer.

"Miss D'Angelo?" The man's gravelly voice echoed in the high-ceilinged room.

I nodded my head and stood up. The man walked over, belly jiggling, and offered his hand. He was at least a foot taller than me. His hands were slightly damp, and the feel of them reminded me of raw pie dough.

I wanted to run into the ladies' room and grab a handful of paper towels. But, as working women all over the world do, I gritted my teeth and smiled instead.

"Hi," said the Dough Boy. "I'm Detective N.C. Newhall. Please come right this way."

Ohhh... *N.C.* Not *Nancy*. "Thank you for meeting with me," I said.

He showed me through the unmarked door, and turned down a corridor. The hallway looked like the ones in every other government building in the United States, painted an uninspiring Band-Aid beige, the ceiling paved with pock-marked acoustic tiles. At the end of the corridor, he opened another door and we stepped into a large room with pale apple-green walls, the floorspace divided up into a labyrinth of gray cubicles.

The occasional sound of a door opening or closing punctuated the chattering hum of busy people rattling away on the phone, or speaking face to face. The whole of the soft cacophony was overlaid with the intermittent buzz of a failing fluorescent bulb.

Newhall led me through the maze to a cubicle unremarkable in its blandness. There were no decorations, no mementos, no family photos on display in his area. His desk was awash with haphazard stacks of papers. Other than that, his little kingdom was as barebones and impersonal as a workspace could be.

Detective Newhall sat down at his desk, and I sat down across from him in a chair upholstered with worn green faux leather. He handed me his card. I couldn't help but stare at it for a couple of seconds.

Norville C. Newhall
Detective
Jackson-Martell Police Department

I suppressed a rude giggle. Norville? Really? No wonder he wanted to be called N. C. It seemed likely that his middle name might be Clarence, or Claude, or something else strange enough to have guaranteed cruel taunts on the nightmarish playgrounds of his youth.

He glanced down at a stack of papers in front of him. "Just to be sure we're on the same page, you are here regarding the death of your aunt, Milagros Minero, correct?"

I nodded. "Yes."

He got straight to it. "On July 18th of this year, at 4:03 in the afternoon, we received a 911 phone call from this number."

He showed me a piece of paper with Millie's cell phone number entered in a box at the top.

"The caller identified herself as Millie Minero. She requested immediate unspecified assistance. The next thing heard was an unidentified sharp noise, which we believe may have been a gunshot, followed by sounds that seemed to indicate the phone may have been dropped, a period of silence lasting a few minutes, followed by the call being disconnected. I can play the recording of the conversation for you if you want to hear it."

I mulled over the notion for a couple of seconds. It seemed like a bad idea. "Is there anything on it that I need to hear?"

He shook his head.

"Then let's not do it, at least not right now." I didn't want to be hearing the fear in Millie's voice playing inside my head in the middle of the night for the rest of my life.

Officer Newhall continued, his gravel-toned voice sounding rather bored with the narrative. "Fortunately, Ms. Minero identified herself to the dispatcher right at the beginning of the call. The dispatcher knew where your aunt lived, so he called for an officer to go investigate." He thumbed the edges of a stack of papers as he spoke, leaving them a little bit rumpled.

"The officer who responded to the call found Ms. Minero a short distance away from the north side of her house. Would it be unusual for her to go walking there?"

"No. She loved to go out in the evenings and watch the sun set over the valley. What *is* unusual is the time of day. You know. It's still really hot outside at four o'clock, in the summer. I would think that she would've waited until it was cooler outside, more towards dusk, if she'd gone out for a casual stroll."

Newhall glanced at the clock on his desk, and plowed on ahead, as if I hadn't said anything. Hello? Was I talking to the wall? My opinion of the man diminished faster than a drop of water sizzling on a hot stove.

"The responding officer, having noted injuries to Ms. Minero, called for an ambulance. As the ambulance crew rendered aid, Linus McFarland drove up in his truck. He stated that he rented a room from Ms. Minero. Is that correct?"

I nodded my head in affirmation to the question. A small twinge in my stomach reminded me that the truth of the situation was a bit more complicated than that. But, Doc had his reasons for saying what he did. The man deserved to have his privacy protected, even in death.

"Yes," I said. "It's my understanding that he'd recently moved in there. Doc was a family friend for years. I'd known him since I was a little kid."

"So, there was nothing unusual about him arriving at the scene?"

"That is correct."

Newhall scribbled something on his note pad. "The ambulance crew made the determination that Ms. Minero was, in fact, deceased, and notified the coroner's office. Dr. McFarland appeared to be in some distress, so the ambulance crew ended up transporting him to the hospital."

Startled, I must have flinched a bit. Greg hadn't told me that part.

Newhall stopped fidgeting with the papers and gave me a long hard stare, as if I'd suddenly turned into prime suspect number one. His face took on a more serious mien, as if reluctant to impart more bad news. "Miss D'Angelo, Ms. Minero was shot with a hunting rifle." He paused, waiting for a reaction from me.

I just sat there looking at him. What could I say? I gave him a slight nod, and he continued.

"We made a search of the area until we ran out of daylight. The search continued the following morning. We didn't find any shell casings. No distinctive footprints were found. The only clear tire tracks that we found in the area matched either Dr. McFarland's truck, or Ms. Minero's car. We also did a search inside the house, and found nothing of a suspicious nature in there, either."

Newhall stopped. He let me think about all this for a moment or two. "Do you have any questions so far?"

I shook my head. He spoke again, his voice harsh. "Miss D'Angelo, who told you that Ms. Minero had been shot?"

"Dr. Hunter did, last Saturday."

Newhall scribbled on his note pad again. "And who is Dr. Hunter?"

A prickle of unease crawled along my spine. I didn't like the tone of cold suspicion that weighed down his words.

I rubbed the back of my neck. "Greg Hunter is, or rather, was, Doc's business partner in his medical practice. He'd also an old friend of my family. He and Doc had known each other for many years. It would have been extremely odd if Dr. McFarland had *not* told him what happened. I don't think there's any way that Dr. Hunter wouldn't have heard the whole story, one way or another."

Newhall kept on writing for a moment. He set the pen down, leaned back, and relaxed. I had no doubt that he'd be checking around to determine Greg's whereabouts at the time of Millie's death. I was ready to bet my last dollar that he'd already checked to see where I'd been. After all, I was the heir to a significant estate.

"Well then," he said, with a self-satisfied half-smile on his lips, "lacking any new information, it appears that your aunt's death was indeed what I originally concluded—the result of a careless accident."

WHAT? Before I could articulate a response to this nonsensical statement, he bulldozed on ahead.

"Because your aunt was shot with a round that is commonly used by deer hunters, it seems obvious to me that this was an accident caused by an illegal hunter. Deer season doesn't open until late September, but poaching does happen. It's not all that unusual. And that would account for the fact that we found no incriminating evidence at the scene, and no indications of suspicious behavior on the part of anyone she knew."

Right. Like he'd talked to everyone Millie had ever known. What kind of professional was this man? I could feel my fingernails digging into the palms of my hands. Careful, careful... As much as I wanted to lash out at him, I knew would do me no good to explode. I'd met this nasty species of human being before. Pushing him would only make things worse.

He tipped his chair back, and the smile on his face turned into a condescending smirk. "The shooter must have been quite some distance away, and most likely completely unaware that they'd hurt someone. And, so, as unfortunate as the situation might be, I rather doubt that we will be able to find the responsible party."

My heart rate sped up. I fixed a death-ray stare on him, but he seemed oblivious to the fact that I was rigid with cold fury. Or, more likely, he didn't care.

Newhall sat forward, gathered his paperwork back into a sloppy stack, and shoved it aside. "Do you have any questions?" His flat tone of voice clearly told me he'd prefer it if I didn't.

I could hold back no longer. "Yes. I do. I do *not* understand how you can assume her death was accidental."

"We don't have any evidence to indicate otherwise." Newhall looked bored again. I half expected him to shrug and add, "You know, shit happens."

"Excuse me." I pitched my voice to an intentionally hard edge. "She was frightened, she called 911, the call connected, and *only then* did you hear the sharp noise that sounded like a shot. So how can this be a random mishap?"

Newhall's face reddened and crinkled into a harsh and threatening glower. "Ms. D'Angelo, I stated quite plainly that we have no evidence to the contrary. I suggest that you remember that the police are the professionals in this instance, and we will exercise our professional judgment. If we say there is no evidence, then there is no evidence."

The man stood up, and leaned forward a bit, in a clear attempt to intimidate me. I had the distinct feeling that Newhall could make things very unpleasant, if he chose to.

I stood up too. There was nothing left for me to say. For now.

"Ms. D'Angelo, I want to thank you for coming in today, and sharing what you know. I think the information that you provided will be very helpful."

At odds with the pretty speech he'd just delivered, Newhall's voice remained harsh, even antagonistic. His message seemed more than clear—he thought I was a pain in the ass. And I needed to back off.

Newhall extended his arm behind my back, in a shepherding sort of motion that felt more like a threat than a kindly gesture. He walked with me over to the hallway door, saw me through it and said, "Good day." The door closed behind me with an emphatic hollow thud.

Propelled by sheer fury, and muttering unprintable insults regarding Dough Boy's ancestry, I strode down the corridor. My heels clicked sharply as I exited through the lobby, and out the double glass doors. The doors closed automatically, denying me the opportunity to slam them. At the bottom of the steps, I turned and stomped my way back to the parking garage.

This was not over. Not by a long shot.

◆ ◆ ◆

Furious thoughts charged through my head as I drove myself home. Newhall didn't tell me that Millie was shot in the back. He did not offer to let me read the autopsy report. What else had he omitted from the conversation?

Perhaps I should have questioned him further. But, deep inside, I knew it wouldn't have made any difference. If I'd pushed him all the way to Timbuktu and back, he wouldn't have told me a single thing more. The man's mind was not only made up, it was set in concrete.

I wanted to tell myself to chill, that things would work out. But I couldn't. This investigation was worse than half-baked, it was non-existent.

Just like the investigation into Rudy's death.

I pulled into the barn, slammed the car door, and stomped towards the house. A folded piece of white paper, stuck in the seam between the frame and the back door of my house, fluttered in the breeze. How strange. I flicked it open.

GO BACK TO NEW YORK!
YOUR NOT WHANTED HERE

I sunk down on the back porch, lilac linen be damned, put my face in my hands, and raked my fingers through my hair. Had the whole world gone insane? This note was... bizarre.

Not even five people knew I'd come home. I jumped up and walked around, trying to understand something that made no sense. I hadn't been here enough to piss anyone off. Or, had I?

Maybe Mark put someone up to this? As soon as the thought entered my mind, I dismissed it. No. This seemed far too crude of an attempt at intimidation to be laid at his feet.

A hot upwelling of anger surged through me. I pulled off my jacket, set it aside, then picked up a flat rock and hurled it side-arm, skipping it across the hard-packed dirt in front of the barn. The explosion of energy felt so good that I hurled another one, and then another one.

My little misspelling friend had picked the wrong person to hassle. They were not going to get the best of me. I turned to face the jagged horizon, took a deep breath, and shouted "NEVER!" The sound of the yell echoed across the empty hills.

I wadded up the note and flung it into the breeze. A gust of wind caught an edge. I watched as the crumpled ball turned and bounced away into the tall golden grass of summer.

I was going to find out what the hell was going on. All of it. Or die trying.

Chapter Eight

As I changed my clothes, the conversation with Newhall kept running around and around in my mind, competing with similarly disturbing thoughts about the strange note I'd found. I couldn't sit still. I couldn't concentrate. Nothing sounded good for dinner.

I grabbed a box of cereal out of the cabinet, poured some in a bowl, added some milk, and called it a meal. I carried the bowl around as I ate, a practice that Millie would have frowned upon, and wandered into the downstairs office.

Sometime in the 1940s, the back half of the downstairs area was remodeled into a kitchen, a pantry, a full bathroom, a laundry room, and an office-library. In the center of the office stood an old oak roll-top desk and matching chair. Back when my father lived here on weekends, before he'd moved back to New York, this room held a bed and a portable closet for him.

Now, the sole furnishings consisted of the desk and matching chair placed in the center of the room, a huge brown leather reading chair and lamp snuggled into one corner, and a wonderful garnet and deep blue Persian rug. Floor-to-ceiling bookshelves ringed the entire room.

Maybe something in that desk held the key to Millie's death. Maybe not. I had to start somewhere.

Was there a clue sitting around that would tell me what had happened that awful July afternoon? If so, I couldn't see it. Any search would have to be slow and thoughtful. And, it would be done... someday. I felt far too restless and angry to even attempt a methodical search.

The bookshelves were tall, massive, and built of oak, with a brass rail along the top for a rolling library ladder to glide on. The shelves groaned with books, short, tall, old, new, thick, and thin. Most days I regarded the collection like a kid eyeing the goodies in a candy store. But not tonight. It would be impossible to focus on words on a page.

"Damn. Where's a TV when you need one." But, Millie hadn't wanted, hadn't needed a television. She had her art, her friends, her workshops, and Doc to keep her company.

I stomped back into the kitchen. I plunked the cereal bowl in the sink without washing it, and took myself upstairs to my bedroom.

I flexed my shoulders, trying to relax, and wandered over to the window that faced north. I let my eyes glide across the view of the granite outcropping on the knoll. The days were growing shorter, the sun setting earlier. I usually loved to watch the muted light of the setting sun as it cast a warm glow over the face of the ancient boulders. But this night, as I looked towards the massive rocks, I froze.

A person, silhouetted against the sky, picked their way across the top of the rocks. Having reached the other side of the outcropping, the person crouched down, glanced over their shoulder towards the house, dropped over the side, and disappeared.

Great. Now what...

I hurtled back down the stairs to the kitchen and locked the back door. I hadn't even thought of doing that since I got here. We never locked the door when I lived here as a kid.

I stood in the middle of the kitchen, took deep, slow breaths, and willed myself to calm down.

Wouldn't a murderer, or any other person with evil intent, avoid walking around in the open, visible against the brightness of the sunset sky? One would think so.

Perhaps the person was just someone who likes to watch the sunset from the top of the knoll? Or, someone looking for a lost dog?

Then again, it could be... someone on a snipe hunt.

Rudy used to sneak around in the dark, scaring the wits out of our friends from town when we had a sleepover. We'd talk them into going out on a snipe hunt. Rudy liked to climb up in the dead tree standing at the top of the knoll, hold himself perfectly still, and freak everyone out by making creepy noises. He was good at it. Some kids refused to stay overnight at our house ever again.

The tree fell over in a storm the day before Rudy died. Fallen tree, fallen Rudy. The two events were tied fast together in my memory.

I double-checked the lock on the back door, climbed the stairs, kicked off my shoes, and flopped down on the bed. I stared up at the dark ceiling and concentrated on slowing my breathing into a normal rhythm.

The presence of an unknown person on the knoll troubled me. I wanted to deny the truth, and brush off the feeling of unease, but couldn't. Well, whoever the Sunset Skulker might be, I knew what I had to do. That decision made, I snuggled down in my bed and pulled the covers over me.

The old house creaked, and I flinched.

◆ ◆ ◆

I woke up early the next morning. Still feeling restless, I went out for a walk. I wandered down the dirt access road for a bit, stopped and gazed back at the house.

Old family letters told us much about the place. At the time it was built, gossip and jealousy over the Minero family's new home had spread like a grassfire through the valley. How could Juan Minero, a man who made his living with his strong back and hands, afford to build such a grand dwelling?

Rumors of a secret gold mine drifted through the town and caused trouble for the family from time to time. Vague stories of hidden gold were handed down within the family.

But by the time we were growing up, the truth, if any, behind the tales had was lost in time, the stories twisted to the point where they no longer made much sense. Which, of course, didn't prevent Rudy and me from spending countless hours digging holes in stupid locations looking for hidden treasure—and getting nothing but blisters on our hands for our trouble. Millie never once told us that we were wasting our time. After a while we figured it out for ourselves.

What a dirty, bedraggled pair Rudy and I must have been after one of those expeditions!

Ah well, I had places to go and things to do. I put myself together and headed down the hill, stopped by the bank, mailed off the forms to initiate my health insurance plan, and did a bit of shopping. Financial independence was yet another thing in my life that felt more than just a little bit weird. Too bad it came at such a price.

◆ ◆ ◆

A few hours later, my errands completed, I proceeded with my plan from the previous night. I pulled my just-washed car into the parking lot of the only automobile dealership in Jackson, got out, and began the countdown.

It took all of five whole seconds for a salesman to pop out of the building and start down the steps to greet me. He stopped, did a double take, and let out a loud yell.

"Alley Cat!" The man came running across the lot grabbed me up and whirled me around. He put me back on my feet and gave me a loopy grin. "Wow. You look great!"

"Well, you look great too, Larry!"

I wasn't flattering him. Larry Smith was a tall, botoxed, dark-haired charmer. To the astonishment of all of our high school classmates, as well as the teachers rumored to regard him as being little more than lukewarm in the brains department, the man was apparently quite successful. Local gossip said that he'd made one spectacular killing on an internet startup company. Even more amazing, he'd then had the good sense to not push his luck any further, sold out, and invested the windfall.

The diversification of his portfolio included the purchase of the automobile dealership, acquisition of an ostentatious house, and lots of flashy gold and diamond jewelry for his wife, Robin. Rumor said that their two kids attended a fancy private school someplace on the East Coast. I avoided asking about any of that. Larry was a bit of a windbag. I'd come on a mission, and was not in the mood to listen to him ramble on.

One of his salesmen ambled over, and Larry turned to him. "Hey Ken. This is Alexandra. She broke my heart. Broke it into tiny pieces, our senior year in high school."

I smiled and refrained from rolling my eyes. I remembered quite well the reasons why I stopped dating him. "Oh, please, Lar. Enough with the sad, tragic story already. You know you owe me."

"Ah," he said. "The woman speaks the truth." He looked at Ken. "If not for Alexandra, I wouldn't have met and wed my Robin."

I knew full well that if I hadn't dumped him, I might have been the one with the shotgun wedding. But, maybe it wouldn't have been all that bad. After all, Robin had gotten herself a nose job and a nice set of fake boobs as part of the deal. Of course, she had a dolt for a husband along with everything else. But that was beside the point.

"Hey, it's great to see you," I said. "but this isn't just a social visit. Let's talk business." We went inside.

◆ ◆ ◆

An hour later, the teenaged lot helper slid into the driver's seat of my car. He pulled it behind the building, and out of my life. After waiting a short while for the mechanic to install a step on the driver's side, I drove off the lot in a brand new, three-quarter-ton pickup truck in boring root-beer beige. The packages from my shopping trip were on the seat beside me.

I'd had a gun rack installed in the back window. It wasn't there for decoration.

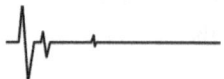

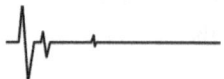

Chapter Nine

The freight truck with my shipment from New York finally showed up. About time. I popped the lids off the crates only to discover that much of the stuff inside looked like artifacts from an alien civilization. And, in many ways, they were just exactly that. Rotating Belgian waffler? Four-person raclette maker? Why the hell had I paid to send this stuff?

My phone rang. The cell signal at my house was so weak that it was close to nonexistent, so I almost climbed right out of my shoes at the phone's sudden blast of an oldie from Metallica. It was Greg.

"Hey," he said. "I'm going to go over to Doc's house to pack up his stuff. I'm not quite sure what's going to happen after that. He must have had a will, because I can't imagine that he wouldn't have, but I've not yet heard from any law firm. The house will probably have to be put up for sale. Anyway, I... I could sure use some company, doing this, if you're not too busy."

Me? Busy? "Be there in about fifteen minutes."

◆ ◆ ◆

Doc had owned an immaculately restored yellow Victorian that sat on a street near the old courthouse. I parked my truck around the corner and walked down the street to the house. Greg was standing at the small wrought iron front gate when I got there, his forehead creased in puzzlement.

A shiny zinc-plated hasp, padlocked, secured the gate. I looked at the lock and looked at Greg. "What the heck is that all about?" Doc never locked the gate.

Greg shook his head. "Beats me. Weird."

It wouldn't be difficult for Greg to climb over the gate—he was tall and agile enough to do it easily—but that wasn't the issue. The issue was that something had changed, we had no idea what, or why, and neither of us were in any big hurry to get arrested for trespassing.

Greg gave a half-hearted little swat at the padlock, and we stood there, mesmerized, watching the shiny metal box swing back and forth. A red Nissan sedan with Massachusetts license plates roared up to the curb behind us, and we jumped.

An older woman with ash-blond tinted hair and fury written across her face launched herself out of the Nissan and stormed across the sidewalk in our direction. She had the tanned skin and the lean, almost stringy, body of an avid lifelong runner.

"And just what do you think you're doing to my gate?" Her thick New England accent grated against my ears. Her wrinkled lips formed a harsh line, almost a slash, across her face.

Greg and I replied in unison. "*Your* gate?" We stood staring at her, probably, in her eyes, resembling the village idiots.

"Yes. *My* gate, to *my* house. And, as I asked you a minute ago, what do you think you're doing? Answer the question or leave." She tapped her foot with exaggerated impatience. "I'm waiting."

The woman sounded like she was doing a very bad impression of Katharine Hepburn.

Greg recovered before I did. "I'm Greg Hunter, Doc's business partner. I'm here to pack up his things." He gestured in my direction. "And this is..."

"My god," said the woman. "Linus' little hussy, in the flesh." She looked at me with venom-filled eyes. "I knew the old goat was running around with a younger woman, but I never guessed that he'd gone shopping at the high school."

"WHAT!" I yelled.

Greg's hands flew up, palms towards the woman, in the classic gesture for *stop*. "Ma'am, I believe you're operating under a very serious misconception. This is Alexandra D'Angelo, and she is..."

"I know who she is." The woman's voice was as cold as New England granite. "And she can take her little hussy self and get the hell off my property."

There's no indignation like bedrock Yankee indignation. I could almost hear the creak of the gallows, the condemning echoes of the Salem Witch Trials in her voice.

"Ma'am..." I said.

"Shut up!"

My mouth dropped open, and I had the vague feeling that I was gulping like a goldfish.

"*Ma'am!*" The chill in Greg's voice doubled hers. I was more than happy to let him rip into the old bat. "Your assumptions are both ludicrous and insulting."

I chimed right in after him, "Not only are you so far out in left field that you're close to outer space, but I'd like to know by what right do you demand that we leave. We are not on *your* property. We are standing on a public sidewalk!" I practically yelled that last sentence.

I heard a distant *thunk-click* of a heavy door closing and looked around. The neighbor across the street had come outside to watch the show. Neither Greg or the woman noticed him. I glared at the neighbor, he slunk back inside, and I returned to the confrontation.

The still-angry woman raised her chin. "In the interest of clarification, allow me to introduce myself," she said with an exaggerated politeness that only sharpened her accent. "I am Suzanne McFarland, widow of the late Dr. Linus McFarland. His heir, and sole owner of this property." She rested her hand on top of the gate. "Therefore, I suggest that you take yourself, and your little cheerleader friend, right up that sidewalk and leave. Now."

I bristled at the snide remark, and very tempted to tear into her one more time. At the same time, I realized that further argument would be useless. She knew she stood on a platform of righteousness and light, and nothing either of us might say would rock her from her stance.

She pulled a small key out of her pocket, unlocked the padlock, and opened the gate. "If you are still here by the time I get inside the front door, I'm going to call the police and have you arrested for trespassing and disturbing the peace. Your word against mine. Good bye."

Mrs. McFarland slammed the gate behind her and stalked up the front walk towards the house.

"Well," I said, still seething. "That was... interesting. But, now we know why Doc and Millie tried to hide their relationship." I added a small afterthought. "Looks like it didn't work out quite as well as they thought."

"Yup," said Greg. "Looks like it."

There was nothing left to do but leave.

◆ ◆ ◆

We climbed into Greg's old pickup and retreated to Demetra's for a cup of coffee. On the way over there, I mulled over a few questions I needed to ask him once we settled in.

The place wasn't very busy, for once. We scooted into a corner table with our cappuccinos, far enough away from the other customers that we wouldn't be overheard.

But still, here I was, in a public place, still married to an absent husband, and in the company of "another man." Mark's threat, his statement that he'd always know where I was, lingered in my mind. Had he figured out where I'd gone? I didn't think he'd waste the money to send someone on a wild goose-chase, to spy on me, but I also couldn't dismiss the idea out of hand. The man always had to win, at all costs.

Well, let him spy. I wasn't exactly living a life of sin and debauchery. If the worse thing he could dig up were photos of me having coffee with a childhood friend, then all he was accomplishing was throwing away money on a private investigator.

I shoved the thoughts of my ex to the side, in favor of a new chain of thought. "Greg, why didn't you tell me that Doc collapsed after the police found Millie?"

His eyebrows flickered with momentary surprise, and his face settled into an odd combination of sadness and chagrin. "I take it you talked to the police. Sorry, I should have said something, but... Well, that whole discussion was so awful, I didn't want to make it even worse."

"I went to the police station last Monday, and talked to Newhall. I'm still upset about it."

Greg sighed, and ran a tanned hand through his hair. "He's a real piece of work, that's for sure. He won't listen to anyone. He and Doc got into one hell of an argument, right there at the scene. Newhall wanted an easy conclusion, accidental death by an unknown hand, slam-dunk, close the case. Doc wasn't having it. He got so upset he collapsed. I supposed we should have all realized that was a precursor to his heart attack, but at the time we wrote it off to simple stress."

"So now what happens? Millie just gets written off?"

"Hell no." Greg lightly smacked his hand on the table. "As soon as I realized the depth of the problem, I got on the phone to the coroner's office. I know the guy. Now, this is just between you and me and the tabletop, 'cause this should never happen, but I talked him into listing the manner of death as 'unknown,' rather than 'accidental.' This leaves the police department an opening to change the initial finding."

A small trickle of relief ran through my body.

"The only reason my friend went along with it is because he knows that Newhall is a flake. He actually referred to the guy as 'No Call Newhall,' as he's apparently known in certain circles. The man does everything he can to avoid taking a call or getting involved in a complex investigation."

"But how can cause of death be unknown? They all know that Millie was shot."

"Not cause of death unknown, it's *manner* of death. Cause of death would be a gunshot wound. Unknown manner of death would mean that it's still unclear whether this was a homicide or an accident."

I thought about this for a moment. "You said that this gives the police the opportunity to change the finding."

"Yes."

"But no guarantee that they would ever do so."

"Yup. You're right. But that's the best that I could do."

I patted his hand to let him know I meant no criticism, and appreciated what he'd done. We finished our cappuccinos, gathered up our stuff, and left.

Greg dropped me off at my truck. All the way home I reflected upon the unhappy fact that I had to depend on a flake nicknamed "No Call" to find out what happened to my Millie.

◆ ◆ ◆

I got into the habit of popping over to Demetra's place every couple of days to check my email and catch up on the news online. While sitting there one day, enjoying a marvelous mocha, I saw "my" Mercedes pull into the parking lot. Temporary dealer plates had replaced the New York ones. Robin Smith stepped out of the car with a flourish.

Dressed in a red silk blouse cut to show off the magnificent body given to her by nature, the gym, and a team of talented plastic surgeons, Robin wore the tightest pair of jeans ever zipped onto a human being. How did she even breathe?

The trailer-trash couture look was marred by the fact that her left arm hung in a sling. A fashion disaster was averted by the fact that the sling was color-coordinated with her blouse.

I recognized Robin only because a framed portrait of her sat on Larry Smith's desk at the car dealership. She sure hadn't look like that in high school.

Back then she was Robina Simkowitz, and quite the little tomboy. Her widowed dad had brought her up to be "one of the guys." By the time she reached high school, Robin could hunt, fish, drive big log trucks, and run the equipment at her father's lumber mill like a pro. In high school, she dressed in boyish shirts and jeans, her hair skinned back into a ponytail, and her face lacking even a hint of lipstick.

Despite her rather plain looks and bare-bones approach to fashion, she was quite popular with the boys. An investigation by Sherlock Holmes was not required to figure out the how and why of that. My very own brother had been infatuated with her. As tempting as it was to believe his fascination with Robin was due to their shared love of the forest.... Ah, no.

The little tomboy had come a long way from where she'd been. Decked out in gold jewelry and designer clothes, her salon-streaked hair arranged just so, her makeup flawless, she seemed engaged in an ongoing piece of performance art, doing everything she could to stun the locals with the kind of movie-star good looks that only money could buy.

Robin came in the door of the shop, made a big deal out of recognizing me, and deposited air-kisses in my vicinity. In New York, I wouldn't have thought twice about such behavior. Now, all the gushing struck me as nothing short of ludicrous.

Robin didn't intend to linger. She tottered over to the counter on her towering stiletto heels and ordered a latte to go. Thank heavens for small favors. I had to wonder—how in the world was she going to drive and sip a latte with one arm in a sling? She must have talents that surpassed the rest of us mere mortals.

While waiting for her order to come up, she wobbled over to my table. That surprised me, to say the least. She and I were never close.

"So, Alexy, what are your plans now that you're back in town?"

Alexy?

The strange new nickname that she'd just invented for me rhymed with "galaxy." Was she messing up my high school nickname on purpose? Or, was she still as dumb as a box of rocks?

Somewhere along the line, Robin had picked up a rolling cadence in her voice that made her sound like a refugee from a junior high school in Southern California. She wasn't known as a rocket scientist back in the day, and I couldn't imagine how things could have improved much in that department.

"I'm not sure." I lied, not wanting to prolong the discussion. "Millie's death was a shock."

Robin nodded with apparent sympathy, but at least she didn't mouth one of the meaningless inanities that people say after a death. I awarded her a point for unexpected good sense.

Despite my earlier intention to keep things short and sweet, I finished the thought. "It's going to take a bit of time to adjust. I just knew that I couldn't sell that house. I love the old place."

"Well, I don't blame you, girl," she said. "That old house is, like, totally awesome, and it's been in your family forever."

Oh really? Gosh, thanks for the news flash. I changed my mind about her having a speck of good sense. As she rattled on and on about nothing in particular, I began fantasizing about stuffing a large wad of napkins in her mouth. I sighed in relief when Demetra called out the number for her order.

Robin waved her hand towards the counter, and winced when she jostled the arm in the sling. "Had rotator cuff surgery. The whole thing was like a total pain." She rolled her eyes. "Well, Alexy. It's great seeing you again. But, I've got to run. Larry and I bought the most *darling* little storefront down on Main Street, and I need to go down there and see how the remodeling work is coming along. It is such a drag to have to go in there and remind the workers like who is the boss and stuff. I mean, really. It's ridiculous."

My heart filled with pity for the unknown crew of remodelers. I bet they just loved her version of "I'm in charge here."

"You really must come to the grand opening!" she trilled. "I'll be sure to send you an announcement. You'll just love what we have planned! We're going to be specializing in custom gold jewelry and other high-end items. You'll love it! Just your style. We've been thinking about doing this for absolutely years, and feel the timing is like totally perfect right now." She paused for a breath. The tight jeans seemed to be taking their toll.

"Well, we'll see you at the grand opening! Ciao!" She blew me a kiss, grabbed her latte, and wobbled towards the exit. She transferred her drink to the hand supported by the sling, put her other hand on the door, then paused, and turned to me. "You're not selling the house, then?"

Hadn't she heard me the first time? "No, Robin, I'm not."

"Oh. Well." She paused for a second, perhaps attempting to get her brain cells to fire in a logical sequence. "If you change your mind, do let us know." She tottered out the door.

I realized that my mouth was hanging open in disbelief. First Pichl, and now her. What was up with people wanting to buy my house? Initially, the inquiries were only annoying. Now the situation was getting creepy.

I leaned back in the booth, took a sip of my mocha, and glanced around the room. A dark-haired man sitting close to the door flinched and jerked his eyes away, as people do when they're caught staring.

The man, wearing East-Coast business casual and tinted glasses, looked jarringly out of place in the land of faded denim jeans. His appearance alone was enough to set off my internal alarm system. Mark hadn't sent any more threatening emails, but still... *Shit!* Suddenly ill-at-ease, I gulped down the last of the mocha and darted out the door.

Not wanting the man to see which vehicle I got into, I dashed across the road into the business park on the other side. I looped around several buildings, then ducked behind a dumpster. I leaned against the heavy metal container, panting.

I threw my head back and stared at the sky. My god. *I'm a fool.* I'd just gone into a full-bore panic because some random guy looked like a stereotypical New York movie mafioso.

I might be a fool, but the pounding of my heart said that the fear was all too real. I needed to get a grip, stop overreacting.

A quieter voice inside told me that perhaps my gut reaction was warranted. I really had *no* idea what Mark might decide to do.

I peeked around the end of the building just in time to see the faux Corleone get into a black Cadillac sedan, and drive away. I sagged back against the side of the building.

A small epiphany dawned. I'd just discovered the strength of my aversion to all things East Coast. Could I go back there? No. Never. I felt safer here in Jackson than I ever would in New York. This was the place I needed to stay, no matter how weird things got.

◆ ◆ ◆

Demetra was true to her word, and that evening I joined five of my old high school friends in the bar at the National Hotel for drinks and munchies. It had been fifteen years or more since I'd last seen some of them, and time had erased most of the commonalities we'd once enjoyed. Demetra and I were the only ones who didn't have any kids, or didn't work as a drone for some faceless company.

All of them were enmeshed in the trials and tribulations of merciless bosses, or diapers, and kindergarten, soccer practice, and lives that I couldn't even imagine living. Snippets of different conversations floated by me. I felt like I was watching a surreal foreign film with bad subtitles. I caught the gist, but not much more.

I had absolutely nothing to contribute to the conversation. Nothing. But, to be fair, my life in New York was as alien to them as theirs was to me. The realization was disheartening. The oddity of the experience was compounded by the evening ending earlier than I'd expected. All the lovely Cinderellas had to leave the ball at the stroke of nine o'clock.

The attempt to re-establish old connections left me feeling more alone than ever.

I drove home, and then went out onto the front porch to look at the stars. In the evenings, I often sat here, in one of the big Adirondack chairs. Well, at least I had one other friend besides Demetra.

I picked up my cell phone, called the number on the back of Greg's business card, and left him a message with an offer that he couldn't refuse.

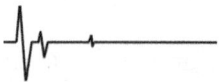

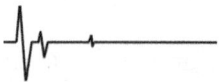

Chapter Ten

The following Saturday evening, near sunset, I drove up the road to Greg's house. I came around the final approach, and I could see him outside, splitting firewood. He must have heard the sound of the diesel engine coming up the drive, because he stopped and peered down the gravel track in my direction.

I drove the truck into the graveled area by the garages, circled around, and stopped a few feet away from him. I swung the door open, and Greg roared with laughter.

I'd dressed from head to toe in brand new western gear, the real deal, not the kind of junk the tourists buy. I had on roper boots, starched jeans with a knife-edge pressed crease, a woven leather belt, and a long-sleeved, peach-colored cotton blouse embellished with flat pearl buttons.

No, the jeans weren't the brand "worn by rodeo professionals." I wouldn't be caught dead in those. The only reason some of the big-time rodeo riders wear those jeans is because they get them for free. Yeah. I know. It's disillusioning.

I took off the straw cattleman's hat that I'd bought at the feed store, stuck it on the dash—the approved and proper place to stash a cowboy hat—and popped the seat belt. He watched me climb down out of the truck, and laughed even harder. Even with a step installed, I had to stretch.

"Hey, Shorty," he said. "Need a stepladder?"

"Dr. Hunter," I said with mock exasperation, "is that any way to speak to the woman who is about to feed you the best damned meal of your life? Not wise, sir, not wise at all. Now could you get your skinny butt in gear and lend some assistance, please?"

He walked over to me, trying with little success to keep a straight face.

"The best meal of my life?" I could tell from his smirk that he had some doubts about my claim, but had decided, in this case at least, that discretion was the better part of valor.

"Behold!" I gestured to a foil-covered pan sitting in a box on the passenger seat. "The nectar of the gods. Or, in this case, the pasta of the gods. It's not every day that you get to eat lasagna made by a genuine half-Italian. A little respect here, please."

"Yes, ma'am, Ms. Half-Italian Rodeo Queen. Or is that Half-Rodeo Italian Queen?" Greg winked at me, and walked around to the passenger side to get the box.

He stopped short and whistled in surprise. There, in the gun rack on the back wall of the cab, sat my brand new short-barreled 12-gauge pump-action shotgun.

He looked at me. "Is it loaded?"

"Heck yes, it's loaded. Double-aught buckshot."

He whistled. "You don't screw around, do you." It was a statement, not a question.

"That's what they taught us in the Girl Scouts. Be prepared. Or something like that. I have another one at home in the kitchen."

Greg paused. "Remind me to not insult your cooking. Ma'am."

"Damn straight. Keep that in mind, City Boy."

Greg, with a small grin dancing around his mouth, retrieved the box from the seat and waited for me to grab another box and a bottle of local wine. I shoved the truck door closed with a swing of my hip, and stood back to admire the house. The place was bigger and more impressive than I remembered.

A classic Italianate octagon house built of granite blocks, it stood three stories tall, with a square tower at the front. The roofline bristled with more chimneys than Toad Hall. A huge Corinthian-columned veranda curved around the entire perimeter of the first floor, the columns supporting a balcony for the second floor. The place was more than a house—it was a flipping mansion.

The suppressed grin broke loose and lit up Greg's face. He seemed pleased with my reaction to the house. "Come this way, Miss Half-Italy. Us disreputable types have to use the servants' entrance."

The servants' quarters formed a separate two-story wing jutting out of the back of the house. He led me up the broad steps from the parking area onto the huge veranda, turned left, and opened a door into a small hallway with a coat rack at the end. "You were here before, weren't you?"

"I just remember the kitchen, probably because that's where the food was."

He gestured in an expansive circle, indicating the whole of the service wing. "This is the best place in the house for me to live. It's self-contained, so it has everything I need. The rest of the house is through the butler's pantry." He tilted his head towards a sliding door on the right.

"There's not much left of the original furnishings," said Greg. "I'll give you the grand tour someday. Not right now, though. Not enough daylight left, and I don't have any lamps in there. It gets downright spooky after dark. C'mon, the kitchen is in here." He opened the sliding door to his left and together we walked back in time.

Except for the modern refrigerator, the kitchen remained true to the original 1915 version that I remembered so well. I'd always loved the color of the pale celadon-green of the ceramic tiles that covered every wall.

I'd never paid too much attention to the old gas range that stood centered on one of those walls. I looked at it with new appreciation—it was close to being a work of art. The stove was an enormous white-enameled beast perched on curved Queen Anne legs, and decorated with pinstriped celadon embellishments. It seemed to be about the size of a beluga whale.

The whale had eight full burners in two rows across the top. One oven of epic proportions sat directly below the burners, perhaps meant for the roasting of whole pigs, or even, perhaps, small elephants. To the right side of the burners was a smaller oven, with a curved-front warming oven right above it. But art was one thing, and functionality another. I surveyed it with not a small amount of doubt.

"Custom built for the house," said Greg. "Runs on propane. It's a champ."

I raised an eyebrow, inviting him to prove it.

He walked across the room to the huge wooden prep table in the center of the kitchen and set down the box holding the lasagna. He pulled out the pan, looked at me, and waited for instructions.

"350 degrees for one hour," I said, "but I don't know how that translates to Moby Dick over there."

"Not a problem. Observe."

Greg picked up a box of wooden matches, struck one, turned a dial on the side to a setting called HOT, and opened up the smaller oven. He stuck the match inside and the gas burners ignited with a muted *whoomp*.

"We let it warm up a bit, pop in the lasagna, and let 'er rip. Because it's an antique, we'll go for an hour and just a tad more. Piece of cake. Or lasagna, whichever the case might be."

I eyed the beast with lingering suspicion. But the lasagna needed an oven, and this was the one it was going to get. "Well... if you say so." I couldn't resist rolling my eyeballs, just for added drama.

I turned and focused on the other food I'd brought. I picked up a small jar containing a two-layered green-gold liquid. Small chunks of minced garlic and herbs rose up from the bottom of the jar and drifted through the mixture.

"What we have here sir, is the top-secret D'Angelo super-powered Italian vinaigrette salad dressing. I can't tell you the ingredients unless you agree to convert to Italianism."

"Hmmm. Gregorio Hunterini. Sort of lacks authenticity, I'd say. But it might be worth it."

"Hell yes, it's worth it. I owe everything that I am today to love songs, and the power of Italian cooking."

"Everything you are today? And that would be unemployed, and living alone in a rundown old farmhouse in the middle of nowhere?

Whoa. That hit a little close to home.

To hide my little shiver of discomfort, I threw a cherry tomato at him. Greg caught it and popped it into his mouth. I glared at him, but he showed no signs of humbled contriteness.

I assembled the salad and stuck it in the fridge. Lasagna and green salad: one of the top-ten all-time great meal combinations ever invented, hands down. The world thanks you, Italy.

Greg picked up the pan of lasagna, slid it into the hot oven, set the timer on his watch, and poured us each a glass of red wine. "Well?" he said.

"Well, what?"

"The secret to the salad dressing. Don't try to weasel out of it. We made a deal."

"Yes, sir, we did. The secret is... C'mon, drum roll, please."

Greg grinned and drummed the tabletop with his fingertips.

"The secret is... the olive oil! Best stuff in the world, or at least the best outside of Italy. It comes from a small family operation up in Coloma. They cold-press it themselves. I'll take you there someday, if you show yourself to be a true believer."

"I'll work at it ma'am. I so promise."

"Yeah, right."

Greg tried to look wounded at my cynicism, then turned and opened the door so we could go back out on the veranda.

◆ ◆ ◆

We stepped outside just in time to catch the peak of the sunset casting ever-changing red and gold tones over the shimmering lake.

A small aluminum boat rocked in the water just below the house. "Seems kind of late in the day to be fishing," I said.

Greg stood up and cupped his hand over his forehead, shading his eyes. "Looks like it's a photographer, catching the sunset. Nice one tonight."

The man in the boat turned and glanced up the hill in our direction. I turned my back to him, and hoped to hell that scenery was all the person wanted to photograph, and not two people having an apparent tête-à-tête on a veranda.

I resented the insidious tentacles of mild paranoia that had recently inserted themselves in my life. But, to throw all caution to the wind seemed foolhardy.

There was my imagination, running away with me again. I forced my thoughts in another direction. "How long has this house been in your family?"

Greg lit some citronella candles sitting on a rattan table. I took a deep breath, relishing the old familiar scent from times long gone. He grinned, understanding the memories evoked.

"It was built in the early 1900s. The Hunters have been here since the Gold Rush—showed up in Jackson from who-knows-where some time around 1850 or so. They started out with a cookhouse in a tent, built a boarding house, opened a general store, and then went into lumber.

"Over the years, the family made themselves a nice pile of cash and decided to celebrate that fact by building the most up-to-date, luxurious house this side of Sacramento. And, so,"—he gestured to the impressive façade of the place— "here we are."

Greg turned and gazed out over the glassy expanse of the darkening lake. "You know, I created quite a stir amongst the locals when I arrived back in town and told everyone that I was moving in here. A lot of Jackson old-timers were placing bets—actual bets—that I wouldn't last one winter in a big old stone house with no central heating. They were all sure that I was just a soft and spoiled city boy."

He chuckled. "After all, I was from Los Angeles, and everyone knows what kind of people live *there*."

"Fooled 'em, didn't ya."

He grinned. "Yup."

We sat in the chairs and talked and laughed about memories of summers past, and other random things. I told him how I'd graduated from Stanford with a degree in music, gone to New York to Columbia Law, and then joined the law firm my dad founded years ago with old gasbag Royston.

"My dad returned to the east coast when I went away to college. I always knew," I said, "that one way or another I'd be heading east too, either to Juilliard or to law school. I'd wondered if I had the chops to make the cut with a major orchestra. But, I never found out. I decided that the law would pay better, plus I wanted to work with my dad. I missed him something awful after he left California. I stayed on with the firm after he died. After a while, I got to the point where I hated the place. It wasn't that hard to leave."

"What kind of law?"

"Corporate," I said, "With a focus on establishment and structuring of non-profits."

"I wouldn't think that would be enough to keep you busy. I mean, how many non-profits can there be? People do like to make money."

"Oh, you'd be surprised. And some of those big non-profits dance just on the edge of the category, at least from my perspective, as they have high overhead expenses and pay their officers rather well. A few of them were downright reprehensible."

I shook my head in rueful remembrance. "But, I didn't get paid to offer ethics counseling, I got paid to keep them within the letter of the law. And while that wasn't the primary reason I got fed up and left, it did play into the equation. After dealing with a few too many slimeballs, I began to feel contaminated by association."

Greg nodded. "I can understand that feeling. I think that the very best doctors are the ones who are attracted to the idea of helping others, of making a difference. The main event is not the income potential. Seems to me that's close to what you were feeling. That's why I initially went into emergency medicine. It seemed important, made me feel needed."

He stretched, and ran his hand through his hair. "You know," he said, "I liked it for a while. I liked the adrenalin rush that came from responding to a critical situation. But, it didn't take me very long to start wondering if I wanted to spend the rest of my life plugging gunshot wounds in snotty little punks, seeing families destroyed by drunk drivers, and telling overweight men with heartburn that, no, they were not having a heart attack.

"So, I ended up deciding to switch my specialty to family practice. Back to school I went. But, it was worth it. At the end of the day, I was a *much* happier person.

"Then, out of the blue"—that infectious grin broke across his face—"the most amazing thing happened. Doc wrote me a letter. He was looking for someone to join his practice, and wondered if I'd be interested. Hell yeah, I was interested. And, so, here I am." Greg swept his arm in an arc. "What's not to love about this place?"

We were both surprised when the beeper on Greg's watch announced the time had arrived to rescue the lasagna from the gullet of the giant stove.

◆ ◆ ◆

A small table in the corner of the kitchen was set for dinner, complete with beautiful old linens and flatware. We settled into the chairs. Greg took a bite of the lasagna and rolled his eyes heavenward. "Whoa. Who taught you to cook? This is amazing."

"My dad taught me. He came by the Italian part honestly, because he was born in Ravenna. Came to the States when he was two months old. He taught Rudy and me how to cook while he sang Italian love songs to my mom. He said it was part of the marriage contract."

He tilted his head, waiting for me to deliver the punch line. I hoped he remembered my dad, the fun-loving guy who enjoyed coming down to the lake to swim with us. All the kids thought he was great. He could make up songs on the spot for every occasion. Rudy and I adored him.

"My dad's name was Romeo. My mom's name was... Julieta."

Greg's face lit up. "You're kidding!"

"Nope. They were set up on a blind date because of their names when they were at Stanford."

"And it obviously worked out."

"Oh, good heavens yes. It did. They were very much in love, until the day she died."

Instead of being carried away by the sappy love story, Greg's face lit up, as if he'd had a sudden thought. "Now, wait a minute here. Hold on. Something doesn't add up."

I looked cross-eyed at him, but the goofy face failed to distract him. He was clearly a man on a mission.

"The other day," he said, "when I was at your house, you gave me all this razzmatazz about your Noble Chilean Ancestor, the Heroic Miner, Juan Minero."

I don't know how he did it, but I swear I could hear the capital letters in his voice.

"So, now you're telling me you're half-Italian. In the interest of full disclosure, doesn't that make you a Chitalian or something?"

I laughed out loud. I couldn't help it. "Nope. Too many generations gone."

"Not buying it."

"No. Really. With all the immigrants that married into the family over the years, if I had a DNA test done, the machine would probably have a nervous breakdown."

Greg burst out with a booming laugh. "So, what you're telling me is that you're really just a mutt."

I laughed too. "Pretty much."

We got busy chowing down on our half-Italian food-of-the-gods. I was surprised when a small flicker of discomfort ran across Greg's face.

"Can I ask you something?" he said. "If you don't want to talk about it, just say so."

"Sure. Go for it."

"What happened to Rudy? I heard that he died in some sort of accident, but never heard anything specific. I asked Doc what happened more than once, but he'd only mutter something vague about Rudy being hit by a truck, and then he'd change the subject."

The question came out of left field and slammed me in the gut. I thought Greg knew what happened. If he didn't, he had a right to know. He'd been Rudy's friend too.

It took a couple of moments to pull my thoughts together. "Well, I'm sure you remember how nutty Rudy was about bugs. That fascination didn't go away as he got older. The science teachers at the high school loved him. He used to roam all over the countryside looking for every little creepy crawly thing he could find. He even had all the right equipment for collecting, preserving, and labeling specimens. He was serious about doing it right."

I took another sip of my wine. "He hauled home some of the grossest, most disgusting things you ever saw: maggots, and stuff like that. I think he loved seeing people freak out. But he had a purpose in doing it. He even corresponded with some researchers at a couple of different universities around the country. He had so much promise..."

My voice trailed off. I had to force myself to refocus.

"Anyway, Rudy loved to go into the forest at night to collect. At first, he would sneak out. Millie busted him for it, thinking he was out smoking pot or drinking with his friends. You know—stupid stuff. Teenage boys are known to do such things from time to time."

Greg rolled his eyes. "True. From time to time."

"Well," I said, "when Millie realized what he was really up to, she got him the right equipment. Rudy would go out in the forest, set up a big white sheet, and tie it between some trees. Then he would turn a spotlight on it, and wait to see what bugs showed up. He did a bug census, sort of, and wrote it up following all the proper scientific protocols. Even published some interesting findings."

I stood up, gathered up my dirty dishes, and carried them to the sink.

"Well, one evening I got home, and found a note on my bed from him. He left it before he went out to the forest. He said he had something important to tell me when he got home." I could see the note in my mind. I still have it, tucked away in my jewelry box.

> You will never believe what I found today. It is BIG!
> And I'm not talking about a bug, either. I'll tell you
> when I get home. Millie is gonna freak, and ask me
> what I've been smoking when she hears about this!

"But... he didn't come home. The next morning a trucker found him dead on a logging road, out near the Simkowitz lumber mill. He'd been run down."

Greg picked up the rest of the dishes and joined me at the sink. "That doesn't make any sense! You can hear the trucks coming for miles out there."

"Exactly. That's bothered me for years. The cops checked all the local logging trucks. They talked to every trucker they could find who'd been down that road. They didn't come up with *anything*. The whole thing turned out to be a wild goose chase. In the end, the coroner ruled it an accident, and that was that."

I had to stop for a moment. After all these years, the anger and hurt still burned my gut. "Doc was furious, and convinced that the autopsy was botched. All of us were positive there was more to the situation than met the eye. But nothing could be proven. It seemed to us that the police department was corrupt as hell. There was a lot of cronyism going on back then."

I wiped my hands on a towel and went back to the table to sit down. A horrible notion raced through my mind, chilling me.

Was I seeing a new cover-up now, with all this "accident" nonsense from Newhall?

I had zero doubt that a cover-up and a shocking miscarriage of justice occurred when Rudy died. Were Newhall's bizarre conclusions a result of something more than sheer incompetence?

Greg sat down across from me, interrupting the tumble of outraged thoughts running through my head. "Police department? Isn't that the county sheriff's jurisdiction out there?"

It took me a moment to pick up on what he was talking about. "You'd think so, wouldn't you? But it's not. The city limits extend way the heck out from the edge of town. City planners must have been overly optimistic at some point or another."

Dare I mention this new suspicion of mine? No. Not yet. I needed to think about this. With all the weirdness going on in my life, I could be getting more than a little bit paranoid.

Focus. Back to Rudy. Finish the story.

"Well, anyway, lots of people around here were super upset about the whole thing, calling it a slipshod investigation, even suggesting a payoff occurred somewhere along the way. The truck drivers were incensed when the police implied that one of them had run Rudy down.

"The coroner ended up retiring and moving away. The police chief more or less got hounded into leaving too." I sucked in a deep breath, then sighed. "It was a mess."

I fingered the gold chain around my neck. A dime-sized natural gold nugget, shaped like a heart, hung from it. I unhooked the necklace, and handed it to Greg. "This nugget was found in Rudy's vest pocket. It's another part of the mystery. We had no idea where it came from, or why he had it."

From the way he turned the nugget in his hand and watched the ambient light shimmer on the lustrous surface, I could tell Greg appreciated the unique beauty of the piece. He handed the necklace back to me, and I fastened it back around my neck.

"I still miss him," I said, "so much..."

◆ ◆ ◆

I helped Greg finish cleaning up. He offered to show me around his living quarters, and a small flicker of alarm burst to life inside of me. Did he think I was flirting with him? Good lord, I hoped not. An entanglement was the last thing I needed.

We climbed the narrow winding staircase to the second floor. Two large bedrooms and a full bathroom took up the floor above the kitchen. The rooms were filled with contemporary furniture that Greg had brought from LA. One glance brought on an inadvertent giggle.

Greg shot me a quizzical look. I needed to explain. "I had the exact same sofa, end tables, and bookcases in New York, when I was in law school! IKEA's finest. But my sofa was red."

I gestured towards Greg's sofa, covered in a striking, geometric black and white print. "I did consider buying that one, though."

A walnut-framed photo of a striking young woman caught my eye. The captured scene showed her standing on a beach, in a tropical location. The sand was a crystalline white, the sea brilliant turquoise. Green-fronded palm trees with curved trunks sat in the distance behind her.

Long-legged, tanned, and fit, she had the lean muscular build of a competitive beach volleyball player. She wore a bright yellow, no-nonsense swimsuit, the kind meant for serious swimming. A diving mask sat atop her head. Her copper-colored hair, caught into a ponytail, curved over her shoulder. A pair of flippers swung from one hand.

The woman was leaning forward, her face lit up by a delighted smile, as if the photo had captured her enjoyment of a wonderful joke.

"She's beautiful, Greg. Who is she?"

"Her name is Claire." Greg turned his eyes and looked straight into mine. "She's my wife."

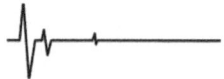

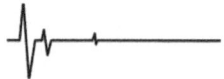

Chapter Eleven

I was surprised, to say the least, and it must have shown on my face. I had no idea that he was married. And I was puzzled as to why he hadn't mentioned his wife up to this point. Greg understood my silent question. His face sagged slightly, and I wondered if the woman had died, or something else equally awful had happened to her.

"It's a long story," he said. "But, there are things... that I'd like you to know. About Claire."

He took my hand and led me back down the stairs to the kitchen. He opened another bottle of wine and poured us each a fresh glass. "C'mon, let's go outside."

The sun had. long ago disappeared, as had the small aluminum boat. Greg stared out at the darkened lake for a few moments, and turned to me.

"I met Claire at USC. I was pre-med, she was a biology major. We fell in love. We married after graduation, when we both received our bachelor's degrees. The picture on the desk is from our honeymoon. While I was working on my MD, she was studying for her PhD in biology, with a focus on ecology and natural systems. Following that, during my residency, she got a teaching position at a junior college. It wasn't what she wanted, but... well, you know. It was a job."

"When Doc wrote to offer me the place in his practice, she literally screamed and ran in circles around the kitchen making fist pumps. She was already interested in this area, and had a friend who was working with the Nature Conservancy out in that forest tract that used to be the Simkowitz property. The friend kept bugging Claire to come check it out. So we did, and next thing we knew, Claire was offered a job too. Not full time, but she didn't care. We pulled up stakes, lock stock and barrel, and came to a new world. She was in heaven.

"Part of her job was to set up a succession survey, see what plants sprouted up first in the areas that had been clear cut, what animals and insects moved in, etc., and keep an eye out for invasive species, so they could be rooted out and destroyed. And, if she found any trash, she'd pick it up and toss it in her truck."

He sat for a few minutes in silence. "One day when she was out there, she was confronted by a man who took exception to her presence. We're not sure exactly what happened. By the time one of her colleagues noticed what was going on, a huge argument had erupted. Her colleague came running up just in time to see the guy smack Claire in the head with a baseball bat. Fractured her skull."

Greg paused again. His eyes were glassy with unshed tears. "Her colleague shouted out, and the guy took off. He had a floppy hat on, like those things the river guides wear, so nobody got a good look at his face. He didn't drop the bat. We still have no idea who it was."

I was shocked, and for more reasons that he could guess. Before I could even process a coherent response, he continued.

"And you know what was so damned fucking weird?" His voice rose, anguished. "The man was flipping out because Claire had picked up an old flashlight, and tossed it in the trash bin. A flashlight!" He closed his eyes, and shook his head. "Never did find out what that was all about. He ran off without it when her colleague arrived on the scene. The police were called, but of course they didn't find him."

He shifted in the chair, and opened his eyes. "What an idiot. If the guy had done nothing, had never gone out there, the flashlight would have just ended up in the landfill with all the other junk they found. But his reaction was so weird, well... I kept the damned thing. Something in the back of my mind tells me that this flashlight is a big deal somehow, but damned if I know why or how." He stood up. "I'll show you."

I got up out of the chair, and I followed him back upstairs.

He rummaged around on the top shelf in a closet, and pulled down a cardboard box. The flashlight was the old-fashioned type, consisting of a floodlight mounted on a metal plate that was in turn attached to the top of a large rectangular lantern battery. The thing looked like a piece of junk. It was dirty, rusty, and splashed with mud. The lens was fractured, and missing a small triangular piece of glass. The flashlight was wrapped in a plastic bag. I picked it up. The thing was surprisingly heavy.

Greg was right. The whole situation was weird. Immediately following that thought came a sudden realization that punched me right in the gut. Hands shaking, I set the light back in the box. As Greg returned it to the shelf, I wobbled across the room, and flopped down on the IKEA sofa. Greg tilted his head, puzzled. "Are you okay?"

I shook my head. "Not really." How could I explain this? "The place

Claire got hurt? That's right where Rudy was found dead."

"Oh, shit," said Greg. "I'm sorry!"

"No, no, it's okay. How could you know?"

We went back down to the kitchen. My knees were trembling, and I had to hold on tight to the railing.

Greg poured me a big glass of cold water, and patiently waited for me to collect myself. Neither of us mentioned the terrible coincidence that I'd just realized. The implications were altogether too sinister, too distressing, to even contemplate.

◆ ◆ ◆

After a few moments of silence, Greg spoke. "Would you like to meet Claire? She's here in Jackson, at a convalescent facility." He looked very somber, his forehead wrinkled, as if gaining my understanding had real importance to him.

"She's still in the hospital?"

Surprise must have shown on my face, because he said, "She was pretty badly hurt. There was significant brain damage."

"Oh, god Greg. I am so sorry..."

He bobbed his head in a quick nod, accepting my condolences.

My emotions hadn't yet settled. A tear rolled down my face, and I brushed it away. I put my hand on his arm. "I'd be happy to meet her."

His offer was touching. Few people knew about this part of his life.

He stood up, walked over to the nearby table, and with a quick pinch, snuffed the last guttering candle. "Okay," he said. "Let's go."

◆ ◆ ◆

Claire sat propped up in bed, staring at the television set mounted on the wall. Her copper hair was cut quite short, almost in a buzz-cut. A wheelchair sat in the corner of the room. Images of an old *I Love Lucy* episode flickered across the screen—Ricky Ricardo, finger wagging, admonishing Lucy for some unknown transgression. The sound had been turned off. Still, the image of the angry dark-haired man gave me the shivers. Too close to home...

"Claire," Greg said. She didn't even blink. "Claire." She kept staring at the TV. Greg picked up the remote and turned off the set. Only then did she seem to sense our presence. She turned her head, blinked, and looked at Greg with blank, jade-green eyes.

The difference between this woman and the luminous woman in the photograph was wrenching, almost unbearable. I couldn't tell whether Claire recognized Greg or not. The expression on her face didn't change.

He spoke to her again. "Claire, honey, I brought someone to meet you." Greg motioned for me to step up to the bed. "Claire, this is Alexandra. She's a friend of Doc's."

Claire kept staring at Greg. He reached out and guided me over, so I stood right in front of him. Her eyes moved from Greg's face down to mine.

"Hi, Claire. I'm Alexandra. I'm pleased to meet you. Greg told me all about you." I extended my hand to her.

Claire didn't respond. She turned her head back to where it had been, stared straight ahead for a couple of seconds, then closed her eyes and settled her head back into the pillow behind her.

Greg picked up the control for the bed, and lowered the head. "Goodnight, Claire," he said in a soft voice. He stroked the stubble of her hair, kissed her cheek, and walked out of the room. I followed him into the hallway. Greg reached around behind me and turned off the room lights.

We went back down the hall. Greg waved to the nurse at the duty station. We walked in silence back to the truck, and got in. Greg, pensive, didn't start it up.

The only thing I could think to say was a soft "Wow."

"Yes. Claire hasn't said anything in a long time, months now. For a while after the accident, she made some effort to speak, but no one could understand her, so I guess she gave up. I don't know if she understands what I say to her, so I assume she does. I've told the nurses to make the same assumption. They're good about talking to her.

"Some kids in a service group at the high school come in once a week to read to her. Right now, they're in the middle of the *Harry Potter* series. The kids, bless 'em, don't get too discouraged by the fact that she doesn't seem to register their presence. It's obvious that a good-hearted someone gave them a solid pep talk about altruism."

He stopped for a moment, and tapped his fingers on his knee. With a tinge of bitterness in his voice, he said, "She has one hell of a great life, doesn't she? Her hair is kept short to keep it from tangling. She had beautiful hair..."

We sat in silence for a moment. Then Greg hit the starter, and drove us back to his place. I divided up the leftovers between us, and he walked with me to my truck.

I shoved the pans inside, then turned, wrapped my arms around him, and gave him a peck on the cheek. "You're a good man, Greg Hunter."

There seemed to be nothing that I could add to that thought. I climbed up into the cab, started up the engine, turned the truck around, and left.

◆ ◆ ◆

I drove the truck up the hill to my house, pulled into the barn, and shut off the engine. I trudged toward the house, wondering if I'd just made a colossal fool of myself, and stopped short. A large... something... sprawled, motionless, across my back porch.

I headed back to the truck, got my Maglite out of the glove box, and pointed it at the porch.

There was a dead coyote on the top step. One of its front legs was mangled, as if crushed by a trap. Its throat was slit. Horrible, red splashes were arrayed in a wide arc across the door, and coagulating blood pooled around the body. Dark stains trailed down the steps and formed ragged splotches where it had spilled over and soaked into the dry soil.

The dead coyote's eyes were open, like dark holes, staring without hope at the cold night sky. The poor coyote, its mouth duct-taped shut, must have been killed right there, on my back porch.

Bile surged up in my throat. Whoever did this wasn't just mildly disturbed. They were downright sadistic.

I stumbled up against the rough stone of the side of the house and drew a deep breath. The scent of blood overwhelmed me. Saliva flooded my mouth, and I swallowed hard, to no avail. I staggered away from the house and vomited.

Oh god oh god oh god... Should I call the police? I really couldn't call this an emergency. But, if I waited to call them in the morning, some scavenger might drag off the carcass during the night.

Damned if I do, damned if I don't.

My quaking legs made the decision for me. I needed to get inside the house, rinse out my mouth, get away from the blank gaze of the animal and the smell of death.

Screw it. I'd call the police in the morning. I fumbled my phone out of my pocket and took a few pictures. If the coyote got dragged away in the night I'd have photos—not to mention the blood all over the place—as evidence that something bad happened here. There. Done.

But, there was no use in walking around to the front door. It was bolted from the inside. The back door was the only one with a key, my only way in.

So, I could spend the night in the truck, curled up with a grimy horse blanket that hadn't been washed in thirty years, or I could deal with it.

I looked around the barn, and found an old wooden crate. I slammed it against the side of a stall. It broke apart enough for me to pull off one of the bottom slats.

I stepped into the blood to get close enough to the coyote to try to move it, and had to swallow a couple of times to fight off the recurring nausea. I put the slat between the door and the animal, and tried to pull it towards me.

Coyotes aren't big, usually weighing less than forty pounds, but I couldn't budge it. Not enough leverage. I switched angles and tried again. No dice.

Well, great. I did *not* want to touch the poor beast. But, sometimes, what you want to do and what you have to do are two different things.

I bent over, grasped a handful of fur in each hand, and stepped backwards as I pulled the coyote towards me. Some tufts of fur ripped out, and the rest slipped through my fingers. I stumbled backwards, but managed not to land on my rear in the bloody dirt. I had a sudden new appreciation for the term "dead weight."

I stepped forward to make another try at moving the carcass, only this time I grabbed a generous fold of skin in each hand. I gave a mighty heave-ho, and the coyote's body slid about a foot. I turned the key in the lock, and managed to get the door open wide enough to squeeze through. I looked down at my feet. My new boots were covered with blood.

I kicked off the boots, ran to the sink, and let my stomach turn itself inside out again.

◆ ◆ ◆

In my dreams that night, the face of the murdered coyote haunted me, dead eyes staring into my soul, asking me why I had allowed it to die. The frozen visage of the animal morphed into the smiling face and warm brown eyes of my brother.

Rudy, up in the old oak tree, laughs in the dark. I watch in horror as he tumbles from the tree, and plunges down the side of the mountain, his calls for help echoing through the night. Millie runs up beside me, and peers over the side, frantic. The tree lurches forward and pushes Millie off the edge of the precipice. She, too, screams as she vanishes into the blackness.

I run down the mountain, searching for them. And I can't find them anywhere.

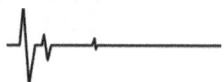

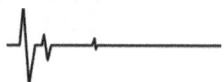

CHAPTER TWELVE

By the time I got up the next morning, iridescent green flies had formed an undulating buzzing cloud around the dead coyote. The stench of the carcass was a stomach-churning cross between spoiled cheese and decomposing skunk. I filled a big bucket full of water, dumped it on the place where I'd vomited the night before, and beat a fast retreat back inside the house. I grabbed my phone and called the police non-emergency number.

To my surprise, the person who answered the phone at the police department didn't give me any flack. I'd assumed that if old "No Call" was a stalwart representative of the quality of the force, then I'd be dealing with the local equivalent of the Keystone Kops.

Presented with evidence to the contrary, a small warm tendril of hope blossomed inside of me. The big question was, of course, how long that hope would survive.

Within an hour after the call, I spotted the trail of dust that marked the passage of a car on my road. I came out of the house by way of the front door. I walked to the car, hoping that old No Call had lived up to his nickname, and I'd be dealing with someone else.

A wave of relief settled over me when a large man I'd never seen before exited the unmarked automobile. "Ms. D'Angelo?"

"Yes."

"I'm Detective Drake. You called about a dead animal?"

A faint hint of puzzlement colored his voice. I hoped that meant he'd reserve judgment until he had all the facts.

Detective Drake looked like he used to be a pro football player, and stood at least six-five. To describe him as physically imposing would be a gross understatement. Detective Drake was a handsome man with deep bronze skin, graying hair, and warm hazel eyes. The kindness in his expression did much to mitigate his overwhelming size.

"It's not just a dead animal, sir, it's a murdered animal. I believe someone left it on my porch in an attempt to intimidate me."

"Oh?" He tilted his head, just a bit. "And why is that?" The comment was not snarky or unkind; he was simply seeking information.

"Let me show you. If a picture's worth a thousand words, this thing ought to be equal to at least an encyclopedia." I gestured towards the rear of the house. "It's back here."

We walked along the packed earth driveway that ran beside the house. We turned at the corner of the building, and the critter's stench hit us. I stopped, not wanting to get too close.

"As you can see, sir, its throat was cut. I really don't think the thing committed suicide."

Drake took a few steps closer to the unfortunate beast and winced. "Do you have any idea why this happened? Any other incidents?"

I started to say "no," but realized that wasn't true. There was that strange "Go back to New York" note, right when I first arrived. I told him about it.

"But as to who or why? I have *no* idea. I just moved here the first of September. I inherited this house when my aunt died. How could I have already upset someone badly enough that they'd do something like this? I don't get it..."

I lifted my hands in the classic gesture of bewilderment. "I can't come to any conclusion about it other than it seems to be an attempt to frighten me. Nothing else makes sense."

He nodded. I didn't know if he was agreeing with my conclusions, or simply acknowledging them. "When did you find this?"

"I ate dinner at a friend's house last night, and when I got home, this was here. I think I got here around ten-thirty or so, maybe a little later than that. I left here just after seven, so it got dumped off sometime in between. I didn't call you guys last night because it wasn't an emergency."

Drake nodded again, and scribbled some notes on a small notepad. "Have you touched it, or disturbed it at all?"

It seemed an odd question, since there were obvious drag-marks in the dried blood on the step. Whatever. I guess he had to figure out who did what.

"I had to drag it out of the way so I could get in the house." I clenched my fingers, remembering the feel of the coyote's cold, damp fur, and resisted a strong urge to wipe my hands on the back of my jeans.

Drake tilted his head towards the front of the house. "Why go to all that trouble when the house has more than one door?"

"The front door is the original. It bolts from the inside. There's no key to it, so I couldn't get in that way. I had to go in the back."

He scribbled another note in his book.

Drake looked down at the poor beast and nudged it a bit with his shoe. The body, stiff and unyielding, didn't budge. I wished he'd walk away from it so we could continue our conversation away from the godawful smell. I stepped back a bit, but he didn't follow. Maybe it didn't bother him as much as it did me.

"Well, as strange as this may seem to you," he said, "I'm going to have an evidence technician come out here and look at it. You don't mind if we bag it up and take it away?"

"You can make coyote stew, if you want. Share it with your friends. Add some carrots and potatoes. It'll be delicious."

Drake's tiny nod acknowledged my pathetic attempt at a joke. He got on his police handset and called someone. He finished his conversation with the invisible person, and looked at me. "We need to discuss a few things. Do you mind if we go in the house?"

Hallelujah. I would have put up with the Spanish Inquisition to get away from that smell. "Not at all. Follow me."

I resisted breaking into a sprint. We walked around the house at a very ordinary pace, and went in through the front door, which I'd left ajar. We continued on back to the kitchen, into the comfy heart of the house. Even here, the stench of death still lingered in my nostrils.

I wanted to run into the bathroom, strip down and stand under the shower, but, instead, I scrubbed my hands and poured us some coffee. We sat down at the kitchen table, and Drake scanned the whole room with an efficient glance. His eyes glided over the watercolor hanging over the fireplace and the wooden kitchen tools sitting upright in the bright Talavera water jug on the stove.

With experience, I guessed that a detective could tell quite a bit about a person from where they lived. But in this case, the five-second scan of the room told him more about Millie than it did about me. I found that fact to be a bit amusing. In my own home, I was the invisible woman. It didn't bother me all that much.

"Miss D'Angelo, there are a few things you need to know, because I believe this incident is related to some events that occurred here before your aunt died. I came here this morning because I investigated those events. It now appears that the case did not close with her death, as we'd assumed."

I sat bolt upright. *What?*

"We didn't know whether some events that occurred over the past few months were associated with Ms. Minero as an individual, or with her home or property. Now, because this happened to you, I think we can assume there is someone out there who has some concerns regarding this land, or this house."

"Concerns? About *this* place?" The idea seemed preposterous, even bizarre.

"Over the past year," he said, "some events occurred here that were similar to what you experienced with the coyote. Ms. Minero wasn't too worried about it at first. She regarded the incidents as pranks. But it came to a point where she had to contact us."

Was that the reason Doc decided to move in with Millie after all these years? Seemed reasonable. But why hadn't she told about it? I'd talked to her on the phone all the time.

"What sort of things?" I asked.

He shook his head. "Early on, the police department made the determination that it would be best to not discuss the specific details of events that occurred here with anyone other than Ms. Minero. Doing so guarantees us that the perpetrator is the sole individual with knowledge of those events.

"I can assure you that up until Ms. Minero's murder, nothing worse than minor property damage occurred. Please keep in mind that we don't know for certain if the pranks, if you can call them that, are in any way related to what happened here last night."

It took me a few moments to process his words, and I wondered if I should mention the bashed fireplace bricks. I decided not to. The damage was odd, no doubt about it, but not overtly sinister.

"The occurrence of pranks, as you call them, doesn't make any sense to me," I said. "The Minero family has lived here, in this house, for over a hundred years. Why the heck would somebody all of a sudden get a bee in their bonnet about it now?"

He shrugged his massive shoulders. "I wish I could tell you. From the pattern we have observed, it does appear to me that someone would like you to sell or abandon this place."

"Over my dead body!" I cringed as soon as the worlds were out of my mouth. Not the best choice of phrases, but it did offer a nice segue to the question that was frantically jumping around in my brain. I plunged right in. "Do you think the harassment of my aunt was connected to her death?"

His face tightened. He inhaled slowly, and appeared to be searching for the right words to say.

Hmm. Interesting. Getting into uncomfortable territory here, are we? How're you going to handle this one without throwing old N.C. under the bus? The answer came pretty fast.

"Ms. D'Angelo, as you know, Detective Newhall is the officer in charge of investigating your aunt's death. And, as you also know, he seems convinced that she died as the result of an unfortunate accident. Be that as it may, we do have evidence that someone was harassing your aunt prior to the fatal incident. We don't know how, or even if, any of these events are connected.

"The best I can do right now is request the coroner's office to leave things open for a while, in case further investigation is warranted."

I felt my shoulders relax a bit. With two people having put a bug in the coroner's ear, it seemed unlikely that the case would be closed too soon.

Drake's eyes traveled over to the new 12-gauge shotgun sitting on the sideboard. "You know how to handle that thing?"

Whoa, slick change of topic there. But, he'd told me enough to let me know that he wasn't going to blow this matter off. A fighter in Millie's corner? Maybe. He seemed like much more like a brawler than old Newhall.

"No worries. My Grandpa John taught me how to shoot both small-bore rifles and shotguns, starting when I was big enough to be able to control the recoil. I used to shoot air rifles competitively in high school, and my grandpa also used to take me skeet shooting."

His face relaxed into a smile. "Good. I've seen some inexperienced gun owners do some very stupid things. I'm glad I don't have to worry about that with you."

He finished off the last of his coffee. "This is just my personal opinion, and I don't want to frighten you unnecessarily, but I believe that this coyote incident marks an escalation in the harassment we've witnessed in the past. You have some choices."

He held up his hand to tick off the reasons on his big fingers. "One, you can find a place to live in town, until we figure out what is going on here. Or, two, you can get someone to come live here with you. Somebody useful, not just ornamental."

I smiled at his choice of words.

"Three, you can stay here by yourself, and be very, very, careful. In fact, be an outright coward. If anything, and I mean *anything,* happens that seems to be the slightest bit off, jump in your car and get the heck out of here.

"If you need to bail out, drive straight to the police department, or to the fire department," he said. "You know. Go to Jail, Directly to Jail. Do not pass Go. Do not hide out at a friend's house. In either case, whether you go to the police department or to the fire station, no one is going to think you're being paranoid. Far from it. People in both places know what happened to your aunt."

He set down the empty coffee cup and leaned back in the chair. "I think you'll have a period of quiet while you decide what you want to do. Whoever dumped the coyote is going to give you time to think about things before they decide to up the ante. So, consider your choices.

"There is a positive side to this event, you know." Drake's habitual smile grew a bit wider. "The person who dumped the coyote here can't be too bright. You'd think that after what happened to Ms. Minero, they would realize that the police are taking note of anything odd that happens up here.

So, this may be the event that starts the unraveling of the knot."

I hoped, to the very center of my soul, that he was right.

"I don't want to put you into overload, but there's one more thing for you to think about," he said. "As you said, the Minero family has lived here for many years, almost as long as the city of Jackson has been around, without any problems to speak of. Then, boom, strange things start to happen. The point I'm making is that something changed. You know it, I know it. Our mysterious friend knows it. The question is *what*."

Drake paused. "Have you gone through your aunt's personal effects yet? You know, paperwork and such."

I closed my eyes and shook my head. I hadn't mustered the fortitude needed to tackle the task.

"When Ms. Minero was shot, my department did a search through her documents, phone records, and so forth, looking for anything that might give us a lead on what happened to her. We found nothing obvious. But that doesn't mean there isn't something here. Maybe we just didn't recognize it." He pushed the coffee mug a short distance away from him. He looked up and locked his eyes on mine.

"So," he said, "as much as you don't want to deal with her stuff, and believe me, I do understand that feeling, sooner or later you are going to have to do it. Please, make it sooner. Not later. Keep an eye peeled for anything that might provide a clue. Anything. We don't have much to go on.

"If you find something that seems a bit odd, or interesting, or whatever, you know where to reach me."

He reached into his suit jacket inner pocket and pulled out a card case. He extracted one and handed it to me.

Donald D. Drake
Detective
Jackson-Martell Police Department

How could his parents be so cruel? I looked up at him, afraid that a combination of surprise and sympathy was written all over my face.

The big detective smiled. "Just call me Drake," he said in an amiable voice. "It's okay. Everyone does. I've even been called Ducky a time or two. I've gotten used to it by now. The important thing is that my direct phone number and my email address are on the back of the card. Feel free to call or email me any time. I mean that. That's why I'm giving it to you. You have a cell phone?"

I nodded, dug my phone out of my pocket, and handed it to him. He loaded his number into it.

Detective Drake struck me as being rock-solid—unflappable and businesslike. I had no doubt that I could rely on him. The man was the very model of compassionate law enforcement professionalism. Thank heavens.

The big man got up from the chair, and we walked out to his car. The evidence technician had arrived while we were inside.

The tech was a slender young woman, dressed in a tan jumpsuit with the word "Police" stenciled on the back. She had a black ponytail tied up in the back and secured with a hairnet.

Moving with smooth grace, like a dancer or a gymnast, she heaved a big gray case out of the trunk of an unmarked car. "Elegant" was the word that came to mind to describe her, but her poise seemed innate, not an affectation.

Drake greeted her with a loud, cheery hello, got in his car, and drove away. She waved back, without glancing up or breaking her concentration. If it had been me, I think I would've flipped him off.

She set down the evidence kit next to the coyote, pulled on purple surgical gloves, surveyed the mess on the porch, and wrinkled her nose.

I didn't envy her. The warm sunshine beaming down on the coyote hadn't made it smell any better. I left her alone to do her work.

◆ ◆ ◆

After the tech left, I scrubbed the porch and door with several rounds of a detergent and bleach solution. No matter how much I scrubbed, the putrid odor of death lingered. I began to wonder if the odor actually remained, or if it only lingered in my imagination. The more I scrubbed, the angrier I got.

I dumped the bucket, scrubbed my hands at the sink in the barn and stomped back into the kitchen, slamming the door behind me. Why, *why* hadn't Millie told me there were problems going on here? How many other "pranks" had been pulled? What was the point in all this?

I picked up my empty coffee mug and hurled it across the room. The mug exploded against the bricked-up fireplace, and jagged daggers of ceramic flew everywhere.

I flung myself down into one of the green chairs, tilted my head back, stared at the old beamed ceiling, and counted to twenty. It didn't do any good. Still irritated, I found the dustpan and broom, cleaned up the mess, and collapsed back into the chair.

Should I have mentioned the damaged bricks to Detective Drake? Good question. Maybe Millie wanted to do something artistic with the fireplace. Maybe... I didn't know what. I tossed my hands in the air, exasperated.

Nothing made sense. Nothing.

Millie was a wonderful person—I wasn't alone in that belief. Even after she'd become rich and celebrated, there was nothing of the diva about her. She wasn't difficult, or demanding, or anything of that nature. In fact, she was as far from being a pain in the rear as anyone I'd ever known. I couldn't imagine why anyone would want to hurt or frighten her, let alone kill her.

Enough. I gave up trying to find any rational explanations for what had gone on, and went and took a hot shower. I stood under the comforting stream of water, and Drake's advice rolled around in my head.

No way would I move into town. And the only person I'd want to come live with me was Greg. But, that might spark some nasty gossip that he could do without. Bertie might be as soft and cuddly as a teddy bear, but she was best experienced in small doses. Demetra had a business to run, and I half-suspected she stayed overnight at the shop more often than not.

I'd been gone so long that I didn't have a strong local support network anymore. So... net result equals zero.

Great. Just great. Maybe a change in scenery would put me in a better mood. I grabbed my keys and my wallet, jogged out to the truck, and drove down the hill.

◆ ◆ ◆

I headed towards Demetra's, where I always felt better. My improving view of the world evaporated a few seconds after I parked in the lot and started towards the door. Focused on thoughts of a caramel latte, I almost collided with Andrew Pichl.

"Hi, there!" I said, with forced enthusiasm, as I tried to walk past him into the shop. He grabbed my arm, then lurched sideways, almost throwing both of us off-balance. Although not a large man, he had a strong grip.

"Oh, uh, hi there, Alexandra. How's it going way up there on the top of the hill?"

The words "all by yourself" were not spoken, but it sure seemed to me they were implied. He reminded me of a gawky teenager trying hard to impress the prom queen, and making a miserable muck-up out of the attempt.

A shudder of revulsion ran through me—irrational, for sure, but I just didn't like the guy. And when did we get on a first-name basis?

"Just fine, Andrew, just fine. You know, you're hurting my arm."

"Oh. Sorry." He relaxed his grip a bit, but didn't let go. "It's not too quiet and lonesome for you out there then?"

I gave him my most dazzling smile, the one I save for real assholes. "Heavens no! I love it. It's so good to be back home!"

It wouldn't hurt to remind him that Jackson was my hometown, not New York City.

"Oh, uh, yeah." The tips of his ears turned red. I didn't feel the least bit sorry for him. "You know," he said, "when you were in my office, I didn't realize you were the niece who'd lived here with Millie. If, uh, you ever decide you want to sell that old place, you let me know."

A jolt of adrenalin hit my system, and my heart thudded. Just a few days ago, I wouldn't have given two cents worth of thought to such a remark, but the world was a different place now.

I wondered if I should flat-out ask him why he was so darned interested in my house, but my gut instincts were screaming at me to get the heck away from him.

I stared at Andrew for a couple of seconds, trying to will him into understanding that he had just said a very stupid thing. It didn't work. So I switched back on the fake-o-matic hundred-watt smile. "Sure will. Gotta run. I've got a lot to do today. See you later!"

I pulled away from him with such an abrupt and obvious motion that he had no choice but to let go of my arm. I bolted into the shop and almost ran up to the counter. Demetra fixed me a latte without even asking.

Her merry eyes crinkled up at the corners and she snorted with suppressed laughter. I lifted the cup to my lips.

"What's the matter, girlfriend?" she asked. "Did our pal Andrew ask you out on a date?"

I darned near choked. "Dear Andrew was just inquiring about my health and continued happiness here in God's Country." I rubbed my arm. "I think he bruised me." I glanced over towards the door to make sure he hadn't followed me inside, and lowered my voice. "The man gives me the creeps." I eyed the brownies in the display case.

Demetra nodded. "I can't stand him either," she said in a similarly low voice, "but don't tell anyone I said so. He's a most peculiar Pickle."

A naughty image danced into my mind. "Kosher dill or gherkin?"

She snorted again. "Girl, you are *soooo* bad! It's a gherkin, honey, gherkin. Like duuuuh! Not that I'm volunteering to do any research to verify, you understand."

She gave me a sassy wink. "If you'll wait a sec, I've got some hot raspberry-filled croissants, right out of the oven. One of those'll fix you right up."

"Deal."

She rang up the order. I slid my ATM card by the machine, grabbed the latte, and sat down to take care of my email. I was muttering dire imprecations under my breath regarding one specific individual (and his gherkin) when Demetra came back with my goodies.

The combined steamy fragrance of butter and raspberry wafting up from the croissant was pure bliss. The woman is the da Vinci of desserts, the Botticelli of buttery things. The smile on her face told me she'd heard my grumbling.

"That's right. Let it out, baby. Just a spoonful of swearing helps the medicine go down." She winked again and walked off.

Who couldn't help but adore Demetra? But then again, we were kindred smart-asses, so of course I liked her.

While waiting for the temperature of the raspberry filling to cool down to less than molten lava, I composed a text message to Drake. Pichl seemed to pop up in my vicinity just a bit too often.

Andrew Pichl asked me about selling my house. Not the first time.

I sent off the text, checked some news sites, and opened my email account. My mind kept wandering back to Mr. Pickle's questions. Was his fixation the simple result of him being weird and socially inept? Or, was he not all right in the noggin? Did I make a mistake by smiling and not taking his head off?

If he acted like that with other people, sooner or later, someone was going to give him a knuckle sandwich. Pow! Right in the kisser. That person would deserve an award. I'd be happy to act as the presenter.

Eager to change my focus, I scrolled through my email inbox. My connections with friends in New York were breaking, one by one. Not too surprising, given the way that real life works.

Forget about just living in another time zone, I now lived in a different world. Or on a different planet. And more than that, I was changing. The brash New Yorker *would* have taken Andrew's head off. The realization was startling.

There was one person in New York who I heartily wished would break with me, but he hadn't. Mark. He'd sent another cheery message.

I don't know why you haven't answered me. What kind of game are you playing? You know you can't win. You'll be sorry if you try.

I sighed with impatience. All I cared about was an equitable division of jointly-owned property. The fact that he couldn't believe that I wasn't after every dime he'd ever made spoke volumes. I didn't want his darned money. I just wanted him to *go away*.

Mark. As I have stated before, please direct all correspondence to my lawyer. Thank you.

I considered blocking his email address, then decided against it. If he got aggressive with his threats I'd need any future nasty communications as evidence. I set up a filter so all emails from him would be automatically sent into an archive.

After thinking about it for a couple of more seconds, I added an auto-response message, a special one just for Mark. Life was too short to put up with his crap.

> You have reached a mailbox that is not monitored. In future, kindly send all written correspondence via US Mail, in care of my attorney. Thank you.

How had it come to this? I'd once loved that man with all my heart and soul. With another small sigh, I closed my email and pulled up the website of the *Argonaut Ledger* to check out the local news. A headline caught my eye.

Suspected Arson Fire Reported

> JACKSON, CA -- An automobile was found on fire in the rural Jackson area early Saturday morning, and police are investigating the fire as arson. Police officers responded at about 1:15 a.m. to a report of a car on fire at the Butte Mountain Road home of Mr. and Mrs. Larry Smith. The officers arrived to find a late model automobile fully engulfed in flames, as well as a tree and some nearby shrubs, police said. Firefighters extinguished the blaze before it could spread further. Officers searched the area but did not find any possible suspects. There was no damage to any nearby homes or other structures, and no one was injured in the fire, according to police. Anyone with information about the fire is asked to call the Jackson-Martell Police Department.

Next to the article was a picture of a burned-out Mercedes. My Mercedes. Or, rather, the one I'd traded in. Had someone torched it, thinking it was still mine?

Or... was I reduced to looking for monsters under the bed? I didn't know what to think. The last traces of my raspberry-induced contentment died away.

There was no point in sitting there worrying about things I could do nothing about. I was about to fold up my laptop and go home when a return message came from Drake.

> Noted. Don't hesitate to contact me any time.

I responded to the text with a short one of my own.

> Thx. BTW, the car torched at Larry Smith's house sure looks like the one I traded in.

I didn't wait for a reply and trudged out to my truck. A horrible thought dawned, and as I considered it, the idea seemed to grow and morph into something dreadful. Did I make a huge mistake by coming home?

No. I could not allow this thought to grow any stronger. It might be true. It might consume me.

I turned around and walked back into the shop. By the time I left, Demetra and I had made plans to put a stake right through the heart of my fears. I hoped it worked.

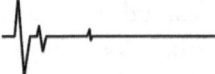

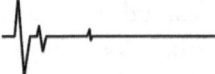

Chapter Thirteen

I pulled onto the dirt road leading to my house. A large animal sat in the middle of the road up ahead of me. Another coyote? No, too big to be a coyote.

It was a dog.

The dog watched my truck, alert, waiting for me. I drew closer, and expected it to run or move aside. But it didn't move. I slowed down. It stood up, and there it stayed, right smack in the middle of the road, looking at me with eyes huge with hope. I had to stop.

He was fairly large with a short, bobbed tail, and rangy, in that gangly way only a younger dog can be. A shorthair with tan legs and too-big feet, he had thick black, tan and gray fur swirled in an abstract mixture all over the rest of him. A merle.

The hair around his neck, chest and shoulders, where a ruff would be on a longhaired dog, was longer and thicker than was usual on a shorthair. I guessed he might be a cross between an Australian shepherd and a traveling salesdog.

The dog trotted around to the back of my truck and leaped into the bed, bouncing off the back bumper like an old pro. He sat down and looked at me as if to say, "So, what are you waiting for?"

I wasn't waiting for anything, so I went. I pulled into the barn, shut off the engine, and went around to the back to inspect my surprise passenger. The dog grinned at me and wagged his stubby tail. The poor thing needed a bath. He smelled of dirt, dry weeds, and a bit of skunkiness.

Life had not been good to this pup. His ribs, hipbones and spine made bumpy ridges under his skin. The red collar around his neck fit too tightly, as if someone had put it on him when he was smaller, and never bothered to see if it needed adjusting. The faux leather had cut into his flesh.

He sat there in the bed of the truck, the skin on his forehead pinched with a bit of worry, waiting for me to do something, anything.

I poked around in the barn until I found an old pail, swished it out at the deep sink in the corner of the barn, and filled it with water. I set the bucket on the floor of the barn and swung down the tailgate of the truck.

The dog jumped down in a graceful arc, ran for the bucket, and gulped down the fresh clean water in huge swallows. His thirst sated, he trotted back to my feet and sat. He stared at me, worried again, with eyes that were about the same amber-brown color as mine. This guy needed a friend.

I knelt down, sponged the skin on his neck with water and an old rag, waited a bit for the skin to soften, and then removed his collar. I took my time, trying not to hurt him, and was glad he didn't object. It was a relief to see the damage to his skin wasn't severe.

I grabbed the big towel by the sink, soaked it, and rubbed him down. He was still dirty, but I made some good progress in the right direction. Only time would take away the residual skunkiness.

That old story about tomato juice taking away skunk odor on a dog is a lie. If you do that, all you'll get is a pinkish tomato-scented skunky dog.

The dog and I walked in the sunshine until his damp fur dried out. He stayed right at my side, looking up at me with trusting eyes. What a sweetie. How could anyone be so mean? We walked, and I contemplated what to give him to eat. I settled upon a gourmet treat—wheat bread torn in chunks mixed with a can of tuna. He looked like he wanted some more, but I was afraid to feed him too much all at once.

"Don't worry, buddy. I'll give you some more in a little while."

I made the dog a bed by piling old musty horse blankets in the back of the truck. If he hung around until morning, if no one came to claim him, and if he demonstrated that he had some manners, he might earn a home instead of a trip to the animal shelter.

Dog stayed the night in the barn. And the next night. And the next. He wouldn't sleep in the house when I invited him in. That was fine with me. Where he spent his time was his decision. On duty all night long, he stayed close to the house and never wandered far. Time proved that I could rely on him to be out there, watching over things.

No one ever came looking for Dog. He'd found a home. I promoted him to Official Truck Dog, and he went everywhere with me.

I hoped he'd keep any more "pranks" from happening.

◆ ◆ ◆

Saturday night arrived—the designated night for Demetra and I to go out and make fools of ourselves. Eat, drink, and be merry. I was free to do whatever I wanted, wasn't I? While not technically correct, as I was still legally married, I embraced the notion.

The scent of Mark still seemed to linger in my nostrils, even after all these months, and I wanted it gone. I wanted to go to a bar, drink Jack Daniels on the rocks, and dance with handsome cowboys. I commanded my broken wings to heal, so I could fly.

Demetra and I dressed to impress. I wore my favorite LBD, and she looked like a siren in scarlet. We went to a new bar in town, one that rapidly established itself as "the place to be" as soon as it opened.

We walked in on a party that was already happening. A band played the best kind of country music, with deep driving rhythms perfect for dancing. In only a moment, we were swept up into a boisterous line dance.

The dance brought out the exuberant and silly side of me that I'd thought lost forever. But, alas, when the line dance ended, no handsome cowboy hero, but a young and gawky kid, all long limbs and pointy elbows, asked me to dance. In the face of all his earnestness, I didn't have the heart to turn him down. We stepped out onto the floor as a bouncy two-step started up.

The guy claimed to be a college student, and over twenty-one, but I had a suspicion that he carried a fake I.D. His sweaty palms spoke of nervous jitters. A large male presence loomed up beside us, and the kid skedaddled as soon as the music ended.

I found myself pulled into a waltz without even a hello. The large dark-haired man held me too close; I strained to keep my distance. "What's your name, sweetness?" the man said with beer-and-cigarette-scented breath.

I growled at him through clenched teeth. "Let. Me. Go."

"Well, that's a strange name, sugar-babe." Suddenly, his left hand clamped around my right wrist like a shackle; his right hand ran down my back, and he squeezed my right buttock.

He didn't know it yet, but he'd called the wrong number. Thank god for my long-ago self-defense classes. I let myself go a little limp, hoping he'd relax his grip. It worked, and I made my move. I spun away from him and took off at a gallop towards the table where Demetra sat nursing a long-neck, laughing with friends.

Sprinting in sky-high heels doesn't work too well. In two or three steps the man caught me. He threw one arm across my front, just above my breasts, and jerked me backwards, pinning my shoulders fast against his chest.

"Where do you think you're going, little hellion?"

No. Oh, no. Agonizing memories flooded my brain. I was no longer in a crowded bar, in Jackson, California. I was alone, in New York City, with a powerful and angry man.

Pure, cold fear washed over me. I screamed, an agonized wail that slashed the air.

The music stopped.

The man dropped me. My knees hit the hardwood floor, and I rolled over onto my side, sobbing.

"Jesus Christ!" said the man. "What the hell's the matter with you?"

I was back in Jackson. Demetra knelt beside me, stroking my hair, murmuring sweet words of soft comfort as my whole body shook with gasping sobs. She helped me to my feet and, with gentle fingers, wiped the tears from my face. "C'mon, girl," she said, "I'll take you home."

The man who'd grabbed me stood there staring at us, as if stunned. I ignored him. As we turned to go, I heard him mutter something that sounded like, "Crazy-ass bitch."

How close to the truth was that? A bit too close, for my money. I shivered at the implications.

We left the bar without saying another word. Demetra took me home, and waited to make sure I got inside before she left.

Demetra called me the next morning. "Hey sweetie," she said, "how're you doing?"

"Fine," I replied. "Really. The guy was just a drunk jerk. You know the kind. No harm, no foul." There, I'd said it out loud, it must be true. But I knew it would be a while before I wanted to go out partying again.

I wasn't as healed as I'd thought.

◆ ◆ ◆

October. I concentrated on trying to weave myself back into the fabric of the town. I attended the City Council meetings, just to stay on top of things going on in the community. I'd even wandered up the hill to the Sutter Creek Chili Cook-off, with a couple of my sort-of-friends from school. And then there was the disastrous evening at the nightclub.

But, despite all my efforts, I still felt very much on the outside looking in. With the exception of Demetra, my attempts at reestablishing my old connections sputtered and faltered. I'd been gone too long.

I kept telling myself that, in time, new relationships would start to form. But, sometimes I still felt very alone, even when out in a public event.

Facing the things right inside my own house felt even more difficult.

Well, that was neither here nor there. Life gives us choices, some of them are worse than others. None are ever perfect. I'd put it off long enough—I had to start going through Millie's belongings.

I trudged up the stairs, stood in the mezzanine, stared at the closed door to Millie's room, and made a decision. The stuff in her bedroom would remain untouched, at least for a while. It seemed all too clear that I was still in an emotionally rocky place. And, I was more than halfway afraid that I'd find something personal, something perilously far into the realm of "too much information." I started with Millie's studio.

A gentle northern light infused the studio, the kind beloved by artists, bright enough to be cheerful, but soft enough to have no glare. Windows stretched across the upper two-thirds of the north wall, end to end. Sheer curtains hung over the glass to moderate the light on hot summer days.

Several completed canvases leaned against walls around the room. A half-finished painting sat on the easel—a watercolor study of the tangled roots of the fallen tree on the knoll north of the house.

Barefoot, I wandered across the wooden floor towards the easel. I stepped on something sharp, and yelped. Balanced on one foot, I pulled the other one up to see what in the world had stabbed me. I ran my finger across the tender spot on my foot and hissed when something stuck in my finger. A drop of blood welled up.

I hobbled over to Millie's chair, and sat down. A small sliver of glass protruded out of my foot. I flicked it off into a wastebasket.

Watching for more glass fragments, I tiptoed from the room and skedaddled across the hall and into my bedroom to slip on my felt clogs. Back in the studio, I retrieved the broom and dustpan from the corner. A careful sweep of the area yielded a few more shards.

Hadn't Greg cleaned up after the police left? After all, he'd taken care of the rest of the house. Maybe it didn't even occur to him. The room looked spotless.

I glanced around. Something about one of the windows drew my attention. I pushed aside the curtain panel. There, in the middle of the window glass, was a round crater about an inch wide, centered with a neat pinhole. The window pane had been shot with a pellet gun.

I had no doubt about it at all—window damage from an air-rifle pellet is quite distinct. I pushed back the other curtains. There were three holes, total. How weird...

I stared at the damaged windows for a few more moments, hoping for a flash of understanding. But none arrived. I turned towards the easel. On a small table beside it, a few paintbrushes were suspended from a metal rack. Next to the rack sat a small basin for washing brushes, the rinse water long gone.

A thin layer of dry pigment coated the bottom of the basin, left behind when the water had evaporated. One lone brush rested in the residue, as if placed in the water and then forgotten.

I jerked as a cold, involuntary frisson ran down my spine. Before me sat a clear violation of one of Millie's cardinal rules.

I'd watched my aunt work zillions of times. I knew her rituals and routines. General housekeeping could go hang, but she always made sure that everything got cleaned up at the end of a painting session. Everything. Always.

No exceptions. Ever.

Millie also used expensive sable watercolor brushes. She would have never walked away and left one of them like that unless...

A sickening realization was born. It grew, blossoming into something unbearable. I had no doubts, none at all. I was looking at a moment in time, preserved.

I knew exactly what Millie was doing just before she died.

Millie, relaxed, stands at her easel. A sharp popping noise distracts her; glass shatters. She flinches, startled, and turns to look at the window. Another pop. Needles of glass spray against a curtain panel, then another pop, and more glass flies. Incensed at someone's carelessness, she slams down her brush and marches forth to find out what the hell is going on.

Millie was set up. She was lured outside by someone taking potshots at her windows with a pellet gun, and then killed in cold blood.

I might have screamed. Or, my howl of agony might have been silent, echoing only inside my head. Tears streaming down my face, I staggered across the hall to my room.

◆ ◆ ◆

I have no idea how long I lay there, collapsed on my bed. But after a while, an unavoidable conclusion crept into my brain: *I've got to let Newhall know what I've discovered.*

Right on top of that came the realization that the asshole probably wouldn't give a shit, one way or another. Or, he'd be pissed off that I dared to offer evidence that might threaten his pet hypothesis.

To hell with him. This was too important to have some bloated piece of human garbage brush it off. I snapped some photos of the windows, attached the clearest pictures to an email message to Drake, and sent it off.

> I think I found out why Millie was out in the sun at the worst time of the day. I think someone provoked her into leaving the house. It looks to me like someone shot at her studio windows while she was working. The glass fragments were never swept up, and her brushes weren't cleaned. She would have never gone off and left her stuff like that without a good reason.

Too bad if Newhall didn't like it, that I contacted Drake instead of him. I was done with him.

I turned and stared at the brushes, the easel, the paints. What should I do with them? What should I do with the artwork? I felt guilty disturbing Millie's things, as if I'd entered the sanctuary at Saint Sava's and got caught mucking around with the sacred items on the altar.

What to do… That question applied to damned near everything in the house.

The vastness of the problem felt overwhelming, as if it had actual weight and might crush me. I picked up the lightweight linen cloth that Millie draped over the easel at the end of a painting session, placed it like a shroud across the unfinished work, and walked out of the room.

A few hours later, Drake called. He didn't state an opinion one way or another, just said my conclusions were "interesting." He said that he would come by to take a look, and thanked me very much for not changing anything, except for cleaning up the glass shards.

I didn't care whether Drake agreed with my assessment or not. I *knew* I was right. Millie's death was no accident. She was executed.

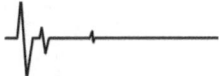

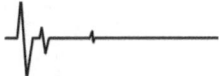

Chapter Fourteen

Drake came by the house the next day and took a look at the studio. I had no idea if I'd stirred up a tempest by contacting him, or if he was trespassing into someone else's investigation. Maybe Newhall had passed the buck? Again.

It didn't really matter. All I cared about was that someone with brains was paying attention. But, it occurred to me that if Drake had encroached on Newhall's territory, I should at least have the courtesy to thank him.

"I'm sorry if I put you on the spot by contacting you instead of Newhall," I said. "I hope I didn't cause any... ah, difficulties."

A crinkly-eyed smile flashed across Drake's face. "No problem. Actually, we've had to readjust our caseloads a bit. Officer Newhall is presently... away, so the investigation of your aunt's death is now assigned to me. So, it's all correct and proper, et cetera. And I have to thank you for having the presence of mind to recognize the implications of what you've found. So far."

I got the hint. I needed to finish going through Millie's things. He was right. Who knew what else remained to be discovered? And, unless I took control, the house would never become mine. It would always be Millie's home, with me living in it.

That thought used to amuse me, but it no longer seemed so funny.

After Drake left, I took a deep breath and went back into the studio. I stood there for a moment or two, struggling to regain my equilibrium.

Focus. Do this. Get it over with.

The small cork bulletin board in the corner caught my eye. Festooned with business cards held in place with colorful pushpins, the board held snips and snaps of the fabric of Millie's life. My eyes settled on the card of Ekaterina Symington, the owner of Millie's favorite art gallery in Sacramento.

Called Kat by her friends, the gallery owner was a tiny, gray-haired, dynamo with a smoky Eastern European accent. She gave Millie her first major break, many years ago, by offering to stage a one-person show for an unknown artist. Millie's legendary career took off that night.

The answer to at least one part of my dilemma smacked me in the face. Kat would know what to do with Millie's lifework.

But I still didn't know what to do about Millie's bedroom.

I squeezed my hands together so tightly they hurt. Tomorrow. I'll figure it out tomorrow.

◆ ◆ ◆

The morning light dawned, and I found my resolution wavering. My thoughts wandered here and there, and then settled, like a butterfly, onto a contemplation of Claire's existence.

Yes. I was being a coward again, avoiding what needed to be done. What was the matter with me? I'd never been like this when I lived the life of a high-powered attorney.

Whatever. Back to Claire.

Did she have enough awareness to understand the true circumstances of her life? Was she miserable? Defeated? Or, did she drift in a Zen-like state, just being? The bottom line seemed clear to me—no matter how much Greg and the nursing staff tried to help her, Claire's life seemed bleak.

Some people might consider my fixation on the woman to be odd. But, I'd have to be a real jerk to not feel compassion for her.

I shoved those thoughts aside, and started going through the paperwork in Millie's studio file cabinet.

◆ ◆ ◆

A few days later, I was in Claire's room, playing my portable electronic piano. No cheap toy, the piano had a rich grand piano sound. It seemed to me that I now knew why I'd hauled it all the way across the country. The keyboard was not destined to sit and collect dust under the bed after all.

Claire sat upright with her head back, staring at a crack on the wall. I had no idea if she comprehended the moods of the passionate music I played just for her. But even if she remained unaware, it didn't matter to me. I had to do this.

Chopin floated from my fingertips and echoed down the hallway. Enveloped in the ethereal magic of the music, I was startled when a soft male voice behind me said, "What...?"

Greg stood in the doorway, his strong body partially silhouetted by the hallway lights behind him. His face was lit with a look of surprised delight. He motioned for me to keep on playing, walked to the side of the bed, and said hello to his wife.

Claire didn't move, refocus, or even blink. He kissed her on the forehead, gave me a jaunty little good-bye wave, and left.

◆ ◆ ◆

Greg called me the next morning. "Hey, piano girl. I have an idea. Can you come by the office this afternoon? After 4:30?"

I flopped down in my big armchair and put my feet up. "Oh, I see," I said, doing my best to sound crabby. "Because I'm, quote, 'unemployed, and living in a derelict farmhouse in the middle of nowhere,' you think I have nothing better to do than come running when you snap your fingers?"

"Hey. Unfair. I didn't say *derelict*. I only implied that your house might be a couple of years older than dirt. And, anyway, why shouldn't you come running? I mean, what better things do you have to do? You gotta admit it's a valid question."

I huffed with exaggerated exasperation, glad that he couldn't see the grin on my face. "I can see why you and Bertie get along so well. Both of you are a pain in the rear."

"But you think we're adorable anyway."

"Yeah, right. But only marginally so. And getting less cute by the moment, by the way. Sounds to me like there's a suspicious plot afoot."

"Your suspicions wound me. No plots, foul or otherwise. You'll see when you get here."

"Hmm. For some reason, my Spidey senses are tingling."

"Would I lie to you?"

"Yeah. You might." I laughed. "But you win. I'll be there."

◆ ◆ ◆

Greg met me at the office door with a goofy grin on his face. He showed me to his small conference room. Bertie was there, hands propped on her soft belly, waiting for us.

I sat down at the table and flung my arms out to the sides. "All right. Here I am. Lead the lamb to slaughter, or whatever it is you're going to do."

"Okay. Since you insist. Have you ever thought about getting a job here in Jackson?"

My head jerked backward in surprise. That was about the last thing I'd expected. "Huh?"

Greg's smile settled down to looking only a bit less excited than a four-year-old on Christmas morning. "Something clicked in my head yesterday," he said, "when I saw you visiting Claire. And I have to thank you for that, by the way. Some people, including her parents, seem to have forgotten that she's still a human being."

Bertie coughed, and it sounded a bit like an editorial comment, but that was neither here nor there.

He ignored Bertie and launched into an impassioned sales pitch. "I've had an idea for a long time, and I think you are the one to set the wheels in motion, to make it a reality. I don't know why I didn't think of it sooner."

He jumped up and meandered around the room, apparently too excited to sit still.

"First of all," he said, "you have compassion, and a willingness to turn that compassion into action. I saw that yesterday. Secondly, you understand non-profits, and know how to structure them, know how they should work."

Good lord, the man sounded exactly like he was giving a PowerPoint presentation to a group of stockholders. I bit my lip to keep from smirking.

He stopped walking, turned, and faced me. "The bottom line is this—I've been thinking a long time about establishing a non-profit foundation in Claire's name, to fund research for solutions to spinal cord and brain injuries. You could put the whole thing together."

"Get real." I shook my head. "You know I'm not licensed to practice law in California."

"Doesn't matter." The big grin lit up his face again. "I don't consider that to be an obstacle at all."

Really?

He must have seen the skepticism on my face because he walked over closer to my chair. "Listen. You have the brains, the determination, the experience, all the necessary stuff. And, best of all, you understand what a law library is and how to use it."

I just sat there, staring at him, with my mouth hanging part way open. What was he up to? Part of the reason that I didn't feel too badly about running away from my job in New York was because much of it was boring beyond belief. But, despite my aversion to mountains of paperwork, he had my attention. I couldn't help but be a bit intrigued.

"I think it's obvious," he said. "You, Ms. New York Super-Lawyer, are the perfect candidate to put together the initial paperwork. Instead of paying a licensed attorney to write the whole thing... Well, bottom line, if you do this we'll be able to save a boatload of money. Then we can hand it over to a licensed attorney to check all the nuts and bolts, make a few suggestions, and roll it out."

Greg plopped himself into the chair across from me, grinning like a puppy with a new squeaky toy.

I, the silver-tongued corporate lawyer, had to show off my totally slick communication skills.

"Oh," I said.

Greg leaned forward in his chair, a sudden earnest look upon his face. "You need to understand though, right up front, there isn't much of a budget to pay you for your work."

Greg and Bertie sat there looking at me as if I held the key to everlasting world peace. But, in truth, after the first few moments of stunned surprise, my brain began to whirl with a multitude of ideas and possibilities.

He was right. Much could be done, *should* be done, for people with injuries similar to Claire's.

And, Greg had hit the nail right on the head. I did need something worthwhile to do with my time. Not that scraping old paint off of windowsills wasn't a rewarding activity in and of itself, you understand.

But this... Right in front of me was an incredible opportunity, mine for the taking. And, I didn't give a damn about the pay.

My mouth went dry. Last chance to change my mind. "Sure," I said. "I'll do it."

◆ ◆ ◆

October edged towards November. I'd become engrossed in the work I was doing for Greg, and relieved that no more strange or frightening incidents had happened at my house. I began to think that someone had done their best to frighten the city slicker, but it hadn't worked. End of story.

Sure, I'd run into Doc's wife a few times around town, and she'd sort of snarled at me. But she was a minor irritation, only hurting herself. What goes around, comes around, especially in a small town.

The "goes around, comes around" notion hit me again, hard, a few days later, but for an entirely different reason. I was, as usual, hanging out at Demetra's, slurping the foam off the top of a nice cappuccino, and looking over the local news on the web. A headline caught my eye.

Local Man Reported Missing

RENO, NV. -- Police are asking for help locating a local man who has not been seen since mid-October.

Authorities are looking for 53-year-old Norville C. Newhall, a longtime resident of the Jackson area. Newhall was last seen in downtown Jackson on Saturday, October 17, at about 10 a.m. He checked into a social media account in Reno, Nevada, on Sunday at about 2:30 a.m.

Since then, he has not responded to phone calls, social media messages or other attempts to contact him. He is known to have been a frequent visitor to Reno for many years.

Newhall is described as being around 6 feet tall, with gray hair and blue eyes, and weighing approximately 275 pounds. He is employed by the City of Jackson as a police officer.

The missing man drives a black Ford two-door sedan bearing California license plate 2GAT143. At this time, the car has not been located.

According to local sources, Newhall was reported missing on Monday, October 19, after he did not show up for work. He was not found at home, and his phone is apparently turned off.

"He's very active in the community and civically engaged. This is not like him," said a friend who wished to remain anonymous.

Anyone with information is asked to contact the Reno Police Department, the Jackson-Martell Police Department, or the California Highway Patrol.

How utterly *strange*. And now I knew why the workload at the police department was adjusted. And I couldn't help wondering if one of Newhall's colleagues had gotten sick of picking up the slack.

◆ ◆ ◆

To get Greg's project rolling, I needed to meet with him a couple of times a week. I had to sit there and admire the depth of his vision. I had to listen to his resonant voice as he outlined his hopes and dreams for the foundation. I had to admire his devotion to Claire and his desire to help others. And I felt my bruised heart was beginning to heal, just a little. I was learning to trust again.

At the end of one rather tiring session, we walked out to the parking lot together, in the twilight, just as the orange-tinged floodlights were flickering to life. We'd been working on the rules for the governing board. It seemed to me that both of us were feeling like we'd wrung our brains dry and were limping along on backup power.

I walked towards my truck, and a small motion caught my eye. A light breeze had set a piece of paper stuck under a windshield wiper to fluttering.

I jerked it free and shook it open. I was only a flyer for a local pizza parlor. Someone had scribbled all over it with a marker. I was about to crumple it into a ball when Greg caught my hand.

"There's something on the other side," he said.

I flipped it over. The message written on the other side wasn't some random piece of nonsense.

GO BACK TO NEW YORK!
you're been warned

My stomach roiled, and I leaned on Greg.

"What's this all about, Allie?"

It warmed my heart to hear Greg use my childhood nickname. "Someone isn't happy with me. I don't know why."

"This has happened before?"

I remembered Drake's warning about not blabbing. "Something like this. Yes."

Greg raised an eyebrow. It seemed quite clear he expected a little more information than I'd provided.

Damn. Greg was a friend, a true friend of long standing. He'd opened up about a very private part of his life with me. Despite Drake's warnings, I couldn't close the door on him, especially when he was standing right in front of me with his forehead crinkled up in concern.

"There's been a few, um, incidents..." My voice trailed away, and I knew I sounded like I was hiding something.

"Incidents? Care to explain that a bit?"

No, not really. "Nothing bad. There's not much to worry about. I'm not trying to be Wonder Woman. The police know someone is harassing me. I'll add this little gem to the collection."

My words hadn't done a darned thing to make Greg look less worried. "Allie..."

"I've not been physically threatened." Well, the dead coyote was an overt threat, but I decided not to go there.

But, he did deserve to know a bit more than that. "Someone wants me to sell the house and leave. I don't know why."

"Oh, Allie..." He took ahold of one of my hands.

As I'd said to him before, sometimes we need someone to lean on when things go south. All I could do was clutch my friend's hand and wonder what was going to happen next.

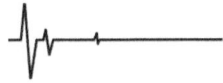

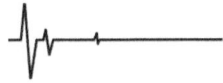

Chapter Fifteen

November. The leaves on the aspens, alders, and the little shrubby mountain willows turned to red or yellow, and fell dead to the ground. The nights arrived early and were dark, cold, and damp. There were far too many nights when the memory of the murdered coyote haunted my dreams, when the threat of an unspeakable *something* sat heavily on my chest.

For comfort and companionship, I'd invited Dog into the house more and more frequently. I'd tried giving him a more inspired name, but he only responded to "Dog," so that was that.

At first, the poor guy acted uneasy about being inside the house, but over time came to realize that he wasn't trapped. I'd let him out when he'd had enough. I flirted with the idea of putting in a dog door, but tossed the idea aside. Raccoons, who'd taken advantage of the easy access, had trashed a friend's kitchen when she'd followed through on a similar notion.

I got in the habit of having conversations with Dog in the evenings. He'd turned into my counselor and maybe even my default Father Confessor.

"So," I said to him one evening, while sipping a cup of coffee at my kitchen table. "Why am I staying here after all these rotten things have happened? I can work on Greg's foundation anywhere."

Dog sprawled at my feet taking a snooze, but looked up at the sound of my voice.

"I can leave. I'm not glued down. But, on the other hand, nothing awful has happened to me. Yet. So... at what point does bravery turn into stupidity? Have I already stepped across that line without realizing it? How will I even know?"

Dog scrambled to his feet and edged up close to my legs. I scratched his head, and he groaned.

"I beg your pardon," I said. "I am *not* whining. I'm thinking."

Dog apparently accepted that answer. He settled his haunches down onto the floor.

But he was right. I was not in a good frame of mind. The amount of courage held inside of me ebbed and flowed, as if pushed by some powerful psychological tide. I'd had plenty of time to think about things since the coyote was left on my porch.

"As much as I hate to admit it, and you know I'm no wimp, a scared little voice inside my head sometimes whispers to me in the middle of the night. 'The time is right for something else to happen.' Do you think that's true?"

Dog licked my hand and sighed.

"Well," I said, "You're right again. All I can do is live my life as best I can. There's nothing to be gained by letting my fears hold me hostage."

His point made, Dog relaxed and flopped onto the floor.

But my doubts didn't go away. Time and again, I asked myself the same question: Am I brave? Or am I a fool?

◆ ◆ ◆

Two weeks had passed since I found the note on my truck. The gallery owner from Sacramento, Kat, had come and gone. A week later, a crew arrived at the house to box up Millie's works—they were to be displayed and sold at a memorial show in December. I turned over most of Millie's paintings except those that were part of the decor of the house.

Kat was stunned by the power of the paintings in Millie's room. She had no idea that Millie had done a body of work so very different from the landscapes that had made her famous.

I agreed that the nudes could be sold, as long as the proceeds were earmarked for a special cause, and that family members could have prints made of any of the paintings, at any time in the future. After all, Millie did have nieces and nephews. The connection was distant, but still existed. All the paintings would be digitized and archived, accessible by any member of the family until the end of time.

One nude would not be going to the gallery. I couldn't part with it. In her younger days, when studying in the UK, Millie did a nude self-portrait, a neat and precise pencil drawing.

The view of the subject was from the back—the figure was kneeling, and half turned to one side. Her long hair cascaded over her shoulders. A soft light illuminated her upturned profile and the side of one breast. A hand extended up in the direction she faced, as if she were accepting the assistance of an unseen person to help her off the floor.

The picture had fascinated me when I was small. After mulling it over for a while, I got up the nerve to ask Millie how in the world she could draw a picture of her own back when, well, it was in the back.

Millie had laughed. "I had someone take a picture of my backside, honey, and then I drew a picture of it, and then made myself look a bit better than I actually did."

Oh, Millie... No way I could part with that picture. I also kept the half-finished painting of the roots of the fallen tree. I wouldn't let go of Millie's last painting. Ever.

Seeing my aunt's works crated and packed into a van turned out to be far more gut-wrenching than I'd anticipated. The day seemed long, full of tumbling emotions. But, she'd left no directions regarding the artwork in her will. And in the end, a sense of satisfaction arose in me. All I could do was the thing that seemed best. It would be silly to leave the paintings stacked against the walls.

◆ ◆ ◆

Later in the day I drove to Demetra's place so I could use the internet. Rocking my shoulders with the music on the radio, I pulled into the parking lot with a smile on my face, finally reconciled and pleased that I had found a solution for dealing with Millie's artwork.

I hopped out of the truck and chuckled at the sight of the carved redwood bears in front of the coffee house. Someone had taped a Burger King paper crown on the top of wooden Baby Bear's head and strapped a cardboard guitar across his body. I stared at the rough-sculptured bear for a moment, and snorted as I got the gag. Ohhh. Duh. 'BB King.'

At that moment, I felt so sure that I was, at last, doing things right that it didn't even bother me that Andrew Pichl, sour-faced as usual, stood staring at me from across the parking lot. I imagined myself flipping the man off with a grand Italian flourish.

Take *that*! Satisfied with the excellent mental image, I went inside to enjoy the best cup of coffee in the world.

As usual, I opened my laptop and pulled up the local news.

Missing Jackson Man Found

CARSON CITY, NV. -- What started as a pleasant weekend visit to Reno rapidly turned into a nightmarish situation when Norville C. Newhall, a 53-year old resident of Jackson, woke up in excruciating pain to notice that he had sustained knife wounds during his sleep.

My eyes stopped at Newhall's name. Holy cow. This should be interesting. I resumed reading, snorted, and then coughed as coffee went up my nose. I had to stop, wipe my face, and blow my nose before I could continue reading the article. The journalist was a comedy writer, and didn't even know it. How in the world do you *sleep* through knife wounds? And then *just happen* to notice them?

> The victim was allegedly drugged unwittingly before he woke up hours later in a pool of blood in a room at the Carson City Val-U-Rest motel. Newhall sustained apparent knife wounds in the lower groin area, leaving him in critical condition.

My eyes widened. Someone cut his balls off? Good lord. I shivered, grossed out despite my antipathy for the man.

> Fortunately, hotel employees were alarmed by the distress calls of the man, who was quickly taken to a local hospital so he could receive emergency care. The man suffered from severe bleeding that could have cost him his life.
>
> Mr. Newhall's condition is now described as stabilized. No information was offered regarding a discharge date.
>
> A spokesperson for the Jackson-Martell Police Department declined to comment on the case, stating only that an investigation is underway in Nevada. It is not known at this time if Newhall knew his assailants. Anyone with relevant information is urged to call the Carson City Police Department.

Well holy cow, I thought. Karma really *is* real. And, here I was, being awful. I supposed that I should be ashamed of myself, but I wasn't. The only sincere response that came to mind was *couldn't happen to a nicer guy...*

◆ ◆ ◆

For the next week, Greg and I worked countless hours finalizing the first draft of the paperwork for the foundation. I was excited. This was going to be real. Good things were going to happen.

A couple of days after I'd last seen Greg, I stood in his office parking lot next to my truck, talking to Bertie. Bundled in jackets to ward off the cold wind of early winter, we'd just returned from eating the famous chiliburgers at Mel and Faye's diner.

Much to Bertie's chagrin, when she approached my truck to speak to Dog, he tensed, and backed away from her. I rolled my eyes, embarrassed. After all this time, he still refused to be charmed by her. What a dork.

Dog's focus shifted to someone behind Bertie's ample silhouette. He bounced around the bed of the truck, making happy little whiny-squeaky noises, his stub of a tail wagging at light speed. I turned around and saw Greg walking towards us.

Why was Dog, who, as far as I knew, had never met Greg, overjoyed to see him?

Greg stopped a few feet away from me. I planted my hands on my hips and looked at him with a challenge in my eyes. "Sir, will you care to explain the cause of this unseemly display?"

Greg pulled back his head, in pseudo-surprise. “What?” His guileless, big-eyed expression could have won points in an innocence competition.

“You know. It seems you’ve employed some nefarious scheme to brainwash my dog.”

Greg's face shifted into the deadpan look of a serious poker player. “Sorry, ma'am, but your dog and I are sworn to secrecy. As always, should the dog, or any of our IM Force, be caught or questioned, the Secretary will disavow any knowledge of the matter. This tape will self-destruct in five seconds.”

He gave Dog a final pat on the head, winked at me, and pivoted around to walk away. He took about three steps, turned, and walked backwards. “I’ve been feeding him treats while you’re in visiting Claire.”

With that, he pivoted around and jogged off towards his office.

I hooted with laughter and turned to Bertie to share the silliness. Her face crinkled into an ugly sneer. I was baffled at her reaction.

Bertie pulled a pack of cigarettes and a lighter out of a jacket pocket and lit up. With a contemptuous jerk of her head, she blew a puff of smoke after Greg.

What was going on here? I’d believed she and Greg had a good working relationship, and, on top of that, I’d never seen her smoke before.

“Bertie...” I said. She knew what I meant.

“Dr. Clean Living is startin’ to annoy me. Seems he doesn’t approve of my life choices.”

“How do you figure that?”

“He sent me home one day, said I smelled like alcohol. Yeah, I’d had a couple drinks the night before. That was all. No need for him to get all excited about it.”

She took a few more deep puffs on the cigarette, then dropped it on the ground and stepped on it, grinding it into the asphalt.

“Well, chickie, as much as I love spendin’ time with you, I gotta go back to the salt mine. Talk to ya later.” She gave me a quick hug and stomped off.

My eyes followed her as she made her way back to the office. If she’d had enough to drink that Greg could smell it on her the following morning, well, she’d put away more than a “couple of drinks.”

Well. And so.

It looked to me like Bertie had gotten into a pattern of making bad choices. I didn’t understand it.

Feeling much more pensive than I had earlier, I started off across the parking lot to the convalescent hospital to see Claire.

◆ ◆ ◆

I entered Claire's room and hauled my portable piano out of the closet. On some days, it seemed to me that she didn't seem so... blank since I began playing for her.

Could my imagination, or my ego, push me to see things that weren't there? I hoped not. The soothing, restorative effects of music are well known. I'd experienced them myself many times. A famous old quote came to mind.

"Music has charms to sooth a savage breast, to soften rocks, or bend a knotted oak."

Can music help heal a broken mind? A seed of hope for the woman had germinated and sprouted in my heart. It kept me going back.

I set up the piano, went over to the bed, and picked up Claire's hand. She turned her head towards me, but today she seemed as out of touch as she had several weeks ago.

"Hey, Claire," I said. She didn't respond, even with as little as a blink. Damn. This wasn't going to be one of the good days.

I returned to the piano, ran my fingers up and down the keyboard, and eased into Debussy's *Clair de Lune*. It seemed the perfect piece of music for this pale and fragile woman. I played a few other Debussy piano pieces, then folded the piano stand and wheeled it out to the hall to complete my rounds for the day.

When I returned, Claire's eyes seemed to focus on me. Her attention was as startling as it was unexpected. Encouraged, I sat down and played more Debussy. After I'd exhausted my repertoire, I put away the piano, and approached the bed.

I picked up Claire's hand, and looked into her eyes. Someone was in there. Claire, focused and intent, reached out to me. I knew what I had to say to the woman.

"Greg loves you, Claire. He really loves you."

Perhaps what I saw was real, or perhaps I imagined seeing a piercing lucidity of thought reflected on Claire's face. She knew. She understood. A small tear appeared from the corner of one of her eyes, welled up, spilled over, and trickled down her face. She opened her mouth, as if she had something to say. A brief imploring look crossed her face.

With an aching slowness, the soft veil of seeming incomprehension, or perhaps defeat, settled back across her eyes. Her face fell slack. She closed her mouth, relaxed her head back into the pillow, and closed her eyes. Her breathing slowed into soft, steady cadences. Had she drifted off to sleep? I couldn't tell, so I gave her hand a gentle squeeze, and left the room.

The enormity of that moment hit me like a hammer to the jaw. In all my self-congratulatory "concern" for others, I was doing nothing more than mouthing empty platitudes. I left the hospital and hurried out to my truck, climbed into the cab, shut the door, and sat there stunned, overwhelmed.

Oh, Claire.

Dog whined, inquiring as to why we weren't going anywhere, so I slid open the rear window. He stuck his head into the cab. I stroked the fur on the back of his neck as my brain came to grips with what I'd witnessed.

I leaned forward and banged my head against the steering wheel, ashamed of myself, mortified by my lack of sensitivity.

My god. What kind of person am I? I'd never honestly considered Claire to be a sentient being. She'd been not much more than a mannequin, or even a shadow. I'd been oblivious. It was a shock to realize that Claire was a real person, with a real life, in real time.

I slid back in the seat and tilted my face towards the ceiling. Dog licked my face, but I didn't push him away.

The quality of Claire's life was debatable. But, nevertheless, she had one.

Now I understood why Greg assumed that she had awareness of what went on around her, and comprehended what we said to her. To assume otherwise was nothing less than cruel and foolish. I slammed my hand on the seat beside me. How had I missed the big picture? Was I coming to visit her just to make myself feel better? I didn't know. I just didn't know...

◆ ◆ ◆

A bit later, I sat up straight, seeking to channel my thoughts into another direction. I had to get out of there before I completely lost it. I drove down the hill from the hospital, picked up my mail at the post office, and stopped at the deli to buy Dog a beef stew dinner.

Yes, I spoiled the beast, but he was The Best Dog Ever. That said, I never bought anything for him from Demetra. Some cooks might be flattered, but I knew she would be insulted. Her creations, served up as dog food? Never.

I set Dog's dinner down on the floorboards to give it time to cool, and sorted the mail. Poor Dog. He whined at me, strings of drool hanging from his mouth. His message couldn't be clearer. "I. Eat. Now."

I patted his head. "Hang in there, buddy. This stuff's hot. You don't want to burn your little goobery mouth."

He whined at me, but I ignored him and picked up an envelope bearing the logo of a local insurance broker. It bore first-class postage, and didn't look like a bulk mail advertisement. I popped open the envelope and pulled out the enclosed letter.

> Dear Miss Dangelo,
>
> Thank you for contacting our office and expressing an interest in purchasing an Accidental Death and Dismemberment Insurance policy.

WHAT? With an angry screech that brought Dog hurrying to peer through the window at me, I wadded the letter into a ball and flung it onto the floor.

It was happening again. This wasn't a mistake. And while the letter was mild, in terms of being a threat, nevertheless, that's what it was, cruel and deliberate. Another small bit of my peace-of-mind was chipped away.

A moment later, hands shaking, I reached down and picked up the paper, smoothed it out on my lap, and read the whole thing. It seemed clear that a woman posing as me had called the insurance broker's office. There was nothing to do but call the office in the morning and let them know they'd been scammed.

Dog poked his head in the window, and nudged me, his forehead wrinkled with worry.

I reached up and rubbed him under his chin. "Well, our special friend has found another way to get under my skin. It's pretty obvious, don't you think?"

Instead of agreeing with me, Dog whined again. I didn't know if he was worried because I was upset, or just wanted his dinner. I leaned back in the seat and closed my eyes.

"How hard," I said to Dog, "would it be to just leave? As much as I don't want to run away, it might be the right thing to do."

Once upon a time, a long time ago, I was accepted at Juilliard. Could I resume my training as a pianist? No... I'd be considered too much of an antique to be trainable. And, anyway, I didn't want to go anywhere near the East Coast. The place was psychologically radioactive.

Dog whined again and tried to lick my face.

"Don't worry," I said. "I wouldn't leave you behind. We could relocate to a coastal California town, or anywhere else in the state for that matter, and I could study for the bar exam."

Or, I could even rid myself of everything, move to Fiji and become a beach bum. A million possibilities were just that. Possible.

Maybe I should call the Pickle Man, and offer to sell him the house...

"No," I said, talking more to myself than to Dog. "Not to him... Never to him."

I shook my head to clear my mind of that distasteful thought. Nevertheless, it seemed quite clear to me that before too long I'd have to make a big decision. I leaned forward and rested my head against the steering wheel again, waiting for my thoughts to clear and my emotions to settle.

Damn it all. WHY was this happening?

Dog, his impatience growing, woofed at me in a sharp, ringing note of chastisement. Since Dog rarely barked, especially at me, I felt a bit guilty. "Sorry, baby. You're not going to starve. Honest."

◆ ◆ ◆

I started up the truck and drove to the grocery store. I parked the truck and carried the beefy treat around to the back. I left Dog wolfing down his dinner while I did my shopping.

I'd been around long enough now that Chairish decided she could chat with me as she ran my purchases through the scanner. The irony couldn't be ignored. Just when I'd started to consider leaving, I found that I'd actually arrived.

I came back out to the truck to find Dog, his belly full, stretched out to take a snooze in the back of the truck. I scratched him on the head again, then drove up the hill towards home.

I tried to push thoughts of the prank with the letter from the insurance company to the back of my mind. It was another taunt, another stone thrown in my direction. I resented being turned into the kind of person who, out of necessity, saw a bogeyman under every bed.

The deepening blue evening sky glittered with the diamond pinpoints of emerging stars. The land around me sat quiet and peaceful. Millie's murder and the incident with the coyote seemed long ago. How could I even consider moving away from this magical place?

I turned off the road onto the dirt track leading to my house. We rounded a bend, and I slammed on the brakes. The rear end of the truck fishtailed in the loose gravel. Good god! I'd almost hit someone. The woman walking in the middle of the road turned and ran away into the darkness.

I could have sworn I'd just seen the snarling face of Suzanne McFarland.

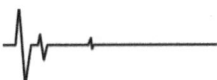

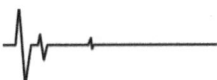

Chapter Sixteen

We were back at the house before the night became completely dark. Dog retired to the barn, and I went inside. In the middle of the night, I heard him bark at some danger, real or imagined. And I wondered, again, what the hell Suzanne McFarland—if it had been her—was doing walking in the dark by herself, on my road.

I guessed I'd never know, because I'd sooner eat maggots than drop by her house and ask her.

The next morning was Saturday, the day I'd marked off in my mind to tackle the papers in the roll-top desk, the next step in the long process of going through Millie's things

When I first moved in, I'd glanced through the desk looking for bills and such. The contents of the drawers looked to be nothing more than old paperwork and keepsakes. The police didn't find anything of significance when they searched. Now it was my turn to churn through the stuff. Again.

Sitting right in the middle of the desk's writing surface, maybe where Millie had left it, was a large accordion-fold portfolio. Might as well start with that. I opened it up. Inside was stack of old-school black and white photos, interleaved with pencil and ink drawings done by my brother Rudy. I grinned, happy to see the artwork, relieved that it hadn't gone in the trash at some point. He'd developed the photos himself, in his high school photography class.

I gathered up the portfolio and took it across to the big leather chair in the corner. I curled up in its comfortable expanse, switched on the lamp, and pulled out the papers.

Rudy had been a gifted artist. From the time that Millie first noted his talent when he was very young, she'd nurtured it. He loved drawing plants and animals, birds and, of course, insects. Millie tried to teach me, too, but I'd never had Rudy's flair for it.

I went through the stack, taking my time to enjoy each sketch. I set aside an exquisite pencil drawing of a little fox so I could have it framed. It was the final semester project for one of Rudy's advanced art classes at the high school. He'd drawn it from life, driving to Lodi day after day during spring break to observe the red foxes at the Micke Grove Zoo.

A few sheets under the fox drawing I found a sketch that was very different from the others. In front of me was a head-and-shoulders pencil portrait of a grizzled old man. I assumed it was a picture of that old recluse who'd lived out in the woods. I'd seen him around once or twice but hadn't known him personally.

Rudy'd come across him while out hunting bugs, and the two had struck up a friendship of sorts. Rudy was always much more gregarious than me; he had an uncanny way of easily making friends. No one ever remained a stranger to him for very long.

I stared at the portrait, trying in vain to remember the old man's name. In apparent reference to some sort of joke between the two, Rudy had scrawled "Old Ben—Obi Wan Cannoli" next to the face.

Oh, that's right. The guy's last name was Kennelly, or Connolly... something like that. What'd happened to him? Some of the photos were also of the old guy, standing in the forest, and outside his strange shack that seemed made of a patchwork of corrugated metal, tarpaper and other found items. Rudy must have used the photos as references for the sketch.

At the very the bottom of the stack I found a couple of pieces of paper that were flipped in relation to the others. The first one I turned over was different from all the rest. It appeared to be a rough-sketched map. It showed the house, the barn, the road, and the old tree at the top of the granite outcropping. The tree was drawn as it is now—tumbled over, flat on its side.

Fallen tree, fallen Rudy.

My heart lurched. Rudy must have drawn this picture only twelve hours or so before he died. The tree had fallen over that very morning. I shifted the paper in my hand, and the one under it slid out and fell to the floor.

I bent over and picked it up. The second paper held a rough sketch of the roots of the tree. There appeared to be some sort of box or rectangular object under the roots. How weird...

I set the stack of drawings on the end table, shot out of the chair, and charged up the stairs like an Olympian. I ran to the studio, flung open the door, and dug out the case where I'd stored Millie's last painting. I flipped open the case and stared at the artwork.

The rough outlines of the painting showed only sand or dirt beneath the tree roots. I dug back into the case. Inside it there were some preliminary sketches and a few photos of the tree roots. Nothing in the photos or sketches resembled the rectangle that Rudy had drawn.

In Rudy's drawing, more of the roots were exposed. Rudy was a very careful artist. So was Millie. A final design might have some fanciful element added to it, the preliminary technical drawings wouldn't.

When I was up there with Dog—had that been just last night? —I'd noticed nothing unusual.

My heart thumped with excitement. This was significant. *Rudy! What did you find? Why didn't you tell us?*

I put the painting back into the storage cabinet, shoved the rough sketches and photos into a manila envelope, and galloped back down the stairs. I set the envelope on the kitchen table and ran out the door without grabbing my jacket.

Calling to Dog, I set out at a fast jog up the little hill. At the top, I stood, panting for breath, and stared at the old tree roots. They looked no different than they did in Millie's sketches. Something did not make sense.

Shivering in the cold air, I turned and hurried back towards the house with Dog. I gasped with a horrible realization. I was jogging along right behind the house.

Right. Where. Millie. Was. Shot.

Seized by pure, unreasoning panic, I again took off running. The barn was closer than the house. I bolted in there, hauled myself into the bed of the truck, and huddled up against the cab. Heart pounding, my breath coming in gasps, I tried to regain my composure. I looked down at my hands—they were shaking like I was running a jackhammer. I clenched them.

Dog leaped in with me, delighted to have company. I pulled Dog's dirty old blanket around my shoulders and sat with my arms wrapped around his warm body. I was now certain that I had discovered something important. I just didn't know what it meant.

I waited for my breathing to slow, my heart rate to settle. It took a while before my brain decided that it might be able to function again.

The first rational thought to come to mind was simple, basic, and smelled of paranoia. Rudy's drawings needed to be stored in a safe place.

I glanced at my watch. It was only a little past noon. The bank stayed open until 3:00 pm on Saturdays. I scooted across the truck bed to the tailgate, but hesitated to leave the barn. My irrational self-preservation instincts were still arguing with my attempts at rational thought.

Inhale. Relax. Exhale. Repeat.

After a while, the part of my brain that told me that no bogeyman lay in wait finally won the argument. I scurried across the open expanse of dirt to the back of the house, wondering all the while if someone was watching me from a distance.

◆ ◆ ◆

Still feeling a bit jittery, I went back into the library, retrieved Rudy's map and sketches, and shoved them into the manila envelope with Millie's artwork. I grabbed my wallet and keys.

Dog and I piled into the cab of the truck and drove down the hill to Jackson. I stopped at the stationery store, made scans of all the documents in the envelope, and stored them onto my flash drive.

I felt jumpy, ill-at-ease, flinching every time someone passed by the table where I worked. The trembling in my hands returned. I fumbled the documents, nervous about handling them in such a very public location, even though they meant nothing to anyone but me.

I hoped. Another thing for my to-do list—buy a scanner.

I left the stationery store, drove to the bank, and locked the originals in my safe deposit box. That task accomplished, I sat in the bank parking lot for a while and tried to think of what I should do next. Top of the list—call Drake, first thing Monday morning, and make an appointment.

This discovery, while not an emergency, warranted a face-to-face discussion. All these things added up to something, even if I had no idea what that might be.

Feeling restless, needing to do something, I walked down Main Street, and found myself in front of my favorite bookstore, Hein & Co. In the window was a display of classic fantasy books, including an autographed collector's set of the famous boy-wizard *Harry Potter* stories.

I'd enjoyed reading the series. I thought about the protagonist, and a simple, painful truth hit me square in the chest. In contrast to the fictional Boy Who Lived of the series, my brother was the real-life Boy Who Died.

Rudy would be known as such forever, maybe not in those exact words, but the truth of that notion seemed inescapable. As long as anyone remembered his name, saw it written on a piece of paper, or happened upon his grave marker in the cemetery, he would be seen as a boy who died too young.

I realized, for the first time, the scope of the long-term consequences of his death. The passing of a child is a wound inflicted on the future.

Like a rip in an intricate web that a spider cannot fully repair, the gash in the fabric of my family's life could never be mended. Broken threads—physical or psychological—do not heal themselves. After all these years, my own actions, even the simple ones taken this very day, were a direct result of Rudy's death.

I knew, if I ever had a child, the weight of this legacy would be passed along to yet another generation. As long as Rudy was remembered, there was no way to avoid it.

A flood of horrified sorrow surged through me and threatened my composure. No longer in the mood to browse, I fled down the street, found the truck and drove home.

I arrived back at the place that should be my sanctuary and found myself still a bit unnerved. Remembering the bite of the vulnerability I'd felt earlier, I parked the truck right at the back door. No longer did I feel safe walking across the wide-open space between barn and house.

The melancholy shadow cast over my mood lasted for the rest of the day.

◆ ◆ ◆

The following day, Sunday, I had an appointment at Kat's place of business, the Ekaterina Symington Gallery, in Old Sacramento. Millie's memorial show was to be staged in December, at the wonderful historic Memorial Auditorium in Sacramento. Details needed to be discussed, plans needed to be made.

So off we went, Dog and I, Hwy 49 to Hwy 16 to Sacramento.

The drive to the gallery lasted a little over an hour, with a bit of freeway navigation required to get to Old Sac. Dog rode in the cab of the truck with me, his head hanging out the passenger-side window, his ears and tongue flapping in the breeze.

I told myself I needed to follow Dog's lead and learn to take more pleasure in the small things in life. Feeling more relaxed than I had in quite a long time, I smiled the whole way there.

We had an uneventful journey, although I discovered that the traffic unnerved me a bit. How soon I'd become accustomed to the patterns of life in a small town! Nevertheless, I always enjoyed visiting Old Sacramento, which is the original 1850s business district of the city. The old buildings and wooden sidewalks, lovingly restored and preserved, evoke those long-ago days. What was it like, when the State of California was new, and anything, and everything, seemed possible?

All the concerns and paperwork related to getting Millie's show put together were addressed within a few hours. Another piece of my inherited burdens lifted from my shoulders, making me feel lighter on my feet, and freer in my mind.

◆ ◆ ◆

The sun had set by the time we got home, but the darkness didn't bother me. Such things come with living in the middle of nowhere. I gave Dog his dinner, fed myself some leftovers, and climbed the stairs to my bedroom. I sat on the couch and read for a while, got ready for bed, and turned out the lights.

The night was crisp and crystalline. The bright light of the full moon once again cast convoluted shadows on the rough plaster wall of my room. I wandered over to the northern windows to admire the night sky. My gaze turned to the granite outcropping. The moonlight cast a magical silvery light over the landscape, rendering everything sharp and clear.

There, outlined in the bright moonlight, just as I'd seen before, someone stood on the rocky knoll, gazing at the roots of the fallen tree. The person had a slender build, their body shape obscured by a bulky jacket. A man? Or a woman? I couldn't tell. I drew in my breath, closed my eyes, and counted to ten. I opened them again, and the person was gone.

Or had the person never there to begin with? Was I losing my mind? It seemed altogether too possible. Why else would Dog not bother to sound the alarm?

I turned away from the window, not wanting to look at the scene one moment longer, and crawled into the bed. It took a long time for me to fall asleep. My dreams filled with images of tree roots, moonlit rocks, old hand-drawn maps, and shadowy figures following me through a dark night.

◆ ◆ ◆

I woke up early the next morning—Monday. I planned to call Drake's office right after 8:00 am. Before I called, I needed to sort out all the troubling thoughts that had given me such a restless night. I crawled out of bed and went downstairs.

After a quick breakfast, I curled in the reading chair in the office with my computer in my lap and studied the scan of Rudy's map. There were marks on the page that didn't make any sense to me.

The map showed a double row of dotted lines running between the house and the knoll. It seemed as if the lines represented a trail or pathway, but I knew for certain no walkway existed there when we were young. Rudy had also drawn a rectangle in the center of the kitchen floor. I couldn't imagine what it represented. The table? That was silly. Why would he draw the kitchen table on the map? It made no sense.

A possible explanation popped into my head. I went into the kitchen and dropped to my knees next to the table. There it was, so familiar to me that it had become invisible: the brass latch embedded in the floor. The latch was on the trap door to the root cellar. It opened by flipping up a flat brass ring and pulling upward.

Millie had shown the root cellar to Rudy and me when we first moved into her house. We'd never gone down there to play, except for that one time. Although the cellar was cool even in the middle of the summer, the place was too dark and full of cobwebs for us. To a child's mind, it was the ultimate monster's closet.

I'd climbed down the ladder on one other occasion, when I was in high school. The cleanout valve for the kitchen drain was located under the flooring. The sink had clogged. I'd stood there holding a lantern for Millie while she opened up the valve to run a plumber's snake through the pipes. I didn't ever want to do that again. It had been mid-winter, and the cellar was damp and cold. It had not been fun. At all.

I got the Millie's red aluminum flashlight from one of the kitchen cabinets, pushed the table out of the way, flipped up the latch, and struggled with the heavy trap door. Finally, it opened, pitching backwards and hitting the floor with a dull *thud*.

That task accomplished, I flopped down on the floor and shone the flashlight around the underground room. It looked no different than how I remembered it. I still did *not* want to go down there.

The dirt floor of the cellar was about twelve feet below the floor of the kitchen. An old wooden ladder, attached to the floor joists at the top, provided access. Next to the ladder was a rope and pulley setup for hauling things up to the kitchen. A deep willow basket was attached to the end of the rope. None of these things had been touched in years.

The root cellar was a square, about ten feet on a side. The light of the flashlight flickered across the rock walls. Shelves, now empty, lined the walls all the way around the perimeter. A room like this, stocked with food preserved over the summer, was a self-sufficient pioneer family's guarantee that they would survive the winter.

I shined the light on every wall in a steady pattern, floor to ceiling. I moved the light, and it revealed a heavy wooden door behind the shelves on the north wall. How odd.

There had to be a way to move the shelves out of the way, but my curiosity wasn't sufficient to drive me down the ladder to investigate. I stared at the door for a few seconds, envisioning the map. The door must lead to an entrance to a tunnel.

A tunnel to where? The top of the hill? Why go to all that trouble? It didn't make sense to me. But, perhaps to a loving Chilean miner father who had survived brutal times, an escape route seemed essential for the safety of his family.

I scrambled up to my feet, closed the trap door with a heavy *thunk*, and secured the latch. I moved the table back into its place, and sat down in the kitchen chair to mull things over. I didn't like the conclusions that my brain kept reaching.

Rudy discovered a tunnel from the house to the knoll.

Millie discovered Rudy's map of the tunnel from the house to the knoll.

Both of them died, right after they found whatever they found. And now, I, Alexandra, have discovered...

"SHIT!" I screamed. My body began to shake again.

Greg... I needed to talk to Greg. Was I right? Was I crazy?

I scooped up my wallet and my keys, called Dog, put him in the cab of the truck with me, and took off down the hill.

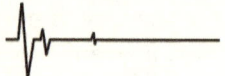

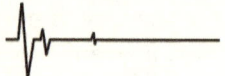

Chapter Seventeen

I could see Greg sitting in a chair on the veranda outside his house. Relief poured through my body. He saw me coming, stood up, and walked with a slow gait to the edge of the steps.

But... wait. For the first time, I realized it was Monday morning. Why wasn't he at work? And, on top of that, the man looked tired, and his shoulders were slumped.

Oh no...

I leaped out of the truck, bounded up the steps, and wrapped my arms around him. He clung to me like a drowning man clings to a rescuer. He was trembling, unable to speak. I stood and held him, just as he'd held me a long time ago in the middle of a dirt road, when he'd explained the circumstances of Millie's death.

I'd needed him then, he needed me now. My problems were born of fear, unproven assumptions, and an overactive imagination. His problem, whatever it might be, was very real.

We walked together to the rattan chairs. Dog sat down beside him. Greg rested a hand on Dog's head, but he was looking at me. His face showed as much emotion as a distressed man with glassy bloodshot eyes could convey.

"Jane Eyre," he said in a soft voice, almost as if he were talking to himself.

Good Lord. Was the man drunk? "What did you say?"

"Jane Eyre. I bellowed your name across the moors, and you heard me."

I remembered reading the book in high school. Jane Eyre falls in love with Mr. Rochester. They plan to wed. She finds out he has a mad wife locked in the attic, and runs away. Disaster strikes Mr. Rochester. In agony and desperation, he calls her name aloud. Despite being miles away, Jane hears him. And responds. They are reunited.

I didn't quite know how to answer him. So I said, "Yes," took his hands, and held them between mine.

"Did Bertie call you?" he asked.

"No. I just came here."

"Just like Jane Eyre?"

"Yes. Just like Jane Eyre."

He heaved a great sigh and stared down at the flagstone floor.

A flash of simple realization lit up my brain. He thought I knew why he was sitting here looking rumpled, red-eyed, and in need of a shave. "Greg, what happened?"

He still didn't make eye contact. "You don't know?"

"No."

"You... just happened to come here?"

"Yes." I could elaborate later. The immediacy of my own concerns had long since faded into the background.

He released his hands from mine, leaned back in the chair, inhaled, and rubbed his fingers across his face. He lifted his eyes and met mine.

"Claire is in critical condition in the ICU."

I stared at him, shocked.

"Pulmonary embolism. The event started Saturday afternoon. Some blood clots broke loose from her lower extremities and hit her lungs. Her physical therapist thought she was having a heart attack, got her right to the hospital and called me. I was at the hospital with her until late last night. Edwina—Claire's neurologist—brought me home.

"I then proceeded to sit down and self-medicate with a bottle of wine, which wasn't the smartest thing I've ever done. But I did get some sleep." He stood up and stretched. "I haven't been up very long. I came out here to get my head clear. I need to get something to eat, and go back to the hospital."

I stood up, linked my arm with his, and towed him towards the back door. He didn't resist being shepherded. Dog followed us to the door and settled down next to it.

"Go put yourself in the shower, Mr. Rochester. I'll find something for you to eat."

Greg walked to the stairs with a gait like that of a much older man. I looked around the kitchen and wondered if he had slept right there on the floor. He sure looked like he had.

I picked up an empty wine bottle off the small table in the corner, tossed it into the recycling bin, and opened cupboards, looking for something to feed him. I assumed he'd want something very basic, so I settled on hot tea and toasted English muffins. He could always get something more to eat at the hospital, or at Demetra's.

After a few minutes, Greg came down the stairs, his hair in a bit of disarray from being towel-dried after his shower. The uncombed hair and tired eyes made him look a bit bedraggled, despite being freshly shaven and in clean clothes. He sat and shoveled down the food dispassionately, almost like a machine.

I put the remaining muffins and unused tea bags back where I found them, and joined him at the table.

Greg managed the smallest of smiles. "Well, I now owe my ninth-grade English teacher a formal apology."

I tilted my head, puzzled.

"I have to confess that I was a real pain in the ass back then, but then lots of fifteen-year-old boys are." A sheepish look darted across his face. "I got into a big argument with the teacher when the class read *Jane Eyre*. I told her that it was just plain dumb—and yes, I used that word—to think that two people could call to each other across miles and miles of open land, and hear each other perfectly."

He reached across the table and squeezed my hand. "But, lacking evidence to the contrary, looks like it just happened."

I squeezed his hand in return. "Sure does. I can't explain it either." I didn't want to tell him that he wasn't making a whole lot of sense.

Greg focused his eyes on my face for a moment, as if trying to determine if I might be poking fun at him. After a few moments, Greg returned his attention to his breakfast.

"Dog and I will take you back to the hospital," I said.

"Dog? That's his name? I was sure you'd give him a fancy name like Sirius, or Argos, or Cerberus, or something ridiculous like that."

"Well, if you like, I can change his name him Pilot, just like the dog in the book. I'm sure he won't mind."

"I'm sure he won't." He stood up and stretched again. "Let's go."

◆ ◆ ◆

The three of us rode to the hospital in silence. I walked with him to the ICU entrance, where he was met by one of his colleagues. The man switched right into support mode, and latched onto Greg's arm, a friend in need. I was relieved. I would have felt like hell leaving Greg there by himself, but I needed to be somewhere else.

I grabbed one of his hands and looked at him. He must have read the hesitation on my face. "You're not coming in?"

"I have to go to the police station. I... I need to talk to them. It's pretty important."

"Okay," he said. "I'll call you." The strong professional part of Greg was back in control.

My heart breaking for him, I left and drove down the hill to the police station.

◆ ◆ ◆

I parked the truck on the top level of the downtown parking structure. Dog could stretch out in the sun in the back of the truck, or watch the cars and people go by. I filled his water bowl and scratched him behind his ears, wondering once again how I ever got along without him. He offered a polite lick on my hand to send me off, after which he settled into the bed of the truck for a nap.

If only my life could be that simple...

I walked around to the entrance of the police department, second-guessing myself all the way and wondering if I'd come on a fool's errand. But, having gotten myself there, I kept on going.

I hoped to hell that Drake was in the office and able to talk to me. I didn't want to meet with someone else—a stranger who would need me to recite chapter and verse. Drake was one fine officer. He wouldn't dismiss my concerns as so much silly nonsense.

At my inquiry, the semi-bored officer at the front desk picked up the phone, gave Drake a call, and invited me to sit down.

The clock in the waiting area made an audible click at the passing of each second. The ticks seemed to get louder the longer I waited, as did the echoes of the doubts that kept popping up in my head.

Why am I here? *Tick.*

Am I paranoid? *Tick.*

Overreacting? *Tick.*

After about forty-five minutes, right when I was starting to think that I was nine kinds of fool, and that I should leave, Drake came through the door that led to his inner sanctum. For just an instant, I saw him as the city of Jackson's very own version of Captain America, a crime-fighting superhero come to life. He did have the height and shoulders for the role.

The knotted muscles in my neck relaxed a bit.

Drake's eyes widened for just a moment as he took in my battered old jeans and faded red Stanford sweatshirt. I'd run out the door without a trace of makeup on my face and with my hair uncombed. The surprise on his face faded into a look of concern.

"Ms. D'Angelo," he said, in his characteristic kind rumble, and extended his hand for a handshake.

I jumped up off the bench, hurried over to him, grasped his hand in both of mine and gave it a brief and gentle squeeze. "I followed your advice. When in doubt, run."

An enormous hand settled on my shoulder, a warm and comforting benediction. "Well, then. Let's talk." He led the way back to his desk.

◆ ◆ ◆

As soon as we were seated, I started the conversation with a question for him. "Did you ever hear about my brother Rudy?"

Drake shook his head. "No." I could see his body unwind a bit, as if he'd braced himself for terrible news and could now settle back into his chair and wait for me to explain myself.

"Rudy was my twin. He died when we were sixteen. Some people said his death was an accident. Maybe it was. Maybe it wasn't. No one knows for sure, but my family always believed there were suspicious circumstances connected to whatever happened to him.

"The important thing here is that this morning I found a piece of paper that seems to indicate that Rudy died about twelve hours after he discovered something."

Drake nodded. "Go on." He kept gentle eye contact with me, and the look of mild curiosity on his face encouraged me to continue.

I drew in a deep breath. "Millie found that piece of paper too. I came across it where she left it, in the desk in the downstairs office. And you know what happened to her."

I dug into my purse, pulled out the copy of Rudy's map. The paper rattled a bit with the trembling of my hands. I handed it to Drake.

He glanced down at the paper, and then returned his focus to my face. "And...?"

"That's a map that Rudy drew. He found something, and then he died. Millie found that same thing, and then she died. And now, I..." My voice trailed off as the horror of this scenario overwhelmed me. "I found this paper, and..." I bit down on my lips and willed myself not to fall to pieces in his office. Drake, bless him, remained the very picture of patience.

I stumbled on. "I think I've figured out what Rudy knew, and what Millie knew. I think that there is something valuable hidden on my property. Whatever it is, it's important enough that someone is willing to kill to keep it a secret. And, as soon as that person figures out that I know something..."

I could feel a big fat tear overflow from my right eye and roll down the side of my face. I flicked it away with an impatient swipe of my hand. I knew I teetered on the edge of losing my composure, and tightened my whole body in an attempt to stay in control.

"I saw someone on my property last night. I think somebody has been watching me, and—"

Drake's deep and gentle voice interrupted me. "Well, if you think there is something problematic located on your property, I guess we'd better find out what it is."

◆ ◆ ◆

An hour and a half later, a police van rolled up the dirt road towards my house with me close behind, and we parked in the open area between the barn and the house. I climbed out of my truck and told Dog to stay in the back. Drake and another officer, a woman, emerged from the van.

I remembered the female officer as Kayla Martinez, the evidence technician who had taken away the murdered coyote. I nodded at her, but Kayla was staring at my house, her hands on her hips. She turned to me and motioned towards the back porch. "Was that over there when you left?"

A large cardboard box sat upside down, flaps outward, in a spot of sunshine on the back porch. I leaned against the side of the police van and closed my eyes. "No."

At this single word, the two officers walked over to the box. The container was an ordinary cardboard box, one that had held something from a major online store, weighted down with a piece of two-by-six lumber. The box had a cartoonish smiling mouth printed in black ink on the end of it. All identifying labels were ripped off. Every once in a while, the box gave a little lurch, as if something trapped underneath was trying to get out.

Great. Now what.

Drake bent down and picked up a small rock. He bounced it off the top of the box, and was rewarded with a distinctive noise from within that sounded a bit like a weed-whacker running in gravel. "Well, that's interesting. At least we know it's not a skunk."

I'd heard that noise before. So had the police officers. Both of them moved a bit backwards, almost by reflex. It's one of those sounds that you never forget.

There was a rattlesnake trapped under the box.

A low rumble from Dog's throat indicated that he didn't like the looks of this situation one little bit. The last thing I needed was to have him bail out of the truck bed and go take care of the situation for me. I opened up the cab of the truck and told him to get himself in there.

He whined a bit, his doggy-sense apparently telling him that this was a very bad idea, but he did what he was told. I pulled the truck into the barn, and left Dog in the cab, with the windows rolled down far enough for him to get plenty of air, but not enough for him to squeeze out.

I exited the barn, and rejoined the officers.

Kayla turned back to Drake and tilted her head in the direction of the snake-in-the box. "What are we going to do about that?" A cool breeze kicked up, and she rubbed her arms.

Drake glanced at the box. "Outside of poison pen letters," he said, "I've never had venomous evidence before." He paused, as if enjoying his own small joke. "We aren't messing with it. This is a job for animal control." He got out his handset and spoke to someone at the police department.

Drake turned and put his hand on my shoulder, in his now-familiar comforting way. "We have here, at the very least, a criminal threat. A criminal threat is defined as 'a serious intent to frighten someone with the implication of physical harm.' This stunt could potentially earn someone up to three years in the slammer. Tack on another few years for the coyote, if the same person is responsible."

A serious intent to frighten someone? No fooling.

On a day-to-day basis, I've never considered rattlesnakes as anything to worry about. They live in the neighborhood. I'd even stepped on one once, and nothing happened, outside of scaring the stuffin' out of myself. Millie had always told us that if you don't provoke a rattlesnake or make it feel cornered, it won't bother you. Usually.

On the other hand, an angry rattler is no joking matter.

The dead coyote was meant to be frightening, but there was no way it could have injured anyone. The snake, on the other hand, had to have been pulled from its den, warmed up until no longer sluggish, then trapped under the box in a sunny spot on the porch where it would stay awake. It would be, therefore, *very* pissed off.

What if Dog had found it first? I couldn't help but shudder at the sickening thought.

Drake put away his handset. "Animal control will be contacted. No estimated arrival time yet." He gave the box a long look, as if weighing something in his mind. "The snake's not going anywhere. If it could have, it already would have. So, back to the reason we came here."

◆ ◆ ◆

Drake turned to Kayla. "As I mentioned before, Ms. D'Angelo has reason to believe that something is buried here on her property, and that one or more outside parties are somehow connected to it, or have interest in it."

I was sure that he was restating the problem for my benefit, rather than Kayla's, just to make sure that everyone was on the same page. I appreciated his thoroughness. Damn, but that snake had thrown me for a loop. Someone had tried to mess with my head, and it worked. I forced my brain to snap back in gear.

He shifted his focus to me. "Where do you think this mysterious whatever-it-is might be located?" "

See the dead tree up there?" I motioned to the knoll. "Down under the roots. Rudy drew a rectangle on the map right there, and it had to be for a reason."

Drake nodded, and opened up the back of the police van. He and Kayla slipped into tan coveralls and grabbed shovels out of the back. We trudged up to the top of the knoll. I knelt down by the tree roots, and stuck my fingers into the gritty soil.

To my surprise, the dirt was loose, and my fingers jammed up against something hard. I brushed aside a bit of the dirt, and found myself looking at a rusty iron plate. Only a couple of inches of soil had hidden it from sight.

"Don't go any further, Alexandra," said Drake. "This is where we take over." He got some stakes and a roll of yellow crime scene tape out of the van, and cordoned off the area.

Drake scooped dirt from the area, cautious shovel-full by shovel-full, sliding it into heavy canvas bags that Kayla held open for him. A sudden gust of wind kicked up a small dust devil that forced Drake to step backwards and turn his head to avoid a face full of powdery grit. The soil in that area was very loose indeed.

In just a few minutes, a rusty iron trapdoor, about three feet square, was revealed. A handle was welded at one edge. Kayla looped a piece of rope through the handle. She and Drake pulled together from the side, and staggered a bit as the door swung up faster than they'd anticipated.

The iron plate dropped backwards, and thudded onto the ground, sending up a small puff of dust that wafted away on the breeze.

Drake squatted down next to the opening and ran his finger along one of the hinges. "Hmm. Looks like the hinges were lubed with Vaseline or something similar. Not much grit in it. Maybe applied not too long ago."

He wiped his finger on his coveralls. "Hand me the flashlight, and let's see what we have here."

Drake beamed the flashlight into the opening, but not much could be seen. The dirt floor was about four feet down. Kayla pulled on a pair of surgical gloves and jumped down into the hole.

"Hand me the light, Drake." She reached up and took the flashlight, bent over, and disappeared.

Her voice echoed up from the pit. "Okay. We have a small, enclosed area here, maybe about five by five or so, framed up with timbers like an excavation might be. One side of it opens up into a tunnel of sorts that goes off in the direction of the house.

"Right here in the immediate area we have some very nice spider webs, a dried-up snakeskin, a decomposed mouse, and a whole bunch of footprints.

"Ah, here's one that's nice and clean. Converse All-Star. I'm guessing size nine." In a lower voice she added, "Glad I didn't step on that one."

Kayla popped back up in the opening, looked at me and said, "What size shoe did your brother wear?"

"His feet were huge. He had to wear at least an eleven or twelve."

"Well, then," said Drake, glancing down at my own stubby little feet. "Must belong to a visitor."

I rolled my eyes, and was tempted to toss a snarky remark back at him. But I wasn't in the mood for levity, and no snappy comeback sprang to mind.

Drake turned and bounded back down the hill, retrieved the van and drove it up towards the knoll, stopping when the terrain got too rocky and steep to continue.

He hopped out and grabbed a plastic box from the back and handed it down to Kayla. She set it upside down over the clean footprint to keep it from getting smeared.

Her voiced echoed up to us again. "I'm going to look around a bit more." In short order, we heard a few thumping noises, a sharp "OW," a pause, and then a loud "Holy shit!"

After a few seconds, Kayla popped back into view. An ear-to-ear grin lit up her face. She held up a fist, fingers clenched around something she'd found.

"Let's try that again. I don't think you heard that right. What I said was, 'Holy cow!'"

She turned to face me. "There's an iron box down there. I tripped over it. It's full of these things."

Kayla opened her hand. Cupped in her palm was a small cloth bag, the white cotton aged to an ivory tan, with a faded red cord as a drawstring. The top of the bag gaped open, revealing a handful of natural nuggets of placer gold.

Most of the nuggets were small, like grains of barley. There were others that were about the size of pumpkin seeds, and one was as large as a nickel. The nuggets were of assorted random shapes, large and small, thick and thin, but all of them shiny, with smooth edges.

The specimens were typical of the kind of gold nugget found in Sierra streambeds and alluvial gravel deposits, burnished to a smooth and silky sheen during a millennium-long downhill journey from the original source.

Drake held out a plastic evidence bag. Kayla tied the drawstring on the cotton bag, plopped it into the larger bag, and set it down by Drake's feet. She grabbed the edges of the iron rim around the hole and tried to pull herself out of the hole. She was too short to get decent leverage, and Drake had to grab her arms to boost her exit.

"Bad news," she said, once she was up top. "That box down there is heavy. It's about twelve by sixteen or so, and maybe three-quarters full, if that, but I couldn't budge it. And it's not bolted down or anything like that. On top of that, the thing is old and rusty. And I mean *really* old. It says Wells, Fargo & Company Overland Express on the side. I'd be willing to bet the bottom will fall out if we try to pick it up. We're going to have to unload it."

Kayla picked up the evidence bag and bounced it in her hand, as if trying to estimate its weight. "There must be an absolute fortune down there."

Where the other two saw riches, I saw blood.

Lightheaded, I staggered over to the fallen tree, and sat down on it with my arms wrapped tight around my knees. I lowered my head and closed my eyes.

I had no doubts about what we'd found. We were looking at the secret that led to the deaths of two of the people I loved most in this world. I knew where the heart-shaped nugget found in Rudy's pocket had come from. I knew what Rudy wanted to show me when he got home from his trip into the woods.

In that instant, I knew the person who'd known about this secret was the one who murdered Rudy.

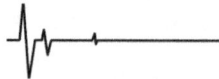

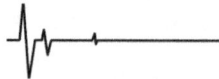

Chapter Eighteen

It was all due to selfish, goddamned greed. Some bastard took out my family because of greed. There was a sudden silence when Kayla and Drake realized I no longer stood beside them. With a bit of confusion, they pivoted their heads to see where I'd gone.

Kayla hurried over and sat down next to me, then gathered me into a warm embrace. Her kindness did me in. I broke down into muffled sobs.

After a few minutes, Kayla looked up at Drake. The evidence bag with the nuggets inside was in her hand. She held it up in the air. In a muted voice she asked, "What are we going to do with this stuff, Drake?"

Drake took the plastic bag from Kayla's hand and stared at it with unmistakable interest in his eyes. "Beats the heck out of me. I've never had solid gold evidence before." Under most circumstances, the joke would have been a good one, but it went flat in the cold air.

"Seems strange that the stuff is still here on your property," he added. "If someone decided to use this cache as their piggy bank, you'd think they would have hauled it all away by now."

He bounced the bag in his hand a couple of times, then handed it back to Kayla. "One thing for sure, now that we've found this, I can't, in good conscience, just leave it here. I'll have to get a directive on this."

Kayla stood up and helped me to my feet. "C'mon, let's go get you some hot tea or something." Her arm wrapped around my shoulders, she walked back down the hill with me.

Drake put the evidence bag into the back of the van and followed us down the hill and into the house. I could hear his deep comforting voice as he talked into his handset. He clicked it off and said to me, "I need to ask you a couple of questions. Is that okay?"

My knees were shaking. I collapsed onto one of the green chairs, and sat with my elbows on the kitchen table, my hands supporting my head. "Sure.

Fire away."

"First, are you sure the box is on your property? It could get a little dicey if it's located on a property line."

I shook my head. "Not an issue. The house is right in the middle of a fifty-acre parcel."

"Good." Drake dug around in a pocket and found his notepad and pencil. He wrote down the information. "In that case, we can assume that whatever we find does in fact belong to your family, unless we uncover clear evidence that it's stolen property."

Stolen property? The idea that one of my ancestors might have pulled a payroll heist on a Wells Fargo stagecoach was offensive, even ludicrous. I felt halfway insulted on their behalf.

"Do you have any idea where that tunnel goes?" Drake's voice startled me, and snapped me back to the here and now.

"Kayla said it looked like it went off in the direction of the house. That agrees with the map my brother drew. I think it might end in the root cellar that's right here, under the kitchen."

Ignoring my still-unsteady knees, I stood up and shoved the table aside. Drake spotted the latch for the trap door and pulled it up, revealing the hole in the floor. The familiar scent of cool, moist earth wafted up from the opening.

"Okay," said Drake. "Whatever's under the house is a whole different ball of wax from what we came here for. There might well be something down there that we need to know about, but one thing at a time. We need to worry about the hilltop first."

He eased the trapdoor back down into the closed position. "I think it's obvious," he said, "that the gold should be moved to a more secure location. Do you agree with that assessment?"

Oh, yeah, he had that right. I nodded my head. "It's pretty clear that what you found is the key to all the things that have gone wrong around here. It needs to be gone."

I glanced over at the clock on the wall. I was surprised to see that it was only a little after twelve noon. It felt like it should be midnight already. "But I don't know how I can move it by myself, though. Who could I trust to help? And where would I put it? Moving it into my house would just make a new target for someone."

"No... you misunderstood me. As far as I'm concerned, we have evidence here of suspicion of trespassing, and maybe even vandalism. I might be able to think of a few other applicable sections of the penal code to throw in. Bottom line—your property was entered without permission, and disturbed. That qualifies as trespassing under California state law. The soil was loosened, the hinges lubed, and we've noted the presence of a footprint that is too large to be yours. Are your aunt's personal effects still here?"

"Yes."

"I'd appreciate it if you can look to see if a shoe that matches the print is among her belongings. If no shoe is found here that matches the print, we can take into consideration the fact that the print was found next to the box, the box contains items of value, and we can make a tentative judgment that a theft possibly occurred.

"In any case, enough penal codes apply that I can justify declaring everything found in the hole as potential evidence. As such, it needs to be stored in a secure location elsewhere."

His words of reassurance were magical. The oppressive weight pressing against my heart vanished. "Thank you," I said. "It'll be a relief to get the stuff out of here. I'll go look at Millie's shoes. Be right back..."

I turned and ran up the stairs. Since Millie kept all of her shoes neatly arranged on a metal rack in the bottom of her closet, it only took a few seconds to determine that a pair of Converse All-Stars were nowhere to be found. I grabbed one of the shoes and checked the size. It was a seven narrow.

I clomped back down the stairs, and reported my findings to Drake.

"Good. That helps to strengthen the trespassing angle. I'll go take a look at the box," he said. "If I can't move it either, I'll call for someone to come help us unload it, otherwise it's going to take all day. Until someone arrives to help out, we can't do much, so we'll go grab some lunch. I'll let you know when things start happening again."

"Okay." Clutching the mug of tea Kayla had made for me, I walked into the office. After setting the mug on the floor, I sat on the edge of my reading chair and tried to make sense of things.

What a mess. Nothing about the gold was even remotely attractive to me. I didn't even care how much it might be worth. Just thinking about it filled me with a bone-deep chill. No pile of gold could bring back Rudy and Millie.

I felt odd, detached from reality, strangely different than how I'd felt when I got the news of Millie's death. I hadn't felt this disoriented since the morning my dad collapsed and died in his office at the law firm. I'd walked in to greet him and found Death—my dad's body sprawled on the floor next to his desk, a surprised look on his face, and a pen still clutched in his hand.

I'd just seen Death again, in the form of the shiny golden nuggets nestled in Kayla's hand.

◆ ◆ ◆

An hour later I noticed the van was back, so I grabbed a jacket and wandered out the back door to see what was going on. I took a quick look down to make sure I didn't kick the snake box, but the container was gone from the porch.

A shrill birdcall above me caught my attention. I turned my face upward. A red-tailed hawk wheeled across the sky against the tumultuous backdrop of darkening clouds above Butte Mountain.

I heard Drake's voice, and glanced around the area, looking for him. He was leaning against the police van, talking on his handset. On the ground at his feet was a clear plastic trash bag holding a crumpled paper bag from a fast food emporium.

Kayla was sitting in the van, and a man I'd never seen before stood at the back of the van, shrugging into the ubiquitous tan coveralls. If they'd just finished lunch, then it seemed probable that I hadn't missed any new developments.

Drake raised his chin and waved to me, so I stopped and waited for him to finish the call. Only a moment later, he clicked the disconnect button and ambled over to me.

"The animal control officer was here. This is what he found under the box."

Drake thumbed the controls on his phone and held it out so I could see the snapshot he'd taken. It showed a man wearing a tan uniform and elbow-length heavy leather gauntlets. His arm was extended, and he held a snare pole with a rattlesnake dangling from the business end. The snake was an enormous sucker, maybe four or five feet long.

That snake would have had a huge strike zone. The thought made my skin crawl. "Someone," I said, "needs to be shot."

Drake didn't reply, but a quirk of his mouth seemed to indicate that he agreed with me. He motioned to the coverall guy, a lean man with copper-colored skin, and thick black hair shorn in a businessman's cut.

"Alexandra, this is Officer Oliver Zachary Deerheart."

He was Native American, for sure. A local guy, maybe from Jackson Rancheria? The conservative haircut didn't spoil the impression that he'd stepped right out of *Last of the Mohicans*. He stepped forward with a grin on his face, and shook my hand. "Pleased to meet you. You can call me Zak."

"Glad to meet you." And I was. I wanted to get the show on the road.

He went back to digging around in the van, and I went over to the barn and let Dog out of the truck. After several minutes spent sniffing the porch with uneasy caution, Dog settled down on the back steps.

"C'mon," said Drake. "Back to it." We piled into the van and rode up the hill.

Carrying a kit for making a cast of the footprint, Kayla dropped down into the hole. I watched as she set up an aluminum frame around the print. She opened a large plastic bag about a third full of white powder, added a bottleful of water, and squeezed it to make sure the mixture was well blended.

She poured the resulting glop around the footprint, letting the thick liquid ooze down and settle itself into the depressions in the soil. I wondered if the stuff was plaster, or something else. It looked like pancake mix. Probably didn't taste like pancake mix.

Kayla left the goo in place and pulled her camera out of her fanny pack. She disappeared into the darkness, interrupted only by a couple of flashes. "Hey Drake, how far down the tunnel do I have to go?"

"Just get the area where we will have to work for right now. Getting this stuff out of here is our immediate priority. We don't know where the tunnel fits in yet, or even if it fits in at all."

"That's good." Kayla's voice sounded a little strained.

"What's the problem?"

"I found out where the snake came from."

Drake burst out laughing. Kayla appeared in the hole, put up her arms, and Drake and Zak leaned over to pull her out. She glared at Drake. "You know, after you went down there to look around, it would have been nice if you'd bothered to mention that there's something *living* in there."

Drake looked down at the ground. Despite his attempt to be noncommittal, mischief was written all over his face. He was obviously working hard to keep from smiling.

Zak tilted his head to one side. "What's living down there?"

Kayla turned to him. "Snakes. Plural. As in 'numerous.' As in 'gobs of them.' As in *Raiders of the Lost Ark.*"

Some of the color drained out of Zak's face. "For reals?"

Kayla sang out in a high falsetto, quoting the old Indiana Jones movie. "Snakes. Why'd it have to be snakes?"

"That's not funny, Martinez," said Zak, his voice stiff with wounded dignity.

"Oh for Pete's sake." Drake snorted, trying without much success to choke back his laughter. "The snakes are hibernating. Hi - ber - na - ting. They're all cuddled up and looking like a pile of leftover spaghetti."

Zak's mouth was set in a hard line. "Okay. Okay. You've made your point." His eyes darted in my direction. I had a feeling that if I hadn't been standing right there he would have said something very impolite.

Drake opened his mouth, then snapped it shut. He heaved a great sigh. "I'll go down in the darned hole and unload the box."

Zak staggered, pretending to swoon with relief. Poor guy. And wouldn't I have liked to know the story behind all that.

Kayla went to the van and came back with a bundle of the heavy-duty canvas bags. Drake, good to his word, pulled on some gloves and dropped down into the hole. He handed up the cast of the footprint, and disappeared down the tunnel.

Zak dropped down the hole, too, but stayed right at the opening.

Drake handed the small cotton bags to him one by one. He, in turn, placed them into the larger canvas bags, making sure not to load them too heavily, and boosted them up to Kayla.

She tagged, numbered, and photographed each one, then put them in the back of the van. Kayla had the best part of the job, I thought, as both the men were tall, and had to work in a semi-hunched posture. They had to be hideously uncomfortable.

I watched them work, and I wondered how many years of hard labor the cache represented. How had the knowledge of this small fortune been lost to the family?

There were so many unanswered questions, so many things that did not make sense, that I hardly knew what to think. One thing was firm in my mind, however. The gold was an abomination, drenched with the blood of my family. I wanted it out of my sight, out of my mind, the sooner, the better.

Once all the gold was out of the tunnel, the two men helped Kayla finish loading the bags into the back of the van. Curious, I went over and picked up one of the bags. Whoa. It was way heavier than I'd expected. Only about a quarter full, it still had to weigh at least twenty-five pounds, maybe more.

In the end, they had twenty-one canvas evidence bags, plus the iron box. It took the team almost two hours to move it all.

◆ ◆ ◆

When they were done, bright yellow barrier tape bearing the words CRIME SCENE DO NOT CROSS was looped twice around the iron trapdoor and tied on the under-side. Ensuring that no human or animal would fall into the hole by accident, Drake dropped the trapdoor back into place. With a jarring *clang,* any secrets remaining within were shut away from the light of day.

The police officers packed up their tools and stripped off their coveralls. Kayla was engaged in an animated conversation with Drake and laughing at something he said.

Something clicked in my brain. There could be no doubt about it. Somehow, I knew that Kayla was in love with Drake.

Her face glowed and her body leaned towards him just a bit. He, on the other hand, was either quite good at maintaining his professional demeanor, or he didn't have a clue. I voted in favor of the "not a clue" option. Guys can be so darned dense sometimes.

Their tasks done, Drake slammed shut the back door of the van. He nodded at Kayla. She hopped in the driver's seat and started up the van to take it back down to the house. He walked over to me. He was rumpled and a bit sweaty, despite the chill in the afternoon air.

"How're you doing?" he asked.

"Better. I took a bit of a nap while you guys were eating lunch."

It would be more accurate to say that I'd sat staring into space, stunned, but I shied away from exposing the depths of my vulnerability. They'd already seen too much of my soul.

"Good. We have a CIT—cash in transit—truck on the way to pick up the gold and transport it to a secure location. Given its value, it needs to be secured in a bank vault or similar facility. Tell you what, while we're waiting around for it to show up, how about we take a look at that cellar of yours."

"Sure," I said. We tromped into the house, followed by Zak, and Drake reopened the trap door.

"Awesome, another bottomless pit. My specialty," said Zak. He stepped towards the hole in the floor, and stopped. "Any snakes down there?" His voice was full of humor, so I knew he was poking fun at himself.

"Weren't any last time I looked. And there's not much of anything else down there, either. No bats, no scorpions—nothing but dust, cobwebs, and maybe a few baby spiders."

Zak flashed a quick grin at me. He eased a foot down onto the top rung of the ladder, bounced a bit, then stepped down to the next one and tested it also. He seemed satisfied that the ladder was in good shape, and disappeared into the darkness.

Not seeing any point in standing around while Zak poked around in the dark, I wandered back outside, threw my head back, and stared at the sky. I was lost in the swirling spectrum of grays in the gathering storm clouds. A touch landed on my shoulder, startling me.

Zak stood next to me, rubbing his forehead, and looking apologetic. "I hate to bother you, but you need to see something down there."

My heart thumped. Now what?

I must have looked alarmed, because he added a bit of clarification. "Nothing bad. You were right. The tunnel does end under the house. I think it's worth you taking a look at it. Consider it another route out of the house, just in case our wacko buddy decides to nail your doors shut or something."

He had a good point. Maybe a bit improbable, but it sure wouldn't hurt me to take a look.

I walked back into the kitchen and flopped down on the floor. Zak disappeared back down the ladder, and I hung my head down so I could see what he was up to.

"See this?" Zak angled his flashlight at a wooden lever mounted on the shelves next to the door in the wall. He closed his fingers around it.

"Okay, all you have to do is shove this thing to the right..." he shoved "...and the latch is released..." a loud thump sounded "...and there you go." He pulled on the shelves, and, with a slight screeching noise, it pivoted out from the wall. "There's no other lock. Just shove the lever, the shelves swing out, and you can open the door. Easy as pie. Got it?"

"Yup. Looks pretty simple."

"To put it back, do all of the above in reverse order." Zak pushed the shelves back to the wall and pulled the lever back to its original position. The latch thumped into place.

"Okay. My good deed for today is done," Zak said.

"Thanks, Zak. I do appreciate it."

Zak came up the ladder into the kitchen, walked across the room and disappeared out the back door. I barely registered his presence. I was already lost in my thoughts again, wondering how the world I'd be able to fight the nameless monster that destroyed my family.

After wrestling a moment or two against the smothering tide of bleak frustration, I straightened my shoulders, counted to ten, and followed Zak outside.

An armored truck rumbled down the access road towards us, a cloud of dust flying in the wind behind it. It rolled around to park in front of the barn. A few scattered raindrops made a haphazard pattern of splats and dots across the layer of fine grit on the windshield.

The uniformed man who clambered down from the cab of the truck wore a sidearm on his belt, and a frown on his face. He crossed his arms and swaggered over to Drake. I didn't know if he was trying to look all big and bad, or if he was ticked off because the dirt road had made a mess of his truck.

Poor baby. Either way, his alpha posturing made him look like a fool.

A few scattered raindrops hit the top of my head. Thank heavens the wet weather had held off until the crew was done mucking around in the dirt. It only took a few minutes for the officers to transfer the treasure into the armored truck. The vehicle kicked up another drifting rooster tail of dust as it left, the rain not yet enough to dampen the road.

Kayla handed me a receipt from the armored truck and an itemized list of everything collected by the police team, right down to the cardboard box that had corralled the snake and the chunk of wood that had weighted it in place.

I fed Dog, went in the house, grabbed a banana and a glass of milk, showered, and put on fresh clothes. I climbed into the truck with Dog and drove to the hospital.

The day had been difficult, all I wanted to do was collapse, but someone else needed solace much more than I did.

Chapter Nineteen

I walked down the apple-green hospital hall that led to the ICU, my shoes squeaking on the linoleum floor, sending faint echoes down the corridor. The familiar scent common to all hospital critical care units assailed me—disinfectant and despair, in equal measures. I hated it. It brought back unpleasant memories.

I approached the nursing station and identified myself. "I'm a friend of the Hunters. Is it possible to see Claire?"

"Your name?" The nurse on duty checked a list, seemed satisfied with the information provided, buzzed open a secure door, and led the way to the room.

Greg sprawled in a chair by Claire's bed, asleep. His head was tilted back, and soft snores wafted from his open mouth. In a low, gentle voice, I called his name. It took a couple of repeats before the sound registered with him.

Greg flinched, blinked, looked up at me, and then glanced at his watch. "Oh dang, I'm sorry. Lost track of the time." He stood up and stretched.

I wrapped my arms around him in a comforting hug, the hug of the friend who shows up when things go south. He looked awful, with faint dark circles under his eyes.

I stood back and looked over at Claire. Her face, yellowish and waxy-looking, was terrible in that way that ICU patients always look. Asleep? Or unconscious? Oxygen tubes were taped to her nose, an IV drip stuck into her arm, and a wide assortment of wires disappeared under the neck of her hospital gown.

"How is she?" I spoke in a low voice, even though there was little chance that I would disturb her.

"Stabilized, but still in guarded condition. We pumped her full of fast-acting clot busters last night, and now we've got her on heparin. She hasn't had any more episodes. She's scheduled for another angiography in the morning, and we'll know more then."

I put my hand on his arm. "Have you had anything to eat?"

Greg's eyes opened wider, surprised. He ran his hand over his face and shook his head. Of course, he hadn't.

I glanced at my watch. "C'mon. Let's go over and see if we can catch Demetra before she goes home. She always has super yummy stuff in the afternoon. If she's gone, then we can figure out something else."

I tugged Greg out into the hallway and waited as he walked to the nurses' station to let them know he was leaving. He joined me, and we left. When we stepped outside, the smell of rain-dampened asphalt greeted us. At least the rain had stopped.

◆ ◆ ◆

The front door to Demetra's place was locked, with the 'Closed' sign displayed. But the lights were still on. I cupped my hands around my eyes, pressed my face up to the glass, and caught a glimpse of my friend behind the counter, cleaning up. I rapped on the door, and she flinched. She looked up, grinned, and came over to let us in.

I gave her a hug. "Anything left? Dr. Hunter has been camped out at the hospital all day."

Demetra looked surprised to see us together, and I could see that her curiosity was piqued. But, bless her, she didn't get nosey. "You're in luck." She grinned and motioned towards the kitchen. "I was about to start packing up the last of my shrimp gumbo to take home. It's still hot. I have a few French rolls left too. Sound good?"

My mouth watered. "Sounds like heaven."

Greg shifted his feet, as if uncomfortable. "Listen, Alexandra, we shouldn't impose. She wants to go home."

Demetra flashed a high-beam smile at Greg. Good lord, she was flirting with the man.

"Oh, you won't be imposing since I'm leaving in about thirty seconds. Stick the bowls in the sink when you're done, and make sure the lights are out and the doors are closed. There's a security timer on the doors. When you leave, they'll lock automatically behind you." She pressed some buttons on a controller box on the wall.

"You'll need to be gone in about thirty minutes or the alarm will go off. Don't forget anything 'cause you won't be able to get back in. Got it?

This wasn't the first time she'd trusted me to close up shop for her. "Got it. Thanks."

We sat down at a small table in the kitchen, as the lights were already turned off in the dining area.

Demetra jogged back into to the kitchen work area and reappeared with two steaming bowls of seafood goodness, the spicy aroma perfuming the air. She grabbed a basket of rolls, zapped them in the microwave, and set them on the table.

She winked at me, beamed Greg another mega-watt smile, grabbed her purse, said goodbye, and went out the back door.

Greg tilted his head. He seemed a bit puzzled. "You two are friends? I mean, I don't think she'd go off and leave her shop with just anyone."

I laughed. "Oh yeah. We go waaay back. We've been buds ever since high school, when I saved her from blundering into a date with a teenaged sexual predator. Captain of the football team, he thought he was nature's gift to females everywhere."

I rolled my eyes. "And he still thinks he is. Poor guy has no idea how much of a fool he makes of himself."

Greg pursed his lips in consideration. "I don't think I'll ask anything more about that."

"Good idea."

The gumbo was exquisite, filled with slivers of green pepper, chunks of tomato, slices of andouille sausage and okra, plenty of plump fresh shrimp, and flavored with the perfect balance of filé powder and hot savory spices.

We ate our dinner with the quickness of hungry people, and made small talk as we cleaned up. As long as we had time enough to make things right, I wasn't about to walk out the door and leave a mess behind.

We washed up the bowls and spoons, and I couldn't help but think about the other times we had done dishes together. We left enough money on the kitchen counter to pay for the meal plus a little bonus as a thank you to Demetra for her kindness.

With just five minutes left on the timer, we switched off the lights, stepped outside, and double-checked the doors with a quick tug on each handle.

We wound our way across the parking lot towards the hospital, skirting small puddles as we went along. "And how was your day?" Greg asked.

I considered what to say. Nothing about my day was even close to being normal. "It was weird, Greg. *Very* weird. I think I found out why Millie was killed."

Greg stopped in his tracks, clearly startled at my nonchalant delivery of this small bombshell. He reached for my hand.

"I came across something when I went through Millie's old papers in the roll-top desk." I told him about Rudy's sketch, and how I'd found it.

"I had the police check it out. Somebody in the Minero family stashed a cache of gold nuggets right there on the property. And, it seems that from time to time, someone has been helping themselves. Millie must have found out somehow, or caught them snooping around."

"What did you do?"

It took me a second or so to understand his question. "The police cleaned the cache out, tagged it all as evidence and loaded it into an armored truck. It's in a vault by now. I think they were going to have to take it down to Stockton or someplace with a more sophisticated evidence-storage facility than we have here. I wasn't paying close attention. I just wanted to get it the hell out of there."

Greg rubbed his forehead. He seemed confused by my reaction.

"It's not a family treasure," I said. "It's a family tragedy."

Greg tilted his head. "I don't quite understand your prospective, but... whatever. I'm not walking in your shoes. What happens next?"

We resumed walking. "Good question. At some point, our mysterious someone is going to find out that the gold is gone, and they are *not* gonna be happy. My guess—my hope—is that they will just go away mad. Match, point, I win.

"There is nothing to gain from trying to chase me off the property now. If they approach me about it, then their anonymity will be blown, and they'll find themselves up to their ass in hot water.

"I think the worst is over. I do want to believe that. One of these days, you'll have to come over, and I'll show you the place where we found the stuff."

We arrived at the hospital, so the conversation halted. I followed Greg back down the echoing hallway. The ICU nurse on duty assured him that Claire was still stable, and nothing had changed since we'd left.

He stood there and considered her words for a few seconds. "Well, I think I'll go home and get some sleep. Please leave instructions that I'm to be called ASAP if anything changes."

The two of us walked back out to the parking lot. I dropped Greg off at his house, and drove home, my mind scrolled through the events of the day.

◆ ◆ ◆

The next morning, I gave Dog a breakfast treat of scrambled eggs. The protectiveness he'd displayed the day before touched my heart. I'd have to be careful not to make him a fat protective dog. He looked sleek and healthy, far different than how he was when he found me. The two of us got in the truck, and I drove back to Demetra's place.

Demetra worked thirteen-hour days, five am to six pm, seven days a week. She rarely took a day off. I didn't know how she did it. I walked into the shop and gave her a hug.

"Hey girl," I said, "I want to say thanks for helping out Greg last night. His wife is in critical condition, at the ICU. The poor guy is close to being a basket case."

Demetra stared at me, bug-eyed. "Wife?" I could almost hear the faint crackle of Demetra's daydreams disintegrating and falling in little brittle pieces all over the floor.

"He has a wife? Holy shit. So you're not his girlfriend?"

"Get real. I've known him since, like... forever, I guess. At least since I was five or six years old. He's more like a brother than anything else. But that doesn't mean that I'm blind."

"Amen to that," said Demetra. "The man's a hunk. I've been seriously lusting after him since he first walked in the door. I should have known a man like that wouldn't be running around unclaimed. Damn, why do all the great guys belong to someone else?"

I nodded in silent commiseration. "I've asked myself that same question many times, believe me."

I almost made a joke about having to settle for Andrew Pichl, but the thought was too repellant to even joke about. I ordered a latte and a lemon-blueberry scone instead, sat down at a table, and opened my laptop.

Demetra waited on several other people, and then came back over to me. She fingered one of the spiral curls that framed her face. "So how did you get to know Greg? He didn't grow up here. Believe me, I would have noticed."

"You, and every other female in Jackson. He didn't go to school here. He used to stay at his grandparents' house at the lake in the summer. His grandpa and my grandpa were buds from college or something. In any case, my brother and I were out at their lake a lot. The three of us used to get into all kinds of trouble."

Demetra laughed. "If he was half as mischievous as Rudy, that doesn't even begin to cover it."

She wandered away to wait on other customers. Hopefully I'd relayed sufficient information to change the focus of any gossip that might get passed along.

Demetra was a sweetheart, but she did like to chat. Her coffee shop provided a one-stop shop for news updates of every imaginable sort. It would be considered hot news that one fine specimen of a man might soon be available to be fought over by the single women of Jackson, just as soon as his wife died.

I found that thought revolting, and, at the same time, an unfortunate truth. Some people do think that way. I must have looked unsettled because Demetra came back over and looked at me, her face tilting in question. "Lexie, are you all right?"

"Yes. Yes, I'm fine. I just... zoned out there for a moment. Greg's wife being ill made me think of my own mom, and when she was in the ICU." I'd indeed had those thoughts, but they'd crossed my mind last night. There was no need to mention that fact at the moment.

She gave me a quick squeeze around the shoulders.

I hugged her back. "Thanks, lovey. You're a gem."

I packed up the computer, walked to the truck and stashed it inside. I checked on Dog and his water supply, rubbed his ears, and then headed off across the parking lot to Jackson Valley Convalescent Hospital.

I went in the side door, as I always did, but instead of heading straight to Claire's room, I went in search of the duty nurse. She had no updates on Claire's condition.

I found it difficult to maintain my cheerful demeanor while I lugged around the piano and visited with the other patients. My mind kept wandering away from me, wondering what was going on with Claire.

When I left, I saw Greg's old pickup truck parked near the front of the hospital. I wondered if I should I go over. Did he need space? Or company? I was torn between wanting to be a friend, and not wanting to suffocate him.

I decided to send him a text message.

Hi. Just checking in. Test results?

Greg would know what I meant to say. I hoped. I walked along the sidewalk, stepped down into the parking lot, and boosted myself up into my truck.

I drove by Demetra's on the way out of the parking lot, and saw Andrew Pichl standing on the sidewalk in front of her place, staring after me. I shuddered in revulsion. It seemed like every time I turned around, there he was. I needed to look up the California legal definition of stalking.

I picked up a few items at the grocery store, stopped to check for mail at the Post Office, and went home. About an hour later a text came back from Greg.

Tests show nothing new. Treatment will continue as started.

And so life was to return to normal. And, just like pressing a reset button, I was back to the question that had hounded me earlier. Am I a fool to stay here?

The first consideration was, of course, the house. Yes, the place was unique and dear to my heart, but bottom line was that it was just a house.

Then there were the piano concerts at the Convalescent Hospital. If I left town to go to Fiji or wherever, the patients might be disappointed, but that would be the extent of it. File it under the category of Things Like That Happen.

Logic couldn't make the thought more palatable, though.

Publicity events were already scheduled for Millie's memorial show.

The show itself would be held on December 8th, just in time for the holiday shopping season. After that, I could leave if I wanted to. Dog could go live with Greg. Or, I could find a good loving ranch home for him. He'd never be happy in Bertie's tiny yard.

So much to think about... What is that poem, or prayer, or whatever the heck it is? I opened my laptop and made an internet search.

God grant me the serenity to accept the things I cannot change,
The courage to change the things I can,
And the wisdom to know the difference.

And right there was the heart of it: *The wisdom to know the difference*. Easier said than done.

What could I change? And what did I have to accept? I pushed myself up from my chair and went into the kitchen to make a cup of coffee. The questions lingered in my thoughts for hours, with no easy answers presenting themselves.

◆ ◆ ◆

That night I slept in restless fits and starts, tangling myself up in my bed sheets. I dreamed of a massive fire, flames shooting one hundred feet in the air, burning up my house, and everything inside of it.

Including me.

Chapter Twenty

The phone rang at six the next morning, startling me awake. A phone call that early is never good news. I heard Bertie's voice, and my stomach clenched. She sounded odd, strained. "Hey," she said. "Sorry to wake ya up, but Greg asked me to call."

"What's happened?"

"Claire's taken a turn for the worse. She suffered a massive heart attack in the middle of the night. She's now in extremely critical condition, on life support."

"Oh, shit."

"You got that right."

A vision of Greg's tired, haunted face flashed into my mind. "How's he holding up?"

"Not well. He put his fist through a wall, and cracked a couple of bones."

My heart raced, full of sudden fear for what else he might do. "Where's he now?"

"One of the doctors took him home, gave him a sedative, and put him to bed."

"Good." I was relieved that his support network had kicked in. At least for the time being.

"Another doctor is gonna go check on him later, so don't go worryin' about him. Well, gotta go, chickie. I have other people to call."

I thanked her for letting me know, but she'd already hung up.

◆ ◆ ◆

Twenty-four hours later, Claire died.

There was a very simple memorial service for her, a few days later, at the Jackson Valley Convalescent Hospital. Claire's parents flew in from

Denver, Greg's father and mother came from Honolulu and San Diego, respectively, and a few old friends drove up from Los Angeles.

I played *Clair de Lune* on the piano. Claire's younger sister, Jana, a copper-haired, sad-eyed sprite, read a beautiful short essay about love, life, and loss. Doctors, nurses and physical therapists hugged and cried along with friends and family.

Even a few of the high school students who had read to her attended the service, their faces stunned, their eyes red. The stultifying fog of grief wrapped around all of us as we contemplated the tragedy of a life that was never allowed to blossom in full glory.

Greg sat through the service, sandwiched between the protective bulwarks of his parents, staring at the cast on his hand. I'd remembered his dad as a hearty bear of a man, with a neat red beard. Now the man looked disheveled, worn, like a Viking warrior gone to seed.

Greg's mother looked much as she always had—like a poised platinum mannequin, with cold blue eyes that elicited visions of frozen Arctic ice. Their marriage had not worked, but they remained united in protection of their son. No one dared to engage Greg in conversation, except to express the briefest of condolences.

He seemed very much in need their protection. The man looked haggard and defeated. Everything he'd done for Claire over the last few years was all for nothing. Greg had put his heart and soul into a battle that couldn't be won.

He probably felt like he'd been bludgeoned. Or worse.

His parents guided him to a car after the memorial was finished and drove him away. I watched the car exit the parking lot and had the horrible sensation that he was being ripped away from me, that I'd never see him again. I couldn't breathe.

This must be how a trout feels when pulled out of a stream.

Greg took a leave of absence from the practice. He closed up the big house overlooking the lake, and hired a caretaker. His dad drove him to Sacramento in his rental car. They both got on an airplane and left. Greg didn't come to my house to say goodbye.

It was the first of December. The chill in the air bled through my skin, deep into my body, piercing me with coldness all the way to my heart. My dearest friend was... gone.

Greg's whole life had fallen apart. And yet, here I was, feeling sorry for myself, knowing that I should feel ashamed and remorseful, because all I could think was *who will I lean on when things go south?*

And I knew that I had fallen in love with Greg Hunter.

◆ ◆ ◆

A week after the memorial service, I stood in the doorway to Claire's room. The bed sat empty, stripped down to the blue-striped mattress. The closet held nothing except for a few empty coat hangers and my folded-up piano.

I stared at the piano, numb. I felt like all my emotions had been pulled from my body and laid out on a bed of crushed ice. I let myself sag against the doorjamb. One of the nurses' aides came up to me and encircled me with her arms.

“It’s okay if you leave the piano here,” she said, her voice filled with gentle reassurance. “We know it belongs to you. We'll take care of it for now, put it away in the supply room. Come back when you can.”

I turned and put my head on her shoulder, returning the embrace. I didn’t know whether my heartbreak was for Claire, for Greg, or for me. My slow steps led me out of the hospital. When would I have the strength to come back here?

I trudged back to my truck, my feet dragging with every step. I gave Dog a half-hearted rub on his head, checked his water, grabbed my laptop computer out of the cab, and headed across the parking lot to Demetra's place.

I ordered a bowl of clam chowder, sat down, and opened up my laptop. The first thing I did was to check my email. There was nothing from Greg.

The chowder tasted like cardboard to me, but I ate it anyway. I stared out into space for a while, feeling empty and disoriented. I knew there was something else I’d wanted to look up on the internet, but damned if I could remember what it was. And so I left.

I slid into the driver's seat of my truck, rested my head on the wheel and whispered, “Greg, where are you?”

It seemed so out of character for him to just walk away.

I pulled out my laptop and found I could pick up Demetra’s wifi signal in the parking lot. I opened up the email program and composed a short message.

> Greg,
> You don’t need to tell me where you are, but I need to know that you are OK. Call me any time if you need to talk.
>
> Allie

I clicked Send, and the message whisked away to places unknown. I packed up the laptop and drove out of the parking lot.

Dog and I stopped at the post office, and the grocery store, then drove home. I walked towards the back door, a big brown paper sack in my arms, and froze.

Someone had been there. Someone angry.

An ugly message was gouged into the solid wood of the old back door.

DIE BITCH

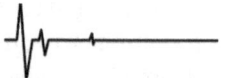

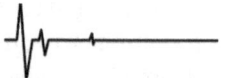

Chapter Twenty-One

Instead of feeling panicked, as I once might have, I was outraged. I turned around, faced the knoll, and flung my arms out. “Here I am!” There was no answer.

“COWARD!” I screamed. “Where are you! Show yourself!”

The only response I heard was the susurrating whisper of the wind over the grass, and the twitter of distant birds.

I was so angry that I didn’t care if someone shot me.

Dog came running out of the barn and circled around me making funny little whuffing noises. He jumped up, trying to lick my face. I hugged him, and was, once more, grateful for his presence.

I got out my cell phone, took a picture of the door, and sent it off to Drake. Then I got up and carried my groceries into the house. Drake called me back within a few minutes, and, an hour or so later, Kayla drove up the road to the house.

◆ ◆ ◆

Kayla got out of her car, and I went out to meet her. “I sure hope you don’t have another coyote here,” she said. “That thing made my car stink for weeks.”

“No dead creatures today, just elegant prose. Our mystery person shows promise as a literary giant.”

I’d had time to reconsider my earlier bravado and realized how foolish I’d been. My defiance had dissolved, and it seemed to me that my voice sounded thin and strained.

I wondered how I sounded to Kayla.

I must have sounded fine, because she laughed and grabbed a big navy-blue nylon bag from the seat of the car. She closed the car door and walked with me over to the back of the house.

She shook her head when she saw the curt message and gave an exasperated snort.

The wood was stained and varnished at some point long ago, but it had weathered, and was no longer very smooth. I hoped the surface had enough integrity for her to get something useful from it.

"Any footprints?" she asked.

Damn. I hadn't even considered that. Had I messed things up? I looked around. "Only that." I gestured towards a scuffed area in the soil. It looked like someone had swiped at the dirt with a rag.

Kayla glanced at it and waved her hand in a dismissive gesture. "Not helpful, dang it. So, who do you think in the past few weeks has touched the door? You know, who can be eliminated, if I find their fingerprints?"

Good question.

There hadn't exactly been a cast of thousands hanging out with me. "Well, after the coyote thing, I scrubbed the heck out of the door. Not many people have been in here since then."

The UPS and FedEx guys? No, they always leave stuff on the front porch.

The guys who packed up Millie's paintings? Or were they here before I scrubbed the door?

"Shit, I don't remember. The guys who installed the security lights were here. You, Drake, Zak. I think that's about it. Man, when you look at it that way, I'm quite the hermit."

Kayla grinned. "Welcome to rural living. Think of it as being self-sufficient. Sounds ever so much better than anti-social. If you think of anyone else after I leave, you know how to find me."

After scribbling down the appropriate names on a sheet of paper, she squatted down and looked at the door again.

"Whoever did this had to put a lot of force into it, so I'm guessing they had to lean against the door a bit. Let's hope they did something stupid, like leave a full set of prints or something."

I must have made a snort or other sort of 'yeah, sure' noise. She turned her head and looked up at me with the same small grin on her face. "You wouldn't believe what we find sometimes. Now, for example, in this case it's pretty obvious that we're dealing with a very angry person.

"People who are angry are not the most careful of folks. A lot of times the person will just flat give themselves away. They might as well send us an email and be done with it. So, let's find out how bright this rocket scientist is."

Kayla put on her surgical gloves. She searched in her bag and pulled out what appeared to be a fat black wand with a small transparent plastic squeeze bottle screwed onto the end. The bottle contained a fine white powder.

She slid back a casing over the handle and revealed a translucent fiberglass brush at the opposite end. Light pressure on the bottle deposited some powder onto the fiberglass filaments of the brush. She moved the brush over the door in the area of the ugly scrawl.

"Old technology," she said, nodding at the white dust, "but for items we can't move, this method is still one of the best ones around."

She worked with a careful, methodical technique, lightly twirling the brush, and refreshing the powder on it now and then with a gentle squeeze on the bottle.

"Okay. We're getting something."

I peered over her shoulder but couldn't see much of anything except a white smudge on the dark wood.

Dog came up and nuzzled my hand, and I jumped. I glanced at my watch. No wonder Dog was whining at me. He was hungry. I went to the barn and scooped out some food for him.

I got back, and Kayla was sitting back on her heels, grinning. "And we have a winner!"

Right there on the door, to the left of the nasty gouges, was a palm print. Someone had braced against the door with their left hand, while they dug into the wood with their right. The top edge of the print was smeared, as if the person had tried to wipe away the print, but missed.

I couldn't help but chuckle. "Way to go, Einstein. Rub out your footprints, but leave even better evidence right here on the door."

Kayla grinned. "See what I mean about sending us an email? Hello?" She shook out the brush, wiped it with a cloth from her bag, and closed it up by sliding the casing back into place.

After taking several snapshots of the prints, Kayla dug into her bag once more. She pulled out a flat rectangular box that looked to be about eight by ten inches. She opened it up and pulled out a thin black rubber sheet. Carefully, she pulled off a clear protective layer and set it aside.

"This is a gel-lifter. I've got to be super careful here, or I'll screw up the prints." Kayla smoothed one edge of the lifter so it stuck to the door above the palm print, and then carefully lowered it, top to bottom, over the print.

"I thought you guys use tape to lift fingerprints."

"Tape works well in some situations, but I'm using this stuff because your door's not smooth enough for good results."

"Oh."

"Now," said Kayla, "we let this sit here for a little bit." While the gel was doing whatever gels do, she dug even more goodies out of her bag. Was there no end to the treasures inside? Maybe a BLT and a chocolate shake? Instead, she pulled out something that looked like a giant toothpaste tube, a spatula, and a sheet of white cardboard.

"Well, I think it's time." In a slow, even gesture, she peeled the gel lifter off the door. The white image of the palm print was captured, crisp and perfect, on the black sheet. She set it print-side up on a piece of plastic sheeting at her feet and set the clear backing on top of it.

"We're going to use some different stuff to preserve the cheery message." As with the fingerprints, the first step was to take a set of photographs. She turned and picked up the fat tube she'd pulled from her bag earlier.

"This is polyvinyl siloxane. Same stuff your dentist uses to take impressions of your teeth. You know, that junk that feels like it is going to run down your throat and suffocate you before the dentist comes back to rescue you."

I snorted out a quick little laugh, remembering that exact experience at the orthodontist when I was in high school.

She squeezed out a strip of the gunk onto the piece of cardboard. Using the plastic spatula, Kayla spread the mixture over the nasty message, pressing hard to make sure the goo was forced into every gouge and scratch.

After allowing a few minutes for it to set, she pulled away a perfect mold of the letters carved into the wood. She set it down next to the palm print.

"Okay, then. You're free to do whatever you want with the door. Putty it, stain it, do whatever you want. Or, paint hearts and flowers around it, varnish it, and save the message as a precious memento of the day we got Our First Big Clue. Your choice."

She tilted her head, and gave me a lopsided grin. "Leave it in place, and you're sure to give all your house guests something to talk about."

I rolled my eyeballs. All my houseguests. Right. We just discussed that.

Kayla bent down and picked up the palm print again. Standing up, she held the print where I could see it. "Don't touch it, but compare the size of your hand to the size of this one. What does it tell us?"

I held my hand next to the print. It wasn't much larger than mine. "Well, I think we can eliminate Drake as a suspect."

Kayla's lips made a sputtering noise as she tried to hold back a giggle. "C'mon. Be serious. What do you think?"

"Our angry person isn't very large. Maybe a small- to medium-sized man, maybe a woman. From the looks of all the old scratches and scars, I'd guess it's not a kid."

"Ms. D'Angelo, you can go to the head of the class." Kayla grinned from ear to ear. "And now we can start eliminating people. Well, you know what I mean, not eliminating them on a permanent basis, although the thought is tempting at times, but eliminating them as suspects. It's about time we got a break on this."

She set the palm print into a shallow cardboard box, and picked up the mold of the gouged message and packed it away also. "This has been a pleasure, believe me."

She gathered up her gear, put it in the trunk of the car, stripped off her gloves, shook my hand, and opened the car door. She looked at me, brows pinched together in thought.

"Listen, Alexandra, I really don't want to scare you, or sound like a fear-monger or something like that, but have you thought about carrying a gun?"

"I have a shotgun in the kitchen, and another one in the truck."

"No. I mean carry one, on your person. A .38 snubbie, or something like that. You don't need one designed to take out King Kong, just one that takes care of business."

"Oh." I hadn't really thought about carrying a handgun. My prior experience with firearms involved small rifles or shotguns. I glanced down at my tucked-in tee-shirt and snug jeans. "Where would I carry it? In my underwear?"

Kayla's smile lit up her face again. "Don't laugh. You can buy exactly that—holsters for your bra, or ones that go down the front, inside your jeans, over your panties. I don't think either of those would be particularly comfortable though."

"Good grief, no. Sounds awful." I had visions of myself bending over and being jabbed in the guts by cold, unyielding steel. *Ouch.* Or worse yet, bending over and shooting myself.

"Well," said Kayla, "you think about it. And if you do decide you want to get a handgun, just don't forget to get a CCW."

I gave her a blank look.

"That's a Carry Concealed Weapon license. You can ask about it at the station." She slid into the car, said, "See you later," gave me a jaunty wave, and drove off.

◆ ◆ ◆

The resulting trail of dust soon disappeared, carried away on the light wind that sprang up and threaded through my already-unruly hair.

I had a new awareness of how very alone I was. Only the whisper of the breezes across the grass, Dog's breathy pants, and the distant sound of a chainsaw broke the silence around me.

There we were. Just me, the dog, and the mountain. Damn. I was indeed a hermit. What could I say? I knew what I was getting into when I signed up for this gig.

Oh well. It is what it is. I grabbed my wallet and keys, hopped in the truck, and went back across the valley so I could use the internet.

There was nothing there from Greg. I still couldn't remember what else I'd wanted to look up. Stress had turned my brain into oatmeal. I had no doubt that complete senility was just around the corner.

I was feeling so sorry for myself that I drove down the hill to get a chiliburger at Mel & Faye's. For the first time ever, the meal in question gave me heartburn.

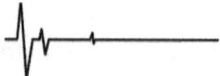

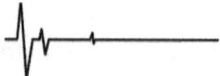

Chapter Twenty-Two

A few days later, I remembered why I'd gone to Demetra's. My brain must have needed a small vacation, or it wouldn't have shorted out on me. But now there was a web search to be done, and email to be checked. I had yet to buy a new smartphone, one that actually had some oomph to it, which would have made checking my email a lot easier.

Maybe I just liked having an excuse to drink Demetra's coffee.

I knew that I needed a solid target to embrace, and a direction for channeling my energies. So, I forced myself to start considering what might be done with the cache of gold once it was released back into my custody.

There wasn't any rush—it certainly wouldn't be returned to me any time soon. But, to be honest, I hoped I could use the windfall to endow Greg's nonprofit foundation. I didn't want to engage in any serious fundraising. My heart wasn't in it anymore.

I had no clue what the gold from the box might be worth. Maybe several hundred thousand dollars? The best use of the unexpected bonanza would be to help those most in need. I could make the ugly cloud hovering over my life grow a silver lining.

So back I went to Demetra's. While slurping the foam off the top of a hot latte, I fired up my computer. I noodled around a bit before getting down to business, looking at the latest memes, and clicking around on all the other silly garbage that we waste our time with on the Internet.

I pulled up a New York tabloid. My stomach flip-flopped. There, front and center, was a photo of Mark, looking as handsome and dashing as ever. The paparazzi had caught him walking into a fancy restaurant with his arm around a very tiny woman. She had long, straight black hair, and looked like she was about fourteen.

According to the photo caption, however, she was a twenty-one-year-old former Chinese gymnast who'd defected to the USA at the last World

Games. Mark had hit the jackpot—he'd found himself a lady love who looked like a kid, even more than I did, but was old enough to take into a bar. Good job, Mark!

I wanted to stand up and cheer. I've been replaced! And I sincerely hoped Mark's new squeeze would keep him happy, at least until the crows-feet started forming at the corners of her eyes.

And, someday, I'd figure out how I could have Mark held accountable for the harm he'd done to his underage victims. It just needed to be done.

Humming a happy little tune, I proceed with my original mission. I poked around on the Web until I found a gold nugget question-and-answer site that looked promising. There were several pictures of odd-shaped chunks of gold that resembled familiar objects—a camel, the head of a scotty dog, a mermaid, and so forth.

Someone had submitted a question regarding the weight and value of a cubic foot of gold. I snorted. Who the hell has a cubic foot of gold?

I almost choked on my latte as a sudden realization hit me. *I do*. For some reason, I hadn't thought of it in quite those terms before.

A single cubic foot of gold will weigh approximately 1187 pounds.

Whoa. I looked at the figures again. Over a half ton per cubic foot. No wonder Drake couldn't budge the old Wells Fargo box! And then there was a bunch of gobbledygook about the weight of gold being measured in troy ounces, not avoirdupois, and blah blah blah. I read the next line.

A cubic foot of pure gold is 17558 troy ounces. At $1171 per ounce, the value is just under 20 million 600 thousand dollars US.

My brain must have lit up like an old-school mechanical slot machine—yellow blinking lights and bells ringing like a stack of wind-up alarm clocks gone amok.

Fumbling on the keyboard with unsteady fingers, I looked up the current value of the price of gold. The current market was much higher than $1171 per ounce. The shaking of my hands went into double-time.

Of course, the figure cited was the value of a solid block of pure gold, and the cache certainly wasn't a solid mass. As to what level of impurities the nuggets contained, I couldn't even begin to guess.

But, still, even if I cut the figure in half, or even into one quarter, the gold found in the old iron box was worth much more than I would have ever guessed. Millions more. I felt slightly light-headed.

No wonder someone was willing to kill for it.

Even more inexplicable was the fact that the mystery person hadn't just hauled it away, bit by bit. It didn't make any sense.

A shadow fell over the computer screen. The fine hairs on my neck raised. Someone stood right behind me, peering over my shoulder.

"Gold nuggets! I love gold nuggets," said a thin, wavering voice. "My father had a collection of fancy nuggets."

I flinched, and closed the laptop, hoping it appeared to be a casual gesture. I took a deep breath and looked up to see the soft white curls and sweet wrinkled face of Amelia Feeney, one of Greg's favorite patients.

Bent from time and fragile bones, she was even shorter than me, and thin as a wraith. Her blue eyes, faded with age, no longer held the alert intelligence they once had, and her expression had a dreamy quality about it.

I sagged back in the chair, relieved I'd not had a more perceptive observer peering over my shoulder. Amelia was well over ninety and seemed to be living in another world most of the time. She reminded me of an aging faery—I always half-expected to see tiny gossamer wings fluttering on her back.

Now she was chatting away about somebody named Mr. Tuggles. My brain struggled to make the shift from gold nuggets to wherever her chain of thought had wandered off to.

"My Mr. Tuggles has gold eyes, you know."

It took me a few very long seconds to figure out that Mr. Tuggles was Amelia's cat. My pulse and breathing returned to normal, and I patted Amelia's hand and excused myself. Since I'd closed my laptop, I had to leave. Otherwise, I'd look like I'd just been ruder than hell to a sweet little old lady.

Which I had been, but that was beside the point. There was no need to end up on the bad end of everyone's opinion. Amelia was beloved by the entire community, and she did have her champions.

I wanted to run for the door, but forced myself to take my time gathering up my things.

Amelia rattled on. "Mr. Tuggles' mother was a purebred, you know, a real Persian princess. Oh yes. He's quite proud of that. Inherited all that lovely fur. But his father was a very naughty boy. A very naughty boy indeed. A bit of a rogue, I dare say."

Not wanting to encourage further discourse, I said nothing. At last, when I did not appear to be fascinated by the soft and fluffy attributes of Mr. Tuggles, nor by his ancestry, Amelia shifted her focus to the man sitting at the next table. She drifted off in his direction and kept on talking.

I hoped she was chatting about cat whiskers or something like that.

Feeling a bit mean-spirited, I hoped that Amelia's short-term memory was completely shot. Last thing I needed was for her to tell half the Jackson Valley that I was researching gold nuggets.

I walked across the asphalt parking lot back to my truck. The entire situation with the cache of gold was bizarre. How could something of such value be forgotten? The knowledge should have been passed along in family lore. But, outside of those vague old stories about some supposed buried treasure, there was... nothing.

You'd think a cache like that would be documented—in a journal, or a note to be passed down through the family, or... *somewhere*. But it wasn't, at least as far as I knew.

I was looking at a diabolical jigsaw puzzle. No matter how I pushed or turned the pieces, they still wouldn't fit together.

And—good lord—this business of Amelia, or anyone else, looking over my shoulder could not happen again. *Would* not happen again. Now, more than ever, I needed to get an internet connection at home.

◆ ◆ ◆

By the end of the following week, I'd signed two contracts. The first one was for satellite internet access. The other was for a closed-circuit surveillance system. A swarm of workers descended upon the house, and at the end of another week my home looked more like Fort Knox than Home Sweet Home.

The satellite dish was unsightly, an ugly gray blister on the front of the house. The surveillance cameras stuck out from the eves, looking, to my mind, like machine gun emplacements. I didn't like it. Millie wouldn't have liked it. Oh well. So be it. I'd had enough.

I checked the email on my laptop for the first time and held my breath. My computer chimed, and I jumped.

I'm safe. Don't worry. G.

A four-word message? Really? He couldn't be bothered to write more than four words? I rolled my eyes. The man was hopeless.

My cell phone rang. No *Jane Eyre* miracle of telepathy this time. The call was from Drake, asking if I could stop by and see him.

I detoured by the post office on the way to the police station. In the mail was a large manila envelope with a Sacramento postmark. I peeked inside and found a raggedy message scrawled onto a sheet of yellow paper.

My shoulders sagged. There was no need to pull it out of the envelope. I'd seen enough. I needed to give the thing to Drake.

◆ ◆ ◆

Drake was all smiles this time when he came through the door to get me. But the good cheer quickly faded from his face. I must have been looking pretty grim. Without a word, I handed him the envelope.

He took a quick glance inside. "Did you touch it?"

"Nope. I did the same thing you did. I didn't have to read it to get the message."

"Well then, let's go back to my desk and take a closer look."

Drake's shoes clicked on the linoleum as we walked down the hall to his cubicle. A whiff of fresh microwave popcorn wafted down the corridor from the far reaches of the building. I settled down into the green-cushioned chair across from him.

Drake rummaged around in a desk drawer, found a new pair of latex gloves, and pulled them on. He slid the message out of the envelope and set it down where we could both see it.

> IF in SPiTE OF This YOU STILL DO NOT LISTEN TO ME but continue To be hostiLe toward me, then in my Anger I will be HOSTILE toward you. And I MYSELF WILL PUNISH YOU for your SINS seven times Over.
> LEVITICUS 26:27-29

My skin crawled. "Well," I said, trying to make light of the strangeness of the message, "I guess all that was too much to carve in the door."

It seemed that my mystery person was more than angry. They were deranged.

"The author of this isn't thinking too clearly," added Drake. "By making threats, the person is just digging their way deeper and deeper into a hole." He shook his head in bemusement. "I'll send it down to be fingerprinted."

He glanced up at me. "Are you all right?"

I shrugged my shoulders. "I'm more unnerved than anything else. Something about this message creeps me out. And makes me wonder why I haven't had the good sense to pack up and move to Santa Barbara."

Even as I said that, and despite my earlier vow, I knew that I wouldn't leave. I'd already given up one home. I'd be darned if I'd be chased from this one too.

"Well," he said, "You're the only one who can make that call. Do think about it. But right now, I want to show you something."

He opened the top desk drawer and pulled out a small clear plastic evidence bag. A gold ring was visible inside of it. "We finished sifting through all the dirt we dug up on your property. And look what we found. Do you recognize it?"

I held out my hand. Drake dropped the item onto my palm. "Don't take it out of the bag," he said.

I held the ring, inside the plastic, pinched between my thumb and forefinger so the light reflected off the top. It was a slim gold signet ring, maybe an antique, of a type that could be worn by either a man or a woman.

The flat surface on top was engraved, but years of wear had made it difficult to tell whether the incised workmanship formed a set of initials, or if the scrollwork was just a design. The ring was pretty, the sort of thing that might have caught my eye in an antique shop, but I was sure I'd never seen it before.

Other than the obvious signs of longtime use—the thinned band, the indistinct engraving—the jewelry looked well cared for, and not like it was kicking around outside in the dirt for unknown years.

I shook my head. "No. I'm sure I'd remember this if I'd seen it before. Sorry."

"Don't be sorry. Actually, that's what I hoped you'd say." He took the ring back and returned it to the desk drawer. "Our Converse-wearing mystery person could be the one who lost it. So, perhaps we have another clue. By itself, it's not much. Let's hope that pretty soon we can start stitching things together."

"Pretty soon?' Nothing more definite that that?" My rising optimism reversed course and ran right down the drain.

Drake's eyes were full of sympathy. "I'm afraid not. But, the good news is that palm print from your door might solve this whole thing. Especially if there are prints on that letter you just got."

"Might?"

"Yes. We've gotten zero matching hits from any of the databases so far. The palm print was distinct, but the fingertips were smeary. So the DMV records and so forth were of no help."

I sighed. The man couldn't magically pull evidence out of nowhere.

"Don't be too discouraged," he said. "We're working on this. 'Going fishing,' you might say. Check out the Lost and Found ads in the *Argonaut Ledger*, starting tomorrow. Seems that someone found a ring."

My eyes widened. "You're kidding me! Would our person be stupid enough to call you up and ask about a ring that they might have lost at a crime scene?"

His mouth turned up in a full-fledged toothy grin. "It's happened before, especially with an object that a person wears or carries on a habitual basis. Often, they're not sure when or where the item was lost. We might luck out this time."

His message was the same one that Kayla had relayed when she lifted the fingerprints—people under stress do really dumb things. Sometimes such persons end up skewering themselves. And here's to someone making themselves into a kabob.

I sat for a minute, contemplating the thought of barbequed suspect served with teriyaki sauce. Sometimes I can be a very bad person. And then another chain of thought drifted in and dislodged the musings on grilled miscreants.

"Listen," I said, "you know I believe Rudy's death and Millie's death are connected. Is there any possibility we can go back over the evidence that was collected when Rudy was found? Can that case be re-opened?"

He didn't look surprised. Perhaps he'd been waiting for me to ask that question. His voice filled with what seemed to be genuine regret. "Unless some kind of new evidence shows up, there's not much we can do from our end. However, if you feel strongly enough about it, you can petition to get the case reopened.

"Be aware, though, unless you can state some very compelling reason for that to be done, the County isn't likely to grant your request."

He folded his hands in front of him on the desk. The gesture had a sense of finality to it, although I was pretty sure that he didn't intend it that way.

"I was afraid of that." No other questions came to mind. "Well, thanks. I'll see myself out."

"See you later then. I'll be in touch."

"Sounds good." I took a couple of steps towards the hallway, stopped, and turned around.

"Drake?"

"Yes?"

"You should take Kayla out to dinner one of these nights. Take her to a nice restaurant, and maybe a movie. And don't talk about work."

With that, I turned and walked away. I glanced back to see him staring after me, his lips slightly parted, looking flummoxed.

I walked to the door with a smug little smile on my face.

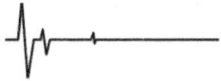

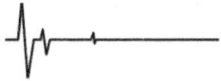

Chapter Twenty-Three

A week before the planned show of Millie's artwork in Sacramento, I drove there for a pair of publicity events, both on the same day. I had my hair cut at a fine salon, and a professional makeup artist applied full war paint to my face. The effect was subtle. I felt gorgeous. I wished I looked like that all the time. Oh well.

I took two of my lawyer-lady suits with me, one for each session, and endured posing for photographs and answering dumb questions about Millie and her artwork for what seemed like hours. But the time spent was worth it.

The journalists came through for me with featured articles in local magazines. The press release from Kat got wide distribution and publication. We were good to go.

PRESS RELEASE

The Ekaterina Symington Gallery is pleased to announce *Farewell to Millie*, an auction of the last works and personal collection of internationally renowned Western Artist Milagros Minero, who passed away in July of this year. The event will be held on December 8th at Sacramento Memorial Auditorium, 1515 J St., Sacramento, California 95814. The evening begins at 5:30 pm with previews and refreshments, followed by a live auction at 7:00 pm.

Farewell to Millie will feature a selection of the western art for which Ms. Minero was famous, plus an outstanding collection of abstract works created by Ms. Minero for her own home.

Proceeds from the sale of these paintings will be donated to the Julieta D'Angelo Memorial Cancer Research Fund and the Claire Nygaard Hunter Memorial Foundation for Neurological Research.

Tickets are $50 for Symington Gallery members, $75 for non-members. All prices go up to $100 after December 1st. For more information, contact us at www.SymingtonGallery.com.

The show was on the road.

◆ ◆ ◆

After all the preparation and waiting, life felt a bit strange when the day of the show arrived, and the nebulous Future turned into the very real Now.

Dog wasn't happy to be left behind in Bertie's yard for the weekend. I didn't like driving away and leaving him, but there wasn't much else I could do.

I couldn't just leave him home with an overflowing food bowl. Like most dogs, he had zero ability to wisely ration his resources.

I checked into the hotel and wished I had the makeup artist again. I shrugged. Oh well. This event wasn't about me. I had high expectations for the evening and hoped they'd be realized.

Millie's paintings would have new homes where they would be loved and appreciated. If all went as planned, a substantial amount of money for two medical research funds would be raised. Kat, the gallery owner who'd organized the show, would get a nice spot of cash for her trouble. And, maybe I'd reconnected with an old friend or two.

Saturday afternoon, I arrived at the Auditorium right in time to see the workers carrying out the art. They placed the pieces on plain black easels scattered around the big wood-plank dance floor.

Built in the 1920's, the building is a beautiful, Moorish-Italian-Romanesque Beaux Arts brick palace. The dramatic landmark was the perfect venue for the art of a dramatic woman.

Kat greeted me with a kiss and a hug, and then dashed off to oversee the staging of the artwork.

I'd decided to wear one of Millie's flowing hand-painted silk scarf dresses. The dress was bright and dramatic—just *so* Millie. She had painted it with sinuous abstract shapes in the same vibrant colors found in the paintings of the nudes.

Mid-calf length on her but ankle length on me, I loved wearing the elegant garment. The dress wasn't the best for wintertime, so I added a ruby-red silk shawl that matched some of the dress's bold streaks.

I also wore some of her chunky jewelry, enameled in the glorious jewel-tone colors that she loved. This whole night was to be a celebration of Millie, and I was determined to carry that spirit down to the smallest detail.

Spotlighted in the center of the room was Millie's old familiar easel. It was set up just as Millie had left it, her unfinished painting resting on it. Her paints and palette were arranged on the small table next to it. The water basin still held the dried residue of paint in the bottom, the unwashed brush returned to the spot where I'd found it.

My eyes prickled with unshed tears as soon as I saw it. A mental image of the glittering shards of broken glass I'd found on the floor of Millie's studio forced its way into my mind.

I pinched my lips together hard. No. I couldn't break down. Not now. This was a celebration. I spun around, turned my back to the easel, and focused on the gilded columns and ornate plasterwork that framed the auditorium stage.

On the stage sat a large object, about five feet wide and fifteen feet long, shrouded in lightweight blue canvas. It was a surprise feature, to be unveiled by the Master of Ceremonies at the precise moment when excitement started to peak. I was crossing my fingers that everyone else would find it as amazing as I did.

Kat and I did meet-and-greets around the floor. An excited buzz arose in the crowd of people looking at the paintings of the nudes. The grace and power of the compositions, the unexpected color harmonies, and the innate drama of the paintings blew them away. They never expected such works from Milagros Minero, Western Icon.

Kat had promised me she would make sure that the Master of Ceremonies for the event would be an individual with strong ties to Jackson. For some reason, that small detail seemed important to me. But I wasn't sure why. With a gentle tug, she turned me to face the stage. The designated MC strode his way up to the microphone. I looked at the man and gasped in delighted surprise. "No *way!*"

"Yes way, Alexandra!" She grinned. "David de León, in the flesh. Local boy makes good, and all that."

"Oh. My. God! He's perfect for this evening! I can't even tell you how many afternoons he spent in our kitchen while the three of us sweated over our homework."

Kat's eyes were dancing. "A little bird told me all about it."

I gave her my best exasperated grump-look.

"To tell the truth, he phoned me way back, right after she died, to see if he could purchase one of Millie's works as a keepsake. He said he owes a lot to her. He's positive that he would've never snagged his university scholarship without the support and encouragement of your family."

"Nonsense. David's brains got him where he is today. The guy's a flippin' genius," I said.

Kat's teeth flashed in a big white grin. "Well, you tell him that then, because I can tell you he's convinced otherwise.

David's warm baritone voice boomed through the PA system, welcoming everyone to the event. He was a familiar figure to most people in the audience, having been a prime-time news anchor for several years at a local station, KSXP, Channel 2.

Tall, olive-complexioned, with black hair and warm brown eyes, he had a commanding presence. Now, all decked out in a tuxedo, he'd come a long way from being the quiet little boy Rudy and I had befriended in the fourth grade. Life was not always easy at his house.

And just look at you now, David. I couldn't help but smile.

After our host offered the standard opening remarks, he said, "First up for auction tonight is the collection of western art paintings owned by the Ekaterina Symington Gallery. The gallery and the Minero family retain rights to produce giclée prints of all original works sold. Following that group, the private collection of Milagros Minero will go up on the block."

He made a swooping open-handed gesture towards the paintings of the nudes. "Buyers will have full rights to these paintings. The family of Ms. Minero will, however, retain rights to have giclée prints made of any of these paintings for their own personal use. All proceeds from the sale of these paintings will be donated to the Julieta D'Angelo Memorial Cancer Research Fund."

A sense of pride surged within me at the mention of the Stanford research fund that my father had created and named in honor of my mother. It seemed appropriate that the money from Millie's personal treasures should be donated in honor of a member of our family.

"Please now direct your attention to the stage for the final item to be auctioned off tonight."

On cue, the cover over the object on the stage slid away, revealing Millie's little station wagon. So many things had changed in my life since I first found it in the barn, covered with dirt and cobwebs. The crowd erupted with a loud crescendo of excited exclamations.

David did his best to read off a description of the make, model, and mileage, but the hubbub of voices drowned him out, as if nobody gave a damn about the mundane automotive details. The exquisite art on the car was the thing that grabbed their attention. Now, that was a collector's item!

The commotion died down a bit, and David, carrying the microphone, walked to the car. "We will proceed with the first two blocks of paintings, and, following that, there will be a short intermission, during which the car may be inspected by potential buyers."

He placed a hand on the hood. "After the intermission, this final item will be auctioned off. All proceeds from the sale of the automobile will go to the Claire Nygaard Hunter Memorial Foundation for Neurological Research."

This was the first step towards making Greg's dream foundation into reality.

David turned the event over to the professional auctioneer. The big sale had begun.

◆ ◆ ◆

When I first conceived the idea of auctioning this car off to raise money for the foundation, I'd pictured Greg standing next to me, resplendent in a tuxedo. I couldn't dwell on that now. He would find out about this soon enough.

Claire's parents had surprised me by agreeing to come to the event. I looked around the dance floor and finally found them, standing off to one side. I'd talked to them earlier in the evening, and they'd seemed touched yet puzzled by my generosity.

I got the impression that they didn't understand how I could have made an emotional connection with their daughter, having only met her after she was injured. As if, after the injury, she had ceased to be a person.

I tried not to judge them, but found it difficult. We had only the briefest of conversations. There seemed to be no common ground between us at all. I didn't let that fact dampen my spirits. Nothing could spoil this night.

As the auction rolled along, the excitement surged. I took a seat in the gallery at the edge of the dance floor, leaned back, and relaxed in the embrace of the soft maroon velour cushions.

I sipped a glass of wine and savored the opportunity to unwind and forget, even if just for a little while, all the nastiness that had swirled through my life as of late.

The room was a kaleidoscope of voices, colors, and sounds. Black-coated waiters darted through the crowd delivering beverages and hors d'oeuvres. People laughed and chatted and exclaimed as the various pieces of art were brought up to the auctioneer.

The bids were not all that important to me. I knew they would be substantial. Everyone understood that this was a once-in-a-lifetime event. To me, the end result—the good that would be done—was the important thing. I watched the people and heard the voices as if seeing a movie from far away.

"Hello, Alexandra."

Startled, I turned my head and found that David de León had parked himself right next to me.

"Oh, David*!*" I put my wine glass on the floor and threw my arms around his shoulders. "Good lord, it's been ages! Thank you so much for doing this!"

David's face lit up in the grin I remembered so well. "I wouldn't have missed this for the world."

We caught up with each other, sharing news of friends and family. His face was radiant with good news. "I just got a great new job and, best of all, Yasmine and I are getting married. The two of us are going to be in Jackson for the next few weeks, so we'll be able to get together. Time for her to 'meet the parents' and all that.

"It'll be interesting, to say the least." A quick grimace crossed his face.

"Even though I've been with Yasmine for five years now, my parents still don't understand why their little boy isn't marrying a nice Mexican Catholic girl."

He rolled his eyes. "Whatever. Anyway, I'll give you my card so you can send me an email or text and we can get together."

"Oh, heck yes." I couldn't wait to meet the famous Yasmine.

The whole time we were chatting, David kept an eye on the easel next to the auctioneer. He came to full alert when one particular piece was placed there. "Ah, that's the one I want. Gotta run."

He handed me a small, cardboard rectangle, planted a quick kiss on my forehead, and vaulted over the low barrier in front of the seats.

I watched as David made his way over towards the knot of people bidding on the painting he wanted, and my breath caught.

When Kat cleaned out Millie's studio, she'd found a large portfolio of the pencil sketches and informal watercolor studies of the type that Millie was forever doing. She created the pieces either as preliminaries for a large work, or for her own pleasure.

The piece that David wanted was a watercolor. It showed Millie's own green kitchen table, with three dark-haired children sitting at it, concentrating on their homework. Tears welled up in my eyes. I wished I could just *give* the darned thing to him. But, that was out of my control now.

I glanced down at his business card, and my eyes widened in surprise. David de León, child of immigrant laborers, was now a correspondent for *Sunday Night America,* the premier national newsmagazine program on commercial television. David had made the big time, network headquarters, New York City. Wow. Just... wow.

By the end of the evening, I knew that the vision formed months ago was realized. The auction had gone well, better than I'd hoped for. Millie hadn't wanted a memorial service, but in essence, she'd just gotten one, and of the best possible sort.

Wearing a satisfied smile, I grabbed my shawl, left Kat supervising the dismantling of the displays, and headed out to walk to the hotel. It was only a couple of blocks away on J Street, so it was silly to engage a cab for such a short jaunt. I shivered in the piercing cold, wishing that I had something more substantial than a silk wrap to keep me warm.

Fog, the winter-time bane of the Sacramento Valley, twisted in gray, wraith-like strands through the streets. As I stood at the corner waiting to cross J Street at 13th, a feeling of deep satisfaction warmed my soul, and defied the near-freezing bitterness of the night. It had been a perfect evening.

A rough arm grabbed me around the neck, and threw me to the ground.

CHAPTER TWENTY-FOUR

My hands skidded along the rough sidewalk as I tried to break my fall. I was shoved downward, and a gritty shoe came to rest on the side of my neck. I couldn't turn my head to see who had me pinned down. Dare I struggle? I had no idea how easily a neck could snap.

From the amount of pressure applied, I guessed my tormentor was a man, or at least a large, strong person.

"Well, little girl," said a low, sandpapery voice, "you and I are going to have a bit of fun. A nice visit, you might say."

"No!" I screamed, *"NOOOO!"* My voice seemed swallowed up in the blanket of fog.

I made a fist, and swung my arm around, trying to dislodge the foot from my neck. My hand bounced off a hard shin bone. The foot didn't move.

I knew I had only a limited time to save myself. *"HELLLLP!"*

"Oh," said the voice, soft and menacing. "So that's how it's gonna be, eh?"

The foot moved. For an instant, I thought I was free. I tried to scramble up, only to find myself slammed flat on the icy cold sidewalk again, then flipped, a knee in my back, my hands pinned behind me, the air knocked out of my lungs.

I tried to yell again. My throat felt too tight, constricted with fear. Other than a gasping rasp, no sound came out. Heart hammering, I struggled to take a deep breath, to try again.

The man who pinned me laughed, jammed his knee harder into my spine, knocking the breath out of me yet again. I tried to roll, but it was impossible to move, to shake off the horrible pressure. My heart pounded in sheer terror.

"Now," said the raspy voice, "We're going to have a little chat..."

"Hey!" Running footsteps echoed through the damp air. From across the street, a voice cut into the quiet of the night. "HEY!"

The heaviness on my back disappeared. Gulping for air, I rolled up into a sitting position, and clutched my shawl around me in unthinking self-comfort.

My assailant vanished in an instant, only the sounds of his footsteps gave a hint as to which way he'd run, into the foggy darkness.

A woman in a security guard's uniform appeared and squatted down next to me. "Are you injured? Do you need an ambulance?"

I shook my head. I gulped in a few more deep breaths. My lips and chin were trembling. "No... I'm okay. Just shook up."

"Can you stand?"

"I think so."

The woman stood and gave me a leather-gloved hand up. I lurched to my feet, legs rubbery, and she grabbed hold of my arm and let me steady myself. "Are you headed for the parking structure?"

"No. I was just going across to the Sheraton."

"Okay. I'll walk with you."

Still holding onto me, she escorted me across the street and into the lobby of the hotel. I collapsed down into one of the plush sofas and looked up at my knight in shining armor. Her uniform indicated that she was from the adjacent Convention Center.

I reached out and squeezed her hands. My eyes brimmed with grateful tears. "Thank you. I think you just saved my life."

She grinned, showing perfect white teeth. "My pleasure, ma'am. I'm glad you weren't hurt." She turned and disappeared out the door, into the night.

◆ ◆ ◆

The morning after the show, I should have felt like Wonder Woman. Unfortunately, despite the triumph of the auction, it was impossible to feel victorious. I'd had a hard night. Endless visions of last night's assault looped in my memory over and over, until my exhausted brain finally shut it down, and I slept for a few hours.

I got up and looked in the mirror. My neck was scratched from the grit on the man's shoe, my back was bruised, and I was haunted by the feeling that I'd only been moments from mayhem and death.

I went to the hotel's fitness center and cleared the gloom from my mind with a pounding run on a treadmill. By the time I'd showered, dressed, and had breakfast, I was ready to think a bit more rationally. And, I was thanking providence that I'd packed a turtleneck to wear. No questions would be asked about my beat-up neck.

I left Sacramento and headed out Highway 16. Inescapable questions dominated my thoughts. Was Millie's killer at the show? Was I followed when I left the auditorium?

Or was the horror visited upon me the previous night nothing more than an unpremeditated attack by an opportunistic predator?

But, if I'd been targeted by a random psycho, why had the man insisted that we needed to *talk*?

Talking would probably be the last thing on the mind of someone who stalked others for their own perverse pleasure. Who was he, anyway? The Midnight Motor-Mouth? I snorted at the ludicrous thought.

Driving by rote, habit, muscle memory—whatever you want to call it—I started an inner replay of the evening's event at the Auditorium scrolling through my memory. The faces of the people I'd talked to drifted by my mind's eye. Had anyone there seemed out of place? Acting odd?

The inescapable answer to that question was a resounding, "No."

Well, one of the waiters was a bit rude.

I laughed out loud at myself. Who did I think was going to show up? Snidely Whiplash, creeping around, looking suspicious, and rubbing his hands together?

I wanted, badly, to believe that I'd been randomly targeted by a deranged stranger. The fact that I found such a notion to be comforting was almost as disturbing as the attack itself.

◆ ◆ ◆

In an effort to clear my thoughts, I tuned my radio to classic rock, and soon found myself belting out a rather loud *Highway to Hell*. Drumming the steering wheel, I drove over the hill, down the grade from Martell, and turned onto the narrow street that led around the hill to Bertie's little robin's-egg-blue Victorian cottage.

I pulled up in front, and could see Dog bouncing around the back yard, his head popping up over the top of the fence only to disappear a second later, then reappear. He looked like he was bouncing on a trampoline. Silly dog.

Bertie heard Dog's excited barking and came outside. She stood shivering on the front porch, rubbing her hands up and down her plump arms to make up for the fact that she'd rushed out without grabbing a jacket.

"Perfect timin'. Come in, come in. I splurged and made some fancy Brazilian coffee, and there're cinnamon rolls just outta the oven."

I hurried up the front walk and onto her porch. She opened the front door, and the aromas of spice and fresh coffee burst out in a cloud of cinnamon contentment.

Bertie's kitchen was a haven for me for years. The sight of the pale lemon walls and white cabinets brought a smile to my face. Soft beams of sunshine, flickering with the motion of the leaves outside the large windows, glinted off the row of copper pans hanging over the spotless white range.

I sat down at the kitchen table and helped myself to the offered goodies. "Ohhhh... I'm in heaven... These rolls are flipping good. As always. Wow, it feels like I haven't talked to you in forever."

Bertie dug into the plate of rolls, too. "So how was the show?" From the bored tone of her voice it was evident that she was asking just as a matter of good form, not out of any real interest.

"Great." I said. "Absolutely great. All the paintings were sold, and I reconnected with a good friend from high school." I reached for my coffee mug, and winced when my abraded hand bumped the hot ceramic.

"What the hell did ya do to your hand?"

I didn't want to tell her about the attack. She wouldn't be sympathetic. All I'd get from her would be a lecture about the stupidity of wandering around by myself in a big city at midnight, and that I should know better, and blah blah blah.

"I tripped and fell on the sidewalk. Dumb. But, fortunately it was after the show, not before." I grabbed the mug, more carefully this time, and took a sip. "How are things with you?"

"Things are so darned slow at the office now. I had an awful mess for a while, with Greg just leavin' like that, but after things settled down I got bored. So, I did somethin' about it. I got hired as a Patient Advocate at the hospital. Greg is gonna be mad, but he's the one who ran off and left me holdin' the bag."

I really didn't think that Greg would care one way or another, but decided to keep my mouth shut. There was no need for me to be obnoxious, and say 'I doubt that, kiddo.' I reached across the table and grabbed my friend's hands.

"Oh Bertie! That's awesome! It's perfect!"

She jumped up out of her chair, scurried away, and then came back with a piece of paper with the list of her responsibilities. "This is just the overview—there's more to it than this, but you get the idea." Her rosy face glowed with excitement.

I scanned the job description. It did seem perfect for her. This change in direction was a huge step for Bertie. She had worked in the medical office for as long as I could remember. Years. The fact she had left her comfort zone to try something new was significant.

I was happy for her. After one last hug, and with a cinnamon roll to go, I loaded up Dog and we left.

◆ ◆ ◆

I got home and walked into the office to check the surveillance system. I fast-forwarded through the images captured by the cameras. The monitor displayed a nice image of a coyote snooping around the outside of the barn, and that was it. Excellent. I hit the delete button, happy that there was nothing on it worth keeping.

I sat down at my computer and sent an email with my contact information to David de León. Then I composed an email to Greg, telling him all about the evening, and offering the email address of the accountancy firm that was handling the purchase transactions.

I wanted him to know how much money had been raised for the foundation, that his dream was alive and well, and had a good chance of surviving. I attached a couple of photographs of Claire's parents standing next to Millie's car, handing over a certificate of authenticity to the high bidder.

In only a few minutes, a reply came back.

Great news! Thanks for including them. G.

Them? I had no idea if he was referring to the fact that I had included Claire's parents in the event, or to the photos that were included in the email.

Whatever. The man was hopeless. Time to think about other things.

I stood up and stared at the desk. I'd never finished going through the stuff. Despite the strange finale to my evening in Sacramento, my confidence and emotional strength seemed to be on the rebound. Everything else that evening had gone well, better than expected, and I chose to fix my attention and energy on the positive.

The time for action had arrived. Drake's hands might be tied, but mine weren't. *Damn the torpedoes, full speed ahead.* I rested my palms on the roll-up cover of the old desk for a second or two, and then pushed upwards to open it.

I opened the small drawers in the upper part of the desk and, finding them empty, moved down to the medium-sized drawers on the left side of the kneehole. Nothing in there except bundles of old family photos. The thought of looking through them was enticing, but I was on a mission, so they'd have to wait for another day.

The everyday stuff of living—old bills and such—were absent. Such things might all be upstairs in the file cabinet, which I'd already gone through. If there were any more of them, I'd find them sooner or later. That left the two large drawers on the right side.

The top drawer was empty. I picked up the big portfolio of Rudy's drawings from where I'd left it, put it in the drawer, and shoved it shut. I opened the bottom drawer.

The space inside was crammed with large manila envelopes. There were far too many to hold in my lap while sitting in the big chair, so I put them on the floor. Settling down onto the worn garnet and deep blue Persian carpet, I picked up the first one.

Millie had saved everything—poems and drawings from first grade, recital programs, ribbons from the County Fair, and awards from school science fairs. While tempted to look through each and every envelope, I forced myself onward. I was sure that everything I needed would be in a single marked packet. Millie would have kept everything related to Rudy's demise, just as she had kept all the stuff related to his life.

It didn't take long to establish a rhythm. Pick up an envelope, check the label, peek inside to verify, set it aside, grab the next one. Then, there it was, right in front of me. I sat there for a moment staring at the label written in Millie's bold handwriting.

Rudy's Death

She hadn't minced words or used a polite euphemism such as "accident." Just as I'd supposed, Millie had saved every clipping, every card, and every slip of paper with any relevant information regarding my brother's murder. Bracing myself against the desk, I got up off the floor. Folder in hand, I walked over to the big chair, flopped into it, and turned on the reading light. I picked up a newspaper clipping.

Hit-and-Run Fatality Reported

JACKSON, CA -- Police are investigating an accident that took the life of Rudy D'Angelo, age 16, in rural Jackson Valley late Wednesday night or early Thursday morning. A truck driver employed by Simkowitz Lumber Products found the victim and summoned police to a private road northeast of Jackson about 7:45 a.m. Thursday. D'Angelo was a victim of an apparent hit-and-run, a Jackson-Martell police spokesman said. A search of the area failed to locate any suspicious vehicles or individuals. Anyone with information about the accident is asked to call the Jackson-Martell Police Department.

Simkowitz Lumber Products... Robin had liquidated the company as soon as she had inherited it. The trucks were sold, the buildings razed, asphalt and concrete torn up and recycled.

The hard-packed dirt roads were deep-ripped and left rough. The forest plantation was freed to go feral, to reclaim the cleared land, to obliterate the road where Rudy died. After all these years, it would be next to impossible to pinpoint the exact location of his death.

In a move that surprised the entire community, Robin had completed the erasure of her legacy by donating the company's forestland to The Nature Conservancy. At the time, we all decided that she must have loathed the old man. But then again, why shouldn't she? Everyone else did.

And, of course, that was where Claire had been assaulted, and so badly injured.

I sighed, and refocused on the papers. I refused to let myself be sad, or even reflective. I poured over each and every one of them, looking for... what? I had no idea. There had to be something in the folder I could grab onto and use as a starting point.

Maybe this? In my hand was a document that appeared to be a photocopy of the summary of the autopsy report. The top and bottom halves of the page had been blocked out with blank sheets of paper when the copy was made.

The copy was faded, and the writing close to being indecipherable. There was an odd smeary blob of white correction fluid that covered up some of the words on the top line. Had someone spilled the bottle? It sure looked like it. If so, they'd done a piss-poor job of cleaning up their mess.

```
                         skull fracture with intracranial hemorrhage
b) Blunt force trauma of torso and extremities, consistent with
   being struck and run over by a motor vehicle.
c) Multiple rib, sternal and spinal fractures with:
      i.    Transection of aorta
     ii.    Cardiac laceration
    iii.    Pulmonary contusions
     iv.    Hepatic and splenic laceration
      v.    Thoracic spinal cord laceration
```

I sat and stared at the document quite a while, waiting for some blinding flash of insight. None was forthcoming.

Other clippings from the paper reminded me of the hostile and acrimonious press conferences and city council meetings that were held at the time. Local truckers were outraged at the implication that one of them had run down Rudy. Most of them knew my brother, either from seeing him in the forest, or because their kids or grandkids were in school with him.

On top of that, there'd been too many questions that the police chief and coroner danced around and never answered to everyone's satisfaction. They always fell back on the position that they were engaged in an ongoing investigation, and it would be quite irresponsible to reveal too much information, blah, blah, blah. Their evasiveness rubbed people the wrong way.

The publisher of the *Argonaut Ledger* wrote a scathing editorial, accusing the pair of incompetence, laziness, and worse.

But, the accusations went nowhere. The virtual stone wall that the police erected withstood all incursions. The incident, despite its suspicious nature, was never classified as a homicide. The police chief declared Rudy's death to be the result of misadventure, and the case was closed.

My stomach churned as I recalled those horrible days. The pattern seemed altogether too familiar. The question foremost in my mind burned with a crystal-clear flame—what was I going to do about it?

I closed my eyes and tried to summon memories that might be helpful. In my mind's eye, I drifted through the cast of characters who had played a role in the drama.

Who'd been caring? Who'd been ready to lend a hand, or a shoulder to lean on?

Abruptly, the answer I sought came to me. I knew who I needed to find.

The investigating officer. He'd be the key.

I remembered him as a kind man, tall, lanky, with sandy hair streaked with gray. He always conducted himself in a professional manner and tried hard to hide his embarrassment at the actions of his superior officers. What was his name? I dug through the papers.

Ah. There. Sunderland. Gordon E. Sunderland. He wasn't a young man at the time of the investigation, probably somewhere in his fifties. No doubt he'd retired years ago. I hoped to hell he hadn't moved to Arizona or someplace.

◆ ◆ ◆

Early the next morning, with Dog sitting alongside of me in the passenger compartment of the truck, I drove along a narrow dirt road that snaked downhill from a ridge above Jackson towards Lake Amador. I hadn't been down this road in years.

My palms were sweaty on the steering wheel, and my whole body was tense. I'd thought a lot about the possible consequences of taking this step, and there were no guarantees as to how it would go. I had no leverage to force someone into cooperating if they didn't want to.

According to the phone directory, the Sunderland family lived down here some place. We came around a sharp bend in the road, and I spotted a man working on a barbed wire fence. His rugged face, punctuated with prominent eyebrows, looked familiar.

I stopped the truck and hopped out. Treading with care along the bumpy, grassy berm, I walked over to him. "Officer Sunderland?"

He turned to face me, brows raised in inquiry. I had no doubt that this was the man I was looking for.

"Yes, I'm Gordon Sunderland, but I'm not a police officer anymore. What can I do for you?"

Tall and lean, he had the look of a man of the land, his skin weathered by years spent in the sun and wind. The brim of his straw cattleman's hat fluttered in the light breeze. He pulled off a heavy leather glove and extended his hand.

I returned the grasp. "Mr. Sunderland, I don't know if you remember me. I'm Alexandra D'Angelo. You investigated the death of my brother, Rudy."

His eyes widened, and the smile on his face faded away. In fact, his entire demeanor stiffened. He hadn't recognized me, but I had no doubt he remembered the case.

"That was a long time ago. I'm retired now, you know."

"Yes, I know. But, if you don't mind, I'd like to talk to you a bit. At your convenience, of course."

Sunderland's eyes grew wary. His focus drifted away from my face to a point in the distance, over my shoulder. "About your brother?"

"Yes. But first I need to tell you why I came looking for you. I'm not looking to cast blame, or find fault with you." I paused for a moment to allow the message sink in.

"You were kind. You were wonderful to my family during an awful time. We were always very grateful for that. You didn't know how much we appreciated you, but believe me, we did."

Sunderland's shoulders relaxed a bit. "Thank you, but I was only trying to do my job to the best of my ability."

"Well, you succeeded in more ways than you knew at the time."

Sunderland's face reddened.

My stomach flipped. The man knew something. And, he was more than a little bit uncomfortable with that knowledge.

"Mr. Sunderland, I've been living in New York for the last several years, but I came back home after my aunt died. You may have heard what happened to her."

He made no comment or motion of acknowledgement.

"In any case, I'm living at her place, just south of Butte Mountain. Some rather alarming things that have happened over the past few months have caused me to start re-evaluating the circumstances surrounding Rudy's death."

He still didn't say anything.

Great. Now what.

I handed him one of my old business cards. No harm in giving the man a few clues about the adult version of me. The New York information on the front was crossed out, and my cell phone number scrawled on the back.

"If you can think of anything that bothered you about that case, any little thing that seemed important to you but was dismissed by others, please give me a call. I'd appreciate it."

Sunderland took the card, studied it for a moment, and stuck it in his shirt pocket. "I doubt that I'll think of anything important. As I said, that was a long time ago. But yes, I'll call you if I do. It is nice seeing you again. And thank you for your kind words. I appreciate it."

He extended his hand again for another handshake, then pulled on his glove, and turned away.

Recognizing I'd been asked to leave, albeit with great politeness, I turned to walk back to the truck. I glanced back at the man before I climbed in.

Sunderland had picked up his fence pliers and was staring at the cold metal implement with a pensive expression. Somehow, I knew that he wasn't looking at the tool, but at the past.

He spoke, his voice so quiet that I wasn't even sure that he was addressing me. "You're a brave lady. Good luck."

He snipped off a loose piece of wire, and it fell to the ground.

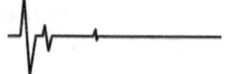

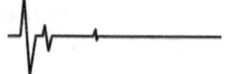

Chapter Twenty-Five

A day later, another large manila envelope showed up in my post office box. There was no return address. I saw it bore a Honolulu postmark, and a rush of relief shuddered through my body. I ripped it open. Inside I found a car window sticker.

DOG IS MY CO-PILOT

I couldn't help but laugh out loud. No note enclosed, but I knew who sent it. Greg was in Honolulu, probably with his dad. He'd thought of me, and that was good enough for now. I put the sticker on the passenger-side rear window of the truck, right above the spot where Dog liked to sit. I thought it a real shame that Dog didn't know how to read. He'd get a kick out of this.

With a small grin on my face, and despite the fact that I now had an internet connection installed at home, I headed over to Demetra's. I did like going there, at least most of the time. Plus, the woman had a way with the food.

I sat down with a cappuccino and checked the email. I saw an email from Greg, and a jolt of adrenalin hit me. I opened it, thrilled to see a long message. Then I realized the email was addressed to Everyone.

"Shit, Greg, don't be so damned obtuse," I whispered. "Somebody here loves you, dumbass." But still, something is always better than nothing.

> Everyone,
> I apologize for not getting in touch with you sooner. I'm at my Dad's house in Honolulu. Thanks to everyone who sent me messages of support and sympathy. I'm very grateful to have such wonderful friends. I do understand my abrupt departure caused some difficulties for those of you who were my patients. All I can do is extend my sincere apologies and hope for your understanding and forgiveness.

> Many of you have asked when I will be returning to Jackson. As of right now, I'm not sure when that will be. However, you do need to know I have extended my leave from the practice until next November. A year is a long time to be gone. I understand that some of you may be disappointed by my decision.

No shit, Bozo.

> I will continue to live here in Honolulu for at least another month, perhaps a bit longer. Following that I will be leaving for Africa...

WHAT? He's doing WHAT? My heart pounded, and my pulse thumped in my ears.

> ...where I will be joining the UNHCR, the UN Refugee Agency, which is dedicated to "safeguarding the rights and well-being of refugees." I will be working with the people who have been displaced from their homes by the ongoing civil unrest in eastern Africa.

Everything around me disappeared into a disconcerting blur of noise and light. I tried to read the rest of the letter. It made no sense. I shut down my computer and packed it up.

I looked up to see Amelia Feeney watching me from across the room. I scrambled to my feet and scooted out the door before the old lady could launch herself in my direction.

I climbed into the truck, closed the door, and screamed, "Shit!" I rested my head on the steering wheel, tears running down my face. I was upset with Greg, and I was upset at myself.

I'd just come *that close* to having a public meltdown. How could I be so damned stupid? I'd gotten the satellite system installed for a reason.

I wiped away my tears. After a while, I started up the truck and drove away.

◆ ◆ ◆

> "And so it was that Greg went to Africa." If our lives were in a goddamned novel, that's how it would read. But this isn't a novel. News Flash – this is real life, sweetie-pie. You're going to go take yourself off to some godforsaken refugee camp on the edge of Hell and risk getting your ass shot off, and for what? The people there are living in the middle of a nightmare, and you think you're just going to sashay in there like the flipping Lone Ranger and save the day? Have you lost your mind?

Nope. Tempting, but not a good idea. Snuggling deeper into my big leather chair in the downstairs office, I deleted the email and started over.

> I have to say I was shocked when I read your email. And, I have to be honest with you about this – it scares me to death to think that you are going to the edge of a war zone. However, I'm sure this decision was made after a great deal of thought, and that you feel that you are doing the right thing.

I didn't much like the new version either. It sounded too namby-pamby, as my grandmother liked to say. But, it would have to do. No one would benefit from a huge dose of sarcasm at this point. I attached a selfie showing Dog and me in the bed of the pickup truck, with Dog sitting, tongue lolling, under the "Dog is My Co-Pilot" sticker in the window.

I added a bit of chatty news, and hit the send button. There was nothing else I could do.

◆ ◆ ◆

To distract myself, I decided the time had come to consider my choices for contacts to make regarding Rudy's case. I don't like making lists, not even for grocery shopping. But making a check-off list of candidates for interviews seemed to be the thing to do. I plunked myself down in my chair, and a horrible realization dawned on me.

If I talked to the wrong person, I'd end up dead.

I'd angered a psycho. Not a good move, to be blunt. Would doing nothing have the same end result as digging around? How could I know? As the old saying goes, damned if you do, and damned if you don't.

Damned if I'd be a coward. And I had to do *something*. That said, I'd never done discovery for a homicide. In fact, I hadn't ever done any kind of discovery for a criminal case. Well, no time like the present to figure out a methodology. And I needed some way to keep track of my thoughts.

For some reason, an old Dorothy Sayers novel I'd enjoyed many years ago came to mind. I'd read it right here in this room, during a series of a rainy days. Peter Wimsey and Harriet Vane, solving a murder. They had some sort of technique they used for sorting facts. They made a chart, or list or something...

Check-off list it was. I sighed. I *hate* lists.

I got up out of the chair and wandered around the perimeter of the room, scanning the bookshelves. Most of the books were older—Millie had taken to e-books with delight when the technology first appeared, and the hardcover library hadn't been updated in quite some time.

At some point in time someone had attempted to put things in a sort of alphabetical order by author. Time and entropy had eroded the system. At last, I found it, Dorothy Sayers, *Have His Carcase*, copyright 1932.

The battered cover featured a rather gory illustration of a hapless victim sprawled across the top of a large boulder, blood streaming out of his body to form a large puddle on the beach below the rock. I winced a bit at the sight of it. It struck a little too close to home.

I paged through the book. Chapter XIII. There. The daring duo made up lists: "Things to be Noted" and "Things to be Done." Peter and Harriet, the brilliant protagonists, always figured things out sooner or later. Would this system work in real life? I sort of doubted it, but what the heck. As I've said before, something beats nothing.

In the book, Harriet said that she started an investigation by focusing on the corpse. I hated to think of my brother as "the corpse." But, what was good enough for Harriet was good enough for me. It's a shame that the poor girl has such godawful taste in men. She seems quite sensible otherwise.

I set up a two-column table in my word processing program. First column, Things to be Noted. I came up with six things to list. Second column, what can be done about those things? I typed in whatever came to mind.

Things to Be Noted	Things to Be Done
1. Apparently found the trap door on the knoll on the day he died.	1. Find out if anyone else knew about it. (a) Like they'd tell me.
2. Must have found the gold because he had a nugget in his pocket. Eureka!	2. Find out if anyone else knew that he had the nugget. (a) Yeah, Sure. Ditto with #1.
3. Apparently killed about 12 hours after he found the gold.	3. I don't know what the hell I can do about that.
4. Was out in the woods when he was killed.	4. Find out if anyone else knew where he was going that night. Good luck.
5. Police say that they investigated the death.	5. Get the police records. Duh. Duh. Duh.
6. Talk to the investigating officer.	6. I already tried that.

Damn. This wasn't working out as well as it did in the book. I added two more lines, the last one blank, in case I thought of anything else.

7. Talk to the police about getting the records. Again.	7. And do something about it this time. Call this Action #1.
8.	8.

Next step, a list for suspects. It seemed like a waste of time. Any list would be like a local version of Six Degrees of Kevin Bacon—Rudy had connections *everywhere*. All the people he knew also had connections, and so on, ad infinitum.

Heck, the murderer might even be someone I'd never met, like that weird old recluse who lived out in the woods someplace, and how the hell would I ever find him? Nope. Not going to work.

I breathed out a whoosh of exasperation, and the hair on my forehead fluttered. Back to item number 5. Getting the records associated with Rudy's case was going to be a royal pain, but it seemed the only available option. As Millie used to say, "If you don't try, you don't get."

A good back-popping stretch is what I needed. I stood up and the book slid out of my grasp, landing upside down on the carpet with a dull thud. I leaned over, picked up the book, and a yellowed piece of paper fluttered out.

I almost balled it up in my fist, thinking it was an old forgotten bookmark. Something made me flip it over. There was a note scrawled on the back, in a more youthful and tidy version of Millie's distinctive handwriting.

Tell Pops that Joe let Spiderlegs borrow the old green book!

Whatever. I hoped Joe got in trouble with Pops, and Spiderlegs, whoever that was, returned the old green book. The note must have been written when Millie was in high school, because her father—called Pops by everyone—had passed away shortly after her high school graduation.

The "Joe" referred to in the note was her older brother, Joaquin. I stuck the note back between the pages, and slid the book back onto the shelf.

I dug my phone out of my pocket and called Drake.

"Hi," I said, surprised that the call hadn't gone straight to voicemail. "I know you must have a million things you need to keep track of, but I was wondering if you'd had a chance to look for the evidence box from Rudy's case."

Drake chuckled. "A million things is just about right. But, yes, the evidence box is still here on the premises."

"Good. That's a relief."

"Not necessarily."

Something about the tone of his voice made my skin crawl. "What do you mean?"

He told me what he'd found in the box.

◆ ◆ ◆

After I'd said goodbye, and disconnected the call, I called Bertie. "You at your house? I need to talk to you. No, nothing awful has happened. See you in a bit."

Dog didn't look happy when I pulled up in front of Bertie's house. He flattened himself down in the bed of the truck, and seemed convinced that he'd become invisible. If a dog could smirk, he was doing it.

"You're a dork, Dog." I scratched his head, turned, and walked up the front steps to the little cottage. Bertie had the front door open in an instant.

"Hey chickie. What's goin' on?" She gathered me into a hug against her squishy body. It was comforting, like being hugged by a teddy bear.

We went inside and trailed though the house into the familiar comfort of the lemon-yellow kitchen. "I need help figuring out some things. You're elected to the figuring-out-stuff-helper-thinker-person position."

"Oooooo. That sounds excitin'." A smile lit up her face. "Do I get an official tee-shirt?"

"Sure." I said. "Got any more of those cinnamon rolls? You do have an endless supply, don't you? No snack, no tee-shirt. I'm playing hardball. 'Obnoxious' is my middle name."

Bertie, hand to chin, momentarily struck a pose like Rodin's *The Thinker*. "You do drive a tough bargain. Hmm..." She straightened up and winked at me. "Okay, you win. They're over there, on the counter, the plate with the foil over the top."

I made a beeline for the counter and lifted the foil.

"You realize that you're committed now," Bertie said. She folded her arms, the very picture of obstinacy. "I want a hot-pink tee-shirt studded with rhinestones, with lace around the neck."

"Deal," I said, the word mushy from talking with my mouth full. "Mmmm. These are *good*. I like the chunks of apple in them better than the raisins."

"Good. Glad you like 'em. I hope you got the one without the arsen... Oops! Now what was I saying? What're we gonna figure out?"

I plopped down at the kitchen table. "I'm not worried about arsenic. I built up an immunity to it the same way I did with the iocaine powder."

Bertie pulled her chair up to the table. "I'll ignore that. What are you goin' to do next about what?"

"Two things. First thing is about the house."

She stuck out her lower lip and chewed on it a bit. "Fine. What about the house?"

She was in such a silly mood I couldn't help smiling. "I'm thinking about making it into a bed-and-breakfast. It's almost all the way there, since Millie fixed up the bedrooms. The upstairs closets are big enough that they could be converted into small bathrooms, and I could put a large armoire in each bedroom to make up for the lack of a closet."

I jumped up, grabbed the notepad and pen that she kept by her telephone, sat back down at the table, and made a rough sketch of how the bedrooms could be reworked. "See?"

Bertie reached across the table for the paper and pensively tapped her fingernail on the table. "Okay. That might work."

I continued explaining my idea. "I'm sure I'll have to have the septic system upgraded to take the extra load of additional showers and so on, but Millie left me enough money that I can do that without taking out a loan. Does all this make sense to you?"

There seemed no point in mentioning that I had more money than I knew what to do with. People generally don't appreciate hearing such things.

Bertie giggled at an apparent new thought. "I guess this means you don't wanna take the California bar and drive old Andrew Pichl outta business. That'd happen about thirty seconds after you hung out your shingle." She tapped her fingernails on the table.

"But seriously, I think I like the idea of a B&B. I don't think you'd have any problem attracting suckers, ah, guests. Your first inmates would all be Western art fans. Oh. Wait a minute. You'd hafta figure out how to keep them from stealin' the art off the walls."

I laughed. "True. No problem, I'll just put up prints. And bolt them to the walls, if necessary. But the jury is still out on passing the bar. I don't see why I can't do both. And Andrew looks to be putting himself out of business. I swear, Millie was probably his only client."

Bertie resumed her chain of thought. "You know, a B&B makes sense. It's a beautiful house. You could fix up the outbuildings. Or leave the old bunkhouse as-is for cheapskates. It would be a lotta work though, day-in and day-out. Are you sure you're up to all that?"

"I'd have to hire a professional housekeeper, that's for sure. And, to tell the truth, I planned on asking you if you want to manage the business end of it, but that was before you told me you got the job at the hospital."

Bertie's mouth dropped open, and then she grinned. "Wow. Lemme think about it. I'm not sure enough about my new job yet. I dunno if I'll have the time or energy to cook the books for you. For now, let's just say I sorta like the idea."

"So you don't think it sounds too crazy?"

"No, not particularly. I'd say go for it. It shouldn't be too hard to figure out how to make a business plan and all that kinda stuff. It seems to me that all you need to do is a little advertisin', and away you go. What was the other thing you wanted to talk about?"

"The second thing is about Rudy."

Bertie drew back her plump chins. "Uh, sweetheart, let me say this as nicely as I can. I don't think there's anythin' that can be done about Rudy. I don't wanna sound harsh, but he's been gone now for quite..."

Bertie's face lit up with a sudden realization. "Wait a minute. I'm sorry. I shoulda known better. Somethin' new's come up, hasn't it."

"Yes. I think so." I stood up and meandered around the kitchen while I considered the best way to explain things. She'd remember it all, wouldn't she?

I leaned back against the white tiled counter. "You know the family wasn't happy with that nonsense about Rudy being the victim of a hit-and-run. I don't know how much you remember of the case, but we never believed it was an accident."

"I remember it quite well," Bertie said with an emphatic jerk of her chins. "Doc was furious with the coroner. I think he woulda tarred and feathered the old nob-head if he'd had half a chance of getting' away with it."

"Good. I mean not good that Doc was mad, but good that you do remember it. That helps." I came back and sat down across from her, mostly to keep myself from eating another cinnamon roll.

"There is no reason on god's green earth why Rudy should have been run down. He wasn't drunk or stoned or anything like that. And back in that forest it's so quiet you can hear the trucks coming a mile away! He went out there all the time. The truckers all knew him. It doesn't make sense."

Bertie leaned back in her chair. "So whadda ya think happened?"

"I think somebody killed him, and then made it look like an accident."

"Oh, c'mon now." Bertie pinched her lips together, like she might be reconsidering her assessment of my mental state. "Someone killed *Rudy?* What in the world for?"

"For things like this." I unfastened the gold nugget necklace from around my neck and set it on the table.

Bertie's eyes widened. She stared at the small chunk of gold for a second, then picked it up and turned it so it gleamed in the light. She fingered its smooth surface and looked back to me. "Go on..."

"Rudy found that. In fact, Rudy found a whole bunch of nuggets right on our property. And he must have shown them to somebody, or somebody was with him when he found the cache. Either way, I think that person decided that those little pieces of gold were an express ticket to the good life. The fact that they were located on my family's property posed a problem, though, so I think that that they killed Rudy before he had a chance to tell us."

Bertie set down the necklace. "How'd you come up with that?"

"Because I found the nuggets, too. Well, first I found a map that Rudy had drawn, and then I found the place where they were hidden. Before that we hadn't a clue why he had a piece of gold in his pocket when he died."

The doubt on Bertie's face vanished.

"Don't worry, it's off the property, all locked up in a safe place now. In any case, I have the time and the inclination to do something about this, so that's what I'm going to do. I'm going to find out who killed Rudy."

"Holy Mother of God. You're not kiddin', are you?"

"You think I'd joke about this?"

Bertie narrowed her eyes, as if she were afraid that I was going to ask her to go snooping around, playing Miss Marple on the trail of a murderer. "And what do you want me to do?"

I reached out and patted her hand. "I just need you to help me think. I thought I'd figured out what I should do, and then realized that what I had in mind was not a good plan. So then a new idea occurred to me, but a problem arose. I need you to help me figure out what I should do next."

"Okay." Her voice wavered.

"So, here's the deal. I thought I'd submit a petition to the County to be allowed to examine the evidence collected by the police when they were investigating Rudy's death. I mentioned that idea to a detective at the police station, and he said he'd have someone go look for the evidence box so he could get an idea of the volume of items involved. They'd have to charge me for copies and such.

"Well, guess what. I just talked to him on the phone a few minutes before I got here. They found the box. But when they pulled it off the shelf and opened it up, the only thing inside was an old Amador County phone book."

Bertie tilted her head as she processed that bit of information. "A phone book? What the heck does a phone book hafta do with anything? And what about the other things that shoulda been in there, Rudy's clothes and such?"

"That, sweet girl," I said, "is exactly the question. The phone book was just in there to add some weight to the box. All the evidence collected when Rudy died is nowhere to be found."

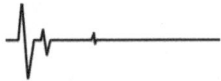

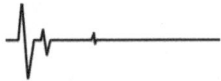

Chapter Twenty-Six

Bertie stared at me. "Holy crap."

"You got that right," I said. "Evidence should not just vanish. If items were destroyed because the case was closed, then there should be a paperwork trail. But there's no directive like that on file. So, now what?"

I padded across the kitchen and grabbed the plate of cinnamon rolls. I offered one to Bertie but she waved them aside.

"Instead of looking for clues regarding only one individual, I need to be looking for clues regarding a rather nasty act of collusion. Because *nobody* should be able to sneak into an evidence locker and make things vanish. And, the fact that more than one person seems to be involved scares the living you-know-what out of me."

"Oh, chickie, honey. I'd be scared too. But that was *years* ago. The police chief is some kinda big deal in State government now, I forget what, and that old creep of coroner is probably dead.

"I'd bet a lotta the others are all retired by now. I mean, I don't think any of those people are gonna pop down to the police station from time to time to ask if anyone's been pokin' around, askin' about an evidence box that's been sitting on a shelf for god knows how long."

"You're right." I stuffed my mouth with another roll. "I don't think the person I'm worried about has any direct ties to the police department, at least not anymore."

Bertie's round-eyed look turned into a thoughtful squint. Her kind, maternal face was etched with concern. "Somethin' tells me that I'm not gonna like what you're about to tell me."

"Yep. You're not going to like this at all, but I have to tell someone." I stopped eating, wiped my mouth with a napkin, and forced a smile. "It's not too late to back out. You just won't get your tee-shirt."

"Nope, can't back out. You committed yourself when you ate the cinnamon rolls."

"All right, then," I said. "Here goes. Millie found the map and the gold too. And that's why she died."

The color drained out of Bertie's face. "Whadda ya mean?" Her voice had gone soft.

"Millie didn't die of natural causes. She was murdered. The police don't want this publicized. That's why the death notice in the paper was sort of vague, and just said, 'passed away unexpectedly at her home,' without any specifics."

Bertie sat there, stock still. I could hear the tick tock of the clock in her front room and the faint twitter of birds outside. Her face had taken on a pale grayish tone.

"Holy Mary, Mother of God," she whispered. "What happened to her?"

I knew I couldn't share that information. Drake had kept things quiet for a reason, and I wasn't about to mess things up for him.

"I didn't get a lot of details because they're still working on the case. Need-to-know, and all that junk. I'll get the full story when they have enough evidence to make an arrest. The one thing that I *do* know is that the cause of death was homicide."

"And you think that the person who killed Millie also killed Rudy?"

I fiddled with the plate holding the rolls, pushing it in little circles. "Yes. Yes, I do. Nothing else makes any sense. I'm guessing they'd dipped their fingers into the gold nugget piggy bank from time to time. They had a good thing going on, sort of like having an unlimited expense account. And then Millie found out about it."

"A serial killer. In Jackson." Bertie's hands were shaking.

"It might be fair to say that. Yes."

"And... And you're the only family member left. You're... next..."

I threw back my head and stared at the ceiling, not wanting to deal with such an awful thought. "No. At least I hope not. The gold is gone now, locked up, so there's nothing to gain by taking me out."

I think I was trying to convince myself more than I was trying to convince Bertie.

"Jesus." Bertie looked at me with horror written across her face. She put her elbows on the table and rested her face in her hands. She looked up, and I could see tears in her eyes.

She reached across the table and took my hands. "Oh, baby girl. You're right. It has to be done. Don't worry. I'll help you. I dunno what I can do right now, but that doesn't matter. I'll help you."

We sat there quite a while, comforting each other, with Rudy's nugget sitting between us, its burnished surface gleaming in the afternoon sunlight.

◆ ◆ ◆

I got home, and there was an email from Greg waiting for me. Well, actually it was addressed to Everyone again, and it was probably sitting in inboxes all over the Jackson Valley. I sighed. Would I ever get a personal message from him?

> Everyone,
> Good morning from the eastern edge of Africa. First of all, I have to assure you that I'm alive and well. It's hard to find a few minutes to write to you, as all of us are busy from the time we get up in the morning to when we collapse on our cots at night.
>
> One thing nice about working for a large international organization is that they have a satellite truck here that allows us to stay in touch with the rest of the world. I'm grabbing a few minutes of time right now, as the sun is just coming up over the horizon.
>
> When I first arrived here, the crush of people flowing into the camp was almost overwhelming. Most of them bore injuries that were not of the type inflicted by war, but were of the type inflicted by a difficult life and extreme poverty. The big crush of people has lessened, but we still have many newcomers arriving daily.
>
> All of the people we see are traumatized in one way or another. Worst of all are the little children with sad, listless faces. They have never had sufficient nutrition, starting before they were born. It is as if they came into this world old and tired. A healthy child should be laughing and smiling. These children are strangely silent. They speak to their mothers in soft whispery voices, as if afraid to draw attention to themselves. At their young age, they already understand the inevitability of death, and seem to be waiting, expecting it to happen at any time.
>
> This job is difficult, but I'm glad to be here. I don't know how much I can help many of these people. Their afflictions are not of the type that can be fixed with a bandage or some antibiotics. The psychological traumas they have suffered are severe. At the very least, however, I can show them some kindness and respect, at least for a few days. They can get showers, clean clothes, and sleep. They need those things as much as the food and medical care.
>
> Please don't worry about me. The combat zone is some distance away, and I'm quite safe here. Best wishes for the New Year to you all.

I stared at his email for a while. There was nothing personal about it at all. No little added note at the end, nothing.

He seemed so far away, on a different planet for all practical purposes. There was twelve hours' time difference between Greg and me. As he sat down to his breakfast, I was thinking about what to fix for dinner. It seemed odd to realize that the sun sinking below the western horizon here was the same one that he could see creeping up into the sky in the east.

How strongly did he feel the pull of home? Impossible to know. People rip up their roots and make a new life for themselves all the time. I'd done it myself.

I let out a long exhale of exasperation. What Greg decided to do would be what Greg decided to do. I didn't get to vote on the matter.

I doodled on a notepad for a while, thinking things over, then typed out a short message to Greg to the effect that I'd decided to open a B&B. News of a B&B seemed so frivolous, so trivial compared to the work he was doing. So, I added an update on his non-profit foundation. I'd gone as far as I could with it, so the paperwork had been passed along to a licensed attorney in San Francisco. And then, after a moment, I decided to mention that I intended to get the investigation into Rudy's death reopened.

It seemed ridiculous to feel the need to include something that showed that I was engaged in "serious" work, too. He hadn't gone to Africa in order to make me feel inadequate.

I sent my email on its way, and hoped he found the emotional healing he sought.

◆ ◆ ◆

Mulled cider weather arrived. The residents of Jackson, for the most part, looked forward to winter, relishing the bite in the air that served as a harbinger of the second of the two annual tourist seasons. Skiers heading up the mountain sprinkle fistfuls of dollars here and there, buying gasoline, food, and lodging. The whole town benefits in the long run.

The Christmas holidays are quite profitable, most years anyway. While others around me seemed to bubble with anticipation, I felt a twinge of the bittersweet nostalgia that the holidays can bring to those who are alone.

My mood was moderated a bit by the hope that next year's winter would be quite different from this one. It had to be. My sanity demanded it.

I didn't want to even consider leaving Jackson, after having decided to stand my ground, and there was no use in fretting over bad things that might never happen. No. I would do my best to think about the future with optimism. The only way to move forward was to just do it.

I ordered a copy of Rudy's autopsy report from the office of the

County medical examiner. It finally showed up mid-January in yet another plump manila envelope in my post office box. I'd developed a small phobia about large envelopes, and was weak-kneed with relief when I saw that the envelope bore the Amador County seal.

I hadn't gotten any more hateful mail since that last envelope that I took to Drake. Had my mysterious tormentor decided to make a strategic retreat? I wanted to believe that. But my logical self said, "fat chance of that, sweetheart."

I sat down at home with the envelope and girded myself for the unpleasant information that I was sure to find inside. I took one quick glance at the autopsy report. That was enough to convince me that studying it was something that I shouldn't do alone.

Lacerations, ruptured organs, fractures... I thanked every god that ever existed that I hadn't ordered copies of the photos.

The following Saturday morning, Dog and I went back to Bertie's house. In the kitchen, I handed Bertie a tissue-wrapped bundle. The bundle held Bertie's decorated pink tee-shirt, but the lighthearted silliness that I assumed would accompany the gifting wasn't there. It seemed that both of us were dreading what came next.

We sat down at the kitchen table. I shoved Bertie's copy of the report across the table to her.

She pulled the docs from the envelope gingerly, as if afraid the words might bite her. "Ah... before we get started on this, I got a question for you, chickie."

"Sure. What's up?"

"Well, uh, last time you were here you mentioned that you think that Rudy's death and Millie's death are tied together somehow."

"Yeah. And?"

Bertie's plump fingers fidgeted with the stack of papers. "Well, you're not gonna make me read Millie's autopsy report too, are you?"

"Oh, hell no. Apples and oranges. I have zero desire to see her autopsy report. And I wasn't invited to do so anyway. The police know what happened, and that's all that matters at this point.

"Rudy's case is a different animal entirely. It was closed, so someone has to poke around and ask questions. The police aren't going to mess with it unless there's a good reason." Something about the tone of Bertie's voice bothered me, though. "Why?"

"Just askin'. No reason in particular. I guess it's because it's so soon."

Now, that I could agree with. I nodded, picked up my copy, and read.

```
SUBJECT: Rudy D'Angelo
The body is that of a normally developed, well-nourished
Caucasian male of normal weight. Physical characteristics
appear to be consistent with the reported age of 16+ years.
The body length is 189.42 cm and the weight is 75.4 kg. The
body is well preserved in the absence of embalming. Lividity
is anterior and fixed. Rigidity is complete.

The scalp is covered by curly dark brown hair up to
approximately 9 cm in length. The irides are dark brown and
the corneae are clear. The head, neck, chest, abdomen and
extremities are normal and unremarkable in formation, with
the exception of areas of significant bone and soft tissue
damage, described below.
```

I found it difficult to read the report, to see every detail of the injuries done to my wonderful Rudy described in cold, technical language. More than ever, I was glad that I hadn't requested copies of the autopsy photos. Feeling sickened and overwhelmed, I skipped to the end of the document.

```
SUMMARY OF FINDINGS:
a) Depressed parietal skull fracture with intracranial hemorrhage
b) Blunt force trauma of torso and extremities, consistent with
   being struck and run over by a motor vehicle.
c) Multiple rib, sternal and spinal fractures with:
      i.    Transection of aorta
     ii.    Cardiac laceration
    iii.    Pulmonary contusions
     iv.    Hepatic and splenic laceration
      v.    Thoracic spinal cord laceration
d) Multiple comminuted fractures of lower extremities.
e) Minor facial abrasions, lacerations and contusions.
```

"Bertie, do you need a break?" I sure needed one.

"Yeah." Despite her years of working with medical documentation, it was obvious from her pallid complexion that she felt more than a bit ill.

I put my hand on top of hers. "Tell you what, put it away for now. I can't take any more either. You can go back to it later, if you want to. If you can't... you can't. No problem."

Bertie sighed. "Thanks, chickie. I've read autopsy reports before, but this one is just brutal. I don't think I can read it again."

"Me either. And I'm not sure that this is telling me anything that I didn't already know. I'll have to think about a Plan B. Or C. Or... something else."

We set aside the documents. Both of us were quiet, and in no frame of mind for idle chitchat, so I gave Bertie a hug, and went home.

◆ ◆ ◆

My unsettled mood persisted long after I got back to my house. I sat down at the kitchen table with the copy of the autopsy report. I stared at the envelope, and a terrible, frightening realization exploded in my brain.

I tossed the envelope on the kitchen table, jumped up, and ran into the office. I pulled open the drawer that held the folder with all the paperwork regarding Rudy's death. I dumped the papers on the rug, flopped down on my knees, and pawed through them with frantic haste.

There! I smoothed flat the photocopy of the autopsy findings that I'd seen before. On the older paper, the list of findings was shorter, and limited to those found on the torso. The head, facial, and lower extremity injuries had been omitted from the copy that my family was given. My memory hadn't failed me or played evil tricks on my emotions.

Why didn't I notice this obvious inconsistency the first time I looked at the older copy? Both copies of the document contained the words, "Blunt force trauma of torso and extremities..."

Extremities. The limbs of a body, mentioned nowhere else in the documents given to my family at the time of Rudy's death. The incongruity should have jumped right off the page and done a dance for me.

Was I looking at a smoking gun, or was this only a casual mistake done by a harried clerical worker?

In my heart of hearts, I knew the answer. This couldn't be a careless error. No way.

And then there was the matter of the skull fracture. I carried the older document back to the kitchen, and set the two copies side by side. Any lingering doubts vanished. The blob of correction fluid on the family copy was placed in a precise spot, to disguise the location of the injury.

Why in the world would the police department alter the document and provide the family with incomplete and misleading information? It struck me that I knew someone who would be able to tell me if the deleted information had any significance.

I grabbed my laptop and pounded out an email to Africa.

> Greg,
> I know that you are up to your ass with problems and traumas. Nevertheless, I'm going to ask a favor of you. Attached is Rudy's autopsy report. I would appreciate it if you could look it over for me. I'm not looking for a translation of the language. What I care about is your expert opinion regarding the big picture. Is there something in this report that waves a red flag, or does not make sense? I trust your opinion in this area more than I trust the opinion of anybody else.
>
> There's no rush to my request. It's been a long time since Rudy died, so a few more weeks won't make any difference one way or another.

Stay safe. I love you.

That evening a reply came back.

Sure. I know how important this is to you.
G.

I didn't expect to see anything further for at least a week, but another email came within thirty-six hours. I'd been hoping that he would respond to the "I love you," but he didn't. Maybe he didn't know how to interpret it. Maybe... I had no idea what to think.

Allie,
I've read the report and thought about it for a bit. The thing that caught my attention right away was the extent of the injuries. Something doesn't add up. If I'm remembering correctly, you said that it was assumed that a logging truck hit Rudy. The severity of the injuries supports the supposition that he was run over by a very heavy vehicle. That kind of truck has a very wide wheelbase, wider than Rudy was tall. I looked it up. According to the report, Rudy was 6'1". If he was accidentally hit, knocked down and run over, the injuries should be in just one basic band or pathway, either his upper body or his lower body, *but not both.* But his chest was crushed *and* his leg bones were fractured. I hate to say this, but it looks to me that he was run over more than one time.

I read those words, "run over more than one time", and a sickening realization settled over me. Greg's conclusion had to be right. Perhaps this was what had bothered me about the report. The injuries were too darned extensive to be the result of a simple bump-and-run. But how could such a thing have happened?

Was there more than one truck on the road? A convoy? No, that was a ridiculous thought. If he was run over by multiple trucks, the injuries would have been even worse.

Also, the skull fracture is very odd. The impact point is towards the top of his head. The location is not consistent with being run over while stretched out on the ground, as his other injuries indicate. It is also a relatively small fracture in terms of area, and reminds me of the type sometimes seen if someone is hit on the head with a hard object such as a hammer or a rock. I saw a few examples of that type of injury when I worked emergency in LA, and the resulting fracture is pretty distinctive.

How... strange. If Rudy had hit his head on something in the road, the injury wouldn't be on the top of his head. I didn't like the direction my thoughts took. An injury that looked like it came from a blow to the head...

Rudy was struck, deliberately, before he fell? I had to stop for a moment and take a deep breath before I could continue reading.

> And, something else is odd that you might not have even noticed. There was a piece of glass embedded in Rudy's right cheek. That's probably the side of his face that hit the ground the hardest, as it had more embedded dirt and abrasions than the other side. He must have fallen on some broken glass. There is a description of the embedded fragment in the report – it's reported as a narrow, triangular, sharply pointed shard of clear glass about a half-inch long, with smooth sharp edges. If that glass had been in the roadway for any length of time, it would have been abraded, and the tip broken off.

I hadn't noticed that detail at all. And, like Greg, I was sure that the glass must mean something. But what? Was the shard from a broken headlight on the truck?

Without the photos from the autopsy, there was no way to know what the piece of glass looked like. And I really had no idea if headlamp glass would shatter into a neat triangle.

I shifted in my chair, and found myself rubbing the back of my neck. The questions kept multiplying, like the water-carrying brooms in *The Sorcerer's Apprentice*. Would I end up overwhelmed, drowning, just like the hapless Apprentice?

> I'll go back and read the report again in a few days, and see if anything else jumps out at me.
>
> Right now, I think we can classify the circumstances associated with this death as 'suspicious.'
>
> Greg

I sat and stared at the final sentence for a long time.

Chapter Twenty-Seven

The following Monday morning, I had another brief phone conversation with Drake. I hoped he'd called to talk about the evidence box. But no. He just wanted to tell me that the lost-and-found advertisement for the ring found in the dirt had yielded no leads. That news was hardly a surprise.

Then, he said, "We got the report from the insurance company that investigated the fire that destroyed the Mercedes. It was definitely arson. Traces were found of an accelerant."

"So, what do you think?" I asked. "Was the fire connected to me, because someone thought I still owned the car? Or was it connected to Robin and Larry? Or... something else?"

"I honestly think that the car fire had nothing to do with you. They'd had the car long enough that it should have been obvious that it wasn't yours any more. Trying to scare you by burning up a car that had the license plate changed and in someone else's possession for several weeks doesn't make sense."

"True," I said. "Do you think there's some kind of insurance scam going on then? It seems sort of silly to risk burning up your house to get a few bucks out of a car."

"Let's just say that the insurance company is still looking into the matter."

He wasn't willing or able to share anything further than that.

As far as I was concerned, his lack of commentary equaled a big fat "Bingo." If Robin and Larry were found to be running a scam, it wouldn't surprise me at all. I'd pegged Larry for what he really was a long time ago. *Slimebucket.*

I didn't bring up Rudy's autopsy report or the email from Greg. The two versions of the autopsy report were not enough to reopen Rudy's case. The disparity could be explained away as nothing more than a careless mistake. The whole situation was damned frustrating, but that wasn't Drake's problem.

"Well," I said, winding up the call, "thanks for the update. I sure appreciate all you're doing."

"No problem. Talk to you later." He disconnected the call.

◆ ◆ ◆

As I stood at the kitchen counter, pouring myself a cup of coffee, Dog's fierce barking alerted me to the arrival of a stranger. It must be the plumbing contractor. I'd asked him to check out the feasibility of adding the bathrooms upstairs—he'd said he'd drop by in a day or so.

I peeked out the window and was astonished to see Gordon Sunderland get out of a metallic green pickup truck. He stood still, allowing the bristling and cautious Dog to sniff his hands. He was clearly a man comfortable with animals, as he didn't seem to be at all intimidated by Dog's dramatic display of faux ferocity.

I hurried over to the kitchen door and opened it. I didn't want to assume that the ferocity would be always faux.

"Dog! Enough. Good boy!"

Dog's head popped up, and he glanced in my direction. He stopped barking and trotted off to his inner sanctum in the barn.

Sunderland walked over and shook my hand. He gestured towards the barn. "That's a darned fine dog you've got there, Ms. D'Angelo. He knows what his job is."

"Why, thank you, sir. I'm afraid that I can't take credit for training him, though. He trained himself. And please, call me Alexandra. Come on in. I just made some fresh coffee. Care for some?"

Sunderland accepted the offer with a small nod of the head, and a quiet "Thanks." He stepped in the door and pulled off his baseball cap. By the way he wadded it up and clenched it in his hand, I guessed that he felt a bit nervous.

We sat down at the kitchen table, sipped our coffee, and chatted about the weather, the house, and the intrinsic value of good dogs.

Having exhausted all other topics, he sat back in his chair. He rubbed the side of his face. "I think you know why I'm here. I've been thinking about things ever since you stopped by. You need to know that I consider Rudy's case my biggest failure."

His statement startled me. "But..."

Sunderland held up his hands to wave off my protests. "Yes, I remember what you told me the other day. Nevertheless, I consider this my failure, but not for the reasons that you might assume. There were things that happened in conjunction with that investigation that were just flat *wrong*.

There were things that happened that were illegal." He paused. "And that has weighed on my mind for years."

The poor man looked tired, drawn. I reached out and placed a hand on one of his. He was trembling. The stress of telling me all this must have been awful.

"My biggest mistake was my decision to refrain from doing the right thing," he said. "I turned a blind eye... No, I have to be honest with you. I did more than turn a blind eye. I was guilty of complicity. I aided and abetted. And now the pigeons have come home to roost."

I stared at him in shock. I couldn't think of a single thing to say.

"It was made quite clear to me that, if I didn't cooperate, there would be a steep price to pay. You have to understand that, at that time, my kids were in college, and my wife was undergoing treatment for breast cancer.

"I couldn't afford to lose my job and my health insurance. I knew full well that I made a deal with the devil, so to speak, but I did it anyway. And I've had to live with that fact. The time has come for me to make things right. I've talked to my wife about it, and she knows what I'm doing."

If I understood him correctly, this man held the keys to solving Rudy's murder. But, in revealing what he knew, he risked going to jail himself. He'd handed me the power to ruin his life. The realization made me nauseous.

I struggled to pull my thoughts together. "The evidence box?"

"Yes. From that I assume that you have already asked to see the contents."

"Correct."

"Right after the case was closed, I was ordered to destroy the contents of the box. I did so."

My nausea got worse, and my hands felt clammy. I looked down at the tabletop, not daring to meet his eyes. I didn't want him to see the sharp disappointment that was surely written across my face.

Beyond that, I really didn't know anything about him. I didn't know how to judge his words.

He seemed wracked with guilt, that much was very clear. I *wanted* to trust him, but there were still too many questions yet unanswered. And, I had yet to understand why he'd come to see me.

"I also made this. Just in case."

Sunderland pushed a piece of paper across the table. "I had it notarized when we were on vacation the following summer, because I didn't dare have it done around here."

I picked it up. It was a copy of a document, dated about a year after Rudy's death. I was surprised to see that it was written on an old-fashioned typewriter. But then, of course, doing so guaranteed that no electronic record of it existed anywhere.

I glanced up at him. "You're sure you want to do this?"

He inclined his head, in a gesture of permission to proceed, so I started to read.

1. My name is Gordon Edward Sunderland. I live on a private access road locally known as Sunderland Ranch Road, which runs southwest from Stony Creek Road to approximately one mile due east of Lake Amador. I am presently employed as a Detective by the Jackson-Martell Police Department. I have been employed by the Police Department for over fifteen years.

2. Over the course of several months ending approximately one year prior to the date of this document, I served as the primary investigator in the death of one Rudy D'Angelo, age 16, who died of injuries sustained after apparently being struck by a large motor vehicle.

3. It was my responsibility to acquire information, evidence and artifacts related to the death of Rudy D'Angelo. All evidence and related artifacts for this case were stored in a standard evidence box in the Jackson-Martell Police Department evidence room.

I stopped right there, and almost asked him what was in the box, but decided that my question was premature. I hadn't read the whole document yet.

4. At the conclusion of the investigation, the death of the victim was declared to be a result of an accident, and the D'Angelo case was officially closed. This was done despite the existence of evidence indicating that the death was the result of a purposeful assault.

Purposeful assault? I drew in a deep breath. I glanced up at Sunderland, but he was studying the painting of the roses that hung over the old bricked-up fireplace. My focus flew back to the paper in front of me.

5. At the time that the case was closed, I was directed by Ralph Ivan Ewing, Chief of Police, Jackson-Martell Police Department, to destroy all documents and pieces of evidence related to the death of Rudy D'Angelo. This directive was contrary to the established Police Department policy of preserving evidence related to violent, suspicious, or accidental deaths for a minimum of fifteen years following the closure of the case.

6. Most of these pieces of evidence consisted of items, such

> as the victim's clothing, that conform to the department's standard list of items to be collected at a crime scene (see attached). I destroyed these items as directed, via incineration, following standard protocols.

Everything. Destroyed. It had been too much to hope for another outcome. A strained heaviness descended on my shoulders.

> 7. Some items were preserved, as I could not in good conscience allow them to be destroyed.

I must have gasped, or made some sort of audible noise. I glanced up, and saw Sunderland watching me. He made a rolling "keep going" gesture with his index finger.

> a. Copies of my original notes, and copies of whatever investigative documents I could easily locate, and without drawing attention to my actions.
>
> b. A handwritten statement by an individual who claimed to have witnessed the death of Rudy D'Angelo. This individual stated that Rudy D'Angelo was in fact deliberately assaulted and left to die. The statement included the names of the individuals whom the witness believed to be the perpetrators of the crime.

A witness statement! I couldn't believe what I'd just read. I had to go back and look at the words a second time. Eyes wide, I glanced up at Sunderland. His lips were curved upwards in a very small smile. My attention again flew back to the paper before me.

> 8. These items are stored in a location known only to myself. I have prepared written instructions to my wife and children directing them to, at the time of my death, turn over these two items to the Office of the California State Attorney General.

Gordon E Sunderland

Gordon E. Sunderland

William J. Fennimore

Notary Public

The documents in front of me simultaneously held the burning light of hope and the dense, impenetrable darkness of nightmares. If Sunderland's statement was accurate, then individuals within the police department had, with deliberate actions, turned a blind eye to justice and broken their vows to uphold the rule of law.

My hands were shaking worse than Sunderland's. I set down the photo and looked over at his troubled face. "Oh dear god," I whispered.

He nodded. He seemed to be looking clear through to the heart of me, into my soul. It seemed to me that he knew that my perceptions of everything related to Rudy's death had just shifted from being supposition to being truth.

Rudy *was* murdered. And the circumstances of Rudy's death had the potential to cast a shadow far beyond the reaches of the Jackson Valley, all the way into the upper echelons of California State government.

Because the present Attorney General of the State of California was none other than Ralph Ivan Ewing, former police chief of the Jackson-Martell Police Department.

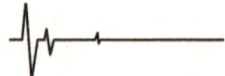

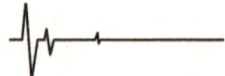

Chapter Twenty-Eight

Long after Gordon Sunderland left, I sat and stared at the copy of the notarized document. I felt sick. I had the power to send a decent man to jail. What a sickening, horrible thought. The more I dwelled on it, the worse the situation seemed. Would whistleblower protection laws shield him? I had no idea.

My heart screamed at me to trust the man. Officer Sunderland had been good to my family during that unbearable time following Rudy's death, when our world had collapsed. He was kind, calm, steady, and reassuring. He provided us with as much information as he could.

Now, looking at him through the lens of our recent interactions, he seemed like a darned nice guy, the sort of person that anyone would want as a friend.

Yes, he'd fallen off the path of justice, but it's hard to fault a man who is only trying to protect his family. He was not seeking power or riches. He was coerced, pushed into doing something that he did not want to do. And he was wracked with guilt. That had to count for something.

Didn't it?

Yes. Coercion did count for something. None of us can know how we will react to an impossible situation until we find ourselves in the middle of it. And, to be blunt, Sunderland was my only hope. In showing me the notarized document, he'd put himself in real jeopardy. The document left no doubt that he was deeply embedded in the fabric of a conspiracy.

Yet, he trusted me. I had to trust him, at least for now.

The document held much more than a confession of Gordon Sunderland's sins. Here in front of me was apparent evidence of serious past malfeasance by the State Attorney General, California's "Top Cop." Ewing's sins were far more egregious than those of Gordon Sunderland. Ewing was the instigator of the evil that had been done.

My family had long suspected that there'd been a cover-up. I never dreamed that unearthing the truth might have such dramatic and far-reaching consequences. Poor Sunderland must have been having nightmares ever since I showed up at his property.

The immediate question that came to mind was almost too awful to contemplate. While the Top Cop is watching over all of us, who is watching over the Top Cop?

Good question. The normal checks and balances of government and law were probably codified somewhere, but why would anyone worry about the integrity of a person with such a stellar reputation? The man was widely admired.

Could Sunderland be lying to me? I doubted it. Doing so would yield no benefit to him. Sunderland's document rang true.

A scalding hot potato had landed right in my lap. I wasn't sure how to handle it without getting burned. Ralph Ewing had risked his entire police career to shield someone who was guilty of murder. Why? He had to have a very powerful motive.

By virtue of his position in state government, Ewing was a powerful man. If I went around asking questions, sooner or later he would hear about it. And then what? I was nobody, from nowhere. I'd be squashed like a bug on a windshield.

Damn it all. Windshield, here I come.

I got to my feet, picked up my copy of Sunderland's statement, and scanned it. I saved the file to my computer and to my flash drive. I grabbed my truck keys and stepped outside.

Dog, alerted by the metallic clinking of the keychain, ran for the truck. We drove into Jackson, and I placed the original copy in my safe deposit box.

◆ ◆ ◆

Instead of going back home, or to Demetra's, I found myself driving to the large quiet park located right off Hwy 49, at the north end of town. I needed to think, and the park was the perfect place to do so.

It was quiet and peaceful there in winter, with dormant lawns and leafless trees. There would be few visitors to break the stillness of a cold Monday morning.

Make that no human there to disturb my thoughts. Dog whined and poked me with his nose after we got out of the truck. I had Dog's old tennis ball jammed in my jacket pocket, but I was in no mood to run around.

Seeing that his efforts weren't working, he gave up the siege and wandered off to investigate the surrounding smorgasbord of interesting smells.

Keeping an eye on Dog's whereabouts, I walked across the grounds.

The dead grass crunched under my feet, and the odor of mud and decaying vegetation wafted up from each footstep. I sat down on a wooden bench, huddled further into my jacket, and stared at the bare trees that were almost skeletal against the winter sky.

In the summer, the park vibrated with the delighted shrieks of children enjoying the swimming pool or chasing each other around the huge lawns. But now the place seemed dead, drained of life just as the pool was drained of water. My own natural optimism was also emptied from my body. I was contemplating an intractable mess, a puzzle with no solution.

A large something bumped into me, and I gasped. But it was only Dog. He settled into the dead grass at my feet, and I reached down and scratched his head.

I stroked the fur behind Dog's ears, and dug into my stored memories of long-ago civics courses. There is, of course, a system of checks and balances in state government, but I could only recall the basics of how it worked.

Then I realized an essential truth. I was looking in the wrong place. The crimes Ralph Ewing committed—allegedly committed—had not taken place during his tenure as Attorney General. These crimes were committed years ago. The crime was a local matter, not a State matter. At least for now.

Dog nudged my feet. I got up and threw his tennis ball as far as I could. I watched my furry friend bound away after it, then frantically sniff around at a bush when he lost track of it. He glanced up at me, as if he suspected some sort of foul plot, and went back to searching.

Keeping half an eye on Dog, I allowed my thoughts to run wild. Since Ewing's crimes were committed here in Jackson, was this a matter for the Amador County Grand Jury? Maybe. But, in order to secure an indictment, convincing evidence would have to be presented. And the evidence that I had in my possession would condemn Gordon Sunderland.

I wouldn't do that to the man, *couldn't* do it. True, he voluntarily opened himself to risk by showing the document to me, but still... The man deserved a medal for his courage in coming forward, not a bullet in the back.

And why shouldn't such a thing happen? Even if Ewing had not killed Rudy himself, he certainly was no innocent lamb. If he could close his eyes to a murder then, he could close his eyes to a murder now.

Dog found the ball, came barreling back across the park, and dumped the slimy thing on the top of my shoe. I picked it up and hurled it in another direction, and Dog was off after it again. I wiped my hand off on my pants. Not that it would stay clean very long with Dog already on a return trip back to me.

And then there was that thing about the witness. I'd have to think about that one. Who in the world would be out roaming around the forest in the middle of the night? One of the truck drivers? That seemed unlikely. They did their daily job, and then they went home.

And, if I did figure out who the witness might be, would I be putting them in jeopardy by the mere act of contacting them?

I threw my head back and stared at the sky. Far above me, three large dark birds rode the morning thermal updrafts. Good god. The vultures were already circling. I closed my eyes.

My cell phone rang, causing my body to flinch in startled surprise. I looked down at the name on the display.

DAVID DE LEON

A bolt of lightning struck my brain. *Holy shit*. Here was the answer! A small flicker of hope ignited in my heart. David just might be the one person in America who could smash this case wide open.

I switched my brain to Social Mode and hit the "talk" icon on my phone. "Hey David! Are you in town?"

Dog came charging back at me and ran into my leg. I almost dropped the phone. He flopped down at my feet and lay there, panting, with a big grin on his face.

David's familiar voice answered. "Close enough. We're staying at the old Hotel Léger in Mokelumne Hill, hoping to see one of the famous ghosts. There's too much dissension on the home front right now to stay with my mom and dad. The hotel's crying ghost can't hold a candle to the daily drama provided by my mom."

Well, I thought, that was certainly the truth. His mom would slap a wandering spirit upside the head and tell it to buzz off. And then go right back to tearing into David over his choice of future wife.

I sighed with exasperation at the woman. "You're kidding. She's *still* on your case about finding yourself a nice Mexican girl?"

"Yep. You'd think she would have gotten the hint by now. I'm hoping our visit will open her eyes a bit. But, in any case, Yasmine and I would like to treat you to dinner tonight here at the hotel. How's that sound to you?"

"Fantastic. I love that place, and I'm dying to meet this paragon of womanhood who's crazy enough to consider marrying you. I can tell her all your secrets, like that time in junior high when..."

David cut me off with a screech of mock indignation. "Christ! Not that! Cut me some slack here, would ya? Some things should remain secrets forever, or at least until after the wedding. I've got her completely faked out, so don't blow it now. How 'bout you meet us in the bar around 7:30?"

I could hear Yasmine laughing in the background. I liked her already. "Sounds good to me. I plan on ordering the most expensive thing on the menu, so I hope your platinum card isn't overextended. See you then!"

I rounded up Dog and headed home, buoyed by a feeling of rising optimism. Maybe, at last, I'd found a way to fight back. It was about time.

◆ ◆ ◆

I got to the hotel a bit early, and made my way to the bar. I caught the eye of the barman, and when he approached, I said, "I'd like a glass of pinot grigio."

He shook his head, and said, "No, you don't."

I said, with real curiosity and only a touch of aggravation, "I don't? And why is that?"

He sighed, and with a friendly but worn-down expression on his face, said, "Because I don't have an open bottle. And nobody else is going to order any, for god-only-knows how long. And, after a couple of days, I'll have to pour it down the drain. That's why."

And there it was, again. Life in a small town. "Oh," I said. "In that case, I'll have a glass of whatever white wine you have open that comes reasonably close."

In New York, I would have gone through the roof. No. Wait. That' not true. In New York, this whole episode would have never happened.

The barman poured me a glass of chardonnay from a local vineyard, and I turned to lean against the bar to wait for my friends. I took a sip. The wine was on the dry side, crisp, and surprisingly good.

In only a moment or two, David and Yasmine walked through the door. It seemed to me, that his good looks were slightly different than they were years ago. I hadn't noticed that when I'd seen him at the auction.

I finally figured out what was different about him, but decided not to ask what had happened to the bump that used to be on the bridge of his nose. Ah, the pressures of commercial television. If Yasmine ever saw any old photos of him, she'd figure it out. Maybe she already had.

I didn't know yet if David remained the mischievous guy that I'd known in high school, or if success had gone to his head. After all, he'd been called up to the major leagues, so to speak, and that fact alone would be enough to bloat an ego. I hoped that the good guy who'd been a true friend to Rudy and me was still alive inside him.

David saw me, and his face lit up with a big grin. "Hey Allie!" He gave me a big hug. "I'd like you to meet the wonderful Yasmine, love of my life."

She was slender, and her exotic good looks spoke of Middle Eastern heritage. The two of them made me think of George and Amal Clooney, if both of the Clooneys were in their early thirties. The young woman stepped forward, grinned, and extended her hand.

David looked at Yasmine with obvious love and pride in his eyes. "We met at work. Yasmine had a position as one of the writers at the television station, but she jumped ship to go to New York with me. I think they're going to miss her more than they're going to miss me."

"Too true," Yasmine said. "The writers are the ones with the brains, you know." She nudged him in the side with her elbow, and turned and winked at me. "He's just the pretty-boy talking head."

David grinned at her and rolled his eyes.

The *maître d'* showed the three of us into the dining room. We settled down to a luscious dinner. David dug into a big ribeye steak, Yasmine went for the colorful vegetarian ratatouille, but I had the best of the lot—jumbo tiger prawns sautéed in brown butter with bacon and chives. It was to die for.

"How long are you going to be in town?" My question sounded quite innocuous, but was far from it.

"We'll be here for a bit," said David. "I don't need to show up in New York until the first of February. We thought we'd stick around here for a week or so, and then if my parents show no signs in budging, we'll go ahead and drive up to Stateline as planned and get married without them. We're keeping the ceremony small. Yasmine's parents will be there, and her brothers, and that'll be that."

His parents' unwillingness to accept Yasmine as his choice of wife was far from a surprise to me. They'd never understood what made David tick. Hence, his habit of seeking refuge at Millie's house. Some things never do change, and one of them was his mom's intransigence.

After a few more minutes of discussion regarding the plans for their wedding, I decided to go for it. "You feel like doing a bit of work while you're here?"

David's eyes widened. His old inquisitiveness was still there, alive and well. "What do you have in mind?"

"Something that will blow your new bosses' socks off. Might as well start your job off with a bang. If you can come up to my house some time, I'll brew you up a cup of coffee and tell you a story that'll frizz your hair."

"Sure," said David. "Sounds... intriguing." He'd practically come on point, like a bird dog. Thank heavens.

I glanced over at Yasmine. She didn't look the least bit put out, and seemed to understand that this wasn't an invitation for a social call. This was work. Nevertheless, I felt a need to let her know that I didn't intend for her to feel excluded. Anyone important to David was important to me.

I leaned across the table. "Since you'll be in town for at least a few weeks, you'll have to come by some time and see where David spent about half his life when we were in high school. And I can show you pictures of what he looked like in the seventh grade before he had orthodontia."

The subject under discussion moaned and put his head down on his arms. "Alexandra! Not before the orthodontia!" He turned his head towards Yasmine. "My teeth looked like they belonged to a demented woodchuck."

David had held down minimum wage jobs during high school, not to buy a used car, as many teenage boys dream of doing, but to have his teeth straightened. He wanted to be in television journalism, and already realized that in the world of mass media, appearances may not be everything, but they had to be agreeable enough to get you in the door. The man's tenacity was legendary—he had shown that drive early on.

I could imagine David's career to-do list. Teeth. *Check.* Nose. *Check.* Dual degree in journalism and mass communications, with honors, from prestigious university. *Check.*

Yasmine's eyes were sparkling with laughter. "Oooo, this I gotta see! Say when, and I'll be there."

David straightened up, threw back his head, and sighed. "I'm doomed. Yasmine will never look at me the same way again."

"Don't worry, honey." She patted David's hand. "I already know that deep inside, you're just a dweeb."

Choking back a giggle, I dug in my purse for the envelope I'd brought and pushed it across the table.

Earlier that evening, after I'd finished getting dressed, I'd printed out a copy of Gordon Sunderland's notarized statement. I then dug around in the desk drawer for a nice new felt marker and blacked out all references to names, including that of the police department. I flipped the paper over and ran the marker over the same areas on the backside. Then I took a ballpoint pen and scribbled tiny loops and crosshatches on top of the marked-out areas.

The incriminating names couldn't be read, even when the paper was held up to a very bright light. That was the least I could do to protect Sunderland, and David was free to show the docs to his bosses. I'd also made copies of the two different versions of the autopsy findings.

"Don't open it now. Read it when you get back to your hotel room," I said. "And then lock it in the safe. Let me know how you feel about digging into it."

David's eyes widened with surprise at the mention of the safe. He reached over and took the envelope from me, and stuck it in an inside pocket of his sports coat.

"I'd love to see the old place again. Yasmine is supposed to go shopping with my mom tomorrow, and, if that actually happens, I think it would be best if I didn't tag along. I'll call you when I know what's going on. Right now, it's still pretty much up in the air."

◆ ◆ ◆

The next morning David arrived at my house about ten. He had a big grin on his face. "Damn, but it's good to be here again! Well, the ladies did take off to go shopping. Yasmine promised me that she would be sure to love anything that my mother loved. It'll be interesting to hear how *that* worked out." He rolled his eyes, anticipating, I had no doubt, a debacle.

"Yasmine's a sensible person and knows how to compromise, but believe me, she's nobody's doormat. This will either be the beginning of the beginning or the end of the end." He sighed. "You know my mom..."

I gave him a sympathetic smile and went to grab the coffee pot.

David made himself comfortable in one of the green kitchen chairs and ran his hands across the tabletop, as if reacquainting himself with an old friend. "Man, this is great. Just like old times."

I poured us each a generous mug-full, and we spent a few minutes discussing how things were going with his parents. David pulled the envelope out of his pocket, extracted the contents and set them in front of him on the table.

"This," he said, thumping the stack of papers with the back of his hand, "is dangerous stuff."

"You got that right," I said, "and the more I think about it, the scarier it seems to me. If you don't want to have anything to do with it, I won't be upset."

That wasn't true, not by a long shot, but I wasn't about to pile on the guilt. I couldn't blame him for not wanting to beta-test a guillotine.

"No, no, don't get me wrong. I guess I was just stating the obvious. I'm definitely interested. And I think my new bosses will be interested. This is just the sort of thing that'll get them salivating.

"And, since I'll be living in New York, I won't be in close proximity to anyone who happens to get pissed off. Assuming, that is, that the bosses give it the green light."

"Honestly," I said, "I don't know how they will be able to resist it. 'Man who apparently covered up a monstrous crime now sits in a position of power in California State Government.' Can't get much juicier than that."

"No question about it. But they don't know me—I'm still unproven in the eyes of the honchos. And you know the New York elite think that they are the most intelligent beings on the planet."

"Good lord, yes. I've seen that species before. But, if they do approve the project, you have to make sure they understand that there is, at the least, one witness who will need to be protected, possibly two."

Even though the network was well-known for its careful investigative journalism, I was not about to let Sunderland be thrown under the bus. Ditto for the mystery witness, if that person could be found.

"Won't be a problem. They have a good track record in that area."

I was hugely relieved and happy that David was willing to stick his neck out. The outcome of our chat was all that I'd hoped it would be. We agreed that when he had tentative approval, and his bosses had assured absolute confidentiality, he'd let me know.

Hopefully, my documentation would be enough for the television execs to give David the green light. If it appeared that he stood on solid ground, so to speak, then he would have to provide full disclosure to his bosses. That was fine with me. There was no other way to get the job done.

We killed a full pot of coffee and talked for over two hours. When David left, his envelope also held a copy of Greg's email regarding the autopsy report, minus Greg's name and other identifying information.

As I watched David drive away, I was on top of the world. I'd found myself my own personal storm-trooper. But, he could only do so much. It was up to me to convince Sunderland to trust a stranger.

And maybe, by some miracle, I'd figure out the identity of the mystery witness.

◆ ◆ ◆

I wandered into my office and snuggled down in the chair. I opened my laptop to check my email. A new message from someone named SJ Hunter awaited me at the top of the inbox. *S. J. Hunter?* Greg's dad?

> Dear friends and family,
> Very early this morning, Greg's mother and I were notified by the UNHCR that Greg sustained significant injuries when a bomb, which fortunately did not explode, hit the building at the refugee camp where he was working.

I gasped, then choked on an inhaled glob of saliva. Coughing, and wiping tears from my face, I read on.

> I was informed that Greg is in stable condition. His injuries are severe, but not life-threatening, and consist primarily of a concussion and broken bones. The person relaying this message was not at the scene, and did not have any specifics.

The lack of information had to be agony for his parents. It was killing me, that was for sure. *Damn!*

> Greg will be evacuated for further treatment at a hospital in South Africa. I'm told that South Africa's medical infrastructure is among the best on the continent. Even though I've been assured that Greg will be receiving care from highly qualified specialists, I will attempt to obtain permission to bring him home. However, I do not know if his condition warrants such a move. At the very least, I will be traveling to Johannesburg to be with him while he is recovering. As further

information is relayed to me, I will pass it along to you.

Sam Hunter

There was a weblink at the bottom of the message. With a shaky hand, I clicked on it.

REFUGEE CAMP IN SOUTH SUDAN ATTACKED

JUBA, SOUTH SUDAN -- According to the United Nations Refugee Agency, the Sudan Armed Forces, or SAF, attacked a UN refugee camp in South Sudan at 2:53 p.m. local time yesterday. Casualty figures remain unconfirmed. A SAF spokesman denied the attack occurred.

At least four bombs were dropped on the camp. Sources on the ground stated that one bomb, which did not explode, fell within the camp, damaging one building, with several more bombs falling in an adjacent field. Witnesses stated that the attack was carried out by the SAF's signature white Antonov bombers. At least three bombs exploded outside the camp: two landed and exploded near the airfield where two U.N. aircraft had arrived earlier in the day to deliver food and other supplies.

The camp is home to more than 22,000 refugees, many of whom walked at least seven days across the border to flee indiscriminate bombing and famine in Sudan's southern state. Since fighting between the SAF and local militias flared up again last July, hundreds of thousands of civilians have fled the country, many into South Sudan.

I went back to the top of the email, and I read the whole thing through again. A "concussion and broken bones." Were the injuries minor? Or was he injured terribly, as Rudy had been, with bones smashed to smithereens?

I typed out a frantic email to Greg's dad, only to get back an automated reply stating that more information would be sent along as it became available.

Frustrated, I smacked my hand on the tabletop, then hissed from the resulting pain.

The next few hours passed in a blur.

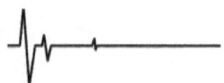

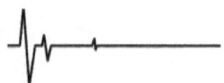

Chapter Twenty-Nine

The distinctive rumbling sound of a diesel engine and Dog's "who goes there" bark snapped me out of my numb haze. I glanced out a kitchen window and saw a dark blue pickup truck that I didn't recognize. Fantastic. Now what...

I was surprised to see Zak Deerheart climbing out of the cab of the truck. He slammed the door, gave Dog a rub on the head, and sauntered over to the back door. He wasn't wearing his police uniform, and had on clothes similar to those he'd worn when I first met him: jeans and a tee-shirt.

Grateful for the distraction, I opened the door.

A smile lit up his handsome face. The afternoon sun gilded his skin, and made his dark brown eyes almost glow. I'd forgotten how tall he was.

"Hi," he said. "Glad you're home. Kayla told me about what happened to your door, so I thought I'd stop by on my way home and take a look at it."

The damaged door was about the last thing on my mind. I stepped outside. "Well, there it is," I said, gesturing to the ugly message. I'd been applying wood filler to the gouges, a little at a time, so it could dry between applications.

"My plan is to fill in the messed-up part, then sand and paint the whole door. I don't know what else to do."

He pressed a thumbnail against the filler. "Well, I'm glad to see you're using the right kind of stuff to fill it in." He studied the door for a moment or two. "I think you're going about it right. Painting it is about the only thing you can do, other than replacing it. And that would be a pain, because I don't think this is a standard size door."

He opened the door and looked at the edge, then rapped on it with his knuckles in a few places. "Solid wood... Putting a veneer on it would be way more work than it's worth. That'd change the door thickness, which would open up a whole other can of worms."

He shot a grin at me. "My dad's a contractor. I grew up doing this sort of thing. What color are you going to paint it?"

"Maybe a nice mallard green. What do you think? I don't want to do boring brown, and I think the green would look good with the house."

He stepped back a bit and studied that side of the house. "Yeah. That would work." He ran his hand over the wood again. "Do you have a power sander?"

"Not a decent one. I found an orbital sander out in the barn that looks old enough to have been on Noah's Ark. It works pretty good, but it's small."

"Tell you what. Give me a call when you get the filler done, and I'll come by with my commercial sander. I can take the door off, and do the thing right. Is that okay with you?" he asked.

"Well, yeah, of course it is, but I hate to inconvenience you."

"No problem. See the red tile roof on that house over there?" He waved in the direction of a hillside a few miles away. "That's where I live. Heck, we're neighbors."

"In that case, sure. Sounds great, in fact. You know, I'd planned on cooking up a big batch of spinach and cheese cannelloni for tonight. You want to stay for dinner?" I asked.

Zak's eyes lit up. I could see I wouldn't have to work to persuade him to stay for a home-cooked meal. I'd originally planned on sharing the bounty with Bertie, but she wouldn't miss something she didn't know about.

"Works for me," he said. "But, I'm feeling pretty grubby. I was doing exciting things all day like going to the dump. I'd like to go home and clean up, so I can feel like a human again."

"Perfect. It takes a while to put it all together. So, if you come back at six, it will be fresh out of the oven, and ready to dig into."

He pulled a business card out of his wallet and scribbled his cell phone number on the back. "Here's my number, in case you need to get ahold of me. See you at six."

A week later, I had a beautiful dark green back door. We were both happy with the outcome, and, more importantly, I'd made a new friend.

Thank heavens. I needed one.

◆ ◆ ◆

February arrived. The long-dead golden grass of summer was bent and shredded, pummeled into the ground by the storms that always come in December and January. The green haze of new growth would soon grow tall and lush, and push aside the spent corpses of last year's grass.

Fresh and bright, the tender new shoots ushered in the time of renewal in the endless cycle of seasons. The storms brought needed rain to the foothills, and snows to the higher elevations.

The colors in the vista from my porch were softened now, muted. Silent fingers of fog crept over the open hills and filled up the valleys at dusk, only to fade away with the gentle winter dawn.

I always loved this time of year. Winter was a time of quiet reflection for me, and I wanted to believe it was a time of quiet for my tormentor also. Perhaps my wish had come true.

Nothing weird had happened since the incident with the door, and I finally began to feel less twitchy when I went out and about on my ordinary business. I hadn't gotten a revolver, as Kayla had urged me to do. It seemed to me that a handgun was as useless as a squirt-gun against someone who liked to take out their targets with a deer rifle.

Still, I remained cautious. It was frustrating to not be able to go out and watch the sunset, or stretch out on my back and admire the clouds, or the stars, as I once had. I didn't like feeling paranoid, but it was stupid to invite trouble. And, sticking to the pattern that I established right after I'd found Rudy's map, I still parked the truck right next to the back door, instead of in the barn.

Sam Hunter finally sent more information regarding Greg's injury. Greg had suffered a concussion, some broken ribs, damaged vertebrae, and a broken pelvis when part of the building collapsed on him, and was receiving specialized care following orthopedic surgery in South Africa. He was dealing with serious shit. The recovery would be unavoidably slow.

I got no emails from Greg, himself. Maybe he was too doped up on painkillers to write coherently. I couldn't even begin to guess the reality of what he was going through.

And I spent many a cold winter's evening searching through Rudy's old school papers, seeking threads and clues, wondering about the person who'd witnessed the last moments of my brother's life.

◆ ◆ ◆

David and Yasmine had gone to New York after parting company with his parents. I had no idea how network television programming worked—how new ideas were developed, how far in advance programs were planned, and so forth. A year, or more? The very idea of such a long wait was painful.

Finally, an email arrived from David.

> Allie, Good news! The documents you gave me blew the socks off the producers, and they've given me the super fast-track to move forward with it. They were not expecting me to arrive with any leads of my own, and the fact that I showed up with something red-hot really got their attention. <grin!>

Fast track? Hot damn! A surge of excitement bubbled up within me.

> Because we can't trust the County file clerks to keep their mouths shut about an inquiry from a major network, please send by overnight express non-redacted copies of all documents that you think might prove helpful. I need to have the honchos and the lawyers look them over, but I think they're sold on the idea. Following final approval, I will be in and out of Jackson over the course of the next few weeks to talk to you, your informant, and anyone else I can smoke out.
>
> I have to tell you, though, that the honchos are not willing to try to connect the one event with the other, as the latter case is still open. I'll try to sneak in a hint, if I can. <wink>

He was, of course, speaking of linking Rudy's death with Millie's murder. The producers set parameters. It was their show; they got to make the rules. After all, they were paying the bills to get this done. All I cared about was that the can of worms would be opened. Even more revelations were bound to come spilling out. How could it possibly be otherwise?

> Please talk to your informant and let him know what's going on. Attached is a password-protected pdf explaining who I am, my contact information, and what I am proposing to do. I'm sure you can get the ball rolling. Will send password separately via a different conduit.

Would Sunderland balk? Should I have talked to him already? It was too late to second-guess past actions. David had done his part. Now it was my turn. I sent David a quick reply.

> Hopefully, the ball will keep rolling. I'll give it a firm nudge (or even a kick or two) and let you know what happens. THANK YOU!

A few minutes later, the password came in a text from David's personal phone. The next step would be for me to talk to Sunderland face-to-face. To discuss such a sensitive arrangement on the phone, or via email would be an open invitation to disaster. I printed David's email and the pdf, put the docs in an envelope with one of David's business cards and drove to Gordon Sunderland's house.

◆ ◆ ◆

The old ranch house was, like mine, been there so long that it seemed at one with the landscape. It too was built of local stone, nestled in a flat spot between two small hills, and surrounded by sheltering oak trees.

I wiped my sweaty palms on the back of my jeans and rang the bell. A woman's face briefly appeared at a window, and I could hear her call out, "Gordy! Someone's here. I think it's that New York girl."

After a few long moments, Sunderland opened the door. His face crinkled with a bit of worry, as if he thought my presence was a harbinger of bad news. Nevertheless, he graciously invited me into his living room.

We settled into two large leather chairs, facing each other.

"What can I do for you?" he said, in a carefully neutral voice.

"I've given a lot of thought to what should be done about the documents you gave me."

His years as a law enforcement officer had taught him to shield his emotions, but it seemed to me that his whole face tightened.

"Don't worry," I said. "I've talked to someone, but haven't done anything that would expose you at risk. At this point, your identity is still shielded. And that's why I'm here. I would like to take some steps forward from where we are now. But I need your permission before anything else happens."

Sunderland relaxed a bit, but remained far from being at ease. "Well," he said, "I expected that you'd take some sort of action sooner or later. But, as I said then, it's time for the pigeons to come home to roost. What do you have in mind?"

"You've heard of *Sunday Night America*?"

Sunderland eyes narrowed. He seemed to instantly understand that I intended to take the case to a national audience. A myriad of complications would then follow, good and bad, expected and unexpected. "Yes," he said.

"A friend of mine from school is now a correspondent for them. He knew Rudy too. This is personal for him, almost a matter of family. He'd love to tackle this case. He's already pitched it to his bosses, with all names redacted. With your permission, he'll move forward with it."

Sunderland exhaled, ran his hand through his hair, and stared up at the ceiling. I forced myself to be patient, and didn't push for a response. What I'd asked of him would take more than a quick moment of consideration.

The implications were immense, not only for him, but for everyone connected with the investigation, even if only peripherally.

"I'll need to talk to my wife," he finally said.

Hope welled up in my heart. He hadn't said "No." I put the envelope in Sunderland's hand.

"Read this after I leave. It's from my friend, David. After you've read it, and thought about it, then the next steps will be entirely up to you. There's no need to contact me about your decision, just do what is best for you and your family."

Sunderland rubbed his neck. "Okay. I'll take a look at it." He set it on the side table next to his chair, and stood up.

I stood too, and said, "One more thing, if you don't mind?"

Sunderland looked wary again.

I smiled, and put a hand on his arm. "It's nothing alarming, don't worry. But, I need to know. Do you happen to recall who the mystery witness was?"

He smiled, and told me what he remembered.

◆ ◆ ◆

Three days later, I got another email from David.

> I got an email from your friend. Green light, all the way.

Sunderland! Bless you, Sunderland. You are a courageous man.

> My cameraman will be coming into town to scout locations, and take still shots. If anyone asks him what he is doing, he'll be just a guy checking out the general area and potential vacation properties, taking pictures to send back home to his sweetie. He may contact you. His name is Demarcus LeMoore. You'll like him. He may need to tell people that he's a friend of yours from New York, so be ready.

Holy cow. It was really going to happen!

> I'll be around too, in and out of town. Might see you soon, might not. Will see you eventually. <grin> My story is that I'm trying to heal the rift with my parents. Which is true. Unfortunately, I'm not too optimistic at this point.

David's parents were shocked when he'd gone ahead and married Yasmine without their approval. I had no idea how they could have been surprised by his decision. It wasn't like he'd given them no warning.

What planet were they living on? Not Earth, that was for sure.

They, with deliberate actions, alienated their own son. And for what? I simply couldn't understand it.

Family is something to cherish. No one knows that better than me.

◆ ◆ ◆

A few hours later, I stared at a pile of pictures in my hand. Based on the information from Sunderland, I was pretty sure that I'd figured out the identity of the mystery witness. But finding him was another matter.

Sunderland had described the witness as "that old coot who lived out in the forest." To me, that had to be none other than Rudy's "Obi Wan Cannoli."

In the pictures that Rudy had taken, the man looked grizzled and worn. I had no idea how old the man was. Was he even still alive?

I fanned the pictures out on the kitchen table. I looked past the man's face, past his ramshackle house, to the landmarks in the photos—the profile of a distant hill in the background, the side of a cliff, anything.

But in picture after picture, there was no view of the horizon, nothing to guide me.

Logic had to govern my search. If the man had happened upon the scene of the crime, I hoped that meant that he didn't live too far from the road where Rudy was killed.

But, on the other hand, perhaps he'd traveled some distance to meet up with Rudy that night.

The road in question didn't exist anymore. But I knew approximately where it had been, and traces of its path should still be visible. Any new trees growing there would still be relatively small.

Back to focusing on the pictures of the man's house. It seemed pretty evident that it was an illegal structure. Then something struck me. The man had pieced together his tarp-draped jerry-built shelter in the center of a cluster of large boulders, perhaps in an effort to help protect his home from the effects of harsh winter winds.

Or, maybe it was an attempt to hide the structure. Whatever the case, the arrangement of the huge rocks looked pretty distinctive. I grabbed my laptop, and opened up Google Earth.

◆ ◆ ◆

Greg remained in South Africa. His dad was correct in surmising that the road to recovery would be a long one. The break in his pelvis was not a clean one, hardly surprising, given what happened to him. Patched together with pins and screws and plates, it would be months before Greg's bones would be able to bear his full weight. His spinal cord had suffered damage too, and no one could predict how it would heal. His future looked... challenging.

I found it reassuring when he stated in one of the emails that the UN staff was extremely supportive during his recovery, and he'd made some close new friends. He wasn't alone. Good.

Because of the distance between the two of us, I was very surprised when I came home from a trip to the grocery store to find a beautiful Valentine's Day bouquet waiting for me on the back porch. I stuck my nose into the middle of it and inhaled the sweet spicy scent of pink and white carnations. I popped the envelope open and found a very simple message.

Happy Valentines Day to a remarkable woman. Your quiet strength is beautiful.

It had been years since I'd received a Valentine wish that was both simple and sincere. Who'd sent it?

I didn't recognize the handwriting. There was no signature. And it sure didn't sound like anything that Greg would say. David would never send me a note like that. And it was crazy to even think that it might be from Mark.

How odd.

◆ ◆ ◆

David did come into town, and he and Demarcus came to the house to record an interview with me. Before we did the interview, the three of us sat and talked for a while.

Demarcus was a short man, with a lean runner's build, and skin the color of burnished mahogany. He was a bit on the quiet side, but once he warmed up, I discovered that he had a great sense of humor. David was right. I did like him. The burgeoning friendship helped me feel a bit more relaxed about being digitized for posterity.

Demarcus showed me the raw footage. "Oh my god," I said. "Do I *really* look like that?" I looked like a frizzy-headed scarecrow.

"Don't worry," he said. "You look just like one of those models at Paris Fashion Week. Only a lot shorter." He said it in such a dead-pan manner that it took a moment for me to realize that he was teasing me.

I reviewed the footage, looking for grease spots on my boat-neck lavender cotton knit shirt. They'd pronounced it perfect, as it added a splash of color that wasn't overwhelming or distracting.

David asked if I wanted to wear the gold nugget necklace, too. Not wanting to share with the nation a zoom-in close-up of my almost non-existent boobs, I declined in favor of cradling it in my hand.

I gave him *that look* along with my answer, and he wisely didn't ask for my reasoning. I didn't want to hear a speech about loving my own body, especially from the guy who'd had his nose and teeth fixed.

Before they left, David reached out and took my hand. "Listen, Allie. We found some pretty graphic police photos of Rudy, ones that were taken at the crime scene. I have to warn you that we plan on using at least one of them in the program. I hate to do it, but I think it's necessary for people to see what was done to him. Visceral response is important. You do understand that, don't you?"

I wanted to protest, to say Absolutely No Way, but I stopped and thought about it for a moment. No, I wasn't real happy with the idea, but David was right.

I sighed. "Yes. Do it."

◆ ◆ ◆

Two days later, I parked my truck at the side of the road, and hiked off into the woods, GPS unit in one hand, a large tote in the other. Night after night of staring at my computer screen had paid off. I hoped.

When I got to my targeted location I looked around. There was no sign of a cabin anywhere.

"Mr. Connelly?" I called out. Connelly was the closest name to cannoli that I could think of.

My voice was carried away on the soughing wind that whispered through the pines. My query went unanswered.

I briefly considered calling out "Obi-Wan?" and then rejected the idea. The nickname might have been Rudy's little private joke, and perhaps unknown, or even irritating, to the old man.

I tried again with the more formal approach. "Mr. Connelly?"

This time a reply came, in the form of the ratcheting sound of a shell being loaded into a pump-action shotgun.

The venture was not going well. I sucked in a deep breath, and tried to remain composed.

"I'm Alexandra," I shouted. "Rudy's sister." Thinking that I needed to add some bit of insider information to enhance my credibility, I added, "He used to call me Allie-Saurus."

I held up the tote bag. I'd brought along a few of Rudy's best insect drawings, and a dozen or so homemade chocolate chip cookies. "I have some things for you."

Silence.

I set down the tote and the GPS, and held my empty hands out to my sides, in a gesture of non-threatening openness. "Can we talk?"

More silence.

I plunked myself down on the soft, pine-needle covered ground, and waited. Long minutes went by. The birds, which had gone silent, started to chirp once more. I was just about to try calling out again when an old man lumbered out from behind a tree.

He was thin, but not nearly as raggedy and dirty as I supposed a hermit might be. His shoulder-length white hair was clean and combed. He had a neatly trimmed white beard. His face, however, spoke volumes regarding his life, and was creased and tanned from years in the weather.

It was impossible to tell if he was sixty or even ninety. He held the shotgun, pointing downward at the ground, in his left hand.

"Mr. Connelly?"

"Close enough. What do you want?"

Chapter Thirty

March came at us like a lion, all right, but it had nothing to do with the weather. Tonight would mark a turning point. I couldn't believe how nervous I felt. This was IT. I'd gone out and purchased a television, for the sole purpose of watching this one specific program.

The announcer's authoritative voice rang out in the small room. "Tonight, on *Sunday Night America,* Murder in a Small Town." The entire hour was allotted for this story alone, which was unusual.

Here we go. I wiped my sweaty hands on the legs of my jeans and thought of Pandora's box. What had been at the bottom of the box? Hope? Dare I hope that something good would come from exposing my soul and risking Gordon Sunderland's reputation on national television?

The program opened with a picturesque overview of Jackson, showing off the natural beauty of the place. There were shots of the shops along Main Street, the huge wheels at the Kennedy Mine, scenic vistas of rolling hills, magnificent oak trees, and the forest where Rudy died.

My hands started to shake. I took a deep breath, and gripped the arms of my big leather chair.

◆ ◆ ◆

The program introduced Rudy. There, before me on the television screen, were the photos that I'd provided to David. Rudy as a four-year-old, studying a trail of ants. Rudy as a seventh-grader, in the junior high school science lab. Rudy, his arm draped around my neck at our sixteenth birthday party.

The biographical sketch led into David's interview with me. I closed my eyes, and flinched at the sound of my own voice.

I hadn't liked the rough cut, but all the rambles and stumbles were edited away, along with the moment when I'd rubbed my nose. I came across as smart, articulate, and determined. I relaxed.

My televised-video-self explained to David how Rudy had not come home from the forest that horrible night so many years ago, and a new image appeared on the screen. My heart pounded.

A sharply focused police photo showed Rudy's body, sprawled face down on a rutted dirt road. Bile surged up my throat.

Yes, David had warned me, but I wasn't ready for it. It was impossible to be ready for it.

There lay my brother, my dear, wonderful brother, legs and arms thrown out from his body at impossible angles, dark swaths of blood congealed in horrible meandering ribbons across the side of his face. I had to close my eyes.

My brain shorted out for a few seconds. A new voice coming from the television set startled me back to awareness, a voice I didn't recognize, for it was deliberately distorted.

I opened my eyes to see the backlit silhouette of a man, a baseball cap perched on his head, all hints to his identity concealed in shadow, speaking of the night when Rudy died.

◆ ◆ ◆

"I was walking down the road in the forest, hoping to find Rudy, because I wanted to show him something interesting that I had discovered the previous day. I guess you could say that I served as a sort of mentor to him. He possessed one of the most promising young scientific minds that I had ever encountered..."

In a flash, I knew that this was Rudy's Obi Wan. He and I had a long talk in the woods the day I'd found him. I'd told him all about David, and my quest for justice. He'd listened carefully, but, in the end, I'd left not knowing if he'd actually talk to David or just chase him off.

My spirits soared. Once again, he'd chosen to do the right thing.

"I came around a bend in the road," the man said, "and saw the headlights of a truck up ahead. I stepped off the road to get out of the way, and was surprised when I saw the truck lurch, as if it had run over something. The truck stopped, and two individuals got out of the cab."

David's voice took on a firm tone, putting emphasis on the importance of the question. "You could see them clearly?"

"Oh, yes," said the man. "One of them carried an electric lantern, and he switched it on as soon as they got out of the truck."

"And then what happened?"

"I was about to run forward, make myself known to them, when it struck me that there was something very wrong with the way that they were acting. They were not the least bit alarmed that they had hit something.

"They walked up to whatever was in the road, and looked at it as if..." The man took a deep breath, "as if they were perusing a display of vegetables at the grocery store, or something like that.

"One of them moved the lantern closer to whatever they were looking at. I was horrified when I realized that they'd run over a person. And they didn't even seem to care! I stepped back into the trees, as I was sure that it would not end well if they saw me. But then... not only did they get back into the truck without rendering aid, but they also backed up over the body while turning the truck around!

"I served in the Army, and have seen people killed, but let me tell you, I'd never seen anything like this. This was a cold, calculated, brutal murder. And once the deed was done, they drove back down the road in the direction from which they'd come."

"They made no attempt to render assistance to the victim?"

"None whatsoever."

"Did you recognize the truck?"

"It appeared to be a truck belonging to the Simkowitz Lumber Company. Their trucks had large, distinctive looping script on the doors. I recognized it when they opened the door to get back in the truck."

I wanted to turn off the television. This was worse than watching a horror movie. But, of course, I didn't.

"As soon as the truck was out of sight, I got out my flashlight, and ran forward to the victim. I was horrified when I saw it was Rudy. And there was nothing I could do to help him. He was dead."

I listened, trembling, and fighting off tears. Horrible memories of the moment when we were informed of Rudy's death came flooding back. I pushed those thoughts aside and focused on the TV.

David asked, "And what did you do then?"

"At that time, I did not have a telephone of any kind. I couldn't call 911. So, I grabbed my bicycle and rode to the police station. It took me a while to get there, since the road is some distance outside of town. I told the officer on duty what I had seen. He had dispatch call for a patrol officer to go out to the site, and requested that I write out as complete a statement as I could. By that time, a couple of hours had passed."

I sat upright, stunned, not believing what I had just heard, scarcely remembering to breathe.

The televised image of David placed a document on a small table in front of the silhouetted man. "Is this a copy of the statement that you provided to the police?"

"Yes, that's it. Signed and dated by me. They made this copy for me at the time I made the statement. I've kept it ever since."

"And your statement was accepted by the police department as potential evidence?"

"Well, at first they had some doubts, as the patrol officer that they sent out to the scene took the wrong road, and didn't find anything. You know, those roads aren't marked. But by then one of the Simkowitz drivers had come across Rudy, and radioed their dispatcher, and the dispatcher called the police department. From that point on the interviewing officer took the whole thing quite seriously."

"And were you able to identify the people who were in the truck? Did you inform the police department who you believed them to be?"

"Yes." He pointed towards the document. I noticed that the mystery witness had on fitted leather gloves, so not even his hands could be identified. "Right here," he said, tapping the paper, "are the names of the individuals whom I believe to be responsible for Rudy's death. To this day, there is no doubt in my mind whatsoever. I knew them both quite well, as they used to come out to the forest with Rudy from time to time."

"David!" I screamed at the television set. "Who were they!" But, of course, he didn't answer.

The televised David nodded to the witness. "And, following that, what happened?"

The silhouetted figure sighed, a deep, despondent sigh that seemed almost a moan. "Nothing. Absolutely nothing."

David said, "And why do you think there was no follow-up?"

The shadowed man replied, "I believe that nothing further happened because one of the individuals I saw has a family connection to the man who served, at that time, as the chief of the Jackson-Martell police department."

Holy shit...

"And what is the nature of the relationship?"

"The person in question is a close relative of the former chief of police. I do not wish to be any more specific than that."

David nodded at the man. "And so, you believe that a cover-up occurred."

"Yes. Without a doubt. I'm unable to come to any other conclusion. I went into the police department immediately after the incident and said, 'Listen, this is what I saw, and this is who did it.' And, as far as I can tell, no action was taken to determine if, in fact, I'd given them an accurate statement. Next thing I knew, they declared the incident to be an unwitnessed hit-and-run.

"To tell you the truth, I became scared at that point. The police chief had my name on the witness statement. It was possible that he knew where I lived. I went so far as to move out of state for a while, until things settled down."

The man shifted in his chair. "To this day, I regret that I did nothing further. But, you need to understand..." He paused, and licked his lips. "Being a witness to a murder makes one more than just a little bit skittish. And law enforcement has a damned efficient good-buddy network."

The man tilted his head and seemed to look off into the distance, as if considering what he would say next. "I have no doubt whatsoever that more than one crime was committed in connection with this incident. I have no doubt that Rudy D'Angelo was, in fact, murdered, and that a cover-up was instigated at the direction of the former Jackson-Martell chief of police."

After a few seconds of silence, the announcer's voice blared from the television set. "Sunday Night America will be right back..."

I sat there, swearing under my breath at the unavoidable necessity for commercials on commercial TV. I'd not invested in one of those magic boxes that allows commercials to be bypassed. Has anyone ever dropped dead from a commercial-induced heart attack? I felt like I was about to find out.

◆ ◆ ◆

The program resumed, and soon I was looking at my own face again. I scrunched my eyes shut, not wanting to see this part, for it was here, I was sure, that David would show me falling apart.

I heard David's televised voice, saying, "Ms. D'Angelo, why do you believe that some sort of cover-up occurred?"

I heard the rustling of papers as my televised-self set the two different versions of the autopsy report summary on the table in front of me.

"I believe that incomplete information was provided to my family so we wouldn't question the extensive nature of my brother's injuries." My voice cracked as I explained how the two autopsy summaries differed. "There is no way that such a large omission could be a careless error."

"And, why do you think your brother was killed?"

I pried my real-time eyes open and peeked at the screen. There was my televised face, staring off into the distance. The tears were welling up, glistening in the harsh light, and then one broke loose and trickled down my face. My onscreen hand opened up to reveal the heart-shaped nugget nestled in my palm.

My televised voice not much more than a whisper. "I have reason to believe that Rudy found a substantial cache of gold nuggets on our property. I believe that either someone was with him when he found the nuggets, or that he disclosed the location. And I believe that someone decided the gold was a ticket to a better life, and that he or she wanted to keep the knowledge of the cache a secret."

David asked, in a gentle voice, "And how did you come to this conclusion?"

I picked up the note that Rudy left for me on the last day that he was alive, the one that started with the words, "You will never believe what I found today." I read it aloud, then set it down and smoothed it out on the table in front of me.

"This..." I had to stop and clear my throat. "This is the last thing that my brother ever wrote." I then placed the heart-shaped nugget on top of the piece of paper. "And, this gold nugget was found in the front pocket of Rudy's jeans. No one in the family had ever seen it before.

"The nugget remained a mystery until not too long ago, when, in my house, I found a map that Rudy had drawn. By following that map, I found, on my property, a large enough cache of gold nuggets to make a substantial change in someone's life.

"Evidence found at the scene indicated that someone had been tampering with it." My eyes looked straight into the camera. "The nuggets were removed, by the police, from the location where they were found. They were placed into the temporary custody of Amador County, and are now secured in a commercial vault somewhere in Northern California. "

I paused, and the camera zoomed in on my face. "No hidden treasure of any kind remains on my property."

The last thing I needed was to have hordes of people swarming all over my property, digging things up, or breaking into my house. I was ready and willing to hire security guards if it came to that.

"Rudy was killed about twelve hours after he discovered the gold, before he'd even had a chance to tell our family what he'd found." Voice breaking, my televised self said, "Greed. My brother was killed because of nothing more complicated than selfish greed."

Another commercial break—I ran to the kitchen and gulped down a glass of water.

◆ ◆ ◆

The program resumed with a shot of David, standing on I Street, a pleasant tree-lined avenue in downtown Sacramento. Behind him stood a tall government building. The camera zoomed in on the California Department of Justice logo, in the form of a massive plaque over the entrance, depicting Lady Justice with a set of scales suspended from her left hand, a double-edged sword in her right.

David made a few introductory remarks, and soon he was sitting down for an interview with the California Attorney General, himself.

"Oh, David," I said, "You're a flipping genius."

Ralph Ivan Ewing, Attorney General of the State of California, beamed at David. It seemed obvious that he was expecting a "local boy does good" sort of interview applicable to himself, and by extrapolation to David, as they were both natives of Jackson.

And that's how it started out.

Ewing had taken a very different career path from most of those who held the position of AG, having begun his career as a cop, and then a police chief, prior to becoming an attorney, then a district attorney, and so forth. He had risen through the ranks in rapid fashion, and was viewed by most observers as being brilliant at his job.

Soon, David had Ewing reminiscing about his days with the Jackson-Martell police department. The man never even saw it coming. David's next question was offered as the very picture of innocence.

"Do you mind if I ask you a question about a case that occurred during your tenure as police chief?"

Ewing looked a bit surprised, but not uneasy. "That was a long time ago. I might not be able to answer the question, but sure, go ahead."

"Do you remember the investigation of the death of Rudy D'Angelo?"

The muscles in Ewing's face become tight, his eyes wary. His focus went away from David, and onto to the desk in front of him. "Vaguely."

I snorted. Yeah, right. Tell another one before that one gets cold.

David continued, his voice pleasant, his manner relaxed. "Can you explain why that death was ruled as accidental when the police were in possession of a signed statement from an eye-witness who stated that Rudy D'Angelo was run down in a deliberate, malicious act, and left to die on an isolated forest road?"

Ewing hesitated for only a moment, then spoke in clipped tones. "If I'm recalling correctly, that case was closed in the absence of evidence indicating that anything other than a very tragic accident had occurred."

David set a piece of paper down in front of Ewing. "Here is a copy of an eye-witness's statement that was turned over to the police department within hours of the incident." He ran a finger over the paper, as if highlighting some of the words.

"You don't recall ever seeing this before? The witness states that a close relative of yours was at the scene, and participated in the injury of the deceased, and yet you only 'vaguely' remember the case?"

Ewing fixed an intimidating glare on David. "I repeat, Mr. de León, the death was ruled accidental, the case was closed due to lack of evidence to the contrary."

The hostile looks were wasted on David. I could tell from the bland expression on his face that big trouble was coming for Mr. Ewing. I'd seen that expression many times before when we were on the high school debate team, when David prepared to slice and dice an opponent. Our team always loved that part. He was relentless when on the attack.

David asked, in an oh-so-innocent voice, "In cases involving unexpected or suspicious deaths, how long is evidence retained?"

Ewing still looked ill at ease, and he shifted in the chair. "It varies from jurisdiction to jurisdiction."

"How long is evidence usually retained by the Jackson-Martell police department?"

"As I recall, the minimum time span was about fifteen years, maybe longer."

"In that case, sir, can you explain why the evidence box from the Rudy D'Angelo case looks like this?"

Someone handed David an evidence box that looked very similar to the ones utilized by the Jackson-Martell police department. He removed the lid, and displayed the contents to Ewing. Inside the box was nothing but an old Amador County phone book.

I whooped with glee. David did not state that this was the actual evidence box. But, from the horrified expression on Ewing's face, it was obvious that the man was startled into believing that's what it was.

Furthermore, he didn't seem to be the least bit puzzled to see a phone book in the bottom of the box.

His shoulders sagged, and he stared at the contents of the box with a stunned deer-in-the-headlights look on his face.

HA! I thought. *Busted!*

David took advantage of Ewing's silence. "Sir, isn't it interesting that all the evidence from the case is missing, and that the box was weighted with a useless item in an attempt to disguise that fact?"

He stopped, allowing that electrifying piece of information to hang in the air between the two men.

Ewing leaned back, lifted one eyebrow in an exaggerated gesture of skepticism, and stared at David. His rigid body language signaled that cold fury had replaced his initial discomposure. His face turned red.

"I have no interest in listening to this nonsense any longer. I have work to do. Good day." With that, Ewing lurched up out of his chair, and stalked out of the room.

Time for another commercial break. I zoomed out to the kitchen, poured myself a glass of wine, and did a little dance back to my chair. Hot damn. This was better than the Super Bowl.

I raised the glass in a silent toast to the power of American network television, and snuggled down in my big comfy chair to watch the remainder of the show.

◆ ◆ ◆

The program resumed, and the scene changed. David faced a different silhouetted figure. Once again, the voice was distorted, but in such a way that it sounded quite different from the voice of the earlier interviewee.

This had to be Gordon Sunderland. Despite being backlit, and in disguise, I had no doubts about his identity. Like the other witness, he was wearing a baseball cap, gloves, and a heavy jacket that filled out his lean physique.

David led him through a series of questions that allowed him to explain, without giving away his identity, how he knew that items were removed from the evidence box and subsequently destroyed.

Oh, Sunderland. I was tense with fear for the man. Despite the efforts made to conceal his voice and physical characteristics, he'd taken a huge risk. Anyone close to the case would easily be able to guess his identity.

As the lead investigator, Sunderland would have been the one who had access to all the puzzle pieces. He would have been the one approached by the chief of police, and ordered to commit a crime.

I sure hoped that prior to this telecast he and his family had taken off for a long vacation in Tibet, or Tierra del Fuego, or maybe Mars.

In short order, it became apparent that something very dodgy had happened at the Jackson-Martell police department during Ewing's tenure as chief. Sunderland explained how officers, who had sworn to uphold the law, were pressured to turn their heads the other way when items critical to the D'Angelo investigation somehow disappeared.

No explicit accusation of criminal activity was stated, but was very much implied. It seemed clear to me that Ewing was guilty as hell. I hoped lots of other people thought so, too.

The program closed with another sweeping view of the Jackson Valley, shot from the top of the hill overlooking the Kennedy Mine. David's voice, in solemn tones, told the audience that, "Somewhere in this peaceful valley, live two ordinary people who work hard, love their kids, pay their taxes, go to church, and believe that they have gotten away with murder."

A still shot of Rudy's tombstone came up, then faded away into a panoramic view of the beautiful little valley.

David paused. The camera panned across the rolling hills of fresh springtime grass. The innocent sounds of twittering birds could be heard in the background. The camera circled around to show David standing in a large open field, the huge wheels of the Kennedy Mine in the background. The camera zoomed in on his face.

"At this time," he said, "it appears that Ralph Ivan Ewing, California's Top Cop, may know who those two people are. It also appears that he may have aided and abetted a serious miscarriage of justice in order to protect them. If these allegations prove to be true, then it is possible that Ralph Ivan Ewing may have acted as an accessory to the crime of murder, in the first degree."

The scene changed to a still image of an empty forest road, similar to the one where Rudy died, and faded to the police photo of Rudy's body sprawled in the dirt. The Mission Statement of the Office of the Attorney General for the State of California was overlaid on the image, with the camera zooming in on these few words:

ENFORCE AND APPLY ALL OUR LAWS FAIRLY AND IMPARTIALLY
ENSURE JUSTICE, SAFETY, AND LIBERTY FOR EVERYONE.

Did Ewing ever stop and really look at those words? Read them, think about them, act upon them? Did he reflect on how well they represented him as a man?

I wondered how he could sleep at night, knowing the things that he knew, and having done the things that he'd done.

Pandora's box was opened. And for the first time, I was frightened about what horrors might come flying out.

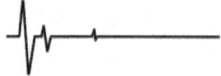

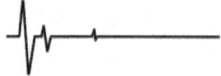

Chapter Thirty-One

The next morning, about 7:30am, I poured myself a bowl of granola, stomped my feet, and belted out the ancient war-chant genetically embedded in the collective memory of all human beings.

Stomp-stomp clap, stomp-stomp clap. We will, we will...

Just as I was digging in with the air guitar, I stopped, alerted by a few vigorous barks from Dog. I looked out the window. A pickup truck pulled into the parking area. Zak, grim-faced, climbed out of the cab.

He had on his police uniform trousers with a white tee-shirt. His uniform shirt hung in a cleaner's bag, dangling from a hook on the passenger side of the truck cab. I opened the back door, and he put his hands on his hips.

"Alexandra, for the love of Mike, what did you *do*?"

I grinned at him. "Can't bring yourself to say 'what the fuck,' can you?"

He didn't look the least bit amused. "Pretty much."

"I take it this isn't an official visit."

"I think that it's obvious," he said, and waved in the general direction of his uniform pants, "that I'm on my way to work. Haven't clocked in yet, so yes, this is unofficial."

His mouth formed a straight, tight line. If a person could shimmer with suppressed anger, Zak was doing it. This was not the reaction that I'd expected from him.

"And you watched *Sunday Night America* last night?"

"The lady scores again! And the crowd goes wild..."

I glared lightning bolts at his heavy-handed sarcasm. "It's rather simple. Drake said his hands were tied. I untied them."

"Is that what you call it? I'd call it running amok with a stick of dynamite in one hand and a lit match in the other. Somebody could get hurt.

You could get hurt!"

I was shocked by the cold fury in his voice.

Of all the people in Jackson Valley, Zak was about the last person I'd expected to lash out at me. I hadn't anticipated an attack so soon, and not from someone I considered to be a friend.

I stood there, dumbfounded, for a few moments. I stepped back into the house and closed the door. I clicked shut the deadbolt lock that Zak, himself, had installed.

I leaned back against the door and closed my eyes. Why was I so upset? Was this simply a case of hurt feelings? Or was I shaken because he spoke the truth?

It seemed altogether too likely that it was the latter case. And I didn't want to think about it. I didn't want to wonder if I'd made a huge mistake.

After a minute or so I heard Zak start his truck and drive away. I walked into the office and turned on the television.

◆ ◆ ◆

The best place to catch the local news was on David's former station, Sacramento's KSXP, Channel 2. The city of Sacramento lives and dies by politics, as it is the State capital, and thousands of area residents are State employees. The television station would be all over any hint of a government scandal.

With an eye on the screen, I started my morning yoga stretches.

To say that David's *Sunday Night America* program unleashed an instant political firestorm would be an understatement. Things were getting very interesting in the Capitol building.

The Governor was waylaid by the TV crew just outside her office and forced into making an impromptu statement. From the look of her ferocious scowl, she was not at all happy about the situation, but it wasn't clear whether her irritation was focused on the TV crew or her Attorney General.

I sat up, stretches forgotten.

Governor Rosewall was blunt and to the point, as always, reminding everyone that "The most fundamental premise of our legal system is the presumption of innocence until guilt is proven in a court of law". She then turned and disappeared into her office.

I got up off the floor and went into the kitchen to get the uneaten bowl of granola. The Governor had my sympathy. She had a narrow tightrope to walk. On one hand, she needed to publicly express belief in the integrity of the Top Cop. On the other hand, she needed to distance herself just enough, in case the allegations turned out to be true. I had a feeling that right now she wished she'd never heard of Ralph Ivan Ewing.

Cereal bowl in hand, I went back to staring at the television. The

Channel 2 political reporter practically glowed. It seemed pretty obvious that his thinking went something along the lines of, "hot diggity dog, let me sink my little pointy teeth into this one."

After providing a brief overview for those who'd had the misfortune to not see David's amazing telecast, he said, "The one thing known at this point is that, from all appearances, something highly irregular occurred during Ralph Ewing's tenure as Chief of Police in Jackson. We will be following this story as it develops."

Hot damn. I was feeling pretty darned puffed up with myself for being the one who launched off this rocket ship.

It seemed for sure that conspiracy junkies would be, as Doc used to say, happier than a puppy with two tails. The evening news was sure to have a more in-depth analysis of the Ewing mess.

◆ ◆ ◆

Just after dusk, I let Dog in for a bit of company and settled into my big leather chair with a cup of after-dinner coffee in my hand. I'd spiked it with a shot of Bushmills. I was feeling giddy. What the hell. Why not?

The Channel 2 political reporter returned for the evening broadcast. He seemed a bit subdued this time. I wondered if he was just tired, or if something else had happened in the case that I didn't know about yet.

He gave a run-down of the information that was presented earlier in the day.

"Proving the truth of the allegations against Ewing will be, of course, much more difficult than simply talking about them," he said.

Ah. That was the problem. The reporter was disappointed. I guess he'd wanted a witch burning or public stoning or something else equally brutal and bloody. I understood those sentiments perfectly.

"It is possible," said the reporter, "that after all the dust dies down, Ewing will not be prosecuted for obstruction of justice, coercion, or evidence tampering. The case will have to rest on an anonymous police officer's word. There are obvious problems with such a scenario. If nothing else, one must wonder about this person's motives, after all this time has gone by."

"Damn," I said to Dog. "The man has a valid point." Dog didn't answer me, but offered sympathy by flopping down across my feet. I reached down and scratched his head to thank him.

"No physical proof of the officer's assertions," the reporter said, "no written threat or directive, are known to exist. State and federal penal codes make clear that the State assumes the burden of proving the accused to be guilty 'beyond a reasonable doubt.' Without any hard evidence, it would be next to impossible to gain a conviction."

Did I care? Not really. It seemed enough that Ewing's career was toast, and his integrity would be questioned forever. All trust in him destroyed and probably never to be regained. Little Ralphie would reap what he had sown. Surely, if nothing else, he'd be forced to resign.

It might be considered unfair that he'd be judged in the court of public opinion rather than a court of law, but oh well... Karma strikes again, baby.

After the news was over, I let Dog back outside, where he'd much rather be. I doubted that he'd ever get used to being a house-dog.

I washed up the dinner dishes and pondered the unknowns—the information that David had not shared, either with me, or with the nation. The biggest remaining question centered on the identity of the actual murderers. David had not named any suspects, and for good reason. The last thing he and his network needed was to be sued for libel.

David's goal was to stir things up and get the case re-opened, not to try a murder case. He'd certainly succeeded in getting peoples' attention.

One thing was for sure. The Amador County Grand Jury couldn't ignore the fact that a person claiming to be an eyewitness to a murder had come forward in a very public venue. National interest would guarantee that this new evidence couldn't be dismissed as being irrelevant or immaterial. The ball was now lobbed out of my court, and into Amador County's.

◆ ◆ ◆

I felt torn. I loved going to Demetra's but I wanted to look at the online news. And I'd sworn off looking at my computer when I was at the coffee shop. So, I sat down in my big comfy chair and pulled up my favorite online local news source, the *Argonaut Ledger*.

Well, well, well. Just as I predicted. Amador County hadn't let any grass grow. Front and center on page one was an article stating that an investigation was already under way. I had a feeling that prior to the airing of the program, David had talked to someone in the higher echelons of the county government, and they had known an explosion was coming. How else could they have responded so fast?

Police To Reopen Investigation

JACKSON, CA -- The Jackson-Martell Police Department has reopened an investigation into the death of teenager Rudy D'Angelo after an investigation by news program *Sunday Night America* uncovered new evidence in the case. D'Angelo, age sixteen, died about eighteen years ago as the result of an apparent hit-and-run accident.

"Following a comprehensive investigation, our conclusion at the time of the incident, and that of the Amador County Coroner, was that the death was accidental and the case was then closed," said Jackson-Martell Police Chief Anna J. Brandt Tuesday afternoon.

A recent investigation by television reporter David deLeon apparently found serious missteps in the investigation, including evidence that an unnamed Jackson-Martell police officer may have been coerced into misstating or omitting key evidence in his reports, and that evidence crucial to the investigation was deliberately destroyed by this officer at the order of then-Chief of Police Ralph Ewing. Ewing is currently serving his second term as Attorney General of the State of California.

"Mr. deLeon shared the evidence that he collected with the Jackson-Martell Police Department and I directed that the case be reopened," Brandt said. "I extend my sincere sympathy to the family of Rudy D'Angelo for their loss and the revisited grief that can accompany the reopening of a case such as this one."

I rolled my eyes. It seemed more likely that she was extending her sincere sympathy to herself, having had a live grenade, so to speak, dumped in her lap.

DeLeon's story aired earlier this month on the Sunday evening televised news magazine, *Sunday Night America*.

Brandt said the Amador County Sheriff's Department will be taking the lead in reexamining D'Angelo's death. "It is my desire that an unbiased, professional review of this case be conducted by a qualified individual who is not a member of our department," she said. "Such an individual has been brought in to head up the investigation."

I snorted. Who were they going to bring in? Sherlock Holmes? The rest of the force must be thrilled to have it implied that they were too incompetent to handle the case.

"Right now, all we have is third-hand information from a reporter who says, 'I have these documents and have statements from these individuals,'" Brandt said. "Until a careful investigation is carried out, we have no way of determining if the allegations are, in fact, true. I assure you that every effort will be made to gain a comprehensive and accurate picture of the events that occurred in conjunction with the death of Rudy D'Angelo."

Why wasn't I elated? I'd gotten what I wanted. Zak's words kept bouncing around in my head. *Somebody could get hurt. You could get hurt!*

I leaned back in the chair and stared across the room. Who would have thought, all those years ago when Rudy, David, and I were all in high school, that David would end up goading the police into reopening a homicide investigation, and the focus of the investigation—the corpse—would be one of us?

For the rest of the day I felt on edge. I didn't sleep well that night. I was up early, and found myself wandering around the house aimlessly. I sure hadn't anticipated feeling so stressed in the aftermath of the broadcast.

But, here I was, sitting smack in the middle of a classic example of, "be careful what you wish for, you might get it." Finally, I couldn't stand it any longer. I went over to Bertie's house. I was shocked at what I found there.

◆ ◆ ◆

For once, there wasn't a plate of fresh cinnamon rolls sitting on the kitchen counter.

"What? You think they appear by magic? That there's some sorta homing device attached to your truck that beeps when you're headed here, so I know to shove some in the oven?" Bertie asked.

"Well," I said. "Yes. Seems reasonable to me."

"Sorry to disillusion you. If you're desperate, I can give you a banana."

"Um, no. I'm really not all that hungry."

And, of course, with me wanting to think about other things, Bertie immediately brought up David's TV show. When I didn't respond to her blow-by-blow recap with any degree of enthusiasm, she tilted her head to the side. "Okay, chickie. What's botherin' you? C'mon, spill it."

Bertie was worse than a terrier for digging up the dirt. She could be relentless, and might as well have had a neon sign on her forehead that said, "Resistance is Futile." So, before I half knew what had happened, my fears all came tumbling out.

"You know, Bertie, when I started all this, I just wanted my questions answered. And now it appears that I've made a mess of things." I couldn't sit still, and stomped around the kitchen, swinging my arms in frustration.

"It seems a sure bet that the people who murdered Rudy will be furious. From what David said, they live right here in Jackson! The crime they thought forgotten made the national news, for godssake."

I felt like an idiot. I should have realized all of this long ago.

"And why I haven't I heard a single word from Drake? Zak is furious with me." I was almost yelling. "Is Drake pissed off at me too?" A glance at Bertie told me I needed to calm down a bit. "Oh damn, I'm sorry. I didn't mean to shout at you. I'm just... wound up."

My body was paying a price for the audacity, or hubris, or whatever it was, that had driven me. Acid reflux had me gulping antacids by the handful. And yet, what else could I have done? In this day and age, nobody should be able to get away with murder.

I ended up in tears, cuddled in Bertie's cushiony arms, with her murmuring comforting sounds. And I felt no better about the situation, even after all of that.

◆ ◆ ◆

Two nights later, I sat on the edge of my bed, pulling off my socks, getting ready for bed. A short, sharp *plink* from the north side of the room startled me. I jumped up and whirled around. I stood there, still, and waited. A few seconds later, came another one. And another.

Oh jeeze. Some jerk was throwing rocks at my window. Was my anonymous buddy trying the same stunt on me that they'd pulled on Millie? Well, sorry Charlie, it's not going to work this time.

Plink-plink. My annoyance increased. But I sure wasn't about to open the window and ask what was going on. And where was the hell was Dog? Shouldn't he be out there chewing someone's leg off, or something?

I padded down the stairs in my bare feet, without turning on the light. I got into the kitchen just in time to hear the rattle of doorknob.

Acid surged up my gullet and into my throat. I fumbled around in the dark downstairs bathroom, grabbed the antacids, and said a silent thank you to Zak, for having talked me into installing a commercial-grade dead bolt and strike-plate. He'd also added a vertical metal plate that extended a few inches past the doorjamb that would keep someone from kicking in the door.

The doorknob rattled one more time, and then the night went quiet. I could only hope that the person had gone away.

Hands shaking, I picked up the shotgun and took it upstairs with me. The gun would live in my bedroom from now on. I'd rather be upstairs, shooting downward at an intruder, than find myself a sitting duck at the top of the stairs, a prime target for someone shooting at me from below, with my own weapon.

◆ ◆ ◆

The next morning, I was bitterly disappointed to see that the surveillance cameras had failed to reveal who'd entertained themselves by trying to freak me out. After paying all that money, what did I get? Images of the top of someone's head, covered with a hoodie. The lights on the house were positioned too high. The face of the person was cast in shadow. There was no way to even tell how tall the person was.

Damn. I was furious. I'd have to talk to the contractor, and see what could be done. He was, after all, supposed to be an expert with this sort of thing. Thanks a lot.

Well if the midnight rock-thrower was someone I knew, it seemed essential to demonstrate that I wasn't intimidated by their little stunt.

I went outside and found Dog. He seemed perfectly fine, not in the least apologetic for having fallen asleep on the job the night before. I loaded up the little traitor, and we drove to Demetra's.

"Fine," I said to him, when we got there. "See if I bring you a snack." He just grinned at me, and didn't seem a bit worried about the threat of imminent starvation.

We pulled into the lot, and I noticed one of the distinctive white Jackson police cars parked near the coffee house. A male officer stood inside at the counter, his silhouette visible through the glass door. Reflections of the sky and clouds across the glass obscured the view, so I couldn't tell who he was. I wondered if Demetra gave a discount to law enforcement personnel. If so, it was a good plan. The place sure was popular with them.

I walked from the truck towards the door with my head down, watching my feet traverse the sidewalk, ignoring everything around me. A hand shot out from nowhere and grabbed my wrist, jerking me to a stop. A sharp yelp burst from my mouth.

I whirled around only to come face to face with Andrew Pichl. An odd, creepy grin stretched across his face. He grabbed my other wrist.

"Get your slimy hands off of me!" I screeched. "Jerk me around one more time, and you're going to get your goddamned teeth kicked in."

He didn't move and gripped my wrists even tighter. My fingers started going numb.

"Let go of me, you stupid twerp!"

I wrenched my hands downwards as hard as I could and out to the side, freeing them, causing Pichl to stumble. I took a step backwards. Shock was written all over Andrew's face.

Sweat popped out on his upper lip. His mouth hung part way open and his eyes were bugged out, making him look like a particularly stupid goldfish. His mouth moved, but no words came out. The only sounds coming from him were short raspy breaths.

"What the hell do you want!" I yelled.

Andrew found his voice. "Uh... I, uh, I would like to offer my sincere congratulations, Alexandra."

"What?"

"Uh, congratulations. You finally found it. After all these years. The gold, I mean."

Finally found it?

A spike of ice-cold adrenalin punched through my guts. "I'm going to ask you again, what the *hell* are you talking about?" I pulled my cell phone out of my jacket pocket.

"You'd better start talking, and talking fast, Pickle-boy, because my finger is right next to the Emergency button on my phone. And your story had better be damned convincing, because I'm only about a half millimeter away from accusing you of murdering my brother."

Andrew's face took on a sweaty, grayish tone. "I don't understand," he said in a soft, faltering voice.

The door to Demetra's swung open, and Zak stepped out. My knees buckled a bit in relief. I wouldn't have to tell my life story to get him to understand what was going on.

"It appears to me that Miss D'Angelo just asked you a question, Mr. Pickle." Zak's voice sounded as cold and hard as snow-covered granite. "On top of that, a whole shop full of customers just saw you grab and restrain her against her will. So. What's it going to be? Are you going to apologize to Miss D'Angelo and explain your actions right now, or do you want to take a ride down to the station where you can explain yourself to my boss?"

Andrew stood there with his jaw slack.

"Ten seconds," said Zak.

Andrew glanced over at me like he expected me to stop Zak and come to his rescue. Yeah, right. In your dreams, Pickle-Boy. How could the man be so effing clueless?

"Ten," said Zak. "Nine... eight... I'm waiting, Mr. Pickle. Seven..."

Zak's hand moved towards the handcuff case hanging from his duty belt.

"It's pronounced Pea-KEL. I was, uh, just congratulating Alexandra on having found that box of gold at last."

Zak raised one eyebrow. "'At last?' Well, that's an interesting choice of words." He turned and looked at me. "Miss D'Angelo, have you discussed with Mr. Pickle any items which may have been recently discovered on your property?"

I was pretty sure that Zak was mispronouncing Andrew's name on purpose, just to be annoying. "No, sir, I have not. And the television program never mentioned anything about a box."

"Well, Mr. Pickle, I think it's time for you to have a nice chat with the officers downtown. Nothing to be alarmed about. If you'll please come with me." Zak grasped one of Andrew's arms, and walked him the few steps across the parking lot to the patrol car.

"No!" Andrew twisted and lunged, trying to slip out of his jacket and escape. "You're making a mistake!" He seemed stronger than I would have ever guessed, but Zak's grip remained firm. "I'm not going with you!"

Zak's mouth settled into a hard line. He'd had enough.

Before Andrew even realized that he'd been outmaneuvered, his hands were cuffed behind his back. Zak recited the Miranda Rights in a calm, matter-of-fact voice while escorting the squirming man to the back seat of the police cruiser.

Andrew, eyes bulging, tried to pull away from Zak. But he was having no more success than a gnat struggling to escape a spider web.

Pichl's law training finally clicked into gear. "On what basis are you restraining me? You have no probable cause! I demand an explanation!"

Zak didn't say a word, placed his hand on Andrew's head, and lowered him into the back seat of the car. The last thing I heard before the door clicked shut was, "It's pronounced Pea-KEL!"

Zak double-checked the door to make sure that it had latched, looked up at me, said something, motioned towards downtown, climbed into the driver's seat, and drove out of the parking lot.

I stood there and watched the police cruiser disappear down the road. I had no idea what Zak had just said to me.

Was I supposed to come to the station in order to make a statement? It seemed the most obvious explanation.

The door to the coffee house opened. Demetra stepped outside, and put her arms around me. "What was that all about?"

"I'm not quite sure," I said, shaking my head, "but something weird just happened."

Demetra gave me a big hug, and then backed off so I could settle down. She stood there a few seconds as if assessing my emotional state, then gave my arm a pat and went back to taking care of her customers.

I got in my truck and drove to the downtown parking structure.

◆ ◆ ◆

Detective Ronald Brownlea, a rather bland-looking police officer I'd never seen before, was waiting for me in the reception area. He had on civilian clothing—slacks and a sport coat—rather than a uniform. He had an unremarkable face, medium complexion, light brown hair, and average height.

The man was the epitome of ordinary. The only thing striking about him were his greenish hazel eyes. Even his clothes were shades of beige. He could, no doubt, melt into a crowd and disappear in an instant.

Brownlea showed me down the echoing back hallway to a small, equally unexceptional cubicle, and pulled out a chair for me.

"Where is Andrew?" I blurted it out without waiting for the niceties.

"Right now, Mr. Pichl is in a holding cell. What happens next is entirely up to you. If you wish to press charges, he will be processed through the system, and a determination made regarding bail, if any."

Brownlea reached across his desk and picked up some papers. He thumped their edges to straighten stack and set them down again. The man seemed like some sort of neat freak.

"At present, there are a few different misdemeanors that he could potentially be charged with—simple assault, perhaps with unlawful restraint thrown in, and theft. The assault charge, of course, stems from the incident outside of the coffee house.

"The theft charge is a bit more complicated, and I will explain that in a moment. We've been having quite an interesting chat with Mr. Pichl."

Theft? What was that all about?

Another thought occurred to me. “Do any one of those charges have the potential of leading to a suspension of his right to practice law, or even disbarment?”

“I'm not an expert in that area, but, yes, I would assume so,” said Brownlea. “I imagine that this incident would not be looked upon with favor, to say the least.”

Poor old Andrew. I could picture him sitting on his butt in a cell, glum and sweaty, wondering if his career was about to tank. Pity seemed more appropriate than anger. I looked down at the faint bruises on my right wrist. Had he hurt me badly? No.

“To tell the truth,” I said, “I wouldn't feel right about pressing charges against him for assault. That's not to say that he didn't grab and restrain me. In fact, he's done it before. I don't believe his intent was to inflict bodily harm. He's just... very inept.”

Brownlea made a few notes. His face revealed nothing regarding his personal opinion of the matter. Maybe he didn't have one.

He finished writing down the statement regarding my lack of desire to press charges for simple assault and straightened up the pile of papers again. I felt sorry for any scrap of paper that might dare to step out of line.

“Okay,” he said. “Now, on to the matter of theft. The actual pilfering of an object from your house took place many years ago. But, in California, in the case of infrequently used items, the actual countdown on the statute of limitations does not start until the thievery is discovered. So, in essence, the clock began running about an hour or so ago.

“Mr. Pichl implicated himself during the process of trying to explain how he knew about the presence of a metal box containing gold nuggets on your property. Ms. D'Angelo, at any time prior to the broadcast of the television show, did you tell Mr. Pichl about the nuggets?”

“No, sir. I did not.” My irritation with Brownlea grew. There was no need for him to ask that question. He'd just told me that Andrew had admitted longstanding prior knowledge. So why ask?

“Mr. Pichl told us when he was younger, he was very active in the local Historical Society. He became friends with your great-uncle, Joaquin Minero. Mr. Minero invited Mr. Pichl to the family home so that Mr. Pichl could look through the old books and journals that belong to your family.

“During Mr. Pichl's visit, he found a very old journal which referred to an iron box containing gold nuggets which was secured in a location referred to as ‘the hiding place.’ Mr. Pichl took that journal from your home under false pretexts.

“He has admitted that he had no intention of ever returning it. And from that intent arises the theft charge.”

I had to hold up my hand to stop Brownlea for a moment. This was a lot to take in. "Wait a minute. You're telling me that Andrew stole from my family? My uncle invited him into our house, and Andrew had the audacity to flat-out steal things?"

Any residual sympathy for him went right down the drain. I could almost hear the loud sucking noise to accompany the picture in my head.

"Yes," said Brownlea. "Mr. Pichl also stated that he'd forgotten he had the book. So, if nothing else, we have conflicting statements that make him sound like he's now trying to wiggle out of taking blame for what he'd done.

"He stated that he'd found the book again right around the time your aunt died. He had no explanation as to why he didn't return it to you as soon as you arrived in Jackson. He had ample opportunity to do so."

I thought of the note that I'd found stuck in the Dorothy Sayers book weeks ago, about the old green book that had been borrowed. I wanted to run down the hall to the holding cell and scream, "Hey Spiderlegs!" at Andrew and see what he did.

At the same time, I knew that Brownlea would never allow such a thing. Taunting prisoners is probably against the rules.

"Now," said Brownlea, "the bottom line is this—based on the entries in the journal, Mr. Pichl became convinced that the nuggets were hidden inside your home, in the bricked-up fireplace in your kitchen, to be exact. And that was why he was interested by the fact that on the *Sunday Night America* program you stated that the gold was discovered by your brother."

"Interesting," I said. "All of this explains his obsession with my house."

Brownlea inclined his head, in an odd combination of curiosity and skepticism. "Can you clarify what you mean by that?"

"He was quite persistent about trying to convince me to sell the place to him." Another thought came rushing into my head. *Whoa.* "I think that you can add suspected vandalism, or whatever the proper charge is, onto Andrew's list.

"After my aunt died, he took possession of the key to her house, and kept it until I could come get it. And when I first walked into the house, I discovered that someone had been chipping away at the bricks in the kitchen fireplace. I'd bet dollars to donuts that Andrew did it."

Brownlea made a note and straightened out the stack of papers again. "Do you believe that he might be the one who is responsible for the other odd occurrences that have happened at your house?"

Ah. He'd done a bit of research before I arrived. Good. But, as much as I wanted to find a culprit, someone to punish, I had serious doubts about Andrew having the cojones to pull off such incidents.

In a vain attempt to get a bit more comfortable, I shifted in the chair.

I tried to imagine old Andrew wrestling with a dying coyote that was bleeding out all over the place.

The idea of a man as prissy as him doing something like that... Nope. Didn't fit.

But, on the other hand, could he afford to hire someone to do his dirty work for him? Probably. But trying to imagine old Andrew as The Godfather didn't quite work, either. He could, however, be quite capable of sending a threatening letter.

"I... don't know," I said. "My gut-level instincts say 'no way,' but sometimes people surprise us. It might be a good idea for you guys to have another chat with him about that. So, let's leave this as an open question for now. There're just too many unknowns still floating around for me to be able to give you a definitive answer."

"And the theft charges?"

"Heck, yes. You bet I will press charges against him for theft. He stole a valuable piece of my family's history and he did it for personal gain. Because he took that book, important knowledge was lost to us, and that led to further tragedies. I only wish we could charge the bast... the man with a felony."

"All right, then." He scribbled in his notebook again. "I'll be having a chat with both Officer Deerheart and Detective Drake. If we decide that further charges are warranted, I'll let you know."

He deemed the paperwork to be completed, and no doubt neat and tidy as well, stood, and extended his hand. "Thank you for meeting with me, Ms. D'Angelo."

"Thank *you*," I said, "for taking this seriously." I had gut a feeling that Brownlea already decided that Andrew Pichl was guilty of many things, and not just of theft.

Outside of the book theft, I had no idea if he might be right, or wrong, about any of it.

◆ ◆ ◆

That evening, I sat on the front porch for quite a while, huddled down in one of the big Adirondack chairs, watching the sun go down.

The sunset was gentle, a muted watercolor of cantaloupe orange, salmon pink, and the soft yellow of a faded rose. I watched, entranced, as the colors faded into the dusty blue of evening.

Dog sat by my side, providing a comforting presence and a warm head on my knee. I felt bone-tired, but my brain wouldn't let go of the confusing events of the day.

I simply couldn't imagine Andrew Pichl as the mastermind behind the murders of my brother and my aunt. Something was missing. Something crucial.

I considered the information brought forward in David's program. The mystery eyewitness stated that there were two people in the truck that ran Rudy down. Andrew was a goofball all right, but I found it hard to believe that he had the stomach for overt brutality.

And, if he'd been one of the people in the truck, then who was his partner in crime? Pichl was a genuine loner, an odd duck who didn't fit in anywhere. He'd never trust anyone to enter into a conspiracy with him.

Nothing connected. Nothing made any sense. There was no way Andrew could have known that Rudy had discovered the cache of nuggets.

I kissed Dog on the top of his dusty head, gave him a small treat from my pocket, and went back into the house.

◆ ◆ ◆

I slid onto the burnished piano bench and opened the cover that protected the keyboard. At first, my fingers wandered over the keys doing basic scales. Then I found myself launching into one of Franz Liszt's ethereal *harmonies du soir*, the Transcendental Etude No. 11.

Music of the evening, indeed. The piece was as majestic and velvety dark as the night sky. The magic of the glorious tones of the old piano cleared my thoughts and eased my mind.

I played until spent, then trudged up the stairs, wandered into my bedroom, stripped out of my jeans and long-sleeved shirt, and set them aside. The familiar and mundane process of settling down for the night was soothing. I folded back the quilted comforter, picked it up, and carried it over to the rocking chair at the end of the room. The nights were now warm enough that I didn't need it on the bed.

I bumped the chair, and the comforter slid off onto the floor. I bent over to pick it up. The window over my head exploded with a body-rattling boom, spraying me with thousands of razor-edged shards of shattered glass and splintered wood.

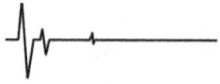

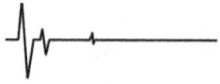

Chapter Thirty-Two

A frightened shriek burst from my throat. My god, the executioner had returned!

The room was fogged with a cloud of fine, chalky plaster dust from where the bullet hit the wall on the other side of the room. I sucked in a panicky gulp of air, and choked and gagged.

Tears streaming down my face, I stumbled across the room to the door, flipped off the lights, and rummaged around in the dark trying to find the shotgun.

Broken glass and sharp spears of broken wood littered the room. I was relieved that I still had on my slippers; my feet would've been sliced to mincemeat without them.

Still coughing, I picked up the loaded gun. I staggered back across the room and slammed myself against the wall next to the remains of the window.

My heart thudded so hard in my chest that I wondered if I would pass out. Remembering my target-shooting lessons, I forced myself to ignore the dust and take a deep steady breath, let it out, and take another.

Half-blinded by grit and tears, I pumped the gun, pointed it out the window and let loose a double-barreled blast of buckshot in the direction of top of the knoll.

There was no place else the shooter could have set themselves up to get such a direct shot into the window. And, by god, they were going to reap what they had sown.

I don't think I expected to hit anything. Blind fury had overtaken my body. The blast was more of an expression of pure outrage and indignation than anything else. Take *that!* Even after receiving a string of overt threats, I hadn't allowed myself to actually believe that I might fall victim to raw violence. But there it was. I had. You sow the seed, you reap the harvest.

Finally, out of nowhere, the commanding voice of instinct burst forth and screamed at me. *Run!*

I dashed out of the bedroom, kicked off the gritty slippers, and pounded down the stairs to the kitchen. I went to the sink, grabbed a glass of water, swished and spit to get the sandy muck out of my mouth, and poured myself another.

I turned around, and gasped, astonished to find a trail of blood across the kitchen floor. I looked down at myself, and choked with surprise.

The whole left side of my body was crisscrossed with cuts from flying glass—glistening ruby streams of blood coursed down my legs, meandered across the tops of my feet and onto the floor. My bra and panties were turning crimson. Only after I saw the injuries did the cuts start to hurt.

Taking care not to slip on the smooth wooden floor, I hurried into the downstairs bathroom. I hopped in the shower, turned on the water, stripped off my underwear and rinsed away the needle-like shards of glass that clung to my skin and hair.

Splinters of wood were embedded in my skin, dark slashes I could do nothing about. Under the pummeling cascade of cool water, the cuts throbbed and hurt like hellfire. The blood swirled in the water and went down the drain, reminding me of the shower scene in the classic old movie, *Psycho*.

I slammed off the water, stepped out of the shower, and stood shaky and bleeding onto the bathroom rug. I was scared to towel off, afraid I'd drive any remaining slivers of glass deeper into my skin.

As much as I didn't want to, I slid my feet into my soft cloth scuffs, then dug a terry robe out of the bathroom linen closet and pulled it on.

I was sure I hadn't lost enough blood to put me in danger of passing out. My adrenalin was buzzed so high that I never once considered that it would be damned reckless to step outside. I wanted to run, get the hell out of there.

I grabbed a bath sheet to sit on in the truck, found my cell phone, wallet, and keys, and ran to the kitchen door.

I heard Dog whining outside the kitchen door. I opened the door, and he attempted to lick the blood off my legs. I shooed him away, and he leaped into the truck.

◆ ◆ ◆

I don't remember driving to the hospital. I found myself there, in the receiving area of the emergency room. The triage nurse took one look at the deep red stains spreading across my terry robe and the blood trickling down my legs, and hustled me through the double doors and into the hands of an ER nurse.

The nurse took hold of one of my arms. "Are you cold?" she asked.

I shook my head, but I'd no idea whether I was or not. She helped me shrug out of the robe, then wrapped me up in a warm flannel sheet, helped me onto a gurney, and plugged me into an IV.

"I need to tell you something," I said. "No. Wait a minute. Two things." I felt like my brain had gone out to dinner and had forgotten to come back, but I seemed to be making some sense. At least I hoped so.

"Call the police department. Someone shot at me. Ask for Detective Drake. He needs to know about this."

She wrote it down. "Okay, got that. And the other thing?"

"I shot at someone too. I shot back at whoever did this. Someone out there... maybe wounded. That person is the one... "

"Understood." The nurse stood up, motioned to someone to come over, gave them the note, and turned her attention back to my injuries. The nurse worked downward, starting with my face. She pulled back the blanket, and began exposing small areas of skin, irrigating my wounds with saline solution, and pulling pieces of glass and wood out of my skin with a pair of forceps.

Dog. I needed to tell them about Dog... But, events overwhelmed me. And I was sure he wouldn't jump out of the truck and run. He never had before.

Whatever the nurse was doing stung like a bitch, tears welled in my eyes, and I bit my lips to try to keep from crying out. She saw my distress, went and got a syringe with some kind of magic solution in it, and numbed the skin before she dug out the worst of the wooden splinters.

She took care of my neck, shoulder, and arm, which had taken the brunt of the blast, then moved on to my legs. She washed the wounds with careful attention, then blotted them dry with gauze pads, and sprayed the whole area with some solution that made me grit my teeth.

She worked, and a man approached. He asked me a series of questions. Exactly what happened, my full name, insurance information, and all the other things they needed to know. I must have made some sense, offered some sort of coherent narrative, because after a while he went away.

Someone else then showed up, murmured gentle reassurances, and stitched the worst of the cuts, and sealed them with Steri-Strips.

I found myself shivering, probably more from shock than from cold. I slid into a hospital gown, transferred to a dry gurney, and a clean warm blanket placed over me.

Another nurse appeared in the middle of the process. Was this the man who had asked me the questions? I had no idea. He handed me a small can of apple juice with a straw stuck in the top. "Drink this, in tiny sips. Stop drinking if you start to feel sick."

He made small talk for a few moments, then asked, "Any family we can notify?"

"Bertie..." I took a deep breath, trying to clear the brain fog. What was her full name? It took me a moment to come up with it. "Alberta. Alberta Strahan. She works here as a patient advocate. She's not actual family, but she might as well be. She's been a friend of my family since forever."

The nurse nodded as he scribbled out his notes. "We'll call Ms. Strahan, and let her know you're here. In the meantime, get some rest. We're going to keep you overnight for observation. In the morning, we'll check over your wounds. If any of them look inflamed, or are unusually painful, we may have to do x-rays to see if there is any embedded glass in there." He stood up, as if he was going to walk away.

"Wait... My dog is in my truck, out in the parking lot. He jumped into the truck when I got in to drive here, and I didn't stop to argue with him. Bertie can drive my truck to her house, because I think the dog will refuse to get in her car."

"OK. When we take care of the call to Ms. Strahan, we'll be sure to pass along the info about your dog. And, we've notified the police department. Someone should be here to interview you before too long."

I handed back the apple juice after a few more sips. "Thanks," I said, and my eyelids drifted shut. I had only a vague awareness of being wheeled down some hallways and lifted into a bed.

◆ ◆ ◆

The faint screeching sounds of someone sliding a chair across the floor filtered into my consciousness. I opened my eyes, blinked at the light, and glanced around.

The walls were painted with a comforting deep shade of dusty blue, with warm cream accents. Despite the pleasing appearance, it still smelled like every other hospital room I'd ever encountered—disinfectant, soap and clean sheets. High-pitched squeaks coming from the wheels of a cart in the hallway echoed into the room.

A few quick footsteps came towards me, only a bit louder than the sounds outside the door.

"How do you feel?" said a man's deep voice.

I was surprised to see Zak, wearing his dark blue police uniform.

"Um, about how you might expect me to feel, I guess. You know, just waking up, and feeling a bit crappy. Not terrible, but I've been better. Are you here to say hi, or are you here to take a statement?"

"A little of both. Do you feel up to telling me what happened?"

"What time is it, anyway?

"Right around eleven p.m."

"Oh." I wondered why he was still on duty so late at night, but didn't care enough to ask. Maybe their shifts rotated or something. Damn, I was tired.

Zak dug a notepad and a pen out of a pocket and sat down by my bed. “What happened?”

“Well, there isn’t too much to tell. You know I was down at the police station earlier this afternoon, talking to that new guy, what’s-his-name.”

“Detective Brownlea.”

“Yeah. Him.” From the tone of my voice, it wouldn’t be hard for Zak to surmise my feelings about Brownlea, but he didn’t say anything. Maybe he didn’t like the guy either.

“Anyway, after I finished talking to him, I came home, did a bit of this and that, went upstairs to go to get ready for bed, and BAM—my bedroom window came flying in at me. Someone shot at me, I think. The whole window frame just disintegrated.”

“And what did you do then?”

“Then I was a damned fool. I grabbed my shotgun and fired back in the direction I guessed the shot came from. Useless, I know. Stupid, too. Nothing more than an angry gut-reaction.

“I only realized that I was injured when I saw blood all over the floor. So, I got in the truck and drove to Emergency. And here I am.”

“You used birdshot?”

“Nope. Buckshot.”

Zak didn’t even raise an eyebrow. For some reason, I needed to add a sort of disclaimer. As if that would excuse acting like an idiot. “I doubt that I hit anyone. The shooter was probably long gone by the time I got the gun.”

“Probably so, but the ER staff will let us know if someone shows up with shotgun pellets in their hide.”

“And that’s it. Like I said, there’s not much to tell. Just like Chicken Little, the sky fell on me.”

“Okay.” He closed his notepad, stuffed it back in his pocket, and scooted the chair a little closer to the bed. His face took on a soft, concerned look. “Now, this part is off the record, strictly personal. I owe you an apology.

“I was way out of line that morning when I stopped by your house. I was upset by the risk you took, and I was afraid that something like this,” he gestured at my bandages, “would happen. I’m very sorry about how I spoke to you.”

He crinkled his forehead in a tentative, almost pleading expression. “Still friends?”

A soft warmth invaded my heart. “Sure, Zak. Still friends.” I reached out and placed my uninjured hand on his. “Apology accepted.”

“Good.” His face relaxed. “Well, I’ve got to go back to the station and file your statement. Some of the guys are up on the hill right now, looking around your property, though they probably won’t find too much in the dark.

Bertie gave us the spare key she keeps for your house. We'll have to talk to you again at the scene, so let us know when you're released."

He took a deep breath, as if he was about to say something important. But all he said was, "Rest well. At least as well as can be expected. Good night."

"Good night."

He turned and walked out the door. His rapid footsteps echoed down the hallway. There was a silent pause, followed by the soft *swish-thunk* of the elevator door closing.

He said "friends." I could sure use one.

◆ ◆ ◆

The following morning, I snuggled under the soft cotton blankets and watched the morning sky turn from indigo to pink outside the hospital window.

A doctor whom I'd never seen before came into the room. She applied gentle pressure to the deeper lacerations, and I had to resist the urge to bellow like a three-year-old.

"How do you feel?" she asked.

"Like I went twelve rounds with a giant cactus."

A small smile curved up her lips. "The good news is that your cuts are looking pretty good. I think we got all of the big pieces of glass out." She made a few notes on the chart. "I don't see that there's any need for x-rays, so I'll start the discharge process.

"Stay aware of what's happening at the points of injury, and if any of them are unusually painful, or don't seem to be healing, let us know. You might get some small areas of localized inflammation from the splinters. They're pretty dirty, and hard to completely remove. So, watch out for any signs of infection, swelling, redness, pus, and so forth. Again, if something looks bad, or hurts, call us.

"We put in absorbable sutures, so they won't have to be removed. Over time, very small pieces of glass may work their way to the surface, so don't be surprised if you find one or two. But, given the fact that your wounds were well cleansed, I doubt that you'll have much in the way of further problems. You did the right thing by showering off."

She finished looking me over. "Everything looks good. Keep the sealed areas dry when you shower. The bandage strips will fall off on their own as the skin heals." She smiled. "Don't worry. You're going to be just fine."

◆ ◆ ◆

I was glad that I had thought to grab my cell phone before I left the house. I sent Drake and Zak a text telling them that I would be released soon, and that I'd let them know when I got home. I followed that up with a text to

Bertie, asking her to bring me something to wear, some underwear, a set of sweats, and a pair of flip-flops to wear home.

My terry scuffs and robe, soaked with blood, had been pitched in the medical waste bin in the E.R. The tops of my feet were too cut up to put on shoes.

Bertie came into the room. "Hey chickie, you look better than I expected. Your truck looked like a damned massacre scene, and your house's even worse. And I taped some plastic sheetin' over the busted window in your bedroom."

"Thanks, lovey." I hoped she didn't screw up the crime scene, and then felt guilty about being critical of her actions. She was only trying to help. I didn't bother to tell her that I hadn't had the guts to look at myself in the bathroom mirror.

There was nothing to do but change the subject. "Did you bring me some cinnamon rolls?" I asked in a sweet, angelic voice. As if I knew what an angel actually sounded like.

Bertie rolled her eyes. Even without cinnamon rolls, I was glad she was there to help me get dressed. I screwed up my courage, went into the bathroom, and forced myself to stare into the mirror. There were small scabs all over my face. I looked like... Well, I looked like I'd been sprayed with shards of glass. I felt very grateful that I didn't look like I was dead.

Dog was standing up, waiting for us in the truck in the parking lot. He jumped around, making his happy squeaky noises. His little tail was going about ninety-nine thousand RPM.

"He spent the night in the truck," said Bertie, "along with a plate of cooked hamburger and a bowl of water. I didn't even try to get him out. He hopped out in the middle of the night to do his business, but other than that, he wouldn't budge."

I doubted that Dog would ever make friends with Bertie. Weird, but whatever. He's a dog. Who knows what dogs think?

"No problem. No point in even trying. It wouldn't have worked."

I gave Bertie a big hug, at least as well as I could, thanked her for helping out, climbed into the truck, sent Drake a text message, and drove home.

◆ ◆ ◆

I heard Drake arrive about forty minutes later. I peeked out the kitchen window, and he flashed me a big thumbs-up sign. That was a bit confusing, to say the least. He was there to talk about the attempted murder of me, for godssake. What was up with the jaunty hand signal?

I hurried out to meet him. Once outside, I threw back my head and drank in the sight of the most beautiful blue sky that had ever been. Damn, I was happy to be alive. I almost skipped over to where Drake stood by his car.

"Hey, lady, you're looking pretty darned chipper considering what happened to you."

"I'm *feeling* pretty darned chipper, considering what happened to me. Just the fact that I'm standing here talking to you is way more exciting than it ought to be. C'mon inside. I'll show you the scene of the crime."

"That's not why I came by. Officer Martinez will be here soon to take photos and locate whatever-it-was that took out the window. I came by to tell you that someone showed up at Emergency with shotgun wounds."

"You're kidding! Who was it?" I bounced up and down on the balls of my feet for a couple of seconds before I realized what I was doing.

The corners of his eyes creased with merriment, and Drake made me wait. He knew me all too well. Just before I felt about to burst, he said, "You know, I shouldn't tell you this, and if push comes to shove, I'm going to deny it. But... Robin Smith came into the ER with shotgun pellet wounds."

My jaw dropped. "You're shittin' me. *Robin*?"

"The one and only."

A cold wave of nausea surged through me. *Oh lord.* What had I done? "How bad is she hurt?"

"She was pretty lucky, all in all. There are only a few impact points on one side of her body. The pellets didn't have too much velocity by the time they hit her, but they still needed to be dug out."

"So, what's her story?"

"She says she was out running over on Clinton Road, cut across a field, and got in the way of some teens shooting at varmints."

It was possible. Weirder things have been known to happen. She is a runner, or at least she used to be, years ago.

Clinton Road was a few miles away, and not too far from where Robin and Larry lived. That particular stretch of roadway certainly wouldn't be my choice of place to go running. It's narrow, with no shoulders. But Robin was a cross-country runner in high school. Maybe she ran *all* the roads, wide, narrow, lousy, whatever.

Maybe I hadn't shot anyone, and Robin was just in the wrong place at the wrong time. It didn't take too much effort to warm right up to that idea.

"Maybe you shot her. Maybe you didn't," he said. "Either way, she was some distance away from the shooter, at the edge of the range within which any real damage could be done. If you want to know the truth of it, you look a lot worse than she does."

The lacerations down my arm decided to throb a bit just then. I wondered if the response was psychosomatic. I thought I looked like I'd barely escaped from a team of knife-throwing ninjas, and he'd just reinforced that impression.

"Now, before we go and get too spun up," Drake said, "I need to know what you had loaded in your shotgun. This could be only a coincidence."

He paused for a moment. "You know, I'm being horribly unethical in sharing all this with you. But, to tell you the truth, I couldn't resist. So much for professional detachment."

He didn't look the least bit embarrassed. I wanted to hug him. So I did. My wounded arm and side stung like the devil, but I didn't care.

I also couldn't help feeling relieved that I hadn't made Robin into hamburger. If I really was the one who'd shot her, that is. Even so, I still felt bad for having done something so stupid. I knew better.

"Well, then." He dropped his arms to his side and swung them back and forth a bit. "Back to the reason I'm here. So where were you standing when you shot at your assailant?"

I led him around to the back of the house and pointed up at the shattered second story window. "Right up there. That's my bedroom. I figured that the shot had to come from the knoll, so that's the direction I shot back."

"Do you have an unexpended cartridge from the same box?"

"Sure do."

I strode over to the back door, held it open for Drake, and followed him inside. He saw the dried blood all over the floor, and shook his head.

At that moment, I realized the blood told a story.

A trail of well-defined, red-brown footprints came in from the hallway, stopped at the sink, which was splashed with bloodstains, and then veered across to the bathroom. More muted slipper-shaped prints came back out of the bathroom and went to the back door.

A pungent butcher-shop scent hung in the air.

"Wow," Drake said. "No wonder you were ticked off. Don't clean that up until after Martinez gets some pictures."

"Don't worry. I won't. I want this mess documented."

For some reason, I got a bit of perverse pleasure out of how gross the place looked. I tiptoed across the floor, taking care not to step on the evidence, and retrieved the opened cartridge box. I took it to Drake and pressed it into his hand.

"Am I going to get in trouble for this?"

Drake pulled out a cartridge and handed the box back to me. "Not if the pellets aren't a size match. If they do match, and all the other facts line up, it's possible that you could be charged with suspicion of negligent discharge of a firearm, or even assault with a deadly weapon."

Whoa... I took a small step backwards. Any future I might have practicing law seemed to be whistling away on the wind. He patted me on the shoulder, then jerked his hand back.

"Oh! Sorry!"

"Doesn't hurt that much." I didn't mind the instant of discomfort he'd caused. I appreciated the gesture.

"Buck up," he said. "No need to panic just yet. California law states that a person can use reasonable force in self-defense, especially in cases where a person feels there is a threat to their life.

"Since your aunt was killed by a rifle shot, and because a gunshot had just missed killing you, it can be argued that you were under extreme emotional duress and had good reason to feel threatened."

He paused and looked at me for a second. "Bottom line, yeah, you could get in trouble. But not if Robin sticks to the story that she was miles from here."

I silently blessed Drake for not pointing out the obvious. When the window exploded, I should have dropped to the floor, found my phone and called 911.

"Make sure that Kayla documents your wounds. I'll let you know as soon as possible what's going on with the shotgun pellets."

Pictures. Great. Just terrific. Photos of me in my ratty old underwear, covered with scabs, on file as evidence, forever. With luck, someone would leak the pics out onto the internet. Every pervert in the world with an injury fetish would love them.

It could be worse. Someone could be taking pictures of my corpse.

I put the cartridge box back where it belonged, then went back outside to say goodbye to Drake.

He left, and I stayed right in that spot for several minutes, gazing up at the wispy translucent white clouds drifting in swirling horsetails across the brilliant azure sky above Butte Mountain.

◆ ◆ ◆

Within the hour, Kayla arrived at the house. She stepped into the kitchen, and had much the same startled reaction as Drake had.

She put her hands on her hips. "Whooo-eee, girl. You did a prime job of making a mess, I'll give you that."

The day warmed up, and the house smelled more and more like rotten meat. I sighed. Cleaning up the coyote blood on the back porch had been awful. This mop-up was going to be way worse.

My mood wasn't helped by the fact that my injuries had really started to hurt. It seemed like the entire left side of my body throbbed in sympathy with my arm.

I must have looked a bit overwhelmed, because Kayla put her arm around my shoulders. I tried hard not to wince.

"Listen," said Kayla. "To use my grandma's favorite expression, don't fret. Call these guys." She wrote down the name of a damage restoration company that specializes in cleaning up crime scenes and handed me the paper.

"They'll do a better job of it than you'll ever be able to do by yourself."

That was the best idea I'd heard in ages. While Kayla photographed the upstairs and dug the flattened bullet out of the wall, I called the company. The customer service rep said they'd be there the following morning. The smell would just have to get worse for a while.

Kayla came downstairs to photograph the kitchen and bathroom. Then it was my turn to be scrutinized. All my clean underwear was on the tired side, and not exactly granny-wear. The universe really didn't need me to provide a female anatomy lesson, so I decided to pose in my turquoise bikini. The swimsuit had about the same amount of square-inch skin coverage as my underwear, but was a heck of a lot more opaque.

Kayla joked and made sympathetic noises over the bruises, scabs and gashes decorating my skin, and the whole session proved less embarrassing than I'd anticipated. She helped me re-tack the plastic sheeting more securely over the broken window, and she left.

Here was yet another individual on the police force who was becoming a real friend. I was glad to have another ally, and imagined us going to the movies on a girls' night out, after the case was finally over.

I went back upstairs and looked at the ugly hole in the wall. A chunk of plaster about the size of a salad plate had crumbled and fallen away, leaving the underlying wooden lath exposed. The wood was split and splintered where the slug had hit.

I felt sick. That could have been my head, blown to bits.

I turned away from the wall. I ran my finger through the whitish dust covering the top of my antique marble-topped dresser, and immediately snatched my hand up. Blood welled from my fingertip. Little needles of glass and sandy fragments of antique plaster covered everything.

I darted across to the bathroom and rinsed my finger. If only the horrible memories of that night could be washed away as easily.

◆ ◆ ◆

Around three-thirty that afternoon, I got a phone call from Officer Brownlea, asking me to come down to the police station. I would have preferred to work with Drake, but there wasn't anything I could do about it.

In any case, working with this guy was infinitely better than working with Newhall.

Brownlea seemed just as uptight as the first time I talked to him. He was dressed, once again, in uninspired shades of light brown. Even his tie was a plain khaki, with only a faint woven-in crosshatch pattern to give it some life.

The man was beyond clueless regarding his style of dress—he was a true sartorial dud. I couldn't help but think that maybe he should change his name to Beige-lea. It would be perfect for him.

He also wasn't much for inane pleasantries, and got right to the point. I wondered how upset he was now that his pet hypothesis, with Andrew Pichl starring as the secret stalker, got shot down. I had to suppress a giggle over my unspoken pun. Time to turn on my attorney face.

"Well, Ms. D'Angelo," he said, "due, in part, to your *actions* of the other night, we've had a significant breakthrough in our investigation."

It seemed to me that it galled him to have to give me partial credit for the recent sudden progress. And it was clear from his odd emphasis of the word "actions," that he didn't approve of the reckless discharge of firearms. Under any circumstance, no matter how dire.

After all, such actions were "against the law."

I bit down on my tongue to keep from making a sarcastic remark about all the progress he'd made on his own. Which wasn't much, as far as I knew.

Brownlea began his explanation. I forced myself to look enthralled, hanging on his every word. I didn't want to screw things up for Drake, since he shouldn't have let the cat out of the bag. Or spilled the beans. Or whatever you want to call it.

"Early this morning, a person of interest presented herself at the emergency room of the hospital, bearing wounds from a shotgun."

I made a surprised gasp.

"She claimed she was out running early that morning, and had decided to take a shortcut through a field on a deer path, back to her car. She stated that she ran into the line of fire of some kids taking potshots at ground squirrels. She screamed, they took off, and she drove herself to the hospital."

I maintained my wide-eyed look.

"At face value, it seems a plausible story. However, the doctor on duty noted that the injuries looked hours old, a fact for which the subject had no explanation. And because we had directed the hospital to be on the lookout for a person bearing shotgun wounds, the emergency room staff called us."

I turned on my patented "very-surprised" look. It had been honed to perfection in the courtrooms of New York State. "Good heavens! I hope she wasn't badly injured!"

"The wounds were fairly superficial. However, some of the shotgun pellets had to be dug out of her skin."

"Eww," I said. "Sounds painful."

"Because the pellets were of the same type as those that you so kindly provided to Detective Drake, we here in the police department decided that further investigation was warranted. We sent a patrol officer out to take a look at the field where the injured party stated she was wounded."

He stopped and fiddled with the paperwork on his desk, making sure all the edges were in perfect alignment. His actions seemed like a stalling tactic. What was up with this guy? After he double-checked the results of his efforts, he resumed his narrative.

"Based on the officer's observations of the area, it was determined that I should go to the hospital and speak with the suspect."

"Suspect? You determined that she should be reclassified as a suspect? Who is it?"

His lips tightened at my audacity. "All in good time," he said, in a withering tone of voice.

I wanted to punch him in the mouth. I added "patronizing jerk" to my mental list of his faults.

"As I spoke with the woman, she became more and more agitated. I concurred with the doctor's preliminary assessment that the suspect seemed to be under the influence of a drug."

I had a sudden mental image of Brownlea as a smug old bishop, bestowing a reassuring benediction on a confused and doubtful doctor. It took a bit of effort to maintain my look of rapt fascination.

Brownlea sat with his hands folded together, perfectly centered in front of his body, which only served to reinforce my mental image of him as a condescending churchman.

"As I continued to speak with the suspect," he said, "her behavior became increasingly erratic. I received the pertinent information from the officer sent out in the field to verify her story, and was obliged to inform her that it would have been difficult for her to have cut across that particular piece of land this morning.

"The field was, at that very moment, being deep-disked. The crew had started their work at sunrise."

I understood immediately the significance of his statement. Disking kicks up a huge volume of thick dust. Visibility in the immediate area would be close to nil. And no sane runner voluntarily risks making mud-pies in their lungs.

"Officer Brownlea. Sir." I leaned forward and allowed a cold, no-nonsense edge to enter my voice. "Who. Was. It."

He stopped and looked me in the eye.

"Robin Smith."

"My god." I collapsed back in my chair and allowed my mouth to go a bit slack. I hoped I wasn't overdoing it.

But, honestly, it wasn't difficult to act surprised. Brownlea held more of the puzzle pieces than Drake had at the time he talked to me. Robin's involvement was now closer to looking like an established fact, rather than speculation.

And, Robin, a druggie? That was a shocker. But maybe she'd just overdone it on pain meds and had a bad reaction. Whatever.

"How well do you know her?" Brownlea's voice sounded less harsh. It seemed that he might be one of those people who likes to push until someone pushes back.

"I know Robin and her husband, Larry, from high school. I wouldn't count them as friends, but they are definitely acquaintances."

He scribbled a note to himself. He set it on a stack of paper, and then straightened the pile so the long edge was perfectly parallel to the edge of his desk.

"A blood sample was drawn to check for drugs. I read her the Miranda rights, the hospital administered a sedative to calm her agitation, and, after an appropriate time interval, she was taken into custody. A search warrant has been requested for her home and business."

I felt chilled inside. I would be lying if I said I wasn't stunned. Prior to my conversation with Drake, I would have never guessed that Robin was involved. This development called for some significant rearrangement of preconceived notions.

Above all, I hoped, with Robin in custody, the harassment would, at last, stop.

But, I really didn't know if we were any closer to finding out who killed Rudy and Millie.

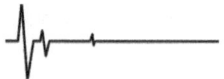

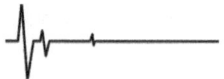

Chapter Thirty-Three

I slept in Rudy's old room that night. Thank heavens the door to that room had been closed at the time of the shooting, so no plaster dust drifted in there. When the restoration company arrived at the house in the morning, I retreated to Demetra's for a few hours to keep out of their way.

I swear the cleaning team used magic spells to get the work done, because when I came back, the place was immaculate. The nasty rotten smell had vanished, and in its place was a light vanilla fragrance.

The scent was pleasant, guaranteed to fade away over the next few days, and I didn't mind it at all. In fact, I was delighted. Who wanted to live in a house that smelled like vulture vomit?

My bedding and lace curtains were taken outside and blasted with compressed air, then bundled up, and ready to be washed. The lace curtains were old, and I wondered if they'd survive the whole process. Oh well. If they fell apart, they fell apart. The whole situation could have been so much worse.

It seemed the best course of action to wash all the clothes in my bedroom. Otherwise, I'd be imagining that I felt glass shards poking into my back even when there weren't any there.

The restoration company did not do structural repairs. I'd have to get someone else to patch the wall and replace the window. Of course, I wondered if Zak could do it.

I spent several hours doing laundry and then settled into my big comfy chair to watch the five o'clock news.

◆ ◆ ◆

The news anchor had on her this-is-serious-news face and delivered the top story in a calm, steady voice.

"This morning, at a Jackson car dealership, a thirty-six-year-old Jackson man apparently took his own life. A spokesman for the Jackson-

Martell Police Department stated that at about 11:30 a.m., police received a call and responded to Larry Smith Downtown Motors, located on Hwy 49-88, in central Jackson.

"The dead man was identified as Larry Smith, the owner of the dealership."

I gasped, then choked on a glob of saliva that got sucked down my windpipe. I fought to hold back the coughs so I could catch the rest of the report. For years, I'd thought of Larry as a spineless weasel, but this... I could scarcely believe what I heard.

"At this time, investigators believe that the cause of death was a self-inflicted gunshot wound to the head. No other details were forthcoming from the police department. However, a local anonymous source told Channel 2 that the shooting occurred after Smith received a phone call at work from the police department informing him that his wife had been booked on a charge of suspicion of attempted murder.

"Other sources have tentatively confirmed this statement as being accurate. A female Jackson resident identified as Robina Smith was detained by the police department this morning about an hour before the incident at the car dealership.

"Records show that Larry Smith was the registered owner of a Ruger .357 Magnum. It is assumed that this gun may be the weapon used in the incident.

"Channel 2 will keep you updated as more information becomes available. Now, in other news..."

I grabbed the remote and turned off the television. I pressed my hands against my eyes. A dull ache erupted in my chest and tightened around my heart.

I was responsible for Larry's death.

◆ ◆ ◆

The next morning, for the first time in my life, I saw the ugly side of small-town life. Word got out that Robin had tried to kill me. People knew what Larry had done to himself. The gossip mill revved up, clicked into gear, and the whispers started.

My first hint that I had moved into the category of "hot news item" came at the grocery store. I turned into the coffee aisle, and the low-pitched conversation between two women I didn't even know was cut off mid-sentence.

They watched me with narrowed eyes as I selected my favorite blend of roasted coffee beans. I disappeared around the corner, and a voice behind me said, "...must have been having an affair. She dated him in high school, you know."

Great. Just *great*. The community had cast me as "the other woman." Never mind that it had been twenty years since I'd gone out with the creep.

The hiss of whispers followed me down the produce aisle. The sound of the letter S in "Smith" and "shot" carried to my ears as I selected my carrots and broccoli.

I went to get a nice cup of coffee at Demetra's, and the hostile stares followed. The situation was unfair, but understandable. I'd thought of Larry as being somewhat like the village idiot, but he was well-liked around town. People were upset.

Try as I might to appear unaffected, the accusatory whispers ticked me off.

I wanted to yell at the gossips and reputation-trashers, ask them what the hell they were thinking. But, of course, I didn't. That would have only added fuel to the fire.

Demetra, bless her, patted my hand. "Ignore 'em."

"Oh, I will, don't worry about that," I snapped.

Demetra blinked, and I realized that I sounded like I was upset with her. I took a deep breath, and gentled my tone. "Sorry, hon. I'm a bit on edge. Anyway, it's useless to deny juicy rumors. It never works, so I won't even try. At least in California there has to be a prompt arraignment."

Demetra rolled her eyes. "Arraignment? Translation please, lawyer-lady."

I grinned. "Oops. Sorry. Robin was taken into custody on suspicion of committing a felony. The prosecutor is required to file charges within forty-eight hours, not counting weekends. At the arraignment, the judge will tell Robin what the charges are, explain what her constitutional rights are, inform her that if she can't afford an attorney, one will be appointed for her, and blah blah blah. Robin will respond to the charges by entering a plea. It's all pretty short and sweet and to the point.

"So, all of this will go down tomorrow morning, and then the judge will decide if Robin can be released on bail. Hopefully, the arraignment will be so quick and so boring that people will lose interest and go back to worrying about whether they need to buy more cat food, instead of making up weird shit stories about my private life."

I hoped.

◆ ◆ ◆

Most court hearings are open to the public, as was the arraignment. But, because I was sure to be a witness when the trial got underway, I had to be content with reading about it in the news feeds.

The article stated that when it came time to enter a plea, Robin stood up and declared, "Not guilty," in a firm, confident voice.

"Liar, liar, pants on fire," I said aloud to the online report.

The judge apparently came to the same conclusion and didn't buy the claim of innocence. Bail was denied. Robin would remain in custody, and the legal process put back in gear to rumble forward.

◆ ◆ ◆

Robin's case went to trial fairly quickly, as these things go, Amador County not having a huge backlog of capital crime cases. And so, one morning, just over eight months later, on a cold December morning, I found myself pacing the floor of my kitchen, knowing that Robin's trial was underway at the Amador County Superior Court building on the other side of the valley.

I couldn't go anywhere because I was on standby as a witness. I might be called first thing in the morning, or I might not be called for days. My stomach felt unsettled, so I made myself hot cocoa with marshmallows on top.

Finally, feeling as if I might explode from anxiety, I grabbed my puffy down jacket, shoved my cell phone in my pocket, and went outside to walk the jitters out of my system.

The overnight temperatures had dipped well below freezing, and each step I took punctuated by the crunch of shattered frost. Up and down my road I walked, Dog innocently gamboling by my side, my mind whirling with horrible memories of the night that I'd escaped death by only a few inches.

Determined to exhaust myself, I don't know how long I had walked, maybe an hour, maybe more than that. Having realized that my fingertips were numb, I'd just decided to go back to the house when a pale green late-model sedan pulled onto my road.

Great. Now what.

It came closer, and I could see David de León behind the wheel. A strong ripple of relief coursed through my body. I didn't want to have to deal with some random clown who was wandering around lost because he was too cheap to own a GPS. I was *not* in the mood.

David rolled down the window and hollered, "Hey! Hop in."

I was freezing, so Dog and I did just that. "Out on a recess?" I knew David was planning on being in court.

"Nope," he said. "Let's get you into the house so you can defrost, and I'll tell you all about it."

An alarm bell went off in my head. David should know better than to discuss the case with a witness. Was I going to have to bite his head off as soon as we got inside?

Best not do it now, or he'd kick me out of the car. I'm not crazy.

Because the case was high-profile, Amador County allowed David's network to tape the trial. The County would own the tapes, but the network could use them for a future television show, provided they followed specific guidelines, such as no extensive editing to skew perceptions and the like. The County agreed to the deal because they got a professional-quality record of the proceedings at zero expense.

David pulled up to the back of the house. While I stood in the kitchen with my hands under the hot water, David hauled a black case from his car into the house. He set it on the table and opened it up. It was a compact video player. He turned it on and punched some buttons.

"All-righty then, check this out, girlfriend."

I stopped in the middle of drying my hands. "Look. You know I can't do that. Technically, I'm sequestered, and all that folderol."

"No problem. I talked to the judge. You'll be fine."

I pulled my head back and blasted him with my very best skeptical attorney-look. "That's usually my line."

David hooted with laughter, pulled out a chair, grabbed me lightly by the shoulders, and sat me down.

"No. Really. It's okay. Watch this. Better than the circus."

I popped back up out of the chair. "David, *no*. I'm *not* going to screw the whole thing up by..."

My cell phone rang. It was somebody at the District Attorney's office, telling me I was off the hook. David was right. The trial was over. What the hell? Now I was dying to see what he had.

I disconnected the call and plunked myself back into the chair. David stuck his tongue out at me, punched the play button, and the tape began to roll.

The camera focused on Robin, sitting up front in the brightly lit, wood-paneled courtroom, at the defense table. She was dressed in a subdued navy-blue suit, with no flashy gold jewelry to be seen anywhere. She wore a minimum of makeup, and her shoulder-length hair returned to its natural shade of drab light brown. Thin and pale, she looked rather ill.

The opening statements began with the prosecution. The county's lead Prosecutor, Franklin J. Dartmoor, a dark-haired man who looked to be in his late thirties, stood up and addressed the crowd.

"Your honor, ladies and gentlemen of the jury, today the people are charging Robina Simkowitz Smith," said Mr. Dartmoor, in a booming baritone, "with violation of California penal code 664, attempted murder.

"Alexandra M. D'Angelo, a resident of this county, was shot at in her home by this defendant, Robina S. Smith, who was, in fact, attempting to kill Ms. D'Angelo."

He turned and flung out his arm, pointing at Robin. She bit her lower lip and looked down at her lap.

"We will call Ms. D'Angelo who will testify that she was inside her own residence when the defendant shot at her without provocation.

"We will call the emergency room doctor who will testify that Ms. D'Angelo sustained multiple cuts and bruises as a result of this unprovoked attack.

"We will also call a Jackson-Martell Police Officer, who will provide evidence that Ms. Smith was present on Ms. D'Angelo's property at the time of the shooting.

"Ladies and gentlemen, the defense may argue that the defendant was under extreme duress at the time of the attack.

"However, we will show that the defendant was quite capable of differentiating between right and wrong, and that she attempted to mislead police when initially questioned.

"At the conclusion of the case we would ask you to find the defendant guilty of this vicious premeditated crime of attempted murder. Thank you."

And then came time for the defense opening statement.

I looked up from the screen to David's grinning face, wondering just when the "better than the circus" part of the tape was going to start.

"Just watch and learn," he said, so I turned my attention back to the monitor.

Robin's legal team's opening statement promised an interesting strategy, the "battered woman defense," but with an unusual twist.

In this case, the twist was that Robin committed violence because of her husband, rather than against him. The defense position was that Robin carried out the crimes because, under threat, she had no choice but to do it.

I could hardly believe what I was hearing. Robin? Confident and forthright Robin? Abused and battered by Larry? This revelation was more than mind-boggling—it was sickening.

Her attorney, Lionel Cantwell, a cocky little man in his sixties, stood up. Bald and arrogant, he strode around the front of the courtroom like a new Napoleon, demanding pity by the bucket-load from everyone.

Cantwell claimed that Robin had been coerced, threatened, forced to do whatever she'd done, under threat of death to her and their children.

"And a woman will do whatever she has to do, in order to protect her children. Is that not correct?"

The camera focused on Dartmoor's face as he listened to Cantwell's diatribe. His lips tightened, and there was visible tension in the rigid way he held his head.

"Larry Smith was a dangerous tyrant!" Cantwell yelled. "Larry Smith was both physically and psychologically abusive!"

It didn't take a genius to see that all the blame for Robin's evil deeds was to be placed on the shoulders of poor, dead Larry.

I felt sickened, chilled to the depths of my soul. It seemed that Robin's life was far more complicated and twisted than I'd ever dreamed.

Dartmoor, looking very much like he was about to raise an objection to Cantwell's histrionics, pushed back his chair and began to stand up.

A feminine voice rang across the courtroom. "No!"

The camera swung around and focused on Robin. She lurched up out of her chair and thrust her arms in the air like a football referee waving off a play. "Stop!"

A stunned silence fell over the courtroom. Robin stood as still as an ice statue, wide-eyed. She looked almost surprised to find herself on her feet.

She took a deep breath, turned and addressed the judge. "Your Honor, I'd like to change my plea to guilty."

The silence of the courtroom was torn apart by a cacophony of shouts and exclamations.

David leaned over and turned off the machine, then turned and grinned at me with a very self-satisfied smirk on his face.

I flopped back in my chair.

"Well," I said. "I'll be damned."

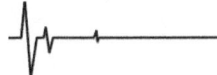

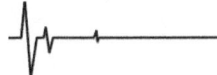

Chapter Thirty-Four

Less than a week later, David de León presented another remarkable interview on *Sunday Night America*. There had to have been one hell of a scramble to put the show together in that short amount of time. But they pulled it off.

The program opened with a view of a cinderblock room—stark white walls and thick metal screens over a handful of small rectangular windows emphasized the uninviting aura of the location. David and Robin sat across from each other at a tan plastic table.

Dressed in an orange jumpsuit, her face devoid of makeup, and her hair pulled back in a stark ponytail, Robin appeared calm. She did not fidget and she spoke in careful, considered phrases.

She had sentenced herself to life in prison by voluntarily confessing to a multitude of felonies, far beyond just the attempted murder charge. And, now she offered to explain her actions, both past and recent.

David and the network couldn't pass up such an opportunity. After a basic introduction and explanation for those unfamiliar with the case, he posed the question everyone wanted to ask.

"Robin, why did you change your plea from not guilty?"

"I pleaded guilty because I *am* guilty."

There were no false dramatics, no claims of abuse and horror. She delivered a blunt and candid recitation of the factors that drove her to kill.

"I originally agreed to the variation on the battered woman defense because there is a strong degree of truth to it. Larry always was able to talk me into doing whatever he wanted done.

"But, that said, I was horrified by the distortions presented in the opening statement at my trial. I needed to cut off that farce of a defense before it got any worse. When I agreed to take that approach, I had no idea that it would be pushed to an extreme.

"Yes, Larry was coercive and manipulative at times, but he was never physically abusive. I couldn't bear the thought of our children believing that their father was a monster, when he was not that way at all. I did this to protect my children's good memories of their father. Their lives are going to be hard enough as it is. I hope..." Her voice faltered. "I hope they can forgive me..."

David showed no reaction to her little pity-party. "So, Robin, you admit that you shot at Ms. D'Angelo?"

She swallowed, squared her shoulders, and said, "Yes."

"Why did you do it?"

"Well, David, there's no simple answer to that question. Are you ready for a long and complicated tale?"

◆ ◆ ◆

Gradually, the story emerged, piece by piece. Robin and Larry had, indeed, killed Rudy.

Robin explained how my brother, believing himself to be in love with Robin, had shown her the cache of gold the morning he found it.

He'd made a huge mistake in doing so. Robin was raised by her tightfisted father in the starkest of conditions. The temptation of easy riches proved too much for her to resist.

"I never had money of my own," she said. "In high school, my dad forced me to wear my brother's hand-me-down clothes, the ones he left behind when he enlisted in the Army.

"I had to work the big machines in the lumber mill, and never got paid for my labor. For years, we subsisted on basic foods like cheap ground beef and oatmeal.

"And it wasn't that we were destitute. That wasn't the case at all. My dad's lumber company did quite well. No, the real problem was that my father was a nasty old miser, and begrudged every cent he had to spend, even on basic necessities.

"He spent night after night, calculating his net worth, using his stupid spreadsheets. That was the only thing that ever gave him any joy—his damned money." She drew a deep breath. "I hated him."

Robin looked down at her hands. "If that gold was mine, I could be free from of my dad. Forever. He could stay in his crappy old shack, and I could have a life.

"I'm afraid," she said, in a soft, regretful tone of voice, "that the idea of riches—free money for clothes, a car, maybe a college education—was too much for me to ignore. The idea of freedom..." Robin closed her eyes and shook her head.

The truth was that she was sexually active with Rudy, but in love with Larry, and she told Larry about the gold. He then concocted the plot to kill

Rudy. She went along with it.

"Larry hated Rudy's guts. There was real bad blood there, deep, and ugly, and I never understood what it was all about. Jealousy? Maybe. Rudy was a lot of things that Larry was not.

"And, as I said, Larry had always been able to manipulate me. After that night, he had a hold on me that could never be broken. He had real power over me."

She inhaled deeply and looked up at the ceiling. "It just now occurred to me... I had just as much of a hold over him." She pinched her lips together, struggled with her composure for a moment or two, and then focused back on David.

"I arranged to meet Rudy out in the forest. I took along my flashlight. It was big, boxy, heavy. Not an obvious weapon. I dropped the flashlight on the purpose. Larry came up behind us, grabbed it off the ground, and hit Rudy over the head. Then he panicked, because he couldn't tell if Rudy was dead or not, so he decided to go get one of my dad's trucks, and make it look like there'd been a hit-and-run."

I gasped. *Flashlight?* The one Claire found? The one that might still be in the closet at Greg's house? My heart raced, and I forced myself to refrain from sending Greg a text right that instant. It was probably only five in the morning in Cape Town. I could hardly expect him to be paying attention to his text messages at that hour. And what could he do about it anyway?

Another thought horrible entered my mind. Was there was a baseball bat, the fine crevices and cracks of the wood-grain stained with Claire's blood, stored in a closet at the Smith house? Not that it would make much difference at this point... I turned my attention back to the television.

A strange far-away look passed over Robin's face, and she shook her head, ever so slightly. "I just realized something else. I have no idea what he did with the flashlight after that... It might be at our house somewhere."

She shivered at the macabre notion, and then took a few seconds to pull herself back together. It seemed clear that she knew nothing about the attack on Claire. Robin's revulsion appeared quite genuine.

"Anyway, *he* was the one who hit Rudy over the head. And *he* drove the truck over Rudy's body. His culpability was just as great as mine, if not more so. And yet, he always made me feel that the burden was entirely on me..."

Despite my disgust for what she'd done, a small flicker of sympathy for Robin came to life in my heart. Larry was as big of a bastard as I'd always thought him to be. Worse.

Her account of the night that Rudy died aligned in all essential points with the statement written by the anonymous witness we'd met on David's previous show.

It was awful, listening to her describe Rudy's death. She remained detached, analytical, her face smooth, and her voice calm, and that made it all the worse.

It seemed to me that Robin had already put this part of her life into a psychological deep freeze. She could pull it out, look at it, and then put it back away, before it defrosted. Before it began to smell.

Would I ever achieve such a state of Zen?

Did I want to?

◆ ◆ ◆

Following a commercial break, David revealed, with the subject's permission, that the anonymous witness was one Owen Benjamin Kennelly, a former natural sciences professor turned forest hermit.

David had contacted him again, and asked him to be interviewed for the show, but Kennelly had declined the offer. One time on television was more than enough, as far as he was concerned.

The firm refusal was disappointing, but hardly surprising. Kennelly did not wish to be photographed either, so David displayed an enlargement of the sketch that Rudy had made all those years ago, the one entitled "Old Ben, Obi Wan Cannoli."

Robin studied the drawing, then looked up from her twisting hands into the camera lens. She took a deep breath, then spoke with a slight tremor in her voice.

"I wish you well, Mr. Kennelly. I hold no grudges. You did the right thing." Her body language seemed out of sync with her words, but I sensed no latent hostility in her voice.

It felt weird, sitting there and watching Robin acting so very differently than the flighty person I'd seen at Demetra's that day, so many months ago. While she was clearly nervous, there was no gushing, no valley-speak, no dramatic flourishes.

Was this the woman she would have been if she'd never gotten involved with Larry?

◆ ◆ ◆

When the program resumed after a commercial break, a new scene opened, featuring an interview with a materials analysis specialist, Jason Abel.

Abel, an internationally recognized expert on the process used to analyze the gold found at the Smith's shop, was not the expert who'd done the analysis for the police department.

No, he resided higher up the food chain from the ordinary techie. How in the world had David come up with someone with such august credentials? The man was amazing.

"Raw gold nuggets," said Dr. Abel, "always contain trace elements that are characteristic of the area where they are found. For example, raw gold from Australia," he held up a sample for the camera, "can be differentiated from gold originating in Alaska." He displayed another sample. Except for basic shape, even in extreme close-up, the two samples looked pretty much the same.

"Detection of trace metals is accomplished through a process called inductively coupled plasma optical emission spectrometry." He displayed a picture of a gas-jet emitting a strange royal blue and magenta flame. "This test is recognized to be so precise that results can be used in a court of law.

"Through such a test," said Abel, "it was determined that a sample of the gold nuggets found at the Smiths' jewelry shop had a statistically significant match with the trace element profile of a sample of nuggets from the iron box found on Ms. D'Angelo's property."

Abel stated that the small cotton bags that held the nuggets found at Smith's shop proved to be identical to the ones from my place, and any lingering doubts regarding the origin of the gold vanished for good.

"Fabric is tested using microscopic fiber and polarized light analyses," Dr. Abel said. He showed a picture of a clump of glowing filaments. No exotic blue and red flame this time. Dang.

"There can be no doubt that all the bags came from the same original batch of fabric, and all were similarly aged."

Perfect match. Bingo.

I was thrilled that this information was presented on a national television show instead of in a small courtroom in an out-of-the-way California county. I silently blessed the day when I'd reconnected with David de León.

The scene then switched to the police department. Detective Drake's familiar face came on the screen, looking rather stern and formidable. I guessed he was in interview mode.

Or maybe he was just ticked off with David. The police department had been blindsided by the previous show. Whatever the reason for his dour formality, Drake explained the rationale and process by which the police department obtained the search warrants for the Smith home and business.

"In the course of our search of the premises," he said, "we discovered that the Smiths had no documentation showing purchases of gold. They also had no gold panning equipment or sluice boxes, no mining claims, and could hardly claim that they'd happened to find that many nuggets just lying around on a hillside.

"When the police asked Mrs. Smith where the gold came from, she failed to provide a specific answer. Her lack of cooperation prompted the request for the spectrographic analysis.

"From those tests came the conclusive evidence proving that random samples of the gold in the Smiths' possession were identical to samples from Ms. D'Angelo's property."

All the dots were connected, at last.

◆ ◆ ◆

There was another commercial break, and then the scene switched back to the prison room.

Now, facing a lifetime of incarceration, Robin no longer had any reason be evasive about where the gold came from. Her life was shattered, her children lost to her, parole unattainable for the foreseeable future. She came right out and admitted that the gold was taken from the secret underground hiding place on my property.

"For years, we never moved the gold because we thought it safe there, more secure than in a bank vault," she said. "Nobody would ask any questions, because nobody knew about it but us."

She and Larry slowly and judiciously dipped into the gold to fund a lifestyle and to purchase investments, including the car dealership. Larry had never made any killing on an internet startup company. That was only a cover story.

"We had to be careful not to cash in too much at any one time or questions would be asked. Opening a jewelry store seemed the ideal solution for turning the nuggets into ready money.

"We hired a British goldsmith who'd either melt down the gold and recast it, or make unique pieces out of the more attractive nuggets. The man did a great job. We loved his work. And, he never asked where the nuggets came from."

Everything was grand in Robin and Larry's world until Millie found Rudy's map. Robin and Larry's little arrangement began to unravel quite by accident.

"I went up the hill one evening," Robin said, "to get a bag out of the box, and there was Millie, staring down into the hole. Even though Millie didn't see me, I think I went a little nuts, and became even more vulnerable to Larry's pressure."

Worried that Millie would find the gold, Larry became more and more antsy about the situation. He pushed Robin into starting the harassment campaign.

"Larry convinced me that we could frighten Millie into selling the place. We were surprised when, after a few incidents, Millie didn't even want to discuss the idea."

To Larry, the solution was to apply more pressure. "Larry could always get me to do whatever he wanted me to do. All he had to do was say one word—Rudy—and I was sunk."

Which showed, I thought, just what a weasel Larry was. Manipulate with guilt. Send someone else—your *wife,* for godssake—out to do your dirty work. What a man.

"After Millie died, a window of opportunity opened. We removed the most gold we'd ever taken at any one time within the few weeks between her death and Alexandra's arrival."

Oh. Nice. My aunt's horrific death was "a window of opportunity." How charming.

"And then, of course," said Robin, "Alexandra moved in and screwed everything up. So the intimidation campaign was restarted."

Screwed things up? "Well, thanks a lot," I said aloud. The little flicker of sympathy I'd had for her sputtered and died.

Robin continued, "I did try to talk Larry into moving all of it, right after Alexandra came back. He said..." she swallowed and turned a bit red, "He said that... Alexandra was 'too damned stupid' to figure it out."

My jaw dropped open. It sounded to me that Larry was the one who was 'too damned stupid.' What an ass.

Robin stared down at the table, and absently rubbed at her left shoulder. "So I decided to move it myself. And ended up tearing my rotator cuff. And that was that. I couldn't move it, Larry *wouldn't* move it. And you know what happened next."

Robin was the one who trapped and murdered the poor coyote. She'd put the snake under the box on the back steps. She wrote the harassing letters. Her palm print matched the partial print from my back door. She'd done all the things that were meant to frighten me.

And, in the course of the police investigation, the police located a photo of Robin wearing the gold ring that Drake and the crew found on my property.

Interestingly, however, she said she had no idea who'd thrown the rocks at my window, and tried to open my back door that one night. I still wonder about that, from time to time.

"My life," Robin said in a moment of unusual eloquence, "was constructed of lies and secrets. Once that foundation cracked, everything around me fell apart."

I didn't feel the least bit sorry for her. Her actions were chilling, unconscionable. Larry may have been a bastard, but Robin had no soul. She'd lived without remorse for years, unburdened about being a thief and a murderer.

No, she only regretted that she'd allowed herself to be manipulated, and that she'd ended up in jail, separated from her kids. She was disgusting.

◆ ◆ ◆

After another commercial break, I was shocked to see none other than Gordon Sunderland appear on the screen.

Sunderland was originally scheduled to offer an anonymous taped testimony at the trial, his name known only to a handful of people. After some intense and drawn-out negotiations, he was granted immunity in return for his corroboration of Robin's earlier sworn deposition regarding her uncle, Ralph Ewing.

He decided to share, with David and the television audience, the same information that would have been entered into the record, had the trial gotten that far.

I never expected him to reveal his identity after all the trouble David had gone to in order to protect him. But, Sunderland laid it all out for the world to hear. I hoped he'd not live to regret his decision.

Sunderland presented example after example of how he was ordered to circumvent the law. He even had a few written notes, scribbled on scraps of paper, to support his story.

I thought about Ewing for a moment or two. How in the world did the man expect to extricate himself from this mess?

◆ ◆ ◆

As a grand finale, the scene switched back to Robin. David asked her, point blank: "Who killed Millie Minero?"

Robin looked confused, raised her eyebrows, and shook her head slightly. "How the hell should I know?" she said.

Robin and Larry Smith had been on a train in Italy, traveling from Florence to Rome, on the day that Millie was shot in the back. There existed not one single shred of evidence to tie them to Millie's murder. Not one.

So, who killed my Aunt?

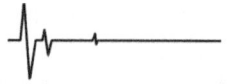

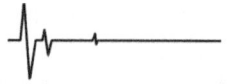

Chapter Thirty-Five

As soon as the television show was over, I sent a text to Greg.

> Is that old flashlight still in the closet at your house? Watch last night's *Sunday Night America*. I hope you have enough bandwidth! This is not a joke. REALLY. Watch it.

About five minutes later, I sent another one.

> !!!

I hoped that would get his attention. I paced around the house, waiting, and waiting and waiting for Greg to answer the damned text. Finally, I gave up and went to bed.

So many thoughts were tumbling through my head that I didn't sleep well. When I got up in the morning, the pacing resumed.

Yes, I'd jumped to the conclusion that the flashlight that Claire found was the same one that Larry had used to attack Rudy. But was it possible that this wild-hare presumption was actually true?

Had Larry panicked when he found out that an organized team of naturalists were poking around in the area where he'd ditched his makeshift weapon? Had he gone out to the forest in an attempt to retrieve it? Was he the mysterious man who'd attacked Claire?

Or had my brain just run down a rabbit hole?

But, dammit, it all made sense! The dirty flashlight in Greg's closet matched the one described by Robin on David's show. The lens was cracked, and it was missing a triangle-shaped shard, just like the piece of glass found embedded in Rudy's face. It *had* to be the same one!

I needed to get my hands on that flashlight.

◆ ◆ ◆

The day wore on. My impatience with Greg was boiling over. *Answer the damned text, pretty boy!* I sent him another message.

> Listen, kiddo, if you can't watch the TV program, here's the deal. I think that old flashlight in your closet is the one that was used to knock out Rudy. I need to get my hands on it, and take it to the police. Can I get in your house?????

And because I thought I was going to explode, I went out to the old bunkhouse to start cleaning it up. If I really was going to open a B&B, maybe there might be people crazy enough to actually want to stay in it. Enjoy the ambience of no air-conditioning, and heating provided via pot-bellied stove. It didn't sound the least bit appealing to me, but what did I know?

I forced the old door open, and looked around. There were twelve built-in wooden bunks in the old building, six on a side, stacked like shelves. The old cotton-stuffed mattresses were still in place, and mice had turned them into deluxe condos. The whole place reeked of dust and mouse urine.

Well, great. Before I did anything, I'd have to get an exterminator in there. And get the place steam-cleaned. Damn. Or burn the whole thing down and build a replica.

I so engrossed in my rambling ruminations that I jumped when my phone chirped. New text message; saved by the bell. I stomped out of the bunkhouse and slammed the door behind me.

The text was from Greg. At last.

> Yes, you can get in the house. Go see Ken at the hardware store. His brother Liam is living in my old quarters as caretaker. I've sent Ken a text and asked him to make you a duplicate key, in case Liam isn't around when you go there. Let me know what happens!

I sent him back a message.

> Super! Thanks! Will do.

I went in the house, cleaned up and headed down the hill to the hardware store.

◆ ◆ ◆

I got the key, and headed to Greg's house. I hoped that Liam wasn't there. A tall lanky man with a long horse-face, Liam was a hard worker, but more than a bit peculiar. He didn't take well to surprises or disruptions to his routine. I felt sure he was a fabulous caretaker, and followed all of Greg's instructions down to the letter. But I doubted that he'd let me in the house, even if his brother called him and said it was okay.

Liam probably would balk, because it was *Greg's* house, not Ken's, and he hadn't heard the words straight from the source. Nice enough guy, but definitely a pain sometimes.

Liam wasn't around. *Whew*. In nothing flat, I was in the house, and up the stairs. I pulled over the chair from Greg's desk, stood on it, and retrieved the box with the old flashlight in it. I shoved the chair back in place and skedaddled. I wasn't in there more than five minutes. Not wanting to linger, I jammed the box in the truck and was out of there.

When I got home, I carried the box out into the bright sunlight, and looked at the old flashlight as carefully as I could without handling it. Dirt and rust encrusted the sides and bottom of the big old battery. The lettering stamped into the lightly corroded metal top said SEALED BEAM EVEREADY BIG JIM WATERPROOF LANTERN. I looked the whole thing over carefully. There seemed to be some scratches on the handle. I wiped the area with a cotton swab. In an instant, my suspicions turned into a harsh reality.

Robin

I pulled my phone out of my pocket and called Drake. And I wondered what the hell I was going to tell Greg he'd had a murder weapon stored in his closet.

◆ ◆ ◆

The next morning at ten I went to the police station. I was a bit nervous, for some reason, even though Drake always took me seriously, and was never dismissive or rude.

I couldn't deny that turning the flashlight over to Drake was not much more than an exercise in futility. After being out in the weather for years, surely any traces of blood or fingerprints were long gone. On the other hand, failure to turn over this apparent piece of the puzzle would be negligent, even immoral. I *needed* to complete the story of Rudy's death.

So there I was.

Drake greeted me, I set the box on his desk, and explained how the flashlight had come to be in Greg's possession. "It stuck me, the other night, listening to Robin on TV, that this exactly matches the description of the item that Robin said Larry used to hit Rudy. And, look..." I pointed at the scratched name on the handle. "Plus," I added, indicating the broken lens, "there was a triangular shard of glass stuck in Rudy's face. It sure looks to me like two plus two equals four."

Drake's forehead wrinkled; caution practically gushed from his pores.

He didn't say a word.

"Yes," I said, "You're right. I know. Rudy's dead, Larry's dead, Claire's dead, and Robin is in prison. So for me to bring this in as evidence now is, frankly, moot. I mean, we don't know for sure who it belonged to. Some other Robin could have dropped it one day when out for a stroll in the woods.

"It might have nothing to do with Rudy or Claire. But, I just *couldn't* let it sit in a box on a shelf at Greg's house. It... it means something..."

Drake tilted his head and gave me a funny little half-smile. "And so, you want it to sit in a box on a shelf here, instead."

"Yep. That's about it."

"Well," said Drake. "Let me think about this." He drummed his fingers on the desk. "Hmmm. I guess when all is said and done, one shelf is pretty much like any other. Leave it here. I'll bag it up, enter it in the system, put it in Rudy's box."

I almost melted with relief. "Thank you." I squeezed his hands, and walked out.

I drove home, one weight lifted from the heavy stack of my emotional burdens, but still a bit unsettled. Always, always, in the back of my mind, there was another question that would not be resolved as easily.

And what about Millie?

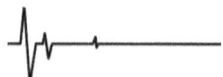

CHAPTER THIRTY-SIX

One morning, a couple of days before the New Year, I sat down to write an email to my single remaining friend in New York, Stefi.

> Another Christmas has come and gone, happily ignored by me. Greg is still in South Africa. He couldn't come back home in November like he originally said he would. Too many of the things that I thought would be settled a year ago are still drifting around unresolved!
>
> The divorce seems on track to be finalized in April or thereabouts. Mark finally settled down and stopped being a jerk about everything. The guy needed to grow up, big time. Maybe he finally has.
>
> HA! Just kidding. That'll never happen.
>
> One major project is almost out of the way. The upstairs bathrooms are close to complete. I finally broke down and hired a contractor. I'll do the painting and other finish work myself. Now, before you go and get pissed off at me for being a cheapskate, I need to

Dog barked ferociously with his "Uh Oh, Stranger" voice, and I stopped writing mid-sentence. I pried myself up out of the chair and went to the kitchen window. A light blue 1956 Thunderbird pulled up behind the house. Demetra?

By golly, it was. She hadn't been to my house in years, and Dog didn't know her. I hurried outside.

She stepped out of her car, and wrapped me in a hug. Dog, seeing that all was well with the world, stopped barking and started sniffing the tires on the T-bird so he could select the best one upon which to pee.

"Hey girl," she said. "Long time no see."

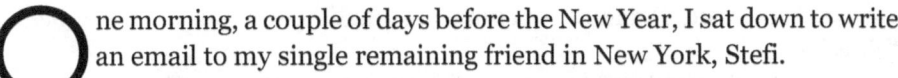

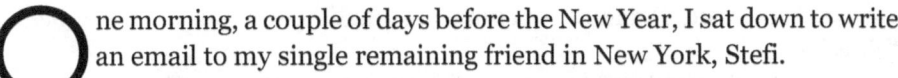

I was touched. She'd had taken time off work to come find me. I'd not gone to her place since before Robin's trial.

We walked arm-in-arm into the kitchen. We settled in at the table, and I ran some coffee beans through the grinder. The wonderful fragrance drifted through the air, reminding me of happier times.

The next thing I knew, instead of pouring coffee, I was pouring out my soul to her.

"I was so sure—so very sure—that the trail that led to Rudy's killers would also tell us what happened to Millie. But, it didn't, and now what?"

Demetra squeezed my hand and let me ramble on.

"I'm haunted by this horrible thought—What a... *colossal* waste of lives. My god. It took a few years for everything to fall apart, but that was the end result. Four lives, thrown away. No. Five lives. Can't forget old Ewing. And then there's the collateral damage to Robin and Larry's kids, and god only knows who else."

I sighed, and rubbed my face.

"So," said Demetra, opening her hands palms-up on the tabletop. "Now what."

"Good question." Leave it to her to zoom right in on the fundamental issue.

I got up and started the brew cycle on the pot of coffee. What this conversation lacked was some of Demetra's pastries, but that was neither here nor there. *She* was here.

"Millie's case is still technically open, but the police have absolutely nothing new to go on. The only thing that I could think of to do was to go through Millie's clothing and personal stuff again."

I sighed again, in frustration. "Goddammit. I suppose I was naïve to hope that I'd find a threatening letter, conveniently signed by the perpetrator, hidden away under a sheet of lavender-scented paper in the bottom of Millie's underwear drawer, or something like that."

Demetra nodded her head in quiet sympathy. Her unspoken question hung in the air. How soon would it be before the police department decided that Millie's case had gone cold, and filed it away in some sort of storage Purgatory?

I had a horrible feeling that it wouldn't be too much longer.

◆ ◆ ◆

January. Gradually, my frame of mind improved. I seemed to be succeeding in convincing myself that I wasn't responsible for Larry's suicide. The pivotal moment came suddenly. I woke up one morning with a startling thought that crystallized the problem in my mind and set me free.

I'm allowing Larry, in death, to manipulate me, and make me feel guilty. Just like he did to Robin, in life.

I sat there, on the edge of the bed, and I knew, right then, that the damage I was doing to myself had to stop. The cuts and scratches on my skin from the shattered window had faded into thin, pale lines. It was time for the scars on my mind to start to fade away, too.

I stood up, and silently told Larry to go to hell, and stay there.

◆ ◆ ◆

It was a crisp February morning, the kind of day when the sky is a rich deep blue and as clear as Irish crystal. I'd finished my breakfast, and was enjoying a nice cup of hot chocolate while looking online at decorating ideas for the new upstairs bathrooms.

I turned on the water in the sink, rinsed the coffee pot, and realized the sink wasn't draining. A small coffee-tinged puddle sat in the bottom of the basin, taunting me.

My shoulders sagged. So much for it being a beautiful day. I could feel tears of frustration rising up in my eyes and trickling down my face. Thank you sooo much, PMS.

The plumbing cleanout was located in the cellar. Of course it would be. Oh, joy. I trudged over to the middle of the kitchen, grabbed a couple of the green chairs and moved them to the side, then shoved the kitchen table after them.

I bent over, grabbed the latch on the top of the trap door, heaved it open, and a burning pain stabbed me in the gut, right behind my rib cage. I flinched. Acid surged up my gullet. *Great.*

But, just like all the other times my stomach rebelled, nothing else happened. So I gulped down a handful of Tums, shrugged my shoulders, and carried on.

I glared at the hole in the kitchen floor. I did *not* want to go down there and play lady plumber. But wishing wouldn't clear the clog. Nobody was going to do it for me.

Dog's half-hearted woof told me that we had company, someone he knew. I rather hoped that some strong, handsome man had arrived to save me from having to brave the dread cellar, but, no, our visitor was Bertie. I wiped my face, and opened the back door for her.

"What's up with the tears, chickie?" She folded me into a big squishy hug.

The uncharacteristic reek of alcohol on her breath surprised me. I'd never known Bertie to be a big drinker, so I ignored it, at least for the moment. I shoved aside the memory of Greg having sent her home from work one day, many months ago now, because she stank of the previous night's booze.

"Hormones." I said. "They make a complete sap out of every woman under forty-five."

"Well, yeah, can't argue with that, but what brought on this particular rainstorm?" She glanced across the kitchen at the open trapdoor. "And what's up with the Black Hole of Calcutta?"

"Plumbing problem. I prefer to think of it as a Yawning Pit of Hell. As in 'Like hell do I want to go down there.' The drain in the sink is clogged up. The cleanout's down below. It's damned annoying, but not hard to fix. I just have to get my rear in gear to do it."

"Not that you have that much of a rear end. Girl, you're looking like a scarecrow." Instead of sounding like her usual jocular teasing, Bertie's speech had a snide tone to it. What in the world was the matter with her?

She smelled of last night's alcohol; maybe she'd topped it off with a morning pick-me up. I didn't think she was drunk, but she sure wasn't acting normal.

I turned and walked back towards the kitchen counter. "How about I brew up a new pot of coffee."

Bertie made a small disgusted sound in her throat. "Only if it's Irish coffee."

The alarm bells ringing in my head got a bit louder. "Sorry, sweetie, no can do." I finished setting up the coffee pot, and turned it on. "Anyway, why aren't you at work?"

Bertie's entire body seemed to puff up with outraged indignation. "The bastards at the hospital fired me. Yesterday afternoon. Can you believe it? After all I've done for them? They got on some big budget-cutting thingy or...or somethin', and gave me the ax. Well, lemme tell you, I'm pretty damned-well steamed about it."

I had a feeling that budget-cutting was only a small part of the picture. "Want to tell me about it?"

"No." For a moment the furrows in her face deepened, making her look like an angry bulldog. "It pisses me off to even think about it. I sat around and moped last night and this mornin', and then decided to come up here and see what's goin' on with you and that worthless dog of yours."

I hoped the remark was nothing more than another poor attempt at a joke. I didn't find it funny, but Bertie seemed unaware that she'd said anything insulting.

"Oh," she said, her face relaxing a bit. "Just thought of somethin'. You might wanna see this..."

She sat down in one of the kitchen chairs, dug around in her purse, pulled out a scrap of coarse paper with raggedy edges, and handed it to me.

It looked like she'd torn it from a newspaper. I smoothed out the clipping on the tabletop. It was an announcement from Andrew the Pickleman, stating that he was retiring, and the office was closing. There was a contact phone number in an area code I didn't recognize.

"Well," I said. "Bye bye, Spiderlegs. I was wondering about how he was going to pull his bacon out of the fire. I don't know if I told you—he entered a 'no contest' to the theft charges, paid a fine, and I got the book back."

"Oh," said Bertie in a flat, uninterested tone of voice, apparently already bored with the topic.

The coffeepot beeped to tell me the brew cycle was finished, so I got up and poured a cup. I offered it to Bertie. She shook her head, but I set in in front her anyway. She ignored it.

I sat down with a mug for myself. "I bet he cut some sort a deal," I said. "This 'retirement' sure looks more like a move to avoid censure or disbarment."

"And good riddance," added Bertie. "Nasty li'l toad." She shifted in the chair, as if she couldn't get comfortable, and glanced around the room.

"When're you gonna ditch this crappy furniture, and make this place look like it's your own? This stuff has been here forever."

"Exactly. That's the whole point. There's no way I'm going to get rid of it." I struggled to keep my voice under control, and not let my irritation show. "Millie's stuff is what will make this B&B unique. Take advantage of the fact that this was her home, and all that. And besides, I like it."

Bertie wrinkled her nose, like she'd smelled something rotten. "Ah. The Shrine of the Holy Martyr, Saint Millie of the Oil Paints. Acolytes from far and wide will come to honor her... her *exalted* memory. Better set up an altar on the grand piano, chickie."

She jerked her thumb in the general direction of the living room, like I'd perhaps forgotten where the piano was located.

"You gotta admit it," she continued, seeming to really warm up to the topic. "Good career move on her part. Get shot in the back, live on in the hearts and minds of worshipers forever."

A terrible silence descended upon the room. "What did you say?" My voice barely rose above a whisper.

"You heard me." Bertie settled back in her chair, relaxed, with a smug little smile on her face.

I stared at her, chilled by the implications of her statement. I had to push aside the cloud of anger that boiled up inside of me before I could speak. "Bertie, the police never released the cause of death."

She had the grace to look a bit flustered, but only for a moment. "Get real, girlfriend. Everyone knows what happened up here. Do you really think those... those jokers on the emergency crew could keep their big mouths shut about somethin' that dramatic?"

A flicker of doubt flared up in my mind. There might be fifteen or twenty people who knew what happened to Millie, maybe even a few more than that. The police, the ambulance crew from the fire station, people at the coroner's office. All these people knew.

And yet, not one speculative whisper had ever reached my ears in all the months since her death. Not one.

"Bertie, who told you that?"

"Hell, I don' remember. That's months ago now."

I searched though my memory. If my aunt's friends or colleagues suspected that a murder had occurred, I would have heard about it. A fuss would've been raised, questions asked. But nothing like that had happened.

Greg had told me the truth about Millie's death, but he hadn't told anyone else. I was sure of it. There was no way he would have jeopardized the police investigation.

I was indeed guilty of telling Bertie more than I should have, that the death was not from natural causes, but I hadn't told her that Millie was shot. I felt a chill, and a light sheen of sweat broke out on my skin.

Bertie adjusted her position in the chair again. "Relax, girlfriend. You're makin' a big deal outta old news."

"Am I?"

"Yeah, you are. Old news about an old bitch." She giggled, as if she'd said something hilarious. I didn't join in, and a defensive sneer curled her upper lip. "What? You know I never liked her."

I sprang up from of my chair and rummaged around in the refrigerator to find something for Bertie to eat. I was now sure she'd had an early morning drink or two, and the woman needed to get sobered up, pronto. And, I needed to do something to keep from clobbering her. I took a deep breath. Control. I need to stay in control...

But, me being me, I couldn't keep my mouth shut. I closed the refrigerator and turned around. "So, then, what was the deal with all the 'Oh my goodness' crap when I told you that Millie hadn't died of natural causes?"

She pulled her head back and narrowed her eyes, as if she had no idea what I was talking about.

I wasn't buying it. "When we were looking at Rudy's autopsy report. You seemed to think I was telling you big news then. You were going 'Oh my god, a serial killer,' and all that shit."

Bertie tapped her fingers on the tabletop as if trying to recall the conversation. "I musta not known then."

Yeah, right. I folded my arms across my chest, almost daring her to continue.

"She stole him from me, you know. Your sainted aunt stole him from me."

What? Who stole what?

Ohmygod... She's still pissed about Doc's relationship with Millie. I wanted to slap her. Instead, furious, I went back to the fridge, pulled out some leftover rice and stir-fry, and tossed the containers onto the counter.

I grabbed my wok, added a splash of my favorite olive oil, and heated it up.

With my back still to Bertie, I said, "What the hell are you talking about?" I was afraid to turn around, afraid that I'd yield to the temptation to punch her lights out.

"Doc. That's who I'm talkin' about. Your bitch of an aunt stole him from me."

I stopped, turned off the stove, moved the wok, took a deep breath, and counted to ten.

"Don't be ridiculous. That's just not true."

"Oh, yeah, it is, and you know it. She stole him from me, crawled inta his bed, wrapped her skinny legs around him and lured him away from me. She got ahold of him, and wouldn't let go."

I turned around and stared at her with the most intimidating glare I could muster. "Bertie. Leave it. You've got it all turned around."

And from the back of my mind, came a horrible thought, based on something that Greg had told me months ago, when I first arrived in town.

"After your aunt died, Doc went into a sort of tailspin. He was a mess. Bertie stepped right up to the bat, and gave him a shoulder to lean on. I was proud of her. She kept him going."

My heart started to thump, faster, faster. My palms were slick with sweat. Bertie hadn't been compassionate. She'd been a spider, luring Doc into her web. She was *happy* that my aunt was gone. And, somehow she knew that Millie was shot in the back...

A wave of fear rolled through me, cutting off my air. I took a deep breath, and stepped back. Bertie... a murderer? I didn't want to believe it, but, there it was. All the puzzle pieces finally fit together. I felt sick, and the acid surged up my throat again.

I had to distract her, find my phone, call the police. I swallowed, and tried to act like everything was just fine. "Bertie, please, just sit back down at the table. I'm going to fix you something to eat. You'll feel better after you get something in your stomach."

"Nah. I don't want anything." She wandered over to the old fireplace and made a show of studying the watercolor hanging over the mantle. "Done by the great artist herself..."

She hooted out a strange little self-satisfied laugh, and all doubt was erased from my mind. She abruptly turned, pivoted on her heel, and stared at me. Her eyes were hard, piercing, with a coldness in them I had never seen before. A strange half-smile crept across her face. I knew right then that she understood that I had realized the truth about Millie's death.

My hands were shaking. A silent mantra started deep inside of me. *Don't panic. Don't panic.* I glanced across the kitchen to the basket on the counter where I usually set my cell phone. It was empty. *Crap!* I'd left the phone upstairs in my bedroom. A surge of helpless frustration rolled over me.

Keep calm, stay in control. I needed to get her thinking of something else, or I'd never be able to sneak up and grab it. My truck keys were up there too. *Damn!*

She took a menacing step in my direction; I flinched. But, instead of confronting me, she shoved me aside and strode off in the direction of the front room. Within a matter of seconds, I could hear odd thumps and bangs echoing down the hallway.

What the hell? It sounded like she was digging sheet music out of the storage area in the piano bench.

No time to look to see what she was up to. There wouldn't be another chance to scramble up the stairs and grab my phone. The thumping stopped, and Bertie's alto voice echoed down the hall, bellowing out Schubert's *Ave Maria*, with altered lyrics.

Ave, Saint Miiiillie
Your old piano is your shrine...

I bolted for the stairwell, and then froze, horrified at what I saw.

"MY GOD," I screamed. "What are you DOING!"

Flaming sheet music crackled on top of the piano. Bertie, singing away, placed more crumpled papers on the pile and held out her cigarette lighter, igniting the new stack.

I sprinted across the room. With a lunge and a desperate sweep of my arm, I hurled the burning pyre off the top of the piano. The burning papers scattered onto the floor by the front windows.

Malevolent spirals of orange fire leaped and twisted up the curtains.

My brain struggled to make sense of the scene before me. And then lucid reality snapped into place. I needed my phone, I needed it *NOW*.

I could make it up the stairs faster than she could. Bertie wasn't one for regular exercise, and I hoped that any alcohol in her bloodstream would mess with her sense of balance.

I turned to run, but tripped over the hallway rug, and stumbled. Those few seconds of wobbling uncertainty were all Bertie needed. She charged forward, and shoved me away from the stairs. I turned to run into the kitchen, but she was right on my heels.

"Bye bye Alexandra." She slammed into me again, and sent me flying. Because she outweighed me by a significant amount, I got the worst end of the deal. I lost my balance and fell.

My head jolted against the floor, and my body spun, sliding in a circle across the smooth oak planks.

And then I fell into nothing.

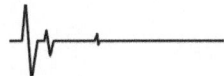

Chapter Thirty-Seven

Pain and darkness. Confusion. Fear. I sprawled face down on the hard-packed dirt of the cellar floor. My hands and face stung, like they'd been sandpapered, and I spit tiny rocks and dirt out of my mouth. How long had I been down here?

I lifted my head, but there was nothing in front of me but shades of orangish black and gray, flickering, as if illuminated from above.

I struggled to push myself upright and gasped as jolting stabs of agony ripped through my abdomen and left shoulder. I tried to lift my left arm, hissed; my whole body jerked at the resulting grinding sting. I ran my right hand across the left side of my collarbone, and flinched. The bone was cracked, no doubt about it.

"Bertie..? BERTIE!"

Holding my breath, I listened for her answer. But I heard no sounds that indicated that anyone was in the house. What I did hear sent chills through my body.

A faint crackling sound, the sound of things burning, filled the air. I glanced up. An undulating orange reflection of dancing flames lit the kitchen ceiling.

No. Good lord help me, *no.*

The cellar was deep—I'd fallen a good twelve feet. There was no way to tell where the source of the fire was without going up the wooden ladder. I reached out and touched the ladder, but when I tried to stand, my left arm shifted, and the pain in my shoulder overwhelmed me. Sparking dots danced in front of my eyes.

I collapsed back onto the dirt floor. I took a deep breath, waited a few moments, and scooted across the dirt on my rear. I grabbed the side of the ladder with my right hand, and pulled myself to my feet.

I leaned against the side of the ladder and, with my right hand, grabbed the rung just above my head. Gripping the wood, I stepped onto the bottom rung.

My left arm swung outward as I moved to put my other foot on the step, and I hissed in pain.

The tiny dots of light and dark sparked across my vision again. Afraid I might pass out. I stepped back down onto the dirt floor, and sagged back against the ladder.

BERTIE!" I screamed. "BERTIE! DON'T LEAVE ME DOWN HERE."

There was no answer.

Well, *shit*. I was going to have to rescue myself. And to do that, I had to find something to support my arm.

The contents of the cellar were cleaned out years ago. There was nothing there that I could use to make into a sling. There was a long rope attached to the old willow basket next to the ladder, but even if I could untie the rope one-handed, I had nothing to cut it with.

I glanced down at the front of my blue plaid shirt, and an idea popped to life. I unbuttoned a few buttons below my breasts, stuffed my left arm into the gap, pushed my hand all the way to my side, and grabbed a fistful of the camisole underneath.

I struggled with the other hand to close as many buttons as I could, trapping the arm in place. My left shoulder still hurt like a bitch, but a small amount of support beat the heck out of none.

Okay. One more time. I grabbed the ladder again and muscled myself up a step. I tilted my head back for another look. The undulating orange light had brightened.

Was I imagining it? Was the whole kitchen on fire, engulfed in crackling, swirling spirals of flame? I couldn't tell.

I tried to pull myself to the next rung, but bumped my bad arm, and almost lost my grip. Gritting my teeth against the pain, I waited for my lightheadedness to subside.

There were still a good six to eight feet to the top of the ladder. I knew I wouldn't make it. I'd never find out if there was a clear path to the back door. Sheer foolishness to even try. The last thing I needed was to pass out and fall again.

I hung on to the ladder with my right hand and slid my foot down, stretching until I found the dirt floor. I stood there, gasping for air, fighting off panic.

The crackling sound in the house above me got louder. This wasn't the way I wanted to die. Buried in a searing rain of flaming timbers and flooring, pinned down in agony, gasping as the fire ate away the oxygen in the room.

"NO!"

I pushed myself away from the ladder and stumbled across the room, away from the opening above me. I clung to a wooden shelving support on the opposite wall and tried to ignore the excruciating spasm of pain that rolled across my collarbone and shoulder.

I found myself crying in frustration and beating my one good hand on the heavy plank in front of me.

The door. There was a door in the wall... Where the hell was it? Despite the flickering orange light from above, it was still damned dark in the cellar. I fought to contain my rising terror and tried to visualize the location of the lever that Zak had shown me all those months ago.

Right... over... there... Holding on to the shelves, I scuttled sideways until I reached the corner. I ran my good hand down the corner post until it hit a protruding piece of wood. I grabbed it and shoved it backwards.

Nothing.

I reset my grip and pulled, relaxing my knees and letting my weight add force to the effort.

Nothing.

My heart pounded, and fear rushed forward to take control again.

Stop. Breathe. *Calm down.*

To the side, he'd pushed it to the side...

I slammed the lever to the right, and the shelves swung out. I stumbled, almost lost my balance, and the grating pain ripped through my shoulder again. A cool breeze swept into the enclosed space and swirled around my body.

A whooshing roar and a flare of orange light from above relayed a horrible fact. The surge of fresh air had fed the fire.

◆ ◆ ◆

I stumbled forward into the dark earthen tunnel. The wonderful flinty smell of cool, clean soil wrapped around me, filling me with blessed relief. I'm safe here, I told myself, sheltered in the embrace of the earth, protected from the flames.

Then I had a horrible thought. Who besides Bertie knew I was here?

No one. Nobody was going to come save me. I leaned against the earthen wall of the tunnel, and tried to clear my mind, tried to focus.

Had it come to this? Could I accept defeat? No.

I had a choice. I could try to make my way to the top of the knoll or I could die here under the house.

I felt my way along the gritty walls until an abrupt whack on the forehead sent me reeling backwards. The sudden impact radiated pain through my head like bolts of electricity.

I gasped, blinked sudden tears, and fumbled around over my head with my good hand. My fingers dragged across rough old wood, and I knew I'd run into a support timber.

I couldn't see a damned thing, but from the increased upward slant in the floor, I guessed I'd reached a transition point. From here forward, it would be a slow climb to the top of the hill. Bent over, afraid I'd hit my head again, I groped my way along the dirt wall in the pitch-blackness.

Oh god. What if I stumbled into a nest of hibernating snakes? Or scorpions? Or...or... I gasped with the beginnings of panic, then stopped and pounded the dirt wall with my fist.

Knock it off! Get in control. My galloping thoughts were not helping in any way.

Shivers wracked my body. I didn't know if I was getting chilled, or going into shock. My legs went rubbery; I collapsed onto the dirt and rolled onto my back. I tried to relax, to even out my breathing, to tune out the agony engulfing me, but nothing helped. No way would I be able to crawl up the hill with only one good arm. No way.

"Goddammit, Bertie," I screamed. "When I get outta here, I AM GONNA KICK YOUR ASS!" There was no answering sound, not even a faint echo.

There was nothing left to do but point myself uphill, and try again. I tried scooting along on my back. The fabric of my shirt dragged on the rough floor of the tunnel, and small rocks pinched and rolled beneath me. I wondered how soon my back would be a bloody, abraded mess. A change in the slope of the floor told me that the tunnel had taken another bend upwards.

Unable to comprehend the significance of the sudden increased grade, I pushed hard with my heels.

My shoulders slammed against the upward slant in the dirt floor. I cried out as my collarbone gave an audible pop and exploded in a flash of unbearable pain, stabbing me, scorching me, like fireworks in the brain.

I'm done... Finished. Nausea curled around me like a crushing serpent. The slightest movement sent jagged shards of pain racing through my shoulder. I'd reached the end of my endurance. I couldn't move. I'd die here, and no one would ever know where I'd gone.

I closed my eyes in surrender. The words of a poem, memorized long ago, floated into my mind. I could visualize the passage by T. S. Eliot. Stark black letters on a white sheet of paper.

AND THIS IS THE WAY THE WORLD ENDS, NOT WITH A BANG BUT A WHIMPER.

Chapter Thirty-Eight

A man's voice called to me. "Alexandra, where are you!"

I opened my eyes, but I was still surrounded by darkness.

"Zak?"

My voice sounded faint inside my head, so I tried again, louder. "ZAK?"

The beam of a flashlight pierced the gloom. A familiar voice called out. "It's me. I'm here." A moment later, a warm hand touched my ankle. "What did you do to yourself?"

"Broken bone." I fought off waves of nausea and pain. "Can't move."

I heard the hiss of Zak pulling in a breath against his teeth. "Okay, tell you what. I'm going to go call the paramedics. We'll get you out of here in nothing flat. Hang in there, just for a bit."

He started to back up, away from me.

"Zak?"

"Yes?"

"Fire. There's... fire."

"Yes. Don't worry. Got it all under control. I blasted the kitchen with my fire extinguisher and called the fire department. I just have to call them back and tell them to send the ambulance too."

"Okay..."

The pain overtook me, and carried me away again.

◆ ◆ ◆

Gentle voices were talking to me. I gasped as I was jostled and bumped. Someone unfastened my pants, and a needle jabbed into my hip. Moments later, soothing warmth spread through me, and the pain retreated into a foggy memory of itself.

I relaxed, only to be jolted again as the mysterious helper eased something under my shoulders, and tied my arm to my chest. Someone pulled downward on my feet, dragging me.

"Nooooo..." I croaked, thrashing my head back and forth. The motion was a big mistake. The throbbing in my shoulder started up again.

"Sorry, hon." I didn't recognize the voice speaking to me. "But we've got to try that again."

"No. Please no." I clenched my teeth as my body was jostled again. It was too much, too much... I closed my eyes.

◆ ◆ ◆

I reached out with my right hand, and it hit smooth, cool metal. A bedrail? Warm fingers wrapped around mine—a thumb caressed my skin with a gentle touch.

I was no longer sprawled in the cold, harsh dirt of the tunnel, but comfortably tucked into a warm bed, looking up at a light blue ceiling. A faint PA system announcement echoed some distance away, paging a couple of doctors.

"Doctor Singh, Doctor Singh. Doctor Volt, Doctor Volt."

I moved my line of sight to the right, towards the voice. A familiar face smiled at me, and an overwhelming feeling of peace filled my senses.

I sighed out his name. "Zak..."

"Hey, Wonder Woman. How are you feeling?"

"Like hell. Haven't we had this conversation before?"

Zak chuckled.

Had I said something clever? I moved my head in order to see him, and sucked in my breath when a sharp twinge shot through my left shoulder. I tried to ignore the pain and reached out my right hand to squeeze his fingers.

I was startled to see bandages on my arm.

"You were burned."

I stared at the white gauze for a few moments before an explanation for the injury clicked into my brain. In my mad rush to save the piano, I'd managed to barbeque my arm.

I looked up into my friend's dark eyes. Explaining it all seemed way too complicated for my befuddled mind to deal with. I opted for a simple question. "What time is it?"

"Almost one o'clock in the afternoon. The more important question would be, 'what day is it.' We brought you in here not quite twenty-four hours ago."

Wrenching memories rushed through my brain, triggering an electric frisson of alarm. *Bertie!*

Ignoring a fierce stab of pain in my shoulder, I struggled to sit upright in the bed.

Zak pressed the button on the controller to raise the head of the bed into the sitting position.

"Is she in jail?"

Zak crinkled his forehead. "Is who in jail?"

A jumbling cascade of panicky thoughts burst from me. "Zak! Listen to me! Alberta Strahan. Bertie. She lives on Argonaut Lane. The police have to get over to her house, right now. And I mean *right now*! She's the one who murdered Millie."

His eyes widened in alarm, and his body tensed. "How do you know that?"

My heart pounded, breaths coming in gasps. "She gave herself away. I put two and two together and she realized it, so she threw me down in the pit, and set the house on fire."

Zak was on his feet. He pulled out his cell phone, checked the signal, and hurried out into the hallway. I could hear him talking. "Yes, it's urgent." I couldn't make out the rest of it.

He came back into the room. "We're putting out a BOLO right now."

"Bolo?" I was confused. What did a string tie have to do with anything?

"'Be On Look Out.' We've got an officer going out to her address right now. A bulletin is going out to the Highway Patrol and all our neighboring agencies. If she's not at her home, someone will find her."

I couldn't believe that Bertie was still out, running around free. "Why isn't she in jail?"

Zak tilted his head, confused. "Why should she be?"

"She was drunk! And she was driving!"

"Well, I guess she made it home."

"Oh." I didn't take the time to dwell on that minor injustice, as it was quickly superseded by another horrible thought. "Where's Dog! He didn't get left there all by himself, did he?"

His reply was gentle. "No. Don't worry. Animal control is keeping him for now, until the doctor says you'll be able to take care of him. The shelter people know he's only there on a temporary basis, and not up for adoption."

Relief rippled through me, and my body relaxed. "Good." Dog would be stressed by his apparent imprisonment, but at least he had somewhere to stay, food and water. He was safe. That was all that mattered.

Zak smiled. "I'm sure he's fine. Probably not too happy about it, but fine."

I glanced around the room. "How did I get here? I was in my house, in the tunnel, and then, all of a sudden, poof, I'm here."

"It's pretty simple. I went by your house, found you, and called an ambulance."

"C'mon Zak." I closed my eyes for a couple of seconds and summoned a bit more energy. "How about the full version, not the Cliff Notes."

"Fair enough. I had some vacation time coming to me, so I decided to take a few days. You know, 'use it or lose it.' Anyway, I was going to make a run down to Folsom and go shopping at the outlet stores.

"I had the notion to stop and say hi, and ask if you wanted to go along. So I turned onto your road, and there was Dog, running around acting crazy and smoke pouring out the front windows.

"I pulled around to the back of your house. The door was standing wide open. I jumped out of my truck and ran inside. There was a pile of something burning on top of the stove, and the over-stove cabinets were catching fire. The living room curtains and the sofa were up in flames too.

"I yelled your name a few times, and there wasn't any answer. I ran outside, called the fire department, and grabbed my jumbo fire extinguisher out of my truck. I went back in and blasted the heck out of everything."

He paused and shook his head. "Someone had crumpled up a bunch of your sheet music, set it on top of the stove, poured olive oil all over it—as an accelerant, maybe?—and turned on a burner. The empty bottle was on the floor next to the stove. I turned off the burner, and I started looking for you.

"Since the trapdoor was open, I looked down into the basement, and didn't see you. Couldn't find you anywhere. I even looked in the barn. Your truck was there, so I went back in the house.

"Things just didn't make sense. And then it clicked. I went down the ladder, saw the door in the shelving was ajar, and found you.

"I called back the fire department, and asked for a rescue crew. As soon as the guys got there, the EMTs scrambled down the ladder, strapped you to a board, and pulled you out."

I was sure it wasn't quite that simple, but it didn't matter. I was here. I was safe.

"How badly is the house damaged?"

"I don't know. The whole kitchen was smoke damaged. I think the cabinets above the stove are pretty much toast, but I really wasn't paying that much attention. And I haven't been back up there to take a look."

I sighed and closed my eyes. My stomach started to ache, and I pressed my hand into the hollow at the bottom of my ribs. How much worse was this whole mess going to get?

"And, as an extra added bonus, we also found out you have a really nasty ulcer. You started vomiting blood in the ambulance. Scared the heck out of us too, 'cause you were strapped down, and the EMTs had to get you flipped over or you would've choked.

"When we got you to the hospital, the doctors found that your collarbone had completely broken through. You didn't have a compound fracture, but the ends were offset, and the whole thing was pretty much a mess."

"Oh," I said.

I tried to think of something clever to say about always being a bloody mess when I show up at hospital emergency rooms, but couldn't manage to come up with anything even halfway witty.

I was much more worried about whether or not the police were going to find Bertie.

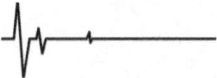

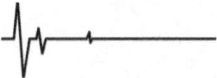

Chapter Thirty-Nine

I stayed in the hospital three days. The Wednesday after I was released, I went to Demetra's house for dinner. I was more than grateful that my truck had an automatic transmission. Even with my left arm in a sling, I was able to drive the short distance to her place from the little rental house Zak had found for me and Dog.

Angel that she is, Demetra had made a meal that was easy on the stomach. She was dying to know everything that had happened, and I didn't mind serving it up. And, of course, the big news was... Bertie.

She'd seen a brief segment on the news stating that one Alberta Strahan had been arrested on suspicion of the murder of Millie Minero, but it hadn't clicked in her head exactly who this Alberta was. So I told her.

"Bertie? *Our* Bertie?" Demetra's head jerked backwards in shocked surprise. She looked at me like she'd just discovered that I was, in reality, some kind of weird blobby creature from outer space. "How'd *that* go down?"

Even now, the whole episode seemed surreal, like an episode from a "true crime" television show. I retold the story, as explained to me by Zak. He'd come to see me every day at the hospital.

"The Highway Patrol found her in Sacramento. After Zak called the police station, an alert was issued. Within a couple of hours, they nabbed her in a traffic stop on I-5, near Sacramento International Airport. She had a boarding pass for a flight to Mexico in her purse."

Demetra shook her head. "Whoa. That was too damned close. Tried to take her ass out of the country, then. That was a pretty stupid move."

"You know it. Zak says that at a minimum she'll be charged with first-degree murder for what she did to Millie, attempted second-degree murder for what she did to me, malicious arson with aggravating factors, and flight to avoid arrest.

"She'll probably end up with a whole stack of felonies lined up against her. The short story is—she's screwed."

"Whoa," said Demetra. "Our Bertie. Who'da thunk it?"

• • •

The trial was months away, but I dreaded the thought of testifying. I was the only witness. Bertie had not come right out and stated that she'd killed Millie. But, even if she had, it wouldn't matter. It was my word against hers.

I knew I'd get torn apart by her attorneys. They'd paint her as a sweet little old lady, and me as a malicious little brat, grasping at straws. And then something weird happened.

About two weeks after Bertie was arrested, Drake called me, and asked me to come down to his office.

I hadn't seen Drake in a while. His face looked far more relaxed than the last time I saw him. But then, to be fair, at that point he was busy trying to control his irritation with David de León.

He met me in the reception area and took me back to his desk. "I'd like you to read something. Don't worry—it's good news. We might have another witness and maybe some hard evidence. If this pans out, a whole lot of weight is going to be taken off your shoulders."

He held out a photocopy of a document. I snatched it out of his hand. Rude as hell, that's me.

> My name is T. Forrest Ashton, and I live at 54434 Camanche Parkway South, Valley Springs. On August 2nd of last year, I saw a woman who resembled the mug shot of Alberta Strahan recently shown on TV. I witnessed her dumping a large black plastic trash bag into Lake Camanche, off the South Camanche Parkway Bridge. I know the date is correct, as it was my birthday, and I had the day off.
>
> I stopped my car and wrote down the license plate number of the vehicle she was driving. It was a dark blue Ford Fiesta with a California plate, 5FAN121. I gave this information to the campground host at Lake Camanche Campground, which is located on Wade Lane, off of South Camanche Parkway, south of the bridge.
>
> T. Forrest Ashton

Startled, I looked up at Drake. My hand was shaking, and the paper rattled, so I set it down on his desk. "How did you get this?" I whispered.

Apparently not offended that I'd grabbed the paper right out of his grasp, Drake reached out and patted my hand. "The guy called me. He saw the report of Bertie's arrest on TV and felt sure she was the person he'd seen dump that bag.

"He thought about it for a few days, but the idea wouldn't let him go, so he phoned us. I asked him to come in and make a statement. He was a real pro about it, and came with his statement already typed out.

"Mr. Ashton was riled up because, first of all, she was trashing the lake and, secondly, he'd reported it, and nothing happened. Then he saw the news report and had a gut feeling that he'd witnessed something significant. Thankfully, he acted upon it."

"So, what happens now?"

Drake grinned. "That plate number was matched to the car that Bertie traded in right after Millie's death."

I was stunned. "And if the bag holds something incriminating..."

"Yep. You got it. I told you, this looks promising. Since the County border runs right along the shorelines of the lake, the Amador County Sheriff is in the process of coordinating a search with the Calaveras County Sheriff's Department. We don't know exactly where she dumped the bag, so both teams need to be on the scene."

I had a mental image of the bridge in question, with a swarm of glistening white cop cars with rotating blue and red lights parked at either end. What exactly did the sheriffs' deputies plan on doing? Walk to the middle of the bridge and shout at each other over the imaginary county line? Well, that was going to be a circus and a half.

◆ ◆ ◆

I was surprised when Drake called me the next morning. I could hear delighted satisfaction in his voice. "Bertie messed up big time," he said. "Out of all the nearby bodies of water in the foothills, she chose the one that's pretty shallow, as lakes go. And, she dumped the bag right where the water isn't very deep."

Well, that got my attention. "They found it?"

He continued, "Yep. Fortunately, we were able to avoid a bunch of jurisdictional hassles because the bag landed closer to the Amador County shoreline than to the Calaveras side. Our sheriff's diver had her hands on it in nothing flat. Bertie would have had to work really hard to find a worse place to dump it."

"Way to go, Bertie," I said. Then, changing the subject, "Wow, you guys work fast."

"Indy racers have nothing on us Amador guys. You want to know what was in the bag?"

"I can't believe you're making me come right out and say it."

"It was one of those great big black bags, like people put their yard clippings in. With red plastic tapes to tie it shut."

"Drake!" I knew he was stringing me along, as he liked to do, so I refrained from adding any insults to the statement.

"Okay," he said. "Stipulation time. I have to remind you not to discuss this with anyone, because closer examination of the evidence may reveal another trail we have to follow.

"That said, the bag contained..." Paper rustled on his end. "...one hunting rifle, wrapped in newspaper, and one pellet gun, also wrapped in newspaper. There's a single visible partial fingerprint on the barrel of the rifle."

I could feel my heart rate going up, but I didn't interrupt him.

"Now," he said, "keep in mind that fingerprints don't generally last too long in water, so it may be too degraded to be of any use. And, of course, there will be ballistics tests done on the rifle."

I had to take a short moment to catch my breath. "Whoa. Thank you, Drake! And bless you, Mr. I-Am-Offended-by-Litterers."

"Heck, yes. I'd give him a hug, but that might offend him, along with the littering. Talk to you later." He disconnected the call.

I slumped back in my chair. The sense of reprieve was overwhelming. Bertie's defense team was going to have a good time explaining this one.

I couldn't believe how badly she'd blown it. Several easily accessed lakes, hundreds of feet deeper than Camanche, lay within very easy driving distance of Jackson. A bit of logical thinking on her part would have ensured that the bag was never found. But she got in too much of a hurry. Maybe she'd panicked.

Here was yet another example of a guilty party doing something amazingly stupid.

I sat there for a little while, thumping my fingers on the arm of the chair. The relief faded after a few minutes, overcome by more serious thoughts.

Bertie had been my good friend for as long as I could remember. But, despite that fact, she tried to kill me. She'd killed Millie. Why? It all seemed so senseless.

Unanswered questions were beating around in my brain like captured birds, unhappy to be caged. And so, even though I hated to impose on my friend, the next morning I called Demetra and asked her for a huge favor.

◆ ◆ ◆

Several hours later, Demetra showed up at the dreary little rental house where Dog and I were living. She didn't look happy. I wrapped her up in a big hug. "Thank you, lovie," I whispered.

She hugged me back, and we sat down at the kitchen table. "Did you get in?" I asked. Bless her, Demetra had gone to the county jail to talk to Bertie.

"Yes," she said. "It was weird."

I was boiling over with impatience, but I bit down on my lower lip and let her tell her tale at her own pace.

"I signed in, and they took me to the visitors' room," she said, her voice soft and sad. "They have a wall with some windows, each with a chair and a telephone handset. They assigned me to one of the windows.

"I waited a while, then Bertie appeared on the other side of the glass. She picked up her handset, and said, 'Hey, chickie,' just like I'd walked through her back door into her kitchen.

"I could *not* believe it. "Demetra shook her head. "Hello? What part of 'it's not a good thing to be in jail' is she missing? I said to her, 'Bertie, what happened?'"

I reached across the table and patted Demetra's hand.

"Now," continued my friend, "this is where it got really... bizarre. I don't know if she had me confused with someone else, or what the hell was going on, but she said, 'I told you. She stole him.' Then she started going off about how nasty Millie was!

"Well, let me tell you, she really pissed me off. So, I said to her, 'Stop it, Bertie. No one can steal something from you if it was never yours to begin with.'"

"And then she says, 'I didn't expect that you'd understand, Miss Uppity.'"

Demetra stood up from the table. She wandered over to the kitchen counter, grabbed the coffee pot, and poured herself a cup. Leaning back against the counter, she sighed. "And that's how the conversation went. She wasn't making a lot of sense. She yammered on and on about some sort of special connection with Doc, and she said some really nasty stuff about Millie, which I will *not* repeat, it was that bad.

"I was getting more and more ticked off, and then it occurred to me that maybe she was putting on an act, in case our conversation was being taped, or audio recorded. It was *that* weird. Like watching a really effed-up movie or something.

"Then, all of a sudden, out of nowhere, she started singing *Onward Christian Soldiers*. Well, that was it. I was done. I hung up the phone and walked out."

Demetra grabbed her mug and came back to sit down at the table.

"Thank you," I said. "That had to be really hard."

"Yep," she said. "Sure was."

We chatted a little longer about this and that, and then she had to get back to work. I walked out to her car with her, my right arm wrapped around her shoulders.

I gave Demetra an extra-big hug, and watched her drive away, grateful to have such a good and giving friend.

Not wanting to go back inside and stare at the walls, I called Dog, and the two of us went for a walk.

◆ ◆ ◆

We picked our way along the uneven asphalt at the edge of the road, shivering a bit in the cooler air of afternoon. I pieced together a probable scenario from snips of memories and from what Bertie had said to me and to Demetra.

It was more than obvious now, that Bertie was in love with Doc, and had been in love with him for years. And then, somehow, everything had gone so very wrong.

I sighed, knowing that I'd never understand how my sweet friend had turned into a murderer.

Dog and I found ourselves at the vacant lot that formed a ratty exclamation point at the end of the road. I plunked myself down on a the cleanest-looking patch of weeds.

I kept thinking of the man at the center of Bertie's imaginary love triangle. I had such fond recollections of Doc. When I was little, I received I-don't-know-how-many hugs and piggyback rides from him. He was always exuberant with his friends. He gave hugs and shoulder-pats to everyone—men, women, dogs, cats, everyone.

"Well," I said to Dog, "I guess Bertie didn't see his hugs as being platonic. Talk about a fundamental misunderstanding. Good lord. How could she be so far off-base?"

Because Dog didn't like Bertie, and hadn't ever known Doc, he didn't answer me. Or maybe he recognized a rhetorical question when he heard one.

Perhaps Bertie's breaking point came when Doc moved into Millie's house. In Bertie's mind, that might have seemed like a betrayal.

"Dog," I whispered, "why do people do such stupid things?" Dog had no answer to that one either, because nobody does.

I reached down and scratched Dog on the head between the ears. How could I have known Bertie for so many years, and never seen how sick she was?

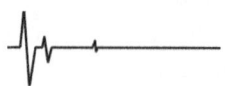

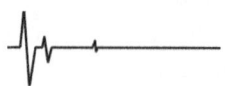

Chapter Forty

In October, more than two years after Millie was shot, *The People vs. Alberta Strahan* finally came to trial. Of course, that month Amador County was pummeled with day after day of cold, rainy weather. The gray and dreary atmosphere created an appropriately somber backdrop for the proceedings.

Bertie's team of lawyers protested her innocence, of course, claiming that on the day of Millie's death, Bertie spent her time shopping and at the library, and then she'd gone home to cook her dinner. Her alibi could not be substantiated, of course.

The burden of trying to prove Bertie's involvement with the crime rested heavily on my shoulders, dragging me down. How had it come to this?

The drizzly Monday morning finally came when I was scheduled to testify. A parade of witnesses had come before me, outlining the case in chronological order. I'd had to spend that time sequestered, forbidden to seek out any news of the proceedings, cooped up in the nasty little rental house that reeked of mildew.

There were moments when I'd wanted to bash my head in frustration against the ugly, floral-papered wall.

The chain of evidence started with the day of Millie's death. First to testify were representatives from the police department, then the coroner's office, then the long-time nurse from Doc's office, to explain the relationship between Doc and Bertie. Finally, at last, came my turn.

I entered the courtroom and couldn't help but stare at Bertie, sitting up front at the defense table with her two lawyers. She was outfitted in a plain gray linen dress with a white mandarin collar.

Was this attire supposed to make an observer mistake her for a sweet little old nun? I rolled my eyeballs. Robin, at least, had looked like she was wearing her own clothing.

I spotted another difference from Robin's trial. Robin had looked down at her lap, grim and unhappy, as the trial got underway. Bertie, on the other hand, was relaxed, and looking around the courtroom as blithe and unconcerned as a seventh grader on a school field trip.

I dubbed Bertie's two-man defense team The Sleaze Bros. Where did she find these turkeys? On a late-night television 1-800-Dial-a-Lawyer infomercial? I shuddered to think about how much money she must have paid for the services of these two clowns, money she could ill afford to squander.

Both men were in their late thirties or so, had carefully tousled, razor-cut hair, and wore slim-fit shantung blazers in complementary colors, as if they'd just stepped out of a Tom Ford catalog. Their languid body language revealed complete belief in their own superior status over the local yokels.

I hoped like hell that their abundant self-assurance wasn't based on a figurative ace up a silk sleeve—knowledge of a crucial "something" that the prosecution might have overlooked or misinterpreted.

We'd all find out soon enough.

It was awful, having to relive that day again. I was seated in the witness box. Prosecutor Dartmoor was pacing the floor in front of the bench. "Ms. D'Angelo, can you explain to the jury how you came to be injured inside your own home?"

My mouth dried, and my windpipe closed up. I had to clear my throat a couple of times before I could speak.

"Ms. Strahan came to visit me. She was a friend of many years. But it soon became obvious that she still regarded my aunt with hate and animosity, even though my aunt was dead.

"She started ranting and raving about perceived injustices done to her by my aunt, and then blurted out that she knew that my aunt had been shot in the back. The police never made that information public. I understood the implications immediately. She realized she'd messed up, and I guess she panicked, and decided that I needed to be eliminated."

I recounted how Bertie set my house on fire, and left me there to die. Surely, no one could doubt Bertie's culpability. She couldn't deny having been there. The security cameras recorded both her arrival and her departure, complete with time and date stamp, as well as the arrival of Zak and the fire department.

The jurors looked grim as I told my story. I was relieved that their faces seemed sympathetic.

It was time for the cross-examination, and Sleaze Bro #1 attempted to pick my testimony apart, implying that all the horrible things that had happened were my own darned fault. His voice dripped with condescending disdain for the little rural courtroom, its occupants, and me.

"So, Miz Dungelo, isn't it true that you fell into your cellar?"

The man couldn't even pronounce my name correctly. Or, maybe he was trying to create a subliminal link between my name and the word "dunce."

Instead of telling him that I thought he was making a fool of himself, I answered the question in a firm, no-nonsense voice. "No, sir. I was knocked into my cellar."

"And you admit that prior to that event, you were heating cooking oil in your wok? Please remember that you're under oath."

Good lord, he was blaming me for setting the kitchen on fire and undermining my credibility at the same time.

"As I previously stated, sir, I turned off the stove when Ms. Strahan showed no interest in the food I offered to prepare for her."

"You can state unequivocally that you turned off the stove?"

"Yes, sir. I *know* that I turned off the stove." And so it went.

The defense team was doing their best to make me stumble, backtrack, and falter. Then it got worse.

"Miz Dungelo, why do you feel compelled to tell such horrible lies about Ms. Strahan, who was for years your close, dear friend?"

My attorney leapt to her feet to object. The judge sustained the objection, but the damage was done. I hoped that the jury wasn't that gullible.

I found myself clenching my hands so tightly that my fingertips started to tingle.

Following my testimony came Zak's turn in the spotlight, then came the Lake Camanche eyewitness guy, and a fingerprint specialist. The last witness was the ballistics expert witness hired by the prosecution.

At last, after days of testimony, everything seemed to be falling into place. The fingerprint turned out to be useless, but the slug that killed Millie matched the rifle found in the lake. And that rifle was registered to Bertie.

I began to have some hope that justice would indeed be served.

A couple more days were taken up with closing arguments and jury instruction, and then the case went to the jury.

I knew the prosecution team was made up of competent individuals, but I couldn't help but worry and wonder how badly the Sleaze Bros had messed with the jury's ability to differentiate between the truth and pure nonsense.

I didn't have to wonder long—the jury came to their conclusions in only twelve hours. I got a late-night call telling me to be in the courtroom the next morning for the announcement of the verdict.

My anxiety was high, my blood pressure surely soaring into the stratosphere when I settled into a seat at the back of the courtroom. I closed my eyes and tried, in vain, to relax.

So much was at stake. It seemed incomprehensible that the jury might let a murderer go free.

I held my breath as the clerk read out, in a steady voice, the statement from the jury. "We, the jury, find the defendant, Alberta Strahan, to be guilty of the charge of murder in the first degree in the death of Milagros Minero."

Relief rolled in waves through my body, and I relaxed a bit in my chair. Bertie would be going to prison for sure, no matter what the jury decided regarding the attempted murder and arson charges.

But, the show wasn't over. I was still a bit anxious, my fingers restless, waiting for what would come next.

Several more times the court clerk's voice rang out. "Guilty." The attempted murder, aggravated arson, attempted flight to avoid arrest, and assorted other charges stood.

Thank god. It was over.

◆ ◆ ◆

In the end, it was the testimony of the guy who saw Bertie dump the bag into Camanche Reservoir that proved critical. Not surprisingly, the defense team claimed the situation to be a classic case of mistaken identity.

The jury, however, could not ignore the importance of the evidence found in the resulting lake search.

Later, when I read the transcript of the trial, I found out that Bertie, in her own defense against the attempted murder charges, had offered a heartbreaking story constructed around a central theme called "poor little me."

That probably hadn't gone over well with the jury either.

Bertie's justification for her behavior on the day she tried to kill me was that she was under the influence of alcohol. As if that made everything okay.

Her pathetic excuses were stopped dead by objections from the prosecution. California State law states, without any ambiguity whatsoever, that intoxication does *not* get you off the hook for a crime committed while under the influence.

Her lawyers should have known better. Maybe they did. I wondered if the Sleaze Bros thought they could pull a fast one on the hayseeds. Oops. Big mistake.

Because Bertie hadn't called the fire department on that awful day she tried to kill me, and ran away knowing that I was in the cellar, it was easy for the jury to believe that the fire at my house was intentionally set, and that she'd meant for me to die.

When it came time for the sentencing, the judge agreed with the jury's findings, and wasn't inclined towards leniency. Bertie received the maximum term of imprisonment on all counts for which she was found guilty.

I could finally sleep at night.

◆ ◆ ◆

What still gives me chills to this day is the fact that had Zak left his place a few minutes earlier, or a few minutes later, Bertie might have gotten away with all of it.

How long would it have been until someone noticed that my house was on fire? Until someone realized that I was missing?

I wasn't the only one whose life was upended by the cascade of events that started so many years ago. There was an article in the local newspaper the other day on former Attorney General Ewing.

Former Attorney General Seeks to Regain License

The California Institution for Men, Chino, California is a long way from Sacramento, both literally and figuratively. Chino is now the home of Ralph I. Ewing, former Attorney General for the State of California. Ewing was sentenced to three years in prison as an "accessory after the fact" in the murder of sixteen-year-old Rudy D'Angelo, a crime that occurred years before Ewing passed the bar.

A true "jailhouse lawyer," he is fighting from the prison library for reinstatement of his license to practice law. The rules of the California State Bar state that a felon can be admitted to the bar, if the individual can provide overwhelming proof of reform and rehabilitation. Since Ewing's crime was far behind him when he was originally admitted to the bar, and he performed admirably as AG, he has persuasive arguments in his favor.

His current activities can also be viewed favorably. In every prison, there are a few problem fixers, also known as "jailhouse lawyers." Ewing is one of those persons at Chino. "I try to fix whatever legal issues my fellow inmates are having," he said, in a recent telephone interview, "criminal appeals, habeas corpus petitions, prison disciplinary appeals... I've gone back to the very basics of criminal law, and am looking at all of it with fresh eyes."

I will be interested in seeing where Ewing's efforts take him. My feelings towards the man remain quite mixed. Part of me wants to hate him, and part of me understands the innate desire to protect family. What I don't understand, though, is how he could not be appalled and repulsed by what Robin and Larry had done.

Bertie is presently serving time at the Central California Women's Facility located in Chowchilla, California. Without question, she'll die there, as she was sentenced to three concurrent life sentences. She was denied the possibility of future parole.

Some people may pity her, but I don't. It's time for her to harvest the bitter crop she planted.

I thought, for a while, that she might file an appeal, based upon the premise that her defense team was made up of incompetent clowns. But, so far, she hasn't. I can't help but wonder why.

Chowchilla is also the place where Robin will spend the rest of her life. Do the prison administrators know of the unfortunate thread linking the two women? I hope so, for Robin's sake. For as certain as anything, Robin will find herself in a world of hurt if she ever crosses Bertie's path.

For all her faults, Bertie loved Rudy fiercely, as she'd once loved me. I feel certain that she will never forgive Robin for what happened to Rudy so long ago, on a cold and lonely forest road.

I'm not very inclined towards forgiveness myself, but I do have a small measure of sympathy for Robin. She was young, and very vulnerable, when Rudy was killed. Her actions stemmed more from a lifetime of abuse, a modest intellect, and susceptibility to manipulation, than from malice. Unlike Bertie, she ultimately took responsibility for her actions and accepted her fate with grace.

I made peace in my heart with Robin. I know better than to allow the corrosive power of hate to eat away at my body and soul, but I will never be able to forgive Bertie.

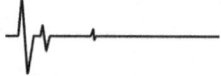

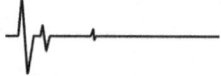

EPILOGUE

09090

I sit here, on the veranda of Greg's stone mansion by the lake, as I write this. Dog is with me, reclined at my feet. Greg is still in Africa. After Greg heard through the Jackson grapevine that my house had burned, he contacted his lawyer. I was presented with legal documents giving me the right to live for the foreseeable future here in this wonderful old place. I was floored when the docs arrived in the mail.

He was more than generous, I'll give you that. There's no cost to me to live here, other than maintenance and property taxes, and whatever I choose to spend of my own money.

Greg stated that there was no point in his home sitting empty when I needed somewhere to live. He said to go ahead and do what I wanted with the place. I had not lost my life-long friend, after all.

I was more than glad to leave the awful little rental behind.

And my house—I hate to even think about what Bertie did to my home, my safe haven. Its future is still up in the air. A fair amount of damage was done to the kitchen and the living room, impacting the overall structural integrity of the place.

Like a wounded eagle being examined by wild-life experts, the damaged house is currently under assessment by structural engineers and historic building restoration specialists.

At some point, I will hold in my hands a written report from the consultants. Because the house is in the register of historic places, the report will then have to be shuffled through layers of bureaucracy. Only after all that will I be able to decide what will happen next.

In the meantime, a fence and a security guard protect the house from further damage.

My rash actions did save the piano, though I will bear scars on my arm for the rest of my life. They are far less painful than the scars burnt onto my soul by Bertie's betrayal. Both injuries will fade over time, or so I am told.

And so, here I am, still in Jackson. I did spend many lonely hours in contemplation while I was recovering, wondering what to do with the rest of my life. Within me lingered a need to do something constructive and meaningful. For as much as I'm a lapsed Catholic, one of the lessons drilled into my head at an early age still resonates.

To whomever much is given, much will be required of him; and to whom much more is entrusted, of him more will be asked. (Luke 12:48)

And from that thought sprang forth the idea for the Milagros School. Just as Millie opened her arms to Rudy and me at the time when we needed her the most, this school will provide a safe harbor for children who are in desperate situations.

In the not-too-distant future, I hope, the big mansion by the lake will ring with the laughter of children given a new chance in life.

◆ ◆ ◆

I hear the crunch-crunch of footsteps; Dog jumps up and his tail starts to wag. Someone is walking across the gravel, coming towards the veranda steps. I turn, and look to see who is there.

It's Greg. His stride is a bit uneven, and he leans heavily on a walking stick. I feel a huge smile stretch across my face, and I leap up out of my chair to go meet him.

THE END

NOTES TO THE READER

Amador County and the town of Jackson, California, are very real places. The Amador Council of Tourism has a colorful website called TourAmador that is loaded with great information for visitors.

A map of a walking tour of historic Jackson can be downloaded at the City of Jackson website, under the Visitor Center submenu.

Calaveras County also boasts a long and fascinating history. The website GoCalaveras offers a visitors' guide and a wealth of information.

Real Locations Mentioned in this Book

Listed in order of appearance

The Old Courthouse

38 Summit Street: The first Courthouse was erected on this site in early 1855, but it burned down in the Great Fire of 1862. The court records were saved, hand-carried to James Hubbard's brick law office, a building that still stands today at 103 Court Street. A new Courthouse was completed by January, 1864. In 1893, an adjacent Hall of Records was constructed. In 1939-40, architect George Sellon designed an art deco exterior to envelop the two buildings and make them one. The remodeled structure was dedicated on June 29,1940.

Former Amador County Courthouse

The National Hotel

2 Water Street: The National Hotel is located on one of the very earliest building sites in downtown Jackson. Ellis Evans established a general store on that spot in 1850. He partnered with others to build a two-story wooden hotel named the Louisiana House that later burned down in the 1862 fire. By spring of 1863 the owners erected a new brick building and called it the National Hotel, a concession to political expedience during the Civil War years.

Jackson Downtown Historic District

Main Street, from 215 Main Street to 14 Broadway: Many of the brick buildings that were constructed following the Great Fire still stand along Main Street.

Main Street, Jackson, in the 1800s

Butte Store (California Historical Landmark No. 39)

State Highway 49 At Milepost 1.4, The Butte Store stands as the last remnant of the community of Butte City. An Italian stone mason constructed the building in 1857 to serve settlers and miners as a post office and general store. The store closed in the early 1900s. The roofless building, still graced with the huge iron shutters designed to protect the store against wildfires, is all that remains of a once-thriving community.

Butte Store

Kennedy Mine Wheels

1200 N Main St: The famous Kennedy Mine, one of the deepest gold mines in the world (at 5912 feet), was original prospected in 1860. True environmental pioneers built the wheels, now iconic symbols of the City of Jackson, during the hard rock mining era of the early 20th century. The massive structures lifted mine tailings from the Kennedy Mine stamp mill, over two hills to an impoundment dam constructed to prevent the tailings from reaching streams and creeks and polluting the valley floor. Today, two of the original four tailing wheels still stand, the other two having collapsed from age. The site was added to the National Register of Historic Places in 1981.

Saint Sava Serbian Orthodox Church

724 N. Main Street: Serbian immigrants built this small, white church that is topped with a Russian Orthodox-style cupola. It was the first Serbian Orthodox Church in North America, dedicated in 1894.

Lake Pardee (Pardee Reservoir)

In the mid-1920s, the expanding communities in the East San Francisco Bay area faced a severe water shortage. The solution to the problem came in the form of Pardee Dam, built across the Mokelumne River, creating Pardee Reservoir. The dam was named for George Pardee, former mayor of Oakland and Governor of California from 1903 to 1907. Water from the reservoir began to flow via pipeline to the East Bay in 1929.

Coloma

Coloma is most noted as the location where gold nuggets were found in the millrace at John Sutter's sawmill, on January 24, 1848. This discovery, made by James W. Marshall, triggered the California Gold Rush. Sutter was a very wealthy landowner at the time. Nearly all of Sutter's workers left him to hunt for gold, or start businesses that would profit from the influx of prospectors. Ultimately, the Gold Rush destroyed the huge, almost feudal quasi-kingdom that Sutter had created for himself, and left him a broken, destitute man. Today, the small town of Coloma is the centerpiece of the Marshall Gold Discovery State Historic Park and National Historic Landmark District.

Sutter Creek

Sutter Creek, known as the "Jewel of the Mother Lode," is located north of Jackson on Hwy 49. The town was named after John Sutter, who sent a work crew to the area in 1846 in search of timber. Today, the delightful town is home to many shops, bed-and-breakfasts, and wineries. The Great Sutter Creek Chili Cook-Off and Car Show is held annually in October.

Reno, Nevada, and Carson City, Nevada

Both of these cities are located at the base of the eastern slope of the Sierra Nevada mountain range, over the mountain from the California Gold Rush Country. The population of both cities boomed following the local discovery of gold in 1850 and silver in 1859. The legendary Comstock Lode was found in nearby mountains.

Old Sacramento

The City of Sacramento was born with the Gold Rush, and was, in the 1800s, the western terminus of the Pony Express postal system, the first transcontinental railroad, and the transcontinental telegraph. Located along the east bank of the Sacramento River, Old Sacramento historical district was the original 1850s business center of the city. Today the area is a National Historic Landmark District and State Park. Virtually all the buildings in this area date from the 19th century, many of them built immediately after the disastrous fire of 1852.

Sacramento Memorial Auditorium

16th and J Streets, Sacramento: Built between 1925 and 1927, the Sacramento Memorial Auditorium, is an architectural delight, and is on the National Register of Historic Places. The architect described his plan to be "a form of the Byzantine," but the building has been variously described as Italian Romanesque, Moorish-Spanish, and Renaissance Revival. Now beautifully restored, today it's a popular venue for plays, ballets, concerts and high school graduation ceremonies.

Mel and Faye's Diner

31 Hwy 49-88: Mel and Faye's Diner is included in this book because it is the author's favorite restaurant in Jackson, and has the very best chiliburgers in the entire universe. Go there. Order the Miner's Special. It's really good.

The Hotel Léger— California Historical Landmark No. 663

8304 Main St., Mokelumne Hill: A California Historic Landmark, established in 1851, the Hotel Léger is said to be one of the oldest continuously operating hotels in California. After restoration following a fire in 1874, the hotel became known as the Hotel Léger. The ghost of the founder, George Léger, who was assassinated in the Hotel in 1879, has been seen in the saloon and in many of the Hotel's thirteen rooms, which are furnished in period antiques. Other ghosts in the Hotel include the Lady in White, who haunts Room 2, crying for her child, and the apparition of a young boy has been seen playing by the fireplace in Room 3. A former owner of the Hotel Léger described seeing phantom smoke and fire in the bar area on multiple occasions.

Mokelumne Hill— California Historical Landmark No. 269

This small town is located south of Jackson off of Hwy 49. Referred to as "Moke Hill" by foothill locals, this area was one of the richest gold mining settlements in California. Founded in 1848, it is said that the placer diggings were so bountiful that miners did not want to leave their claims to travel to Stockton for supplies, and risked starvation just to stay on site. Local lore says the first man to establish a store in the area became quite wealthy. Once a booming city, Moke Hill now has a population of only about 650. The whole town is a California Historic Landmark.

Stateline, Nevada

Stateline, Nevada, is located on the Nevada side of the state border with California, on the shores of Lake Tahoe. Stateline is the home to the famous Tahoe-area casinos, and is a popular place to get married. Some of the big casinos have elegant wedding chapels that overlook the lake.

Camanche Reservoir

The reservoir was named after the former Gold Rush town of Camanche that now lies beneath its waters. The East Bay Municipal Utility District evacuated the town in 1962 in order to build the Camanche dam. The Camanche Reservoir is fed primarily from the Mokelumne River, and is located downriver from Pardee Dam. The maximum depth of the lake is 150 feet, and is far shallower than that under the shoreline bridges. Water from the Reservoir flows by pipeline to slake the thirst of East San Francisco Bay area residents.

Fictional Locations Based on Real Places

Alexandra's house

I imagined Alexandra's house to be located on a rolling grassy hilltop on the south flanks of Butte Mountain. The outside appearance of the fictional house is roughly based on the old Gold Rush-era "Dogtown House" formerly located just outside Clements, California. After serving as stage stop for many years, it was given a new life as a family home.

Glen Oaks Ranch House, Glen Ellen, California

Time and dry rot eventually won, and the building was condemned and demolished in 2014. I was not able to find a picture of it. Of similar appearance, but newer, is the Glen Oaks ranch house in Glen Ellen, California, above. The Dogtown House was more rough-hewn and rugged in appearance.

Greg's house

The exterior of Greg's great stone house is based on the Bidwell Mansion, now a part of the Bidwell State Historic Park in Chico, California. The mansion, located at 525 The Esplanade, is open to the public on selected days of the week. There is a small admissions fee. Note the octagonal wing of the house and the blockish servants' quarters jutting out to the left.

The Bidwell Mansion, Chico, California

Character Based on an Actual Sentient Being

Dog

The character Dog was based on a real dog, although that wasn't the name given to him. How this sweet pup came to live with Alexandra is an accurate retelling of how he came to live with the author and her family. He hopped right up into the back of the pickup truck, and said, "Here I am."
The poor guy was thin, dirty, hungry, and rather skunky at the time. He was grateful for his rescue, and for years vigilantly protected us from the terror of ground squirrels, gophers, and other wild beasts. Best. Dog. Ever.

Dog

Historical Note

The Chilean War of Calaveras County

The fictional character, Juan Minero, was said to have fled to Jackson following the Chilean War of Calaveras County, which was a very real event. Along Highway 49 between San Andreas and Mokelumne Hill, sits California State Historical Marker No. 265, memorializing events that are now referred to as the Chilean War of Calaveras County. The marker states that the area known as Chili Gulch was the "Richest placer mining section, extending five miles, in Calaveras County."

In December 1849, Anglo-European miners in Calaveras County drew up a mining code that called for all foreign miners to leave the country within 15 days. The Anglo miners were angry and jealous of the success that Chilean miners were having working the rich deposits at Chili Gulch. They wanted the claims for themselves.

The controversial foreigner expulsion decree lead to protests and violent attacks. The Chileans sought legal remedy and obtained a court order protecting their claims.

The miners' historic victory was short-lived. Despite the fact that the Chileans were recognized as having a valid legal standing, fighting broke out. The Chilean War of Calaveras County resulted in several deaths and the forcible expulsion of all Chilean miners from the area.

California State Historical Marker No. 265

About the Author

I was lucky enough to live for many years in Gold Rush Country, on acreage outside of a small town overlooking the Mokelumne River Valley. There my husband and I raised two wonderful kids, tended a small pistachio orchard, and (over a span of many years) enjoyed the company of two mutts and ten Australian shepherds.

The area where we lived was just off of the old historic road that ran from Stockton to Jackson, California. Tangible pieces of history were everywhere around us. It was very natural for my hubby and me to load the kids in the car and go roaming around the foothills from time to time, looking for the odd, the beautiful, and the historic.

Even before we lived in the area, we'd spent many a summer night camped near the old towns of Volcano, or Jackson, or Sutter Creek. One of my kid's favorite places in the whole world was a little rock shop in Volcano, which had on display (delighted giggles!) petrified dinosaur poop. Ah, kids.

They also loved visiting Cave City, where clever Gold-Rush-era residents set up housekeeping inside of a network of caves, and provided themselves with natural air conditioning in the hot foothill summers.

The end-result of all these excursions was the development of a true love for the Gold Rush region. I've worked hard to convey the magic of the area in my books... rolling hills covered with golden grasses, the huge old oak trees with dusty blue-green leaves, the giant granite boulders littering the landscape, left behind eons ago by melting glaciers.

Well, time goes marching on. The kids have grown up, and the orchard is now receiving tender loving care from new owners. But, from time to time, it is still fun to hop in the car and drive to Jackson, enjoy the scenery, check things out at Hein & Co Used Books, and eat the best darned chiliburger in the world at Mel and Faye's Diner.

◆ ◆ ◆

I'd love to hear from you! Visit *SusanMSoule.com/contact* to say hello. And please do let me know if you find any errors, factual or otherwise, and I will jump right on them.

If you liked this book, a review with a few kind words will be greatly appreciated.

www.ingramcontent.com/pod-product-compliance
Lightning Source LLC
Chambersburg PA
CBHW020903200626
46814CB00001BA/144
* 9 7 8 0 9 9 8 8 7 9 5 1 2 *